# DRAWN TOGETHER

# DRAWN
# *Together*

MERCEDES RON

SIMON &
SCHUSTER

London · New York · Amsterdam/Antwerp · Sydney/Melbourne · Toronto · New Delhi

First published in the United States by Atria Books, an imprint of Simon & Schuster, LLC, 2026

First published in Great Britain by Simon & Schuster UK Ltd, 2026



1 3 5 7 9 10 8 6 4 2

Simon & Schuster UK Ltd, 7th Floor,
199 Bishopsgate, London EC2M 3TY



Simon & Schuster Australia, Sydney
Simon & Schuster India, New Delhi

www.simonandschuster.co.uk
www.simonandschuster.com.au
www.simonandschuster.co.in

The authorised representative in the EEA is Simon & Schuster Netherlands BV, Herculesplein 96, 3584 AA Utrecht, Netherlands. info@simonandschuster.nl



A CIP catalogue record for this book is available from the British Library

UK Paperback ISBN: 978-1-3985-6173-1
eBook ISBN: 978-1-3985-6174-8
Audio ISBN: 978-1-3985-6175-5



Originally published in Spain as *Marfil* by Penguin Random House Grupo Editorial, S.A.U. in 2019.
English translation © Frances Riddle 2026
Published in agreement with Writers House.

Printed and Bound in the UK using 100% Renewable Electricity
at CPI Group (UK) Ltd

*To my father,*
*thank you for teaching me*
*that the sky is not the limit*

# CONTENT NOTE

This novel contains themes that may be sensitive for some readers, including kidnapping, violence, and power imbalance. Reader discretion is advised.

PROLOGUE

# SEBASTIAN

If someone had asked me what the hell I was doing there, I could've given eighty thousand different answers, and none of them would've been totally true.

The work demanded so much of me that I sometimes asked myself why I continued to do it, why I didn't just quit, leave that world for good. But when I thought about what it would mean to throw it all away, I simply silenced my conscience and got on with it.

The other men there would've killed me without thinking twice if they even suspected my doubts. But for years my mind had been my stronghold, and I knew how to control my thoughts so that no one could so much as glimpse the reservations I sometimes felt.

In the world I run in . . . doubts can mean death.

From a distance, I checked that my aim was lined up. No one was covering me; I was on my own . . . although more than fifteen men surrounded me.

As soon as shots began firing, I knew everything had gone to hell. But one single shot would change absolutely everything.

## CHAPTER 1

# MARFIL

TWO WEEKS LATER

I looked at the Colombian peso coin I held between my fingers. As I waited for Liam, I had only one thought: The two sides of that coin made up a whole, but they would never see each other face-to-face. It seems silly, a coin is just a coin, but I couldn't help but identify with it. Did I have two completely opposing sides that would never merge into one? Sometimes I struggled to understand myself. If I could view my life from the outside, I'm sure the only thing I would think in most situations is . . . What the hell are you doing?

My sister, Gabriella, insisted that spending our entire childhood and adolescence at a boarding school four thousand miles from home had scarred us. Thankfully, I had already left that period of my life behind. My sister, on the other hand, still had two long years of strict rules and cloudy skies. She would be sixteen in just a few months, and her biggest concern was that she had never kissed a boy. She said that if she continued living with all girls for much longer, she was going to end up dating one. Imagining my father's face at the mere suggestion made me smile.

Scars . . . a subject I could talk about for hours. The deepest one still caused me to wake up in the middle of the night with my heart racing and tears streaming down my cheeks like I was four years old, not twenty. It was incredible how some memories remained forever engraved on our minds and others disappeared without leaving a trace. According to Pixar—yes, the animation studio that made the movie *Inside Out*—our brain erases the memories that no longer serve us and retains those that it considers important. But I have to ask myself: Does it serve me to remember my mother being killed right in front of me? Clearly, no matter what Pixar says, the brain does whatever it wants.

As my thoughts wandered aimlessly, I became aware that the group of guys at the bar to my right were staring at me. Without hesitating, I lifted my head and looked at them, refusing to avert my eyes. It had been my intention to intimidate them, or at least make them stop staring so shamelessly, but two of them started laughing, and the third, tall with light brown hair, held my gaze unwaveringly.

I hated being the first to look away, no matter who it was. Only one person on the entire planet could make me lower my head on demand: my father. But he was far away, and I didn't have to think about him. So began the most epic staring contest in all of human history. Well, maybe it wasn't that dramatic, I tend to exaggerate, but it felt intense. The more he looked at me, the more curious I became, and the more I looked at him, the more I could imagine what was going through his mind. Maybe I could have some fun with this guy.

"Hey, Marfil," came a deep voice behind me, although it was the feel of his hand on my back that caused me to jump and look away.

Shit! I'd just lost.

My frustration vanished as I turned to see my best friend. Liam Michaelson was almost six feet two, with hair black as night and bright blue eyes. His smile was famous for its ability to break hearts, and the worst part was that he knew it. His eyelashes, long and dark, the envy of every woman, and the hours he spent in the gym working out created the perfect storm.

Women lost their heads over Liam. A real heartthrob. No, he wasn't gay, and yes, he truly was my best friend. Stranger things have happened.

"Did I keep you waiting long?" he asked, looking over my head to the guys at the end of the bar.

"Long enough for you to have to buy me a drink." Legally, I couldn't drink alcohol, much less buy it, but fake IDs were so readily available that the law seemed ridiculous.

Liam smiled sweetly and called the waitress over. He ordered our usual drinks, which she brought over a few minutes later.

"And to what do I owe the half-hour wait?" I asked, twirling the olives in my martini.

Liam raised his beer to his lips and rolled his eyes. "You don't want to know."

"Virginia? Oh, no, wait . . . Rose?"

"Tessi," he said.

I couldn't help but laugh. "Tessi? Do you call her that for any reason in particular?"

"That's what she wants me to call her. Shit, she's unbearable."

Liam was a guy that, well . . . he was a guy. The end. Guys, as a general rule, just want to have a good time, and generally speaking, we women also want the same, plus a whole lot more, although I don't include myself in that statement. But I understood why Virginia, Rose, and . . . Tessi wanted something more from my best friend. He was a great catch, if he could stop hitting on everything that moved, of course.

Liam and I met during my first year of college. I'd just moved to New York after eight years at boarding school abroad, surrounded by all girls and nuns; I only spent a couple of months a year at home in Louisiana. Liam and I had both been studying economics at Columbia University. He was three years older than me, which meant he'd been in his senior year.

It took a lot of effort, but I managed to convince my father to let me move to New York City on my own two years ago. You could say I went a little wild when I first found myself with so much freedom. All that repression during my teenage years had been very unhealthy, and I lost my head a bit, but I liked to think that that period was behind me now, for the most part.

Liam was my first kiss. I had just turned eighteen and discovered what I was capable of when it came to seducing men. My father had always kept me hidden away from the world as if I were untouchable, although Liam touched me . . . everywhere.

We didn't sleep together, but we did other things, until we ultimately realized that we were better off as friends, even as perfect as I might be for him, and as perfect as he might be for me.

After Liam, I had a brief, more serious relationship with a guy named Regan. But then I learned that he and his friends had bet ten thousand dollars to see which of them could sleep with me first. That's right, ten thousand dollars. Pathetic. The fact that my father had been right all those times he told me to never trust men made me more furious than anything. After that, something changed inside me; I became unrecognizable. I decided that I would take exactly the type of physical pleasure I wanted from men and give them nothing in return, cut and dry.

"The dude from the bar is coming over," said Liam, half an hour and three martinis later. "Should I pretend to be your boyfriend?"

"That might be fun, but no," I said, curious to see what the guy had to say. I sensed someone behind me, but I played it cool.

Liam, on the other hand, turned around to look at him. "Can I help you, man?"

"Actually, I wanted a quick word with your friend here."

I turned around with a smile. He was very handsome, more handsome than he'd looked from across the bar. He was tall, with dark blond hair, and he exuded that same confidence that almost all the men I knew carried, a confidence obtained from simply having been born with silver spoons in their mouths.

He blinked a few times. "Fuck . . . you're even hotter up close."

I didn't have to look at Liam to know he was rolling his eyes.

"Yes?" I asked calmly. Compliments meant nothing to me.

The guy stuttered, then took a business card from his shirt pocket and handed it to me. "I'd love to buy you dinner sometime," he said, his voice now a bit steadier.

I looked at his card. His name was Harry, and he was an architect. He probably had no idea I was only twenty years old. That's what I got for going out on Wall Street.

"I'll think about it," I answered.

Harry smiled, and I noticed a dimple in his left cheek. I smiled back, and he waved goodbye. He hadn't even asked for my name. I put the card in my purse and turned back to my friend, who was looking at me with a mixture of amusement and annoyance.

"Sometimes I'm horrified by how similar you are to me."

I shook my head. "We are nothing alike and you know it."

Liam sighed. "The guy who finally gets to sleep with you will be one lucky dude."

I glared at him. "Shh, don't tell anyone my deep, dark secret."

"It's nothing to be ashamed of. Do you care that dudes lie about having slept with you?"

Yes, it bothered me.

"If they have to lie to make themselves feel more like men, let them. If anyone wants to know the truth, they can ask me."

"You're like a praying mantis. You know that, right?"

"I've never eaten anyone; I simply take what I want and discard the rest."

Liam laughed. "You're so naive. One day some dude's going to make you lose your mind, and you'll have to swallow all those feminist ideas of yours."

"It has nothing to do with feminism. Men have used women since the beginning of time; they take what they want and move on. What's wrong with me doing the same thing? I'm not going to let someone else enjoy my body; I want to be the one doing the enjoying."

Liam looked at me like I was clueless. "Any man on earth would enjoy just looking at you, Marfil. Touching you would be like winning the lottery for them, believe me."

It's not like anyone had ever taken me to the point of ecstasy, ever. But Liam didn't need to know that. No one did.

I fell silent for a couple of minutes, then finally said, "You're the only person I'd be willing to go further with, because we're friends."

Liam choked on his beer. "And that, right there, tells me that you're drunk. Come on, let's go; I'll take you home."

I wasn't lying about Liam being the only man I'd consider offering myself up to completely. Out of all the guys on the planet, he was the only one I trusted. I had thought about it many times, because even though I had plenty of experience in everything that came before sex, I was afraid of taking it all the way. From a young age, my father had instilled in me the notion that a woman's virtue was the most important thing she had. And the nuns at boarding school had spared no details about every awful thing that could happen to us if we gave in to the sin of lust. For some reason, that was the only thing from boarding school I took to heart. Everyone around me seemed so obsessed with virginity, and losing said virginity, and even though I desperately wanted to rebel, and did in some ways, I was still incapable of taking that last step.

Liam drove me home in his gray Audi. He'd just recently bought it, and the seats still had that new-car smell. Unlike a lot of students, I didn't live on campus. My father allowed me to move to New York for college on the condition that he would decide where I lived. My apartment was located on the Upper East Side, one of the most expensive parts of town, and was only a train ride from campus. I might sound spoiled, but I couldn't have cared less about living in one of the most exclusive buildings in Manhattan. I'd been surrounded by luxury all my life, and even though many people thought I was an idiot for even going to college when it was clear I'd inherit a fortune, I had always known I would try to forge my own path.

I was great with numbers, so economics made sense. But for pretty much the entirety of my teenage years, I'd begged my father to let me join the New York City Ballet. His answer was always a resounding no, and when I tried to stand up to him, I ended up regretting it. I'd been forced to give up my dreams of being a professional dancer, but if having an entire apartment to myself was good for anything, it was being able to dance as much as I wanted at home.

I gave Liam a kiss on the cheek, and we promised to hang out before the weekend. I waved to Norman, the doorman, as I crossed the lobby of my building to the elevator. Living alone in New York City might seem brave for a young woman, but my neighborhood was very safe, mostly families of bankers who had made obscene amounts of money on Wall Street. My father was one of them.

My apartment was minimalistic, with almost no decorations except for a few bright pink throw pillows. My motto was: *The less you have, the less you have to clean,* and I followed it religiously. I was lucky to have such a large apartment, at least by New York City standards: two bedrooms (not including the staff's room), two bathrooms, and an open-concept living-dining-kitchen. Since I lived alone, I'd set up a dance studio in the second bedroom, where I spent most of my time at home. I had even installed a ballet barre and large mirrors that returned my gaze as I relaxed to the rhythm of the music.

On one of the living room walls, my other best friend, Tamara, had begun painting a mural I could stare at endlessly. It was a conglomeration of quotes from our favorite books, pictures of us, song lyrics, flowers, and most of all eyes, of all sizes, showing all types of expressions . . . Tami studied people's gazes, and I was amazed by her ability to transpose them almost perfectly onto any flat surface, as long as she had something to paint with. She once drew a Minion for me on a Starbucks napkin using only a stirring stick and the foam from my Frappuccino.

I set my purse on the island and went directly to the fridge, although I'm not really sure why. I was a disaster in the kitchen. I once tried to make myself a shepherd's pie using my former stepmother's recipe, but I forgot about it in the oven and almost burned down the entire apartment. It was safer to order takeout.

I had a microeconomics exam coming up, so I decided to sit down and study. I put on some classical music, and before I knew it, the hours had flown by. When I opened my eyes, I realized that I'd fallen asleep in a very uncomfortable position. I sat up, wishing someone could carry me to bed like a little girl.

I was not so lucky.

I set my textbook on the coffee table and dragged myself to the bedroom. As soon as I was all curled up under my white down comforter, a feeling of loneliness came over me. It wasn't that I was sad, exactly, but I had always lived with lots of people around me. At home, Lupita, the housekeeper, had been like a mother to me. There was also Peter, the driver; Frank, the gardener; and even Logan, my father's bodyguard, whenever he was home. At boarding school I'd shared a room with four other girls, including Tami, so we were almost never alone. Being on my own in that apartment sometimes triggered irrational fears; the slightest sound could project a horror movie onto my mind. I hated days like that.

I closed my eyes, burrowed under the blankets, and began to silently count: *One, two, three . . . eighteen . . . forty-four, forty-five . . . two hundred six.* At some point around 543, I finally fell asleep.

---

Friday came before I knew it. I'd been invited to a single's Valentine's party at a club, but I declined the offer. Not because I don't like going out—I love it—but I decided I'd rather stay home and dance or watch a movie, solo.

After spending more than two and a half hours at the ballet barre doing pliés, I put an oversized white shirt on over my leotard and took out Harry's business card.

I could call and ask if he wanted to do dinner. That would save me from having to order another pizza from the place around the corner. But then I remembered that he hadn't even asked for my name. What was I going to do, text and say: *Hey, I'm the random girl from the bar. Want to have dinner on Valentine's Day?* No fucking way.

It was still light out, so I pulled on some leggings, threw on a sweater, put on a pair of gloves and my favorite sneakers, and headed out for a run. I normally ran for over an hour every day, but never in the mornings, because I hated waking up earlier than strictly necessary. Also, I loved seeing the sunset over the Central Park Lake.

I waved to Norman with a smile and went out into the early evening. Central Park was always bustling with people—families taking their kids to the playground, others walking their dogs, feeding the ducks, or enjoying some time under the shade on warmer days. When the sun started to sink low on the horizon, the park began to clear out, except for the runners. I recognized a few other regulars, and we nodded as we passed each other. I had made the mistake once of going out with one of them, and I vowed never to do it again. I hated having to change my jogging route so as not to run into past flings.

After an intense, longer-than-normal run, I slowed to a walk to begin cooling down. The day had given way to a gorgeous clear night, with the lights of the skyscrapers glimmering on the water. I loved this city. A lot of people complained that it was too busy, that people never stopped moving, so on and so forth. I had lived my entire life in the countryside, and being there, in the big city, made me feel like I was part of something exciting.

I was leaning over the stream of a water fountain's cool water, pulling my long ponytail out of the way to keep my hair from getting wet . . . when it happened.

I didn't even have time to scream.

A hand grabbed me around the waist and pulled me backward while another hand covered my mouth with a damp cloth that smelled repulsive. I tried to resist with all my might, panic flooding me, body and mind. I struggled as hard as I could to break free, but the person holding the damp cloth over my face acted swiftly. My eyes began to feel heavy; my limbs lost all their strength. I felt myself falling backward, collapsing against someone tall and muscular.

"Put her in the van."

That was the last thing I heard before losing consciousness.

## CHAPTER 2

# MARFIL

I opened my eyes in a hospital room. There was no one around, just the beeping of a machine to keep me company. Looking down at my body, I saw that I was wearing a green hospital gown with an IV tube sticking out of my left hand and a bandage on my right one. My heart began to race, but since I wasn't connected to a monitor, I was the only one aware of the incessant pounding.

What happened?

The door opened, and a nurse approached my bed. "Miss Cortés? How are you feeling?"

I blinked several times, stunned. "Where am I? What happened?" I tried to sit up. I don't know where I thought I was going to go, but my instincts were telling me to get up and run for it, to flee, to keep myself safe . . . From who, though?

"It's okay, you're fine," she assured me.

I felt my eyes fill with tears, and my mind whirled as I conjured the last images I could recall. Jogging in the park, stopping for a drink of water, someone covering my mouth, darkness, and then . . .

Before I could ask what had happened, the door opened again, and to my relief, my father entered the room.

"Marfil . . ." he said, walking over and putting his arms around me. I buried my head in his chest and breathed in his scent: Eau Sauvage by Dior combined with the tobacco he'd likely been smoking nonstop. "Thank God you're awake," my father said, smoothing my hair.

My father and I weren't very close, and not just because I'd lived most of my life abroad, but I'd never been happier to feel his arms around me as I did in that moment.

Once I'd calmed down, he explained what had happened.

"You were kidnapped, Marfil," my father said grimly, his mouth a thin line.

I'd been found unconscious outside a hospital in New Orleans, an hour and a half from my family's home near Baton Rouge. Luckily, I still had my wallet, which allowed the doctors to identify me and contact my father.

"They didn't leave anything, not even a note; they didn't ask for ransom, either. I realized something was wrong when I called you Sunday and it went to voicemail five times."

Sunday! *God! That means I must've been out for almost three days at least.*

"When I found out you weren't in your apartment and that no one had seen you come back from your run Friday evening, I knew something terrible had happened."

I shook my head, unable to wrap my mind around it.

"The police would like to speak with you. There are two officers outside. They've been waiting for you to wake up."

My father left the room and came back with the two officers. I sat up, nervous, as they started asking me questions. My father kept his eyes on me the entire time. I had never seen him so worried in my life.

"I don't remember anything," I said, feeling my mouth go dry and my palms begin to sweat. "All I remember is the moment they grabbed me . . ."

"You didn't regain consciousness at any point?" one of the officers asked.

I shook my head, racking my brain, but nothing.

"Anything you might be able to tell us would be a big help, Miss Cortés."

I looked nervously to my father, and then at the nurse. "I'm sorry . . ." I said in a trembling voice.

My father took a step toward me, staring straight into my eyes. "Is there any possibility that they did anything to you?"

My lip began to quiver, and I bit it, trying to control the terror coursing through my body. I didn't want to think about that possibility, horrified at knowing I'd lost all sense of what was going on around me, that I could've been in the hands of murderers or rapists . . . Anything could've happened.

"Answer."

I looked up from the bed and met my father's gaze, frightened. "I don't remember anything . . ." I said again, hating the fact that I had no idea what might've happened to me.

"I want you to give her a complete examination right now. Whatever you've done before, I want it done again."

The police looked at my father, and then at me. They seemed uncomfortable, as if the notion that someone might've sexually assaulted me scared them as much as it did me.

"I'll leave my card—anything you remember, as insignificant as it might seem, don't hesitate to call and notify us down at the station," one of the officers asked.

I nodded without speaking, fearing that my voice might break if I tried.

Once the officers left, the nurse asked me if I thought I could walk, clearly taking my father's request seriously. Standing without any pain, I felt somewhat relieved. If I had been sexually assaulted, I would surely feel something, as minimal as it might be, but that wasn't the case. I followed the nurse to a gynecological examination table, where she asked me to put my feet in the stirrups. I made an effort not to cry, wishing this nightmare would end.

"We need to check for traces of . . . any bodily fluid. There were no exterior signs that would indicate sexual assault, but before we proceed, we need to make sure you're okay with this. Even if your father insists, you're over the legal age, so the consent must come from you. . . ." the doctor explained kindly as she examined me.

I understood that my father would want to double-check. It was important for me, as well, to rule out the things I imagined could have happened to me.

"The examination did not reveal any visible physical injuries or foreign DNA," she assured me. "We got your bloodwork back and the results of the HIV test."

AIDS? I opened my eyes wide in terror, but the doctor smiled reassuringly.

"Not AIDS, HIV. But don't worry, we just had to check, it's standard procedure. I know this was a scary, horrible experience, but you're perfectly fine. You can rest easy now."

I nodded, and after a while, a nurse brought me clothes so that I could change out of the hospital gown. I wanted to go home and forget any of this had ever happened.

Once discharged, Peter Vertès, my father's driver, was waiting for us outside the hospital to take us home. My father rode up front in the passenger's seat, talking on the phone the whole way as I tried to process the fact that, just three days ago, my biggest concern had been a microeconomics exam.

I couldn't help but glance around nervously when I stepped out of the car and walked up the stairs to the huge white mansion where I'd grown up. Lupita, who had practically raised me from the time I was a baby, came out to greet me with tears in her eyes. She hugged me tightly, and I returned the embrace, holding back my own tears.

"Miss Marfil!" she said, wiping her face with her apron. "You have no idea how worried about you we all were."

"I'm fine, Lupita; I'm home now," I said, trying to put her mind at ease but equally happy to find myself safe inside those walls.

"I'll make you something warm for dinner, okay? You go take a shower, baby."

My father had disappeared down the hallway, cell phone glued to his ear, wearing a face that said he wasn't to be interrupted. I was grateful that he was trying so hard to find out why the hell someone had kidnapped me without asking for anything in exchange.

As I stood under the shower, I couldn't shake the feeling that this wasn't over yet. Something told me that the kidnapping had merely been a warning to my father. But to warn him of what? It was no secret that my father had a lot of money, which was why it made no sense that they hadn't asked for ransom. Why else would someone kidnap the daughter of Alejandro Cortés?

After I showered, Lupita brought me a cup of steaming-hot soup and a plate of roast beef with potatoes. I hadn't realized how hungry I was until the smell flooded my senses. I had dinner in bed with the TV on in the background as a million thoughts raced through my mind. Liam had sent me a thousand messages, so I called him so he could stop worrying.

"When your father called me, I almost had a heart attack, fuck!" he exclaimed. "He grilled me, like I had something to do with your disappearance. My God, Marfil, I was so worried!"

"Don't pay any attention to him. Apart from Tami, you're one of the few friends I've mentioned to him, and he didn't know who else to contact."

Liam wanted to know everything, asking me to describe what happened, what I remembered and what I didn't, but that was the last thing I wanted to do. I needed to rest. My eyes felt heavy, and despite the fact that I was now safe at home, my fear had not diminished.

"We'll talk when you get back to New York," Liam said.

Why the hell had someone moved me from New York to New Orleans, and better yet, how had they done it?

I played these thoughts over and over in my mind as my eyes closed of their own accord and I fell into a deep, restless sleep.

---

I woke up to a stormy day, as if the weather were a reflection of my mood. I looked out the window at the extension of green lawn that surrounded my father's mansion. I always enjoyed being here; knowing that my mother had been the one to turn this large and imposing estate into a cozy home made me feel warm and fuzzy inside. The hardwood floors throughout the entirety of the house, the furniture, the fixtures. But out of every room, my favorite was the huge kitchen, where my sister and I spent most of our time as little girls, making cookies with Lupe and stealing lumps of sugar to give to the horses. It had also been designed by my mother, who believed that the kitchen was the heart of the home. Now that we were no longer at school together, the living room, with its large fireplace, had become our favorite spot to hang out during the holidays, when Gabi and I would sit around scorching marshmallows and catching up on each other's lives.

I got dressed, quickly pulling on leggings and a sweatshirt, and went down to breakfast as I searched for the next possible flight back to New York on my phone. I had already missed a few classes, and I was going to have to talk to my microeconomics professor and pray that he'd let me retake the exam I'd missed. I should've been more concerned over what had happened to me, but I was still unable to remember anything. I was scared, but since I couldn't even visualize it, it felt unreal.

I entered the kitchen to find Lupita peeling potatoes. The smell of coffee filled the space, which meant that my father must still be home. I had never met anyone as addicted to caffeine as he was. I, on the other hand, had not inherited his passion for the dark, bitter drink; I preferred a glass of warm milk with honey for breakfast.

Lupita smiled when she saw me, and before I could count to ten, she had breakfast in front of me. "Your father wants you to go see him in his office when you're done eating, sweetie."

I nodded, bringing one spoonful of cereal after another to my mouth, finishing my breakfast quickly and thanking Lupita. I crossed the living room, furnished with dark brown leather sofas, a thick Persian rug, a sixty-inch TV, and a long dining table where we ate on special occasions: Christmas, Thanksgiving, my birthday or Gabriella's, if she wasn't with her mother.

I walked the long hallway that led to my father's office, hating every step of the way, as the walls were lined with the mounted heads of dead animals. My father was a big-game hunter who spent a fortune traveling to the most remote corners of the world in search of unique trophies to hang on his wall. I still remember the time he insisted on taking me with him. Not only did he force me to kill a deer, but he then "baptized" me by drenching me in blood from head to toe. He and his friends laughed as I stood there sobbing; I still had nightmares about it. My sister and I were both fervent animal lovers, and we were disgusted by the fact that our father spent his free time hunting them for his own enjoyment.

I knocked on the door before entering. My father was sitting at his huge desk, and in front of him stood Logan Price. Logan had been in charge of my father's security team for as long as I could remember. Anytime my father went anywhere, Logan went with him. It was something so normal that I'd never stopped to ask what dangers he needed protection from. My father, Colombian by birth, had emigrated from Colombia to the United States at just twenty years old. He was a brilliant man, who had made a multimillion-dollar fortune out of nothing. He'd purchased land in Colombia when prices were so low they were practically giving it away, and he planted vineyards that now supplied fine wines to a large part of the southern region. He also had a very close relationship with the Colombian president, with whom he had long talks over cigars.

Yes, Alejandro Cortés was a successful man, but he was highly reserved with us; he hardly ever talked to my sister and me about his work or his endless travels. He'd met my mother in Russia, and they'd married a month later. A year and a half after that, I was born. Hanging over the mantel, right there in his office, was a framed photo of her. Paulina Kozlova had been a dazzling beauty, a gorgeous woman with high cheekbones, full, seductive lips, golden-blond locks, and large emerald-green eyes. I looked like her, though I'd inherited my father's dark hair. My heart twisted in my chest every time I saw that picture. I hated the fact that I had only one memory of my mother: her lifeless eyes staring back at me as blood pooled on the ground all around her.

Logan turned as I closed the door behind me, greeting me with a dry "Good morning, Miss Cortés" as he pulled out a chair for me.

My father rested his elbows on the desk and looked at me. "We've been talking about what happened, Marfil, and the only conclusion we can come to is that someone kidnapped you and brought you here without asking for anything in return simply to send a message. To show me how easy it is to get to you and to let me know that they could do it again anytime they want."

No *How are you feeling, honey?* My father went directly to the point, as always.

I clenched my fists, trying not to show how much it scared me to think that something like this could happen again. "But why? What's the reason behind it?"

My father leaned back, shrugging. "Plenty of people resent my success, hate me, even, Marfil. I guess they were trying to get to me through you."

Logan had been staring out the window, and he now turned to us with a serious expression. "Until we can figure out who it was and what they were trying to achieve by kidnapping you, you'll need protection, to make sure this doesn't happen again."

No . . .

My father knew what was coming before I even opened my mouth. "You begged me not to hire security for you, Marfil, and I was a fool to agree. I didn't listen to my security team's warnings, and now look what's happened. You could've been raped . . . or killed!"

I swallowed, feeling the blood course through my body. "But . . ."

My father stood up and went to the bar beside his desk. "No buts, Mar," he said, opening a bottle of scotch and pouring himself a glass. "I'm not going to take any more chances. I never should've given in to you in the first place."

I looked to Logan and then to my father. They both seemed very serious, decided.

"I can't live a normal, everyday life if I have a bodyguard with me all the time, Dad."

"Would you prefer to let this happen again?"

I had no good argument, and I hated having to just sit there in silence.

"Until we've cleared up what happened, you need to be guarded twenty-four hours a day. I'm reinforcing my security as well, and Gabriella will have a guard, too, when she comes home. She's safe at school for the time being, but I don't plan to let anyone take one of my daughters ever again."

"So you plan to have someone watching me day and night?!"

Logan stepped forward and answered for my father. "Only until we can clear up what's happened, Miss Cortés," he said. "We already have the best private investigators looking into who could've kidnapped you."

"Private investigators? Wouldn't it be better to leave it to the police?"

"The police are slow, honey; they're overworked and underpaid. I prefer to pay for services instead of sitting and waiting for them to be carried out incompetently," her father said.

I closed my mouth. I didn't want something like this to happen again. Still, I felt defeated. I had fought so hard to convince my father that I didn't need security, and it had all been for nothing.

"We got you the best bodyguard we could find. He served in the US military and was decorated with honors. We were lucky he's agreed to accept the job."

I sighed, knowing the battle was lost. "I don't want anyone at school to know I have a bodyguard, Dad."

"We've already thought of that. He'll be undercover; no one will know why he's there unless you tell them. We have informed the university, and he'll be able to pass as a student and escort you everywhere. You won't have to worry about a thing; it'll be like he's not even there. I promise."

This was somewhat of a consolation, although I doubted that some soldier could pass unnoticed in a crowd of mostly young students.

"Your apartment has two bedrooms and a separate room for staff. I've already sent someone to make space for Mr. Moore."

Shit, my dance studio. I couldn't help feeling frustrated and angry. It wasn't that I didn't appreciate what my father was doing for me, but it annoyed me that I would have someone hovering around me all the time. Yes, I was still scared, but I didn't want to live in fear. I didn't want a constant reminder of the fact that someone could hurt me again, or at least try to. But I knew that, given the circumstances, there was nothing I could do.

"How long do you think it will take to figure out who's behind this?"

My father sat back down. "I don't know, but I can assure you it's my top priority."

I nodded, ready to leave. "Can I go?"

My father agreed and looked back at his computer.

I hadn't even met this Mr. Moore, whoever he was, and I already disliked him.

CHAPTER 3

# MARFIL

My father made arrangements for Logan to fly with me back to New York the next day, where Mr. Moore would be waiting to meet me. We weren't able to take the private plane because my father would be leaving for Puerto Rico very early. Not that I cared.

I couldn't help but feel safe with Logan seated beside me in first class. I wasn't a huge fan of flying, so I always preferred to travel with someone else. But beyond my fear of flying, I was also still shaken by what had happened, which was at the forefront of my mind. I just wanted everything to go back to normal, but I'd been kidnapped so close to home that the city I loved so much now felt like an enemy.

As I got off the plane and switched my iPhone out of airplane mode, I received a message from Liam saying he would bring dinner over and not to worry about anything because he would take care of me as if I were his girl. That made me smile. Sometimes I wondered why we weren't a couple, but then I thought about our friendship, and any ideas of taking it further vanished from my mind.

I was not at all excited about sharing my apartment with a stranger, and if this Moore character had to be around, I'd feel more comfortable with Liam there, at least until I got used to him. Bodyguards made me nervous; they were a constant reminder that something bad could happen.

When my mother was killed, my father tightened up his security to an extreme. He never went anywhere without Logan, even if he was just stopping to buy a bottle of water. Gabriella and I had never had our own bodyguards, but only because we were locked up at boarding school where there was no need. Also, unlike our father, a well-known figure, we had always been hidden from the public eye.

Things changed when I moved to New York. It wasn't like back in England, when my father was more permissive than I had expected. But now that I had been kidnapped, there wasn't a person on earth who could convince him not to assign me a security detail. This annoyed and relieved me in equal measures. I'm not going to lie, the whole thing scared me, and it was even scarier knowing that the reasons for my kidnapping were still a mystery. And I still couldn't shake the nagging feeling that the worst was yet to come.

I tried to push those thoughts aside as I followed Logan down the long airport corridor. So much had happened in such a short time, and all I wanted to do was take a steaming hot bath and crawl into bed, then wake up and discover it had all been a bad dream.

"Miss Cortés, I won't be seeing you back to the apartment—my flight leaves in two hours. Mr. Moore will take care of you from here on out, all right?"

*He'll take care of me?* I suddenly felt like I was three years old.

I nodded and remained silent until we reached the automatic doors that opened onto the arrivals hall, full of travelers and men in suits holding signs with names on them.

As I walked toward the very handsome person who would now be my bodyguard, holding a sign with my name on it, my heart began to pound. Logan stepped forward and clapped the man on the back as if they already knew each other, while I stood there unable to breathe, all the air suddenly sucked out of my lungs. Never before had a man's physical looks caused my body to react in such a way. *Ever*. I could try to describe it, but words wouldn't do it justice.

"Miss Cortés," he said, holding out a hand, "I'm Sebastian Moore. I'll be in charge of your security from here on out."

Sebastian . . . Fuck. Did his name have to be so incredibly sexy, too?

It took me a few seconds to snap out of it and lift my hand to shake his. My stomach did a flip as our skin made contact. Was this the feeling Liam had told me about?

I felt clumsy, small, and insignificant . . . a sensation that was totally foreign to me. Sebastian, on the other hand, stared blankly at me, like someone looking at a freaking park bench, utterly indifferent.

I hurried to put on my sunglasses. I needed to organize my thoughts and keep from showing how much meeting this man had affected me.

"I'm leaving you in good hands, don't worry," Logan said to me before shaking Sebastian's hand.

I looked on as Logan said something that I couldn't hear and didn't care to. I was drinking in the sight of Sebastian Moore. He was tall, a few inches taller than Liam—whom I had to stand on my tiptoes to kiss—and looked strong enough to pick me up with one arm . . . just the way I liked them. He had light brown hair, a hint of stubble on his chin, which I imagined was prickly to the touch, a square jawline, and an athletic build, with large biceps visible even through his nice suit jacket. He honestly could've passed for one of the millionaire New Yorkers who lived in my neighborhood, although he seemed incredibly young.

How old was he? Twenty-five? Twenty-six? Suddenly, I was dying to know everything about him . . . What was happening to me?

Surprisingly, I was able to be coherent enough to say goodbye to Logan. But as soon as he left, I was hit with the realization that I was now alone with my new bodyguard. I began fidgeting with my hair, unsure of what to do or say. Fortunately, I didn't have to stress for long.

"I didn't park too far. Come on, I'll grab your bags."

Whenever I was with my father, we always had a driver pick us up and drop us off, but in New York, I'd always gotten around just fine by taxi, Uber, or even the subway. This time, however, Sebastian had a black Audi waiting for us in the airport parking lot. He walked to the driver's side as I waited for him to open the passenger door.

"You sit in the back," he said over the hood of the car.

I blinked several times. It had sounded like an order, which was a bit strange, and he hadn't opened the door for me either. It's not that I was some princess, far from it, but I was so accustomed to my father's strict protocol for his employees when they were around me, that this guy's mannerisms took me by surprise. Lupe was the only one who would drop the formalities from time to time, and only when we were alone.

I rode in the back seat, glancing constantly at his reflection in the rearview mirror. He didn't seem to have any trouble orienting himself, and in just three minutes, we were heading into Manhattan. We still had to cross all of Queens, which would take us over half an hour. Did he ever plan on speaking to me?

"I'd like to know what orders, exactly, my father gave you . . ." I said after fifteen minutes passed, silent as the grave.

Sebastian took his eyes off the road and rested them on my sunglasses for a fleeting instant. "Orders?" he asked.

Suddenly, the word sounded insulting.

"Well, instructions, directions, guidelines, whatever you want to call them."

"It's my job to protect you and keep your father informed

on anything that might come up unexpectedly while you're with me."

While I'm with him. Of course, not the other way around.

I didn't want to talk anymore. His cold, clipped tone was starting to irritate me, and at the same time, his deep, baritone voice was giving me goose bumps.

We reached my street in record time. It was clear that speed did not figure among the safety risks he was concerned with protecting me from. We parked the car in the garage and, as he followed me into the elevator, I remembered that I was going to have to share my apartment with him.

Fuck.

The silence inside the small space of the elevator was deafening. Never in my life had I been quiet for so long in another person's company. Liam would've been proud.

Eventually, what felt like twenty minutes later, the *ding* of the elevator indicated we had reached my floor. Sebastian led the way, stopping in front of my apartment and taking a key from his pocket. Opening the door, he motioned for me to go in first.

So, chivalry wasn't dead, but . . .

He had a copy of my key?!

Hold on.

Had he already been here?

"Not now," he said, as if reading my thoughts. "Come inside."

I did as he said, and took in my apartment. It looked like it always did, but it didn't feel the same, and I wasn't sure if and when it ever would again. The last time I'd left the house, my only concern had been whether or not I should call that guy from the bar whose name I'd already forgotten.

I set my bag on the kitchen island and, feeling restless and uncomfortable, turned to look at my new roommate. "This is strange," I said.

Sebastian took off his suit jacket and hung it on the coat rack beside the door. It was then I noticed he had a gun in a holster, like a cop.

"Just act like I'm not here."

Piece of cake! Except he practically took up the entire room.

"Look, I don't know anything about you, but if you're going to live here, hovering around me twenty-four hours a day, there are some things I need to know."

"You can ask me anything that has to do with you and your safety."

"How old are you?"

Seriously, Marfil?

Sebastian frowned, looking confused. "That has nothing to do with your safety."

"You're not going to answer?"

"No."

I pursed my lips, annoyed. "I don't like having a bodyguard. I should warn you that it's going to be hard for me to get used to you."

"You will."

I took off my sunglasses, realizing I still had them on. I looked into his brown eyes, bordered by thick black lashes. I had the urge to look away, intimidated, but I remained firm. "So I should just pretend like you're not here?"

"Exactly. Just let me know if you're going to go out."

Great.

"I don't know if you saw the guest room, or . . ."

"I didn't touch your dance studio, don't worry."

"I spend a lot of time in there. I know the other bedroom is a lot smaller, but I'd like to keep practicing in my studio, as I've been doing."

"It's your room. I don't care how you use it."

That was a relief. I'd been afraid my father had sent someone to clean out my dance studio and that Sebastian would've already set up his bedroom in there. I was aware that he was doing me a favor, since the other room was much smaller and less comfortable, but I didn't want to give up my favorite part of the house. It was my apartment, after all.

"Well . . . I'm going to my room," I said, and then turned around and walked away without waiting for him to respond. He made me too nervous.

My bedroom was a mess, just as I'd left it. For some inexplicable reason, I decided to clean up, entering into an almost manic fit of organizing. I don't know if I did it because I felt so anxious or because I couldn't just go out into the living room and lie on the couch like I usually would. I felt like I was losing my mind, but I kept cleaning until the room was spotless.

Satisfied over what I had accomplished, I finally allowed myself to take a look at my phone. I had a text from Liam, letting me know he would be here in an hour. At least that would give me an excuse to take back the living room.

After my shower, I changed into my favorite blue jeans and a white comfy shirt, then stood in front of the mirror examining myself carefully. What did Sebastian see when he looked at me?

For as long as I could remember, everyone around me had always complimented me on my looks. The other girls at boarding school either hated me or envied me. It took me a long time to gain the acceptance of my classmates and the nuns, who had once been brutal, always saying I was a walking sin. I didn't fully understand what they'd meant until I met Liam and he finally explained it to me.

"Do you have any idea what a babe you are?" he'd asked me once, lying in my bed—me in nothing but a long-sleeve T-shirt and underwear, and him in sweatpants, shirtless—the night we did more than just kissing for the first time.

"I know that whatever it is you see has nothing to do with what I am," I'd answered, without feeling flattered.

Sure, I was pretty, but when being pretty meant that people never looked beyond your appearance, beauty could become your worst enemy, especially with a rebellious personality like mine. It wasn't until later that I discovered the power I had over others and learned how to take advantage of it. If men were going to treat me like an object, not like a sentient being with a brain, I would treat them no differently.

I walked out of my bedroom feeling like an intruder in my own home. I had stayed in there for longer than my restless personality could bear.

The living room was empty, but when I looked down the long hallway, I saw a dim light under his bedroom door. I imagined he'd spend most of his time in there.

I sighed and made my way over to the fridge. I should've gone grocery shopping days ago. There was absolutely nothing in the apartment—even the toilet paper had run out.

As I put on my sneakers, I began to make a mental note of everything I needed from the store. It wasn't cold enough for my big jacket, so I left it on the hook and grabbed my bag. Once at the door, I paused for a few seconds. Did I have to tell him I was going to the store? It was only a block away . . .

My instincts told me I should let him know.

I walked down the hall and timidly knocked on his door.

This was so strange.

He opened it a few seconds later, casually leaning on the wall with one arm and slightly holding the door ajar with his other, as if intentionally keeping me from peeking inside. I couldn't help but take him all in, from his rolled-up sleeves to his right arm covered in tattoos to the thick, black-framed glasses, which made him look intellectual and caused my brain to temporarily short-circuit.

I was painfully aware that by staring like this, I was becoming the same kind of objectifier I despised, but he had me completely spellbound. Besides, it wasn't like I knew much else about him.

Clearing my head, I forced myself to focus. "I need to go to the store to pick up a few things."

Sebastian nodded. "Give me just a second, please."

He turned around, and I took the opportunity to glance into the room. It looked nothing like the storage dump it had been a week ago. Granted, all I could see from the doorway was a black leather chair and a pretty white rug, but still. I watched as Sebastian sat down in front of an open laptop, typed something quickly, and then closed it with a frown.

Had I interrupted something important?

"Right behind you," he said, snapping me out of my trance.

Outside, on the street, it felt very strange to have him walking beside me. My father's security guards had always either walked behind him or out in front of him. But Sebastian did so right next to me, as if he were my friend.

"Is it always going to be like this?" I asked as we entered the small supermarket.

"Is what going to be like this, Marfil?"

Hearing him pronounce my name sparked too many emotions to ignore, although I did everything possible to go on talking as if the guy next to me in the shampoo, makeup, and tampon aisle was just some regular guy. Tampons . . . shit, I needed those, too.

Was I going to have to buy tampons in front of him?

"Like, you always with me even when I just need to go to the deli."

"Yes," he answered curtly.

I looked at him, annoyed by his response.

I grabbed shampoo and toilet paper but left the tampons

behind, then pushed the cart over to the wine section. I picked up a bottle of white and put it in the cart. Sebastian didn't say a word, so I continued shopping, picking up a pack of Heineken and then stopping in the fruit section. As I carefully selected some strawberries and apples, it dawned on me that Sebastian would have to eat, too.

I was about to say his name when I noticed his eyes were fixed on the shop entrance. I looked in that direction. Two guys, more or less his age, had just entered.

"Do you need anything?" I asked him.

"What?" he replied, now facing me, distracted.

"Food. There's nothing in the apartment unless you get it delivered."

Sebastian shook his head. "Don't worry about me. I'll take care of my own meals."

I shrugged and continued filling my cart with potato chips, olives, milk, sugar, and a pie from the bakery section. As I waited in line to pay, I noticed that Sebastian had not stopped scanning the place the entire time; his eyes had never been still. His presence was more imposing than any bodyguard my father had ever had, and as the cashier eyed him suspiciously, it dawned on me that with his body like a Greek god, he probably made other people wary.

I looked at his black suit pants and white shirt. How the hell was I going to take him to school with me looking like that?

After I paid for the groceries using my father's Centurion card—or rather, my extension of it—Sebastian picked up my bags and carried them in his right hand, leaving his left free. I hadn't bought that much, but there were some bottles and other heavy items. I offered to help him, but he refused with a simple shake of the head.

My mind raced as we headed back. There were so many things I wanted to know about him. That was why I'd never liked bodyguards; it was impossible for me to be around another person without talking to them. As a little girl, before being sent away to school, my nannies would have to change shifts hourly because I was so exhausting. Or so my father told me when listing his reasons for sending me to boarding school abroad.

"Sometimes, Marfil, you don't realize how annoying you can be. You're just a girl—it's understandable—but keep quiet in my presence," he'd said to me more than once.

Eventually, I'd learned to stay silent, but only for short periods of time.

"Are you left-handed?" I asked Sebastian as we walked side by side.

He looked at me with furrowed brows.

"You're carrying all the weight in your right hand. Not because you're right-handed, but because you want to have your left hand free to grab your gun if you need to, right?"

He tilted his head slightly, and I noticed a hitch in his lips that almost looked like a smile, *almost*. "I'm ambidextrous, but yes, I'm a bit more comfortable with my left hand."

Ambidextrous . . . I looked at his hands, the left hanging loose at his side, the other carrying the bags as if they were filled with feathers instead of full bottles.

Without warning, I imagined those hands gripping me tightly, moving down my back, up my legs . . .

I put my sunglasses back on and ignored him for the rest of the walk home.

---

Fortunately for my mental well-being, Sebastian went straight to his part of the apartment and left me to put away the groceries. He offered to give me a hand, but I wanted to be alone. I assured him that it wasn't necessary, and he didn't insist on helping.

The doorbell rang just as I was finishing putting everything away in the fridge. I knew it was Liam, so I rushed to the door, excited to see my best friend. But as I crossed the hallway, I crashed straight into a human wall, much harder than I thought possible. Large hands wrapped around my forearms, halting my rush to open the door.

"Are you expecting someone?"

His touch caused me to feel chills all throughout my body. Sebastian, however, quickly pulled his hands away, as if my skin burned him.

"It's a friend of mine," I said, stepping forward.

He placed a hand on the door above my head, stopping me from opening it.

I turned toward him, frowning.

"Who is it? They didn't even use the buzzer."

"He has keys."

Sebastian shook his head and pressed his lips together. "You give out keys to just anyone?"

"I give keys to my best friend."

"Hey, Mar! Open up, fuck, I'm gonna go crazy if I don't see you."

I put my hands on my hips.

"What's his name?"

I rolled my eyes, exasperated. "Liam."

"Your father made it clear to me that there would be no men in the apartment."

I laughed. "Yeah, sure! And I'm Bluey."

Sebastian seemed lost.

"From *Bluey* the TV show . . ." I said, but still no response.

He probably didn't have any younger siblings.

I shook my head and pulled the door open, ignoring the presence of the gorilla behind me.

Liam barely gave me a chance to get a look at him, his arms

instantly lifting me off the floor, squeezing me tightly against him. I inhaled his scent, which smelled like home. "Fuck . . . you scared me to death."

I felt my eyes well up with tears. I'd been holding it all in. Ever since I'd gotten back, it had felt like my life was no longer mine, my home was no longer my home. Now, with Liam here, everything seemed to fall back into place, and I finally felt relaxed, comfortable.

"I still can't believe what happened . . ." I said into his neck, not wanting to let him go.

Liam nuzzled his face in my hair, then tensed a few seconds later. In a single movement, he put me down and fixed his gaze on Sebastian. "Who is that?"

I huffed, hating the fact that his arms were no longer around me. "My new bodyguard."

Sebastian looked Liam up and down. I closed the door behind me, and the temperature in the room seemed to drop by several degrees.

"I need to see your ID," Sebastian demanded.

Liam looked at him in disbelief. "Isn't it enough that she says she knows me?"

Sebastian barely blinked. "Your ID, please."

Liam rummaged in his pocket and pulled out his black leather wallet. He removed his driver's license and handed it over.

Sebastian studied it for a few seconds, then gave it back. "I'm going to have to ask you to return the keys to this apartment. For security reasons, we can't have them circulating. There's a chance someone could steal them from you and try to get in."

What? No! Why would anyone try to get in? I hadn't even been kidnapped at home.

Liam looked shocked and offended. "I would never place

her at risk. I have a key in case there's some emergency and she needs me."

"If there's some problem or Marfil needs help, I'm here now."

They stared at each other for several endless seconds.

"Liam, just give him the keys. My father's the one behind all this, and the last thing I want is to give him a reason to do something crazy, like force me to move back home, for example."

Liam let out the breath he was holding in and turned toward me, a scared look on his face. Then he did as Sebastian asked. As soon as he had the keys, the bodyguard excused himself and went into his room, after reminding me that I should let him know if we went out.

"Do you want a beer?" I said, focusing back on my friend.

Liam nodded as he sat on the couch and looked down the hallway. "I can't believe what happened, Mar," he said, resting his elbows on his knees and smoothing his hair.

I sat down next to him as I handed him a cold beer and brought mine to my lips. "Me neither . . . It's been terrifying, but at the same time it's like it was all a nightmare, like it's not real. I was drugged the whole time, so I guess that's why I feel like it happened to someone else."

"But why? Fuck. Why would someone want to kidnap you?!"

It was obvious that I came from wealth, but I never talked about it, and Liam could tell it made me uncomfortable, so he never asked. His mother was an elementary school teacher, and his father owned a pet shop. He owed everything he had to his brilliant mind, having been accepted to Columbia on a scholarship, and he'd had to work nights at the trendiest clubs in the city to pay his bills, since the scholarship didn't cover everything. I admired Liam because, as opposed to him, it didn't matter how much I achieved in life, everyone would always see me as a little rich girl, born with a silver spoon in her mouth, never having to lift a finger.

My father had so many companies that I couldn't even name them all. He owned Banco Cortés, one of the most important banks in Latin America, and he raised Appaloosas, a desirable breed of horses. All that, along with countless other investments, had made him into something of a public figure, and it was no surprise that people envied his fortune. That was why my father had always kept Gabriella and me away from the limelight. He had never let us attend his parties, and we didn't know any of his business associates. My father rarely discussed work; all he ever talked about with us was horses, which he'd taught us to love and respect from a young age.

"I don't know . . . no one knows. My father thinks someone was just using me as a way to threaten him. The fact that they didn't ask for anything in return and they also didn't send a note, nothing, is almost more confusing than the kidnapping itself."

"And now you're going to have this guy around all the time?"

I nodded, pursing my lips.

Liam placed a hand on my cheek and set his beer on the table. "Your father did the right thing. You were kidnapped right here in Central Park, Mar. They could do it again if they wanted, especially if they were to find out about the other parts of town you frequent," he said, a displeased look on his face.

Liam and I had argued about this issue countless times. I realized I was going to have to inform Sebastian and beg him not to say anything to my father.

"I won't get kidnapped again. I'll be careful. The only thing that worries me is my father . . . and my sister . . ."

"Gabriella is in London; she should be safe there."

"If I told you about the things she gets up to at school . . . Fuck, I have to warn her not to leave!"

I felt like I was about to have a heart attack as I raced to my bedroom and found my cell phone. It was nine thirty here, two thirty in the morning there. She should be asleep, so I opted to send her a text instead:

Don't even think about leaving school. Something's happened. Call me when you get this. It's urgent.

Our father hadn't told Gabi about the kidnappings, because he hadn't wanted to worry her, but he had no idea that I'd taught her all the best ways to sneak out of school. She could cross the woods and get to town without anyone knowing. If anything happened to her, it would be all my fault!

Leaving the room with my cell phone in my hand, I watched as Sebastian's door opened and he stepped out into the hall, as if he'd read my mind and knew that something was wrong.

"What's going on?"

Liam stood up from the couch and came over.

"My sister has no idea about the kidnapping. My father didn't want to tell her, but what he doesn't know is that she sneaks out of school. She goes into town with a few other girls and they meet up with friends . . . If they came for me, they can do the same thing to Gabi."

"She's probably asleep now, Mar—you can talk to her tomorrow and explain everything," Liam said, though I couldn't keep my eyes off Sebastian.

A few seconds later, he finally spoke. "I'll make some calls. I know someone in London. I'll ask him to make sure nothing looks suspicious. I'll talk to your father tomorrow and inform him."

NO!

I stepped forward and grabbed Sebastian's arm as fear took

hold of every single one of my nerve endings. "You can't tell him! He'll kill her!"

Sebastian studied me for a few fleeting seconds, during which, although it might seem impossible, we communicated without a need for words. He walked away without a sound, and I knew that my sister would be safe.

## CHAPTER 4

# SEBASTIAN

I went back to my area of the apartment and made several calls. If what Marfil had said was true, we were going to have to keep a much closer eye on the youngest of the Cortés sisters.

Wilson answered on the second ring, and after explaining the situation, he took the necessary measures for the time being, until we could get one of Alejandro's more experienced men to London. I knew the girl would be safe with him looking out for her.

The day seemed like it would never end. I had only been on the job a few hours, and I already felt claustrophobic. I would've never chosen to serve as bodyguard for Marfil Cortés, but the boss had given me the order, and there was nothing I could do about it. Babysitting a spoiled brat was not on my list of career ambitions. I had received the highest possible score on the C-SORT and the physical tests to become a Navy SEAL. This job should be nothing compared to any of that, but I was beginning to think it might require more mental effort than all the military intelligence tests combined. Working for Alejandro Cortés was proving more difficult than I'd ever imagined.

Almost without realizing it, I found myself watching the computer monitor linked to the camera I'd set up in the apartment's living room. Marfil was lying against her "friend" on the brown leather couch as he rubbed her back until her eyes closed. No one had alerted me to the existence of a possible boyfriend; I should've been informed.

I looked at the ebony color of her hair, contrasting magnificently with the ivory skin that did justice to her name. Her enormous eyes, with their long eyelashes, seemed to follow me everywhere I went. Her body surpassed any standard of beauty to the point that I sometimes lost my concentration whenever she was near. The need to gaze at her, as if I were in front of a work of art in motion, became increasingly difficult to ignore. She was beautiful. Even Samara couldn't hold a candle to this girl. I wasn't usually too impressed by beautiful women, but I understood why her father wanted to keep her locked away.

I went to the mini fridge I'd brought in for my personal use, opened a beer, and took a swig. With the computer in front of me, I clicked through the camera feeds in other rooms of the apartment. I had placed cameras everywhere except for her bedroom and bathroom, which made me nervous, since it would be pretty easy for someone to enter through the bedroom window. Marfil didn't know about the cameras, and my instincts told me not to mention them for now. I had a feeling that, sooner or later, her ignorance of them might benefit me.

My left hand unconsciously moved to my rib cage, to the spot right between the fifth and sixth ribs. The wound should've healed by now, but the infection had been bothering me for a couple of weeks.

I looked back at the living room feed and wondered, seeing her lying there asleep, if she had any idea of the danger she was in.

CHAPTER 5

# MARFIL

I opened my eyes and realized that I was lying on a wrinkled sheet of paper. I picked it up, half asleep, and read the note Liam had left me.

*I didn't want to wake you. You need your rest. I'll see you next Wednesday for dinner and a movie. Love you, babe.*

I smiled. I liked feeling that things were still the same. Well, more or less. Our Wednesday movie night might still be in place, but my inner voice told me that something had changed. I looked at the time. Eleven thirty!

"Shit!"

I jumped up and threw on a pair of jeans and a red-and-white-striped T-shirt. Then I stepped into my motorcycle boots and went to the bathroom to wash my face and brush my teeth. I had a mark on my right cheek from where I'd slept on Liam's note, but I couldn't waste time putting on makeup.

I rushed out of my room and shrieked when I saw Sebastian standing there. He was dressed in light jeans, a dark T-shirt, and white Nike sneakers. Was this the same guy who'd picked me up at the airport yesterday looking like a bank manager? He lifted one of my white coffee mugs with hearts to his lips, and I felt so dizzy that I had to hold on to the wall behind me for support.

*Sorry, you're not scary; I was just startled by how hot you are,*

I would've liked to explain. But I still had some self-respect, so I tried to play it off with as much dignity as possible.

"I'm running late," I said as I walked to the kitchen and stood on my tiptoes to reach my pink thermos, when an arm stretched over my head and grabbed it for me. I turned to face him and found him much closer than I'd expected, that it took me a few seconds to snap out of it and take the thermos he was holding out to me. "Th-thanks," I said, walking around him to heat up the milk. Once warm enough, I added honey, then poured it into my thermos at lightning speed. "Can we go?"

Sebastian nodded, picking up a jean jacket and putting it on.

I opened the door without looking back and pressed the button for the elevator. His presence made me uncomfortable. I couldn't help it; I was extremely attracted to him. We stepped onto the elevator, and as the doors closed, his Hugo Boss cologne filled my nostrils. I thought I might finally experience an orgasm right then and there.

I was anxious about what it would be like to have him following me around all day on campus. He was dressed enough like a college student to blend in, but what would people think if he was always right next to me, watching me at all times? I didn't want anyone to know he was my bodyguard, so when we got to the car, I ignored his orders and climbed into the front passenger seat.

"You should sit in the back, Marfil."

Once again, that tingling feeling returned when he said my name.

"You're not my driver, Sebastian," I said, enjoying the feel of his name on my lips. "I don't want anyone to know what your job is. If I show up to school in the back seat, my friends are going to start asking questions."

"The windows in the back are bulletproof; it's for your safety."

I put on my seat belt, ignoring him. "No one is going to shoot me."

Sebastian clenched his jaw and looked forward. He started the car and I smiled, happy that I'd gotten my way.

"We have to think about what we're going to say when people see you with me," I said a few minutes later.

Sebastian acted like he hadn't heard me.

"You might pass for a student, but if my friends see us always together, every day, they'll think we're a couple."

"What others think should be the least of your concerns."

Maybe that was true, but I didn't want to give people any more reason to talk about me. They did that more than I was comfortable with already. "I don't want anyone to know I have a bodyguard."

"Well . . . tell me what you expect me to do, because *I am* your bodyguard."

I looked at him, annoyed by his condescending tone. "Pull in here," I said as we neared the parking lot that was farthest from my first class, where no one would see us.

Sebastian shot me a confused look but did as I asked.

I grabbed a notebook out of my backpack and ripped out two pages. "Here's a schedule of my classes and a map of campus. Don't talk to me; keep a safe distance without looking suspicious. We'll meet back here after I grab some lunch."

I got out of the car without waiting for his response. If I didn't take control of the situation, Sebastian Moore might get the wrong idea about me. I was the one who would be calling the shots; I wouldn't let anyone boss me around, and I had a feeling Sebastian wasn't going to like that one bit.

When I entered my Intermediate Microeconomics class late, the professor looked irritated. Silently excusing myself, I went straight to my favorite seat at the top of the room, right by the hallway door. Only after I'd taken out my laptop and opened my notes did I allow myself to look around. Sitting to my right, like he belonged there, was Sebastian, scanning the classroom until he spotted me. For some reason, I didn't avert my gaze when my eyes met his across the room, but I should have. It turned out to be almost impossible to concentrate knowing he was watching me.

---

The rest of the day flew by. Asking the professor to let me make up the exam I'd missed because of the kidnapping was useless. I didn't want to tell him the real reason for my absence, and my excuse of being sick was laughable to him.

"You'll have to make up for it with the midterm and final, Miss Cortés, that's all there is to it."

I stormed out of class, making my way to the closest dining hall. As soon as I landed on the third floor of Lerner Hall, my bad mood turned worse. Regan, my betting ex-boyfriend, was leaning against the cafeteria glass wall, surrounded by all his asshole friends. They had to comment when I walked past, as always. "Hey, Marfil! We missed you. Some of us had to go back to watching porn."

I ignored their stupid comments, crossed the cafeteria, bought a salad with arugula and cheese, then went straight to my usual table, where my friend group sat. Lisa and Stella were classmates more than friends, but they were some of the few girls I could more or less tolerate. I'd met Lisa at orientation and Stella in the campus infirmary, where we'd both landed with epic hangovers after our first college party.

I liked them, but it was hard for me to open up.

"Where have you been?"

"I was sick," I lied as I took a sip of water. I watched as Sebastian sat down at the table next to ours after walking across the cafeteria with his eyes on me. I observed him as he took a bite of a cheese sandwich. I liked seeing him eat, proof that he wasn't actually a Greek god, just a mere mortal like the rest of us.

"Who are you looking at?" Stella asked, following my gaze until landing on Sebastian.

"No one," I answered, quickly looking away.

"Who is that?!"

Lisa turned, and her eyes lit up just as Stella's had.

"Who?" I said, playing dumb.

"What do you mean, who?" Lisa said, looking incredulous. "That snack over there in the corner. I've never seen him around! He's so hot!"

"Ooh, he *is* a snack; I'd like to dunk him in my glass of milk," said Stella, shameless as ever.

I looked at my two friends. I didn't want them to even look at him, and my irrational jealousy concerned me more than the fact that, when I glanced around, I noticed they weren't the only students eyeing Sebastian. Several other girls were stealing glances at him.

Fuck, Sebastian Moore had just become the talk of Ferris Booth Commons, and an object of sexual desire for half the students. Wasn't he supposed to pass unnoticed?

We didn't make eye contact again until we reached the car. I sat down, furious and exhausted, my emotions close to the surface for reasons I didn't fully understand.

"Is it really necessary for you to come to all my classes and even eat in the exact same dining hall, at the exact same time as me? You could wait outside—nothing's going to happen to me here on campus."

"My job is to protect you twenty-four hours a day, Marfil."

I sat in silence as he drove. I wasn't used to a man being so indifferent to me. Sebastian seemed immune to my presence, whereas his presence drove me crazy.

We didn't exchange another word, but in my mind, I was beginning to formulate a plan. Although I knew that, if I was successful, it would only cause more problems.

---

Back at the apartment, Sebastian went into his room, and I locked myself in my bedroom with a single objective in mind. I wasn't going to deviate from my daily routine, although I did spend a few minutes longer than usual choosing my dance outfit. I finally settled on my favorite leotard—black with a lace back—chose a matching skirt, and finished it off with tights, leg warmers, and my pink sweater.

Ready to set my plan in motion, I knocked on the door to his room, and he told me to come in. Like some practical joke destiny was playing to give me a taste of my own medicine, I found him standing before a boxing bag in sports shorts and a white sleeveless shirt that left his muscular arms bare. In place of boxing gloves, he had white tape over his knuckles. My eyes paused on his tattoos. I wanted time to study them, to ask him about each one . . .

Seeing me enter, he stopped the bag, which he must've hung from the ceiling the day before, and stood looking at me without a word. To my satisfaction, his eyes scanned my body down to my legs and then back up to my face. I didn't usually display myself to men, but I felt a smug satisfaction to see that, even if Sebastian Moore seemed to be from another planet, I could still get some type of reaction out of him . . .

"I'm going to be dancing for a while . . ." I said.

He didn't say a word or even so much as glance back in my direction. Instead, he resumed pounding his knuckles against the boxing bag, the sound echoing through the silent room and immediately reawakening my frustration.

Once in my dance studio, I tried to forget that he was right outside. It wouldn't do any good to keep brooding over it; Sebastian was there to protect me, nothing more. I turned on the waltz from *Masquerade* Suite by Aram Khachaturian, a Soviet composer who always made me feel better on days when I needed to forget about the world and let myself be transported far away. I warmed up for twenty minutes, and even though I hadn't done quite enough stretches on the barre, I didn't care—I needed to dance.

I began to move around the room, the tips of my toes totally perpendicular to the floor, my pirouettes and arabesques almost perfect. I longed to dance with another person . . . to jump up and be lifted through the air in the arms of my dance partner before an audience that valued my effort and dedication the way I'd always dreamed.

My mother had been a prima ballerina with the Bolshoi Ballet in Moscow, one of the best dance companies in the world, if not *the* best. The fact that my mother had been a star in the ballet world gave me a sense of infinite pride. Ballet was something we both shared, something I had inherited from her and that no one, not my father or my uncle, had been able to take away from me. Dancing was my one true passion, and I would do it forever, even if that meant finding the courage to defy the people who wanted me to quit.

Exhausted, I flopped onto the floor and was trying to catch my breath when my cell phone started to ring. I sat up, relieved to see that it was one of the people I loved most in the world: Gabriella. I turned off the music and answered the call.

"You were kidnapped, Marfil?" she shouted after I'd explained the reason for my message the night before.

"Don't worry, Dad is taking care of it. But you can't leave school; they might try to do the same thing to you, although I'm sure you're safe there in London."

"I want to see you," she said, and I could picture her already packing her suitcase and begging our dad to let her miss a few days of school.

"I'm fine, Gabi, really. They've assigned me a bodyguard."

There was a momentary silence on the other end of the line, followed by "Poor guy."

I laughed, knowing that she was relaxed enough to make fun of me again.

"But for real, I want to see you. Can't you talk to Dad? Even just for the weekend; it's been so long since we've seen each other, Mar."

"I know . . . but it's not a good idea for you to come back right now. You'll be safer there, at least until we know who was behind the kidnapping."

My sister, like me, was very stubborn, but I was finally able to make her understand that it wasn't the best time to ask our father for favors. We couldn't talk much longer, since her school limited phone calls to fifteen minutes, so we said goodbye and promised to talk again soon. Even though Gabriella seemed worried, I felt relieved knowing that she was going to put an end to her escapades beyond the confines of the school grounds.

When I walked out of my studio, I saw that Sebastian's room was empty. I found him in front of the stove, cooking. His hair was still wet, and he was no longer wearing his shorts or sleeveless shirt. Instead, he now donned a pair of gray sweatpants and a plain black tee.

"What are you making?" I asked, walking over and taking a look at the vegetables simmering in the pan, filling my apartment with an unfamiliar yet welcoming aroma.

"Sauteed mushrooms with vegetables and shrimp."

Was he going to invite me to eat any of that delicious dinner? Or would he serve himself a dish, take it to his room, and leave me to my greasy noodles from the Chinese restaurant on the corner?

"I'll make you a plate, if you want."

Oh, well, he did have some manners, at least.

"I'd love that, thanks."

I went to my room. I couldn't stand to be so close to him, nor his coldness. After showering, I put on my pajamas and went back out to find the living room was once again empty. On the table sat a plate of food, a glass, and a perfectly aligned knife and fork, waiting there for me so that I could have dinner . . . alone.

---

The next afternoon, I let Sebastian know I was going out for a run. He didn't seem thrilled with the idea, or with anything I did for that matter, but I set out, with him behind me, toward Central Park. I wasn't sure why, but I felt a need to return to the spot where the kidnapping had occurred. I needed to confront my fear in order to return to some sense of normalcy. It made me furious that someone had converted my favorite place in New York into something I had to fear. I was even more furious that I hadn't even been able to defend myself; I didn't stand a chance in a situation like that one due to a total lack of self-defense training.

We reached the water fountain at almost the same time of day as when I'd been kidnapped a week prior. I stopped and looked around. It was the ideal spot for an attack, with trees and an outcropping of rocks that hid the fountain from view of the path. I noticed that, a short distance away, the road that looped around the park could be seen through a wrought iron gate. I stepped toward it, heading deeper into the trees, until a hand caught my arm, stopping me.

"Marfil, don't try so hard to tempt fate."

Sebastian seemed more annoyed than nervous. I knew perfectly well that if I were in any real danger, he wouldn't have let me get that far. No, he had some other reason for stopping me. And while I was curious about what truly concerned him, I was more interested in understanding how somebody had managed to carry me out of the park without anyone noticing.

"You just do your job; that's what you're here for." My words came out ruder than expected, but he was curt with me all the time. I pulled loose from his grip and walked through the trees until I reached the gate.

"It's locked . . ." I said, more to myself than to him.

I tugged at the padlock, attached to an iron chain. On the other side of the gate, cars sped along the road boardering the park.

"Whoever did it must've had access to this key . . ."

"You don't know that. They could've just broken the lock," he argued.

The chain and lock were both rusted.

"If they had broken it, the replacement lock would be new, not one that looks like it's been here for years." I turned to Sebastian, an uneasy feeling in my stomach. "There's something strange about this whole fucking thing . . . It doesn't add up."

Sebastian barely blinked. "Do you remember anything?"

I shook my head. "Maybe if I saw the people again . . . I might be able to identify them. I have a dream every night about someone chasing me. I hope that whoever did that to me ends up behind bars."

I moved away from the gate and started jogging back home. For some reason, I was suddenly anxious to be back within the confines of my apartment. I didn't feel like talking about the kidnapping or who'd done it, much less my dreams, with someone who, at the end of the day, was a stranger to me.

I sped up, letting my mind clear and forgetting about the man trailing behind me.

When I reached the entrance to my building, I realized that Sebastian was nowhere in sight. My heart started pounding even harder as I looked around, confirming that I was alone. But someone was watching me; I could feel it.

Was I being too trusting of Sebastian's presence as protection?

"Fuck!" I heard someone say behind me. Sebastian, furious, the veins in his neck standing out from anger as much as from exertion, finally appeared.

"I thought you were right behind me."

"Just go inside."

I did as he said, but he stayed behind, carefully observing my street for a moment before following me into the elevator.

We were both panting, trying to catch our breath. I could tell by the tension in his body that I had managed to piss him off. Well, it was about time.

We entered the apartment, and he closed the door harder than necessary. "You can't run away from me. Do you not understand how much danger you're in?"

"You're here to protect me, aren't you? Well, then do it! And do it in a way that doesn't interfere with my life and my exercise routine."

"No fucking idea . . ." he said under his breath. He headed to his room, where he'd probably lock himself away for the rest of the night.

I rushed to beat him to his door and stood in the middle of the hallway, blocking his path. "I'm not going to let you talk to me like that."

Sebastian exhaled through his nose and looked down at me. He was so tall that his chin almost touched his chest in his attempt to return my stare. "I regret to inform you that the word *tolerance* is going to have to begin to form part of your vocabulary, beautiful."

I blinked. Sebastian Moore had lost his cool! I almost enjoyed seeing him strip off his mask of infinite self-control.

"You work for me," I reminded him.

As he moved me aside to pass, he cupped my chin and pulled at my lower lip with his thumb. The movement was so fleeting that I might've even imagined it.

"I work for your father," he clarified.

Then he walked around me and disappeared into his room.

## CHAPTER 6

# SEBASTIAN

Shit!

I got in the shower with my head spinning and the image of Marfil hijacking my thoughts. Ever since I'd seen her dancing over the security camera feed, I'd begun to view her differently.

I had been captivated by her movements, gestures, the way her legs and body—squeezed into those tight dance clothes, leaving so little to the imagination—performed impossible motions. I had been surprised by my irrepressible urge to touch her, even if only for a few seconds, to see if her skin was as soft as it looked. Resting my finger on her bottom lip had been a mistake I was sure I'd pay for dearly.

*Keep your distance from her. Don't fall at her feet like everyone else*, I told myself. But how could I not give in to the attraction when she looked like she'd been dropped straight down from heaven, endowed with everything necessary to launch a man straight into hell in one swift kick?

Just another reminder as to why I could never let what she did at Central Park happen again. She'd run away from me when I'd stopped to look at the rusted, unbroken chain in the park. Marfil was very clever, and she was right; the kidnapping could've only happened if someone had a key to that gate. By the time I realized she was gone, she was already a good distance ahead of me. She was fast as a bullet, but if I hadn't been distracted by the lock, she would've never gotten a head start. That mistake could've cost her life. Which is why I was so mad;

I had neglected my duties, and now, to top it off, I'd let her see a part of me that I needed to keep hidden.

If I wasn't careful, Marfil Cortés might find out more than she needed to know, and in a case like this, anyone who wagged their tongue could end up losing it . . . for good.

## CHAPTER 7

# MARFIL

That night I dressed up a little more than I normally would to go to the movies. It wasn't Liam I was trying to impress, but someone else . . . Sebastian's fleeting caress had meant absolutely nothing, I'm sure, but no one had ever made me feel so much with a simple touch.

I had never talked about it with Liam, because I was embarrassed to admit it, but I'd almost always had to pretend that I liked the way guys touched me. That was also one of the reasons why I went through them so quickly. I wanted to find someone who made me feel what I'd read about in books or seen in movies, that boundless passion that could lift me to the heavens and leave me trembling against the sheets. Only two guys had ever come close to making me feel something like that, my best friend and my ex, whom I wished I could forget entirely.

But just looking at Sebastian made my body tremble, my heart race, and my hormones run wild. If I wasn't careful, I could make a stupid mistake, and with him more than anyone, I wanted to be smart.

Tami had sent me a message asking what I was doing that night. Tami was my polar opposite. While I loved going out partying, meeting guys, and dancing all night, Tami was more chill. She hated anything to do with parties and loud music; her favorite pastimes were painting, chatting, especially over coffee, and, well . . . not much else. I adored her. We told each other everything . . . Well, *almost* everything. I was convinced there was something underneath her unshakable calm that she hid from me and the rest of the world.

Liam couldn't stand her. I'd introduced them one night, so excited that my two best friends would finally meet. But World War III had almost broken out. Tami was uncomfortable the entire time we were with him, and when Liam lost his patience over the fact that she barely participated in the conversation and answered everything in monosyllables—something that irritated me, too, on that occasion—they started shouting insults at each other.

I hated that conflict between them because I adored them both. But whenever one of them got wind that I could be making plans with the other, they started fighting to get my attention. And there was no better example of that than today. Tami had texted asking if I had plans, suggesting we go out for dinner somewhere nice. I had already promised to go to the movies with Liam, but we hadn't hung out in weeks, and I wanted to see her, too. In the end, I decided to just do exactly what I wanted, which was to see them both that night. So I invited Tami to the movies, leaving out the fact that Liam would be there.

When Sebastian saw me, all dressed up to go out, he simply said he'd get the car keys. It wasn't that I was surprised by that indifference, the only reaction I'd received from that man since I met him, but I had taken extra care with my hair and makeup, putting on my favorite black dress and strappy gold sandals just to impress him. Maybe his fingertips brushing my lips had just been my imagination after all . . .

I got in the front passenger's seat once again, against his objections. "I get carsick if I ride in the back," I said, shrugging. I was an expert liar, a skill I'd learned early in childhood.

Sebastian asked me where we were going and I gave him the

address. As we drove, I started asking him questions again, as if I were talking to a friend.

"Do you like movies?"

Silence.

"I love them. I go almost every Wednesday; one week I choose the movie, and the next week Liam chooses. He mostly likes movies about superheroes or cars that go a hundred and fifty miles an hour. I can't stand them; I prefer rom-coms. I know, it's a cliché that women like those dumb scenarios that would never happen in real life, but I love them. Especially when the male lead is tall, strong, and handsome . . ." I was letting my personality loose, blabbing away like I was talking to someone who actually cared, but nothing. "What kind of movies do you like?" I asked.

"I like to drive in silence, Marfil," he said calmly, making an impeccable right turn.

"Silence means there's nothing to say."

"Exactly," he said, satisfied.

"And I always have something to say," I said at practically the same time.

"Sometimes you can say more with silence than a conversation that goes on for hours."

"Oh yeah? Then what are you saying, since you're always so quiet?" I asked, enjoying the excuse to turn and admire the profile of his straight nose and his square jaw . . . I could've spent hours looking at him.

"You don't want to know."

"But I do."

He stopped at a red light and graced me with a cold sweep of his brown eyes. "You don't need to get to know me, Marfil. I'm not here to be your friend."

I actually wanted something much more than friendship and much more pleasurable from him.

"Do you like my dress?" I asked, ignoring his last comment.

Sebastian cursed between his teeth and looked back at the road.

I smiled, amused by his reaction. I was driving him crazy, and I loved it.

---

Liam was waiting for us outside the AMC Theatre on 19th and Broadway. We both loved movies so much that we paid for a monthly subscription that allowed us to watch up to four movies a week for only thirty dollars a month. I was a movie fanatic. I would even go by myself, I didn't care.

Sebastian and I had stopped to pick Tami up from campus, and the poor thing almost had a heart attack when she saw him, but I explained the situation on the way to the movie theater.

We got out of the car, and I linked arms with my friend. Liam's eyes narrowed in annoyance as we approached, and Tami's steps slowed as she spotted him.

"You didn't tell me he was going to be here," she complained quietly. My friend was not often combative, which was why I'd been so surprised by her fight with Liam; I had never seen her so mad. I couldn't even remember what he'd said to her, just that he had been messing around.

Liam, on the other hand, thought that shy, quiet girls like Tami were boring. That's why he and I got along so well. It occurred to me that Sebastian would be thrilled to guard someone like Tami instead of me, and I couldn't help but turn to look at him. He walked several steps behind us, glancing around as if daring the universe to lay a hand on me. Deep down, it was a great feeling to know I was being protected.

When we reached Liam, I let go of my friend and gave him a big hug. He picked me up off the ground, as he always did, and whispered very quietly in my ear, "You're going to pay for this, babe."

I laughed and turned to my two friends. "A truce, just for tonight. If you promise to behave, I'll let you pick the movie."

Liam sighed and Tami remained silent. I suppose the fact that I'd been kidnapped made them more willing to give in to me. I noticed that Liam was eyeing Sebastian, and I tugged on his arm so that he would focus on what was important.

"Are you seriously going to make me watch a movie about a man who turns into an ant?" I complained a few minutes later.

"Don't try to sabotage it. It's throwback night—when will we be able to watch *Ant-Man* in a theater again? Besides, we get to choose the movie," said Liam, who, to my surprise, was being fairly cordial to Tami.

She, on the other hand, had hardly said a word. I watched her as she walked away to buy popcorn. Her golden-blond hair, almost white, brushed her waist with every step she took. She was beautiful, adorable; I didn't understand why she had decided to stay single. I'd had to convince her not to become a nun, almost beating her over the head with a lamp to make her see reason when she'd shared the thought with me at boarding school. In the end she decided on her own that it wasn't the right path for her, but I spent several months worried.

"Your friend is strange."

I elbowed him in the side. "That 'strange' girl is the only true friend I had until you came to darken my doorway."

"It's thanks to me that you're not like her. You should be more grateful."

He was right about that. Even though I'd always been fairly rebellious, moving to the Big Apple after spending practically my entire life as a recluse hadn't been easy.

"Maybe you could teach her a thing or two," I said, smiling.

Liam turned his back to my friend and looked at me,

amused. "Helping you become the heartbreaker you are now is my greatest achievement, don't expect me to do the same with just anyone."

"But she might be an even bigger heartbreaker than me . . ."

Liam smiled in that seductive way of his that used to drive me crazy but now just made me laugh. "I don't think there's enough patience in the world for that, babe," he said, touching my nose and turning back to look at my friend. "What would they say in that virgin factory of a boarding school?"

I glanced behind me, hoping that Sebastian hadn't heard that last comment. He was staring at the entrance, as always, alert for any sign of danger.

I sighed.

---

The movie was as boring as I'd remembered it being. To make matters worse, I ended up sandwiched between my two friends, both of whom could not stop commenting on what was happening onscreen to the point that I couldn't even follow along.

I stood up to go to the bathroom without a word, and I noticed that Sebastian was getting up to follow me.

This could be fun.

I waited until he was beside me to speak. "Are you liking the movie?"

"I'm focused on other things. Why are you leaving?"

I kept walking, gesturing toward the bathroom sign with a tilt of the head. I smiled to myself when he stopped at the door to the ladies' room. "You're not coming in?" I teased.

Sebastian leaned against the wall and crossed his arms. "I'll wait here."

"What if there's someone in there who wants to hurt me?" I asked, taking a step toward him, feeling brave.

"Scream."

I stopped, gave him a once-over, and, almost as a reflex, he did the same. That was enough for me.

I turned around, flipping my hair, and went into the bathroom.

Why was it so hard to get him to pay attention to me? Did he really take his job that seriously? Or was he absolutely not attracted to me at all? I briefly considered screaming like a scared little girl to see how he'd react. Would he break down the door? Would he draw his gun and barge in like James Bond?

I didn't do it, not because I didn't dare—I would welcome any emotion from him, even rage—but I didn't want to be the boy who cried wolf. I'd been in danger, and if anything were to happen to me, I wanted to be sure that Sebastian didn't doubt for an instant the genuineness of my cry for help. Instead, I washed my hands and left the bathroom.

"There was a door at the end of the stalls," I informed him. Sebastian peeled his back from the wall as his only response. "It was locked . . . Although apparently that won't necessarily keep someone from kidnapping me."

"Leave that to me, Marfil. Now, go back in and watch the movie."

"The ant one? No fucking way," I said, studying the showings for the other throwback movies. I scanned past several that didn't interest me until I reached a Nicholas Sparks film. I grinned at Sebastian and went inside.

The theater was packed, but I found two seats in the last row on the right. I knew he had no choice but to stay close and make sure nothing happened to me. When I sat down and saw that he was taking the seat beside me, an unhappy expression on his face, I almost squealed with joy.

The movie had already started, but I didn't care. What mattered was that I was on a "date" with my bodyguard seated beside me in the dark, where I could fantasize about him for the rest of the hour left in the Marvel movie my friends were watching.

"Do you think she's pretty?" I asked as an excuse to lean close to him and take in his masculine scent, a mixture of leather and aftershave.

Sebastian ran a hand through his hair before answering. "No."

I smiled, amused. "You're much more handsome than that guy." And that "guy" was none other than Liam Hemsworth, if you can believe it.

Sebastian glared at me through the darkness of the theater. "Watch the movie, please!"

I did as he asked and, when the sex scene between the two main characters started, I thought I was going to have a heart attack. The guy pushed the girl against the wall of her bedroom. Liam was so tall and broad-shouldered that he almost covered the female star completely from view, but that only intensified the effect the director wanted to achieve with the scene.

I peeked at Sebastian out of the corner of my eye. The poor guy looked more bored than anything. I studied his enormous hand on the armrest. What was Sebastian like with women? Would he be the kind of guy who touches a girl tenderly, or would it be passionate and rough, like the scene we were watching? Suddenly I had the urge to run my fingers down his arm to his wrist, and feel my hand disappear in his gigantic palm.

What would it be like to be kissed by him? What would it be like to feel his body pressing me into my mattress, almost suffocating me with his weight, flooding me with pleasure? Before I had the chance to do anything I'd regret later, my phone started to ring. The incoming call from Liam was ruining the hot sex scene taking place before my eyes. I rejected the call as several people in the theater glared at me disapprovingly.

Where are you? For your information, the next time you want to come to the movies with me, you can't take off in the middle of the movie and leave me alone with your friend. She left all pissed off, of course.

Oh shit! I quickly replied to his message.

What happened? Don't be mad, I just popped into the theater next door to see part of the Nicholas Sparks movie! I'll come out now.

I hadn't even stood up before he sent me another message.

It doesn't matter, just keep watching your movie, I'm already on my way home.

Fuck. I'd just pissed off my two best friends.

---

The ride home would've been silent if it weren't for the fact that I played my music over the stereo. I felt guilty for having left Liam and Tami alone to watch another movie because of my ridiculous desire to be by myself with Sebastian. I didn't understand what could've happened, as they'd seemed so engrossed in the film.

When we entered the lobby of my building, Norman handed me a medium-sized FedEx box. "You received a delivery, Miss Cortés."

"Thanks, Norman," I said as I took the package, wondering if it was the shoes I'd ordered online.

Sebastian called after me as I went straight to my room and tried to call Tami, but she didn't pick up. Liam hadn't either.

I set the box on my bed and got undressed, tying my bathrobe around myself and sitting on the edge of the bed in front of the package as I waited for the bathtub to fill.

I barely had time to see what was inside the box; my hands touched something sticky, and when I instinctively pulled them out, I saw they were covered in a red liquid. I screamed so loud that I'm sure the building across the street must've heard it.

I jumped from the bed, flipping the package over and spilling its contents onto my white comforter, bathing everything in blood. I brought my hands to my face, trying to cover my eyes.

Inside the box was a dead animal.

Before I had time to react, the bedroom door flew open, banging against the wall, causing me to scream again. Sebastian entered, gun drawn. He moved over to me and, after checking that there was no one in the room, he looked at the box on my bed, then at me.

"Are you hurt?" he asked, slipping his gun in his jeans and grabbing my face to examine my head and then my hands, both stained with blood.

I started shaking.

Sebastian, on the other hand, seemed to relax when he saw that there wasn't a scratch on me.

"Try to calm down," he said, cautiously approaching and wrapping me in his arms.

I didn't even register the fact that the thing I'd wanted from the moment I'd met him was finally happening. All I could think about was the image of that dead animal on my bed and the blood staining *everything*. I began to sob uncontrollably. Sebastian placed a hand on my head as he took out his cell phone and made a call. He said something so quickly that I couldn't even understand him. Then he took my hand and led me to the bathroom, where he sat me on the closed toilet and picked up a towel. He proceeded to turn off the water, which was about to overflow, and wet the tip of the towel.

"I'm going to clean your face, all right?"

I didn't answer; I just let him do it. I was so shocked that I didn't even hear what he was whispering in his attempt to calm me. My entire body shook, tears rolling down my cheeks. When he'd finished cleaning my face, my white towel stained a strange pink color, he started wiping my hands, his strong fingers attempting to erase every trace of blood from my skin. But even though he did the best he could, my hands were still stained.

"Those sons of bitches," he said to himself.

I looked up and stared at him. "What happened?" I didn't even recognize my own voice.

"Wait here." He stood up and left my bedroom.

I ignored him, getting up to look at myself in the mirror. My pale skin contrasted grotesquely with the reddish stains on my cheeks, eyelids, and even part of my lips.

I grabbed the soap and desperately started scrubbing my hands and face.

Nothing.

The blood wouldn't come off, like a nightmare that wouldn't end, that refused to leave me alone.

I heard the door open and saw Sebastian appear with a bottle in his hands. "It's alcohol," he said. I noticed that he also had a small sponge. "Let me clean you up."

I let him softly rub the sponge over my cheeks, eyelids, and lips. When he finished, he moved on to my hands. His jaw tensed forcefully, but his hands were gentle as he carefully cleaned me up.

"Why would someone send me something like that? I don't understand."

Sebastian didn't answer until he'd finished what he was doing. "They want to scare you, that's all."

"But who? Why?"

Sebastian released my hands and moved for the door. "I don't know. But your father is putting every possible measure in place to find out who wanted or wants to harm you. Get in the bath to warm up; you're freezing. I'll clean up the mess in your room."

He didn't give me time to respond; he simply closed the bathroom door and left me alone. Shivering with cold, I did as he said, taking off my robe and plunging myself into the hot water.

Eye for an eye.

That's what the package had said; I'd read it before seeing the rest.

What was happening? What had my father done to make someone want to get revenge on him through me?

I closed my eyes and let the water cover my head.

## CHAPTER 8

# SEBASTIAN

Those fucking bastards.

I had a bad feeling from the moment I saw the FedEx package. I couldn't say why, but something didn't feel right, maybe the delivery time. When I heard Marfil's scream, I feared the worst. Opening the door to her bedroom, the only room in the apartment without security cameras to monitor her, I saw her standing there, covering her face with her bloodstained hands and her emerald eyes frozen in a mask of horror. It was then I understood that I had failed her.

Those bastards had mixed the bird's blood—it was a fucking condor that they'd sent her—with red paint so it would be harder to clean up. Her white face, almost the color of porcelain, had looked so grisly with those red stains.

The poor thing was horrified and shaking so hard that I was afraid she might faint. Seeing all that blood, the dead animal, and the message they'd sent must've been the worst thing that had ever happened to her. Or maybe not, considering her recent past.

I got to work, making sure that by the time she was done with her bath, there would be no trace of that scene that looked like something out of a horror movie. I put the bird in a plastic bag, intending to have it sent to a lab to be examined, along with the box.

I took the cover off her duvet and saw that the down comforter was completely ruined as well. I put it in another plastic bag and went to get mine. Once everything was clean and organized, I heard the bathroom door open. She walked out fearfully, wrapped in a white robe with her jet-black hair dripping down her back. Her incredibly green eyes were red from the tears she'd shed, and her cheeks, although surely hot from the water, were pale under the superficial warmth of her skin.

"I gave you my comforter. I had to throw yours away."

She nodded, looking warily at her bed. "Did you talk to my father?"

"I called him, but he didn't answer. I talked to Logan. Tomorrow I'll send the evidence off so they can try to find something that might lead us to the people trying to scare you."

Marfil sat down at her dressing table. I watched her reflection in the mirror as she opened her mouth to speak. "Did you see what was in the box?"

I pressed my lips together, furious.

"They're taking revenge on my father through me, and we don't even know why."

I had no idea how much Marfil knew. Her father had clearly specified that I not divulge any information that could scare her. I felt a stab of pain in my side and was reminded to keep focused on my job.

"Don't worry about that right now. Do you want a cup of tea or something hot?"

She shook her head, eyes lost to her reflection in the mirror. "Would you mind lighting the fireplace?"

I did as she asked, and after checking her room one last time to make sure everything was in order, I left to give her some privacy.

I made a cup of coffee, feeling that I needed to remain alert. When I was almost finished with it, the door to her bedroom opened and she appeared, barefoot, adorable in her pink pajamas. She looked better, not a trace of red paint on her skin, and she had dried her hair, which hung straight and loose down her back.

"Are you all right?" I couldn't help but ask.

She seemed to hesitate for a moment before opening her mouth to ask me something. "I'm sure you'll laugh at me, but . . ."

I set the coffee cup on the kitchen counter, giving her my full attention.

"Could you stay with me for a little while until I fall asleep? When I close my eyes, all I see is . . ."

"No problem."

I followed her into her bedroom and sat on the chair in the corner. After what had just happened, it was as if something had changed between us. Her eyes never left mine as she lay her head on her pillow and pulled my comforter up to her neck. She breathed in my scent on the blanket, and we gazed at each other until sleep overcame her and she closed her eyes.

I sat watching her for a long time, with only one thought on my mind: *I'll do anything to keep you safe, Marfil. That's a promise I won't allow myself to break.*

## CHAPTER 9

# MARFIL

I dreamed the same dream I've been having since I was a little girl. The blood pooled on the ground in front of me, my mother's head lying on the cement step, cracked open, her brains splattered all around her.

That was the last image I had of her. The only one, in reality, because I was just barely four years old when my mother was murdered in front of me. All I remembered was the sound of the gun going off, the touch of her hand gripping mine tightly, and then letting go as she fell to the ground.

I'm not sure how long I stood looking at that scene; it could've been minutes or even hours. What I do know is that I didn't move until my father came to get me. The attack on my mother, according to the police, had been a random robbery. Colombia is not a country where a family as wealthy as mine can go out on the street without certain precautions. They killed her and stole her diamond engagement ring, valued at half a million dollars at the time.

Would the same thing happen to me? And if so, would they kill me for even less?

I looked at my hands. I never used rings, but on the rare occasion when I did wear jewelry, it was never worth more than a hundred dollars. My father used to get mad at me because I never wore anything he bought me, not even the ones for birthdays or Christmases; years went by until he finally stopped insisting on giving me jewelry and started giving me a check instead, which I would then donate or stick in a drawer and forget about.

What if my mother's murder had been something more than a simple robbery? What if someone had been trying to hurt my father back then the way they were trying to do now? Was it revenge for some failed business deal or simple jealousy? People would do crazy things for money, and my father had enough to buy a small country.

I looked to the chair where Sebastian had spent the better part of the night. I never would've imagined he'd agree to watch over me as I slept, but there he sat until my eyes closed. I had tried to fight off the heaviness of my eyelids—on one hand, because I knew that I was going to have nightmares, and on the other, because I didn't want to give up the privilege of looking at him. His eyes never left mine for an instant, and during those long moments that we gazed silently at each other, I imagined what it would be like for Sebastian to fall in love with me.

I'd always fantasized about love, true love, not one based on physical attraction. I was attracted to Sebastian, very attracted to him, but for some reason I found difficult to explain, I couldn't help but wonder if my untrusting heart could possibly fall in love with him.

---

Sebastian wasn't in the kitchen when I came out fully dressed and ready to head to campus.

Great, just my luck.

I was anxious to get to my classes and get them over with because I had my private ballet lessons afterward. I taught dance to twelve-year-old girls who couldn't afford to attend a ballet academy. For the past two years I had thrown all my energy into teaching them everything I knew, preparing them to hopefully one day receive scholarships to the School of American Ballet.

I was so close to banging on Sebastian's door when he entered the living room. "Ready?" he asked, picking up the keys off the counter.

I nodded in silence, grabbing my backpack and the sports bag that held my dance stuff.

He didn't mention any of what had happened last night at the movies, and I didn't either. My father would resolve the matter; I was sure of it. I only hoped that no one would send me any more dead animals. I wouldn't be able to handle it.

I climbed into the passenger's seat, and this time Sebastian didn't even blink. At least we were now in agreement on that matter. I had no idea how I was going to tell him that I planned to take the subway to Brownsville that afternoon. It was known as a fairly rough neighborhood in Brooklyn, but to me, it was just another neighborhood in New York; nothing would happen to you as long as you were careful. Still, I hoped that Sebastian was unfamiliar with the area and its reputation. I didn't know where he was from, but it definitely wasn't Manhattan; he used Google Maps to get around from time to time.

As always, he parked the car in the lot farthest from campus. We walked to class, and I hated having to stay in front of him. I liked being beside him, accidentally brushing against each other, or at least looking at him and imagining that our relationship was more than strictly professional.

And that thought persisted throughout class. I was so distracted, I could hardly pay attention. Afterward, I walked halfway across the Morningside Heights campus to find Tami in the fine arts building. No matter what else was going on in my life, I needed to know that things were okay between us.

I poked my head into her oil painting class and found her concentrating on the canvas in front of her—messy bun, no makeup, wearing blue jeans and a white smock stained with different colors. In the middle of the room, three models posed half naked so that the rest of the class could paint them.

I waited for class to end, then went inside to admire my friend's work. It was spectacular.

I snuck up from behind Tami and wrapped my arms around her. She jumped but immediately knew it was me, since no one else would snuggle up to her like that.

"Are you still mad at me?" I asked against her back. She was shorter than me, and her hair smelled like lavender.

"I'm busy right now, Mar," she said, picking up a paintbrush and pulling away from me.

At least she'd called me Mar, that was a good sign.

I looked toward the door, where Sebastian was watching the entrance.

"There's something I have to tell you. Something happened last night and I'm worried," I said, trying to get her attention.

Tami glanced at me over her shoulder, her messy bun almost falling off her head from the weight of her hair. "What happened?" My friend was too nice not to worry about me, and even more so after the kidnapping.

I recounted everything I'd been through the previous night, and her hand never left her mouth, scared and horrified.

"Why would someone do something like that?"

"No idea," I answered, shrugging. "All I know is that this isn't over. My father hasn't even called, and I don't know if that's a good sign or a bad one."

"You know how your dad is, Mar. Unless you're dying, he'll keep going on with his life."

Her words were harsh, but Tami had never liked Alejandro Cortés. Not because she wasn't accustomed to seeing a distant father, since hers was cut from the same cloth as mine—Tami came from a very wealthy London family who had locked their daughter up in boarding school as soon as they could—but precisely because she'd been blinded by the illusion of the perfect family, with a father who was caring and affectionate. It was my father who made her realize that wasn't the case.

"Sebastian talked to him. He's doing everything he can to find out what's going on."

My friend said nothing in response, and after apologizing again, we said goodbye in order for me to make it in time to Brownsville.

"Sebastian," I said, stopping at the intersection across from the subway. If we turned left, we would reach the parking lot, which wasn't what I wanted. "I give private ballet lessons to some girls in Brooklyn every Monday. It would be better to take the subway—it's faster."

Sebastian frowned and leaned over to speak to me quietly. "The subway could be dangerous for you. We'll go to Brooklyn by car." He moved to continue walking, but I grabbed him by the arm.

"Where I'm going, it's not smart to go by car, trust me. It would be better for us to take the subway. And whether you believe it or not, it's safer than driving on the highway."

"No."

I growled in frustration. He was supposed to be following me, not the other way around.

I didn't even make it to the corner before he'd stopped me, holding me back by the arm.

"My God, make my job a little easier, Marfil."

I looked at him without backing down. "I told you I wasn't going to change my life because of what happened. I can't afford to, Sebastian! There are a bunch of amazing little girls waiting for me to give them dance lessons, to provide them with an activity that could potentially help them in their future. So you can either come with me or I'll go by myself."

Sebastian frowned, looked over my shoulder, and then let go of me. "Where is this class, exactly?"

I tried to keep my cool. "In Brownsville."

The expression on his face made it clear that he was familiar with the area I was talking about.

"Have you lost your mind?" he asked, fuming. "You're going to just walk into one of the most dangerous neighborhoods in the city, knowing people out there are trying to hurt you?"

"No one has hurt me yet. They could've shot me in the head if they'd wanted to. They've had more than enough opportunity, but they're simply playing at sending absurd messages so that my father freaks out and I get too scared to leave the house, something I don't plan on doing." I pulled away from him and crossed the street to the subway entrance, praying he believed in my bravery.

I knew where I was going. You just had to be cautious and not let anyone think you had money. That was the reason for my simple outfit that day: black leggings, sneakers, and gray sweatshirt. Even my gym bag was secondhand; I'd bought it at a flea market for this very purpose. No one would suspect that, inside that bag, I carried ten pairs of ballet slippers worth fifty dollars each. The girls were going to be thrilled.

Just as I expected, Sebastian was right behind me as I got on the train. It was an hour-long trip in total, during which Sebastian was so tense that it ended up affecting me. I had never been afraid to go to the girls' school, but I was freaked out by the suspicious glances Sebastian threw at everyone who entered the subway car and the way he repeatedly, although very discreetly, reached for his gun. By the time we exited the train station, my heart was racing a mile a minute.

"I've been coming to this neighborhood for a year and a half, and nothing has ever happened to me, so can you relax?"

He didn't answer, too focused on examining the street. I let him do his job and walked ahead.

When we got to the school—an old, dilapidated storefront with a mirror that took up an entire wall and a ballet barre Liam had helped me install—the girls were waiting for me excitedly, sitting on the floor warming up.

Almost all the girls came on their own. They came from families with very few economic resources, and I knew that my classes brought them a moment of calm and a bit of hope. When they saw Sebastian, they all began to whisper and laugh. Lili, a ten-year-old girl with an incredible talent for ballet and modern dance, ran up to give me a hug. Her pink leotard was a bit big on her, but her mother had bought it that way intentionally, so that she could use it for a few more years.

"Hello, girls!" I said with a smile as I set my bag on the table with the sound equipment.

They greeted me, glancing repeatedly at Sebastian, who, so tall and wide, seemed totally out of place in that room full of little girls in pink and white leotards.

I took off my leggings and sweatshirt to reveal my ballet clothes underneath: a black leotard and white tights that made me stand out from the girls. I turned toward the mirror to gather my hair into a bun and slip on a short transparent skirt. As I did, I saw that Sebastian was staring at me. I would've preferred him to wait outside, but he was so uptight that I didn't feel like pushing him.

"Girls, this is Mr. Moore, and he's here to make sure we're safe. Right, Mr. Moore?"

Sebastian glared at me with his brown eyes and remained at his post beside the door, guarding the entrance.

"Today I've brought a surprise that I know you're going to love," I said, opening the sports bag after tying up my pointe shoes.

The girls went crazy when they saw what was inside. The Capezio bags flew around the room, and in a matter of seconds, they had all taken off their old shoes and slipped on the new ones. "Thank you so much, Miss Marfil!" they shouted in unison, excited.

"You're welcome, you're welcome—now, let's see if you can show me everything you've been practicing at home," I said, stepping up to the barre and encouraging them to do the same.

With the music of *The Nutcracker* booming through the room, I spent an hour and a half teaching them to place their arms in the five ballet positions, correcting their posture, showing them how to improve their pirouettes. The girls were very eager to learn, and I loved teaching them everything I knew with equal parts excitement and dedication.

At the end of class, as I gathered my things and the girls said goodbye with smiles that warmed my heart, Lili came up to me with a worried expression.

"What's wrong, darling?" I asked as I slipped on my pants and let down my hair.

"I don't think my mom is going to be able to pick me up today. She told me to stay home, but I didn't want to miss class, Miss."

Lili's mother had three jobs and four kids to take care of, another sad example of the system failing those who need it the most. Lili was the youngest, the only girl, from what I understood, and for some reason, I'd always gravitated toward her the most. Her older brother, Caleb, was always getting into trouble. This little girl had witnessed things not even adults should see, and I always worried about her.

"No one can come pick you up?" I asked, checking the time and realizing that within the next half hour it would be dark and it would be unwise to remain out on the street alone.

Lili shook her head.

I looked at Sebastian, who was waiting impatiently beside the door, and walked over to him.

"We have to walk Lili home; she lives only a few blocks from here."

Sebastian looked at little Lili, then cursed between his teeth. "You're playing with fire, Marfil."

I took that as a yes, and together we went out into the cool evening. Lili trustingly slipped her hand into Sebastian's. He seemed to make her feel safe, and she immediately started asking him questions. My kind of girl.

"Why are you so tall?"

"Because I am."

"Can you give me a piggyback ride?"

"No."

"Do you like ballet? Do you like chocolate? Why do you have an earring in your ear? Why do you have so many tattoos? Did they hurt? Why did you come here with Miss Marfil? Are you her boyfriend?"

I had fun watching him control his temper with Lili, even as I replayed that last question in my head. And the more I thought about it, the more I found myself wishing the answer was yes.

A few minutes later, we dropped Lili off without any problems, and her mother thanked me profusely for bringing her home.

Back on the street, Sebastian took out his cell phone and quickly dialed a number. "Yes, in Brooklyn, Sutter Avenue . . . Thanks."

"Who were you talking to?"

"A car service."

"You ordered a car? To take us all the way to Manhattan? Are you crazy?"

Sebastian whipped around and glared at me. "Right now, you're going to do exactly what I tell you to."

I narrowed my eyes; I didn't like the tone he'd used with me at all. "I make my own decisions, Sebastian. I'm an adult."

"You're not coming back to this neighborhood ever again."

"Of course I'm coming back! What I do here is the only thing in my life that has any meaning."

"Too bad," he said without even looking at me.

The taxi arrived, and he opened the door for me to get inside.

"Stop telling me what I can and cannot do. You're not my father." Just then, my cell phone started to ring.

Still standing outside the taxi, I saw that it was said father calling. That couldn't mean anything good.

I looked at Sebastian, who stared back as coldly as a marble statue. Nothing.

I got in the car as I answered the phone. "Hi, Dad, how are you?"

Sebastian closed the door behind me and got into the front passenger seat.

"What the hell are you playing at?" my father shouted from the other end of the line.

I remained silent.

"Listen carefully, young lady, you're going to do exactly what Sebastian tells you, or I swear to God, I'll lock you up in this house tomorrow and you won't so much as see the light of day. I have more than twenty men working on your kidnapping, and you can think of nothing better to do than go prancing around the most dangerous part of the city? What the hell is wrong with you?!"

"But Dad . . ."

"But nothing, dammit!" he shouted so loud that I started to shake. My eyes met Sebastian's in the rearview mirror, and my mind went black. "I have a thousand problems right now to have to add being worried about you. Do not give me another reason to call you again!" He hung up before I could say anything else.

I lowered my hand and looked at the blank cell phone screen.

---

Sebastian and I didn't exchange a single word the entire ride back home, and I didn't even attempt to pay for the car when it stopped at the entrance to my apartment building. Let him pay for it!

I jumped out of the car before it had even fully stopped, but I didn't care; all I wanted was to get as far away from Sebastian as this ridiculous situation would permit.

I greeted Norman with a slight nod, no smiles that night, and got into the elevator without waiting for Sebastian.

I entered my apartment, still fuming. I don't often get mad, being a woman who preferred to talk more than anything else, but I felt betrayed. To make matters worse, it was by someone I whose presence I was beginning to like more than I would ever admit, which only further complicated things.

My idea had been to lock myself in my bedroom, but I didn't. Instead, I waited, arms crossed, for him to enter the apartment. When he walked in—so tall, so handsome, so mysterious that I wanted to shake him—my blood began to boil at what he had done.

"I know you're mad, but it was necessary."

"It's never necessary to call my father!" I shouted, his words stoking the fire blazing inside me.

"It is when you won't listen to what I say and instead choose to do whatever you want," he replied, taking off his jacket and hanging it on the coat rack beside the door.

"Those classes aren't for me; they're for those little girls!"

"You can restart them once things have calmed down. For the time being, I can't guarantee your safety in that part of town."

"Well, then I want a different bodyguard, someone better than you!"

Sebastian clenched his jaw. I'd hurt his pride, and I loved it. "You're behaving like a spoiled child."

His words only made me more furious. I suddenly felt so hot that I ripped off my sweatshirt and tossed it onto the couch as I stepped closer, pointing my index finger in his face. "I don't plan on letting those girls down, not for you and not for—"

He cut me off, grabbing my finger and spinning me around, pressing my back against his chest. His arm encircled my waist, and his other hand gripped me by the neck.

"Two more seconds and you'd be dead if I wanted you to be," he said quietly into my ear.

My breathing was agitated, not only from the surprise of finding myself trapped against his body, but because every part of my anatomy was in contact with his. His arm was right under my breasts, covered only by the black leotard I was wearing that afternoon. I didn't even need to check to know that my nipples had just gone hard of their own accord, making my excitement evident. I tried to pull away, but he gripped me tighter.

"You should thank your lucky stars it's me that's here protecting you and not someone else." His voice, deeper than normal, caused every hair on my body to stand on end. He then gripped my neck tighter, almost cutting off my breathing. "And next time you wait for me before coming up to the apartment." His lips brushed the sensitive skin of my ear, and I froze.

I didn't know how to feel. I was so vulnerable in that position, angry over what he'd done, but at the same time, I didn't want him to ever let me go.

Then, Lili's face flashed in my mind, followed by the faces of the other girls. I wasn't going to be able to continue giving them classes, and it was all his fault.

"Let me go," I hissed into his fingers that were still cupping my chin.

He did as I asked and, so that he wouldn't further see how aroused I was by his tight embrace and his whispered words against my skin, I rushed to my room, slamming the door behind me. Once inside, I leaned against the wall and slid down to the rug.

I'd just had a dose of what would soon become the most addictive drug in history . . . at least for me.

CHAPTER 10

# SEBASTIAN

I shot daggers at Marfil's back as she walked away and slammed her bedroom door. I hadn't been able to resist the temptation to show her exactly who she was dealing with. The girl had no idea.

Calling Cortés had been necessary. I didn't plan to keep giving in to her tantrums that could cost me not only my job but also her life.

On second thought, it was a relief when she locked herself in her bedroom. I wouldn't have been able to continue that absurd discussion with her standing there half naked, her nipples showing through the thin fabric of that ridiculous outfit. Pressing her against my body had also been a mistake; the warmth of her skin and the smell of her hair had caused me to have an erection that would've been difficult to hide had I not been wearing jeans.

Seeing her that afternoon, dancing and interacting with those little girls, had allowed me to see a new side to her personality, very different to what she normally showed me. Marfil Cortés could test the patience of even a saint—she'd certainly tested mine—but with those girls, she'd been all patience and sweetness, calm and discipline.

Discipline was my middle name, something I couldn't live without, something I demanded in my daily life. Having spent the better part of my formative years serving in the US military had given me a lot of practice in self-control, although I also had to admit that since I'd been working as Marfil's bodyguard, my self-control had gone out the window several times. The more time I spent with her, the more I realized there was something about her, apart from her beauty, that managed to send me off the rails.

My phone pinged, alerting me to a text message.

Identity of bedroom attacker confirmed. They didn't even bother to try to hide it. This is the closest they have been to her. Don't let it happen again. If she goes down, we do, too.

The last thing I wanted was to lose my job.

## CHAPTER 11

# MARFIL

Tuesday was uneventful. I didn't say a word to Sebastian all day, not even when he asked me to lend him a pencil to jot something down. He seemed to understand that it was better to start back over from the beginning: using only monosyllables.

I took advantage of the silence to think of ways to continue with my ballet classes, but it would be impossible if I wasn't allowed to return to Brownsville for the time being. The girls would never forgive me. In the end, I convinced Tami to take over for me. Tami danced ballet, too. We had taken classes at school from the time we were little girls, and although she wasn't that into it, she covered for me on occasion when I couldn't make it to class because I was sick or had an exam.

A few days later, on a Saturday afternoon, I was out for a run, Sebastian trailing behind me, obviously, his eyes glued to the back of my head as always. I decided to pick up the pace, force my body to go faster, wanting to make him sweat, to make him suffer, but there was no shaking this man; his long, muscular legs easily kept the pace.

In the end I was the one who had to stop first, exhausted, to catch my breath and take a sip of water. Although I'd been living alone for a while and had gotten used to it, I felt lonelier and more isolated than ever now that I'd stopped speaking to Sebastian.

I gave him a quick look out of the corner of my eye. Sweat dripped onto his workout shirt, and his gray athletic shorts showed off his muscular legs. Still, there was no sign he was out of breath. I couldn't stand the fact that I felt so attracted to him, even more so than before, despite how much he infuriated me.

The feeling of his body pressed against mine and his hands on my neck had stayed with me since that night, leaving me unsatisfied, wanting more. A part of me considered trying to seduce him. I wanted to drive him crazy, make him obsess over me twenty-four hours a day, like I was doing with him.

With that in mind, I bent down and grabbed my ankles to stretch my arms and legs, showing off my flexibility. My ass was right in front of his face, and I loved seeing how he averted his gaze, looking toward the opposite side of the park.

I smiled, satisfied.

Just then, my phone rang, putting an end to my attempt at seduction. It was Stella, inviting me out that night; the guys from the soccer team were having a party on the penthouse floor of a building along Park Avenue. A party organized by the soccer team was never my favorite activity, but I had nothing better to do, so I accepted the invitation.

I didn't mention the party to Sebastian until I was dressed and ready to go. I had decided on a short red dress that fit me like a glove. It was revealing but at the same time elegant and feminine. For my hair, I went with a high ponytail, giving it a wet-look effect with what was quickly becoming my favorite product—one I'd bought at Harrods on my last trip to London. I picked up my black Louboutins and matching purse and went out into the living room as I tucked my phone away and called out to Sebastian. When he stepped into the hallway, dressed in a tracksuit but with his hair wet from the shower, I knew I'd just screwed him over good.

"I'm going out," I informed him.

Sebastian looked me up and down, disapproval written all

over his face, which was not the response I'd hoped for after two hours of preparation.

"It's ten o'clock. Don't you think you could've told me sooner?"

I shrugged. "I forget you're here, sorry," I said. I was being bitchy and I knew it, but I was still mad at him for taking me away from my girls.

"And where are you going?"

"Does it matter? I'm going out, and that should be enough of an answer."

"Given you're my responsibility, yes, it does. Now tell me."

"To a party on Park Avenue, at a penthouse. Happy? Now, can I go?"

"Give me ten minutes."

I waited patiently for him to get dressed. What I didn't expect was for him to come out in slacks, a dress shirt, and sneakers, looking so good I almost fell on my ass. My friend karma was paying me back yet again.

As we stepped into the elevator, I couldn't help but look at our reflection in the mirror. We made an incredible couple. Rarely was a guy so much taller than me in heels, but Sebastian still loomed over me. Feeling brave, I stepped closer to him. The minty scent of his shampoo instantly came to me in waves, making him even more irresistible. He was so masculine, so sure of himself . . . and so totally immune to me.

That night, I'd taken extra time with my makeup to highlight the bright green color of my eyes. It had always been easy for me to leave men staring, to feel desired, so it irritated me that Sebastian couldn't give me one damn compliment, but what bothered me most was that I was offended by his lack of flattery. I had always hated being valued only for my physical appearance, wanting to be seen beyond the packaging . . . And yet, there I was, having spent two hours getting ready—

something I rarely did—all for what? Sebastian was only here to protect me; nothing else interested him in the slightest, not my personality, opinion, or my looks. He wasn't going to touch me or even look at me inappropriately because he worked for my father, someone you did not want to cross, as I knew from personal experience.

A specific memory of my father tried to come to the surface, but I forced myself to banish it from my mind; a single image of that day would be enough to make me start shaking. I had learned it was better to leave bad memories tucked away in the back of a locked drawer.

We arrived to the party fifteen minutes later. I had called Liam to invite him, but he hadn't answered. I wanted to see him in person to make sure we were all right, but his silence every time I called made me worry he was still mad at me. Tami had been friendly with me the other day, but I knew something must've happened at the movies to make them both leave so abruptly and angrily. Sometimes I asked myself how it was possible that my two best friends could both get along so well with me but then hate each other.

We went up to the penthouse's rooftop of the building and were met by a large group of college students jumping around and dancing to the rhythm of electronic music. The party was being hosted by the new team captain, Andrew Davis, which meant that his best friend and my ex-boyfriend, Regan, was surely lurking around there somewhere. I hoped I wouldn't run into him—that asshole always put me in a bad mood—so I went the opposite direction and started looking around for my girlfriends.

Stella was in the kitchen, passing out Jell-O shots and pouring drinks, which could only mean one thing: she'd gotten back together with Andrew. She let out a shrill squeal when she saw me and started jumping up and down. I laughed and gave her a hug.

"You look amazing!" she said, looking me up and down. "Is that Dolce?" she asked, eyeing my dress.

"Versace," I answered, picking up a beer and checking out the rest of the party. Sebastian seemed to have disappeared, although I imagined he was watching me wherever he was. It was a relief to feel like I was alone, even if just for a few hours. "Where's Lisa?" I asked. If she wasn't with Stella, she was most likely hooking up with someone.

Stella's face fell, and she suddenly seemed nervous. "I didn't want you to find out like this, but . . ."

Before she could say anything, Regan entered the kitchen, dragging a fairly drunk Lisa behind him, her lips swollen and her lipstick smeared. Regan seemed surprised to see me, and as his eyes ran down my body, I regretted having worn something so daring. The last thing I wanted was to get that asshole's attention.

Regan let go of Lisa's arm and came over to me. Lisa, drunk as she was, didn't seem to notice; she picked up a beer and started dancing with the group that was jumping around in the middle of the room.

Had they hooked up?

"Look who we have here. The queen bee," he said, hovering around me like an annoying mosquito.

I faked a smile. I wasn't going to give him the satisfaction of knowing he got to me, even though he always did. He had humiliated me and made me believe he was in love with me, only to gloat about it with his friends and lie about things we never did.

"Don't get too close; I might sting you."

Regan smiled in that way that used to drive me crazy. "You look superhot, as always."

I took a sip of my beer and tried to ignore him.

"What's wrong? You can't even look at me anymore?"

"I prefer to pretend you don't exist."

Regan laughed and stepped in front of me, inches away from my face. "Are you ever going to forgive me?"

I looked at the traces of Lisa's red lipstick on him and almost laughed out loud. "Forgiving you would mean admitting that I give a shit about you, Regan, and that is far from the truth. Now go away so I can enjoy the party."

Regan seemed unaffected by my words, placing his hands on my hips and pulling me toward him. "You weren't this cold when we met, Marfil, maybe that's why I didn't fall for you . . . You were a little girl straight out of high school, so innocent, so *pure* . . ." His fingers slid down my back to my ass. "Now you walk around like you're the queen of the universe, creating and destroying things at your will . . . I can't deny that it turns me on, a lot." He pressed his body to mine, and I could feel his erection against my stomach.

I remained still. Shamelessly, part of me liked knowing that he was still capable of falling under my spell. "You missed your chance," I said, so close to his lips that I could smell the whiskey and cigarettes on his breath.

"It's not about chance, Marfil. This is about the score we still have to settle." He moved his hand up my side and wrapped it around the underside of my left breast.

It was then that I decided to put an end to this interaction. I placed my hand on his chest and pushed him away. His body was hard from how built he was, and instead of doing as I said, he simply smiled.

"I'm not moving an inch until you let me taste your lips again."

"I'd rather become a nun before I ever kiss you again, Regan." I pushed him harder, but his legs pressed into me, trapping me in place.

"Nuns are chaste, baby, and you and I both know you're anything but."

What an idiot.

Then, out of the corner of my eye, I noticed that Sebastian had appeared, making his presence known by calmly leaning against the kitchen wall. His expression said it all: He was asking me if he should get this guy off me or keep his distance.

I wanted to prove to Sebastian I was capable of handling things on my own. So I tried lifting my knee in order to hit Regan in the balls, but the idiot saw it coming and blocked the hit, using incredible force to hold my leg.

"Let go of me. Now," I said through clenched teeth. The joke had stopped being funny, and the fact that Sebastian was witnessing something so pathetic made me embarrassed and angry in equal measures. I didn't want to need him; I didn't want to have to ask him for help.

"Or what?" Regan whispered in my ear, blocking my view of Sebastian.

Before I could even think of a comeback, a shadow fell over us, giving Regan no time to react. In a matter of seconds, he was on his back, looking up at the gigantic man who had just pushed him off me.

"Get lost," Sebastian said, surprisingly calm.

Regan clenched his teeth in response. "Who the hell are you?" he asked, jumping to his feet and stepping in front of Sebastian.

He looked down at Regan without blinking and calmly answered his question. "Your worst fucking nightmare."

Before anything else happened, or rather before Regan attempted to punch my bodyguard, Sebastian had pinned Regan's arm behind his back and pressed his head into the wall.

"Come at me like that again and you'll be crippled for life. Do you understand?"

Regan let out an unintelligible grunt, and Sebastian, after

twisting his arm a bit farther into that unnatural position, let him go. I won't deny that I enjoyed seeing someone put that asshole in his place. Luckily for Regan, there was no one else in the kitchen; if it had happened in the main room in front of all his teammates, it would've damaged the bad-boy reputation he had so carefully cultivated. It was pathetic how quickly Sebastian had been able to pin him against the wall, and I was reminded that my bodyguard was much more skilled than a spoiled college athlete who lifted weights in the gym to bulk up and tighten his pecs. Sebastian was trained to kill, and thinking this, a strange sensation crept up my skin.

Regan looked at us with a look of loathing on his face, first at Sebastian, then at me. "One more for your list, huh, Mar?" he said, walking backward and smiling, despite being short of breath from the shakedown Sebastian had just given him. "Hot tip?" he said now to my bodyguard, who appeared annoyed. "Stay away from her—she's so frigid, she'll freeze your cock."

I didn't see Sebastian's reaction to Regan's last words, because I turned around and walked out the other door.

I had once believed I was in love with Regan. Opening my heart had been a mistake I would not make again.

*Frigid.* That word haunted me.

Feeling like shit, I crossed the crowded living room to the drinks table. I took three tequila shots in a row. The last one almost made me gag, but instantly, a curtain lowered on the thoughts crashing around in my head and allowed me to focus on the party happening all around me. I hadn't come here to be insulted. I'd come here to have fun.

I don't know how it happened, but I ended up on top of a table surrounded by guys who kept shouting how hot I was. I couldn't make out what they looked like—they were all blurry to me—but I liked being high above them, where they could look at me but not touch me.

I chanced a glimpse at Sebastian in a corner of the room, then continued to dance for what felt like hours. When I finally grew tired of dancing, someone helped me down from the table, as I struggled to do so on my own, and guided me to the bathroom.

"Are you okay?" Sebastian asked me before I shut the door in his face.

I looked at myself in the mirror and tightened my ponytail, which had come almost completely undone. I ran my hand under the faucet and wiped cool water across the back of my neck. When I went back out to the party, the heat felt dizzying, and I decided it was time to leave. I went directly to the elevator, but as I reached for the button, a huge hand appeared and pushed it for me. I turned to Sebastian.

"Are you all right?" he asked, more out of duty than real concern for me, I'm sure.

"What do you think?" I answered, blinking to clear my vision.

"Get in the elevator, Marfil," he ordered me, as if bored.

I hated his condescending tone.

"You know something?" I said, jabbing a finger into his chest. "What you did back there made you look like a total jerk, like a little macho man from the last century . . . I don't need you to rescue me. I can do it all by myself."

Sebastian nodded. "Understood. Now get in the elevator."

I got in the elevator, not because he told me to, but because I needed to get some fresh air.

When we stepped outside, a light drizzle was falling onto the streets of Manhattan. I looked up at the immense skyscrapers surrounding us, lit up with different colors. The cool rain felt refreshing on my feverish skin.

After a few seconds, I opened my eyes and found his fixed on me, observing me without the slightest attempt to hide it.

"Let's go home," he said, and this time it sounded more like a request than an order.

*Home* . . . That ordinary word falling from his lips produced a sensation of warmth that I'd never felt when thinking about the apartment I lived in.

"I want to walk," I answered, spinning on my heels and heading down the street. The buildings in that area were beautiful, majestic, with elegant entryways. It was horrible to think that just up the street people were dying of hunger.

I kept walking until a lighted storefront pulled me toward it like a magnet. I had always wanted to get a tattoo, but I'd never had the nerve.

I pushed open the door, and Sebastian followed me in with a sigh. The place was painted entirely black, even the furniture was of the same color, and there were hundreds of different pictures displayed—some grotesque, others small and cute. Before I could get a good look, a tattooed man with huge plugs in his stretched earlobes appeared behind the counter.

"Let me guess, you want matching tattoos?" the man asked.

"No one's getting a tattoo. Marfil, can we go?" Sebastian said.

"He wishes," I said, looking at the tattoo artist. "But nope, it's just me."

The man gave me a crooked smile, picked up a rag off the counter, and wiped his hands as he looked at me with an amused expression. "A body like that doesn't need any art." Then he looked to Sebastian. "Get her out of here—she's drunk; she'll regret it tomorrow and blame you."

Sebastian tried to take my arm, but I pulled out of his grip.

"Actually, I'm not drunk, and I know exactly what I'm doing. I want a tattoo, okay? I'm tired of people telling me what to do. It's my body. I'll tattoo my entire face if I want."

"That would be a shame," the man answered, looking at me with lust, "but do whatever you want. What'll it be?"

I moved to look at the catalog he had open on the counter, but Sebastian gripped my wrist and held my gaze, searching for some kind of inkling that this was a joke. "Marfil . . . a tattoo is for the rest of your life. Don't do it just to prove something."

I blinked several times, dazzled by how handsome he was due to the concern I could read in his eyes.

"You have your whole arm covered in them," I said, challenging him with my gaze, "and I'm sure you have even more in other places, don't you?"

Sebastian looked away and released me. His silence was enough of a response.

"Show them to me. I want to see them."

"No," he said, cursing between his teeth and running a hand through his hair.

What other tattoos did he have? And more importantly, where?

"So you can get tattooed, but I can't?"

"A tattoo should mean something."

He was right about that. But I did have something very important in my life, something that never ceased to amaze me.

I flipped the pages until I found what I was looking for. "This. I want this tattoo."

Sebastian looked at me with pleading eyes. "Please, don't do it," he said in a kinder tone. "This man is right—your body doesn't need any ink to make it prettier."

Was that supposed to be a compliment?

"I'm just like you and him. I want a mark that will serve as a reminder of something I feel truly passionate about."

The tattoo artist, paying no mind to the conversation, gestured for me to go into the little studio. I did as he said, Sebastian stepping into the room with me, which I hadn't been expecting.

"You can wait outside," I said.

"In your dreams."

I rolled my eyes, and when the man asked me where I wanted the tattoo, I thought for a few seconds. "On my back, right in the middle, under my neck."

"All right. I'm going to go make some sketches. In the meantime, you can take off your dress and lie down on the table."

I hesitated. If I'd been wearing a shirt, I wouldn't have had to get fully undressed. I didn't want to lie there with nothing but a thong and my ass out in front of them.

The tattoo artist seemed to understand my dilemma. "Don't worry, I'll cover you with a sheet."

"How about I cover her and you come in once she's lying on the table?" Sebastian suggested in his usual cool tone.

"Jealous boyfriend, huh?" He laughed. "Don't worry. That's the standard procedure."

Sebastian didn't answer, and I didn't feel like explaining that he wasn't my boyfriend but my bodyguard, who was currently looking at me like he wanted to kill me.

The tattoo artist laid a white sheet on the table and left the room.

"Are you sure you're not going to regret this later?"

"Totally sure, and don't you dare mention this to my father," I said, starting to take off my dress. He let out a soft "I won't," then turned around as I slipped it over my head and stood there in my matching red bra and underwear. I picked up the sheet and lay face down on the table, covering myself. "You can look now," I said calmly, wishing, not for the first time, that the tattoo artist's comment about Sebastian being my boyfriend were true. I liked him; there was just something so sexy about the way he protected me, albeit annoying at times, and I wanted so badly to break through his impenetrable façade. "Can you pull the sheet up a little higher?" I asked him. "Oh, and unhook my bra, please."

If he was at all affected by my request, he didn't show it. He leaned over and lifted the sheet to just above the end of my spine, his fingers brushing my naked skin. It was a fleeting caress, but it made my entire body tingle. Then, with one smooth motion of his fingers, he unhooked my red lace bra. I closed my eyes and imagined him running his hand up and down my body, from the base of my neck to the end of my back.

But he didn't.

The door opened, and the tattoo artist got to work. First, he cleaned the area where he was going to tattoo me, the cold alcohol giving me goose bumps.

"Are you cold?" he asked, running his hands up and down my back the way I'd wanted Sebastian to do.

I tensed, and Sebastian noticed.

"Keep your fucking hands still," Sebastian said.

The tattoo artist laughed and raised his hands in a gesture of surrender.

Sebastian then grabbed a stool and, to my surprise, sat beside me, where he could see the man's hands up close.

"Let's get started," the tattoo artist said after placing the outline of the image on my skin.

The buzzing of the machine scared me, and I suddenly had second thoughts.

"It's going to hurt," Sebastian said. "It's a tricky area because there's hardly any fat, just skin and bone."

That gave me a clue.

"Is that where you have one of your tattoos?" I asked as I felt the touch of the needle against my skin. I closed my eyes tightly. Fuck, it hurt.

"Not in the middle of my back, but on one of my shoulder blades," he confessed, and I knew he was saying it to distract me.

"What do you have there?"

"The Japanese symbol for bravery. And before you ask, I got it as a tribute for a fallen comrade."

"Just that? You don't have any more?"

"I have a full sleeve on my arm. That's not enough?"

"I get the feeling you have more tattoos than you're telling me."

"I might have a few more."

"How many in total?"

"Just three others."

"Will you show me one day?"

"Definitely not," he answered, although I thought I saw a hint of a smile on his face.

That brief moment of conversation was followed by an hour of suffering. The tattoo was small, but it consisted of intricate details and line work. Even though I hated every second of it, I didn't back out. In fact, I was so excited when I finally sat up, covering my breasts with the sheet, and saw it in the mirror.

"I love it," I said, unable to stop smiling.

"I'm going to cover it up now. For the next week, you'll need to wash it three times every day with unscented soap and apply a dab of antiseptic lotion. I'll give you the name of a good one."

"Thank you," I said, unable to stop looking at it.

They left me alone so I could get dressed, but I took my time, admiring the tattoo in the mirror. Eventually, after a few minutes, I left the room and paid. Two hundred dollars didn't seem like a lot for a ballet dancer on her toes, arms in fifth position. She'd come out perfect.

We left the tattoo parlor, walking back to where we'd parked the car. I was still on cloud nine, and still very much curious about Sebastian's tattoos.

"Why a full sleeve?"

"Once you start, it's hard to stop."

I stood in front of him, blocking his path. "Will you let me see them?"

Sebastian hesitated for a few seconds. "It's late."

I knew it wasn't going to be easy to get him to divulge something so personal.

"Did it hurt?"

"No," he admitted as he picked up his pace. "I have a high tolerance for pain."

His response surprised me, but I let it go.

"When did you get your first one?"

Sebastian looked down at me for a few seconds. "At sixteen."

"You were a baby! Your parents let you?" He didn't answer, and I froze, realizing that I'd just put my foot in my mouth. "I'm sorry," I said.

"You have nothing to be sorry about. I never even met them."

My God, Sebastian Moore revealed something about his past.

"What happened to them?"

"I don't know."

His tone told me that it was best to stop prying.

I felt sad as we got in the car, the adrenaline of the tattoo draining out of me as I remembered my mother. I also hated that Sebastian had grown up without a mother, too. Without anyone, really.

Had he grown up in some orphanage? In foster homes?

He must've noticed I'd gone mute because before starting the car, he turned to me and said in a soothing tone, "Hey, it's okay. You can't miss what you never had."

That was a lie, and he knew it. There wasn't a day when I didn't miss having a mother to take care of me, to give me advice, to ease my fears. Even so, I could imagine how he must feel, since my father had never paid much attention to me, but at least I had Gabriella.

"Hey, Marfil, I'm serious; don't feel sorry for me," Sebastian interrupted my thoughts, clearly trying to distract me from them. "Let's talk about something else."

I let out a sigh, suddenly no longer in the mood to talk. "Sure. You pick."

"Okay. Your name."

"What about it?"

"It's unique. Why Marfil?"

I hesitated, then shrugged. "It's the Spanish word for *ivory*. According to my dad, it came to my mother the moment she held me in her arms." I let out a small laugh. "I didn't like it at first. I thought it made me stand out too much. But over time, I grew to love it. It was chosen by her."

"It suits you."

I chuckled. "What's that supposed to mean?"

"Do I really have to elaborate?"

I toyed with the edge of my sleeve, suddenly unable to stop the words from spilling out of my mouth. "I used to be obsessed with elephants when I was little. Still am, honestly."

"Elephants?" His smile widened.

"Their tusks, they are made of ivory," I said. "Or at least that's what Lupe used to say to me all the time." I paused. "They're gentle, loyal. They remember everything. They grieve. They love deeply and never forget the ones who matter."

Sebastian was quiet for a beat, then softly said, "That tracks."

"With what?"

"With you."

He didn't elaborate, and neither did I, but the weight of his words followed us back to the apartment, where we said good-night to each other with a cold "See you tomorrow."

At least he'd told me a little bit about himself, and cared enough to ask me about me, which also happened to be the reason why I lay awake practically all night.

## CHAPTER 12

# MARFIL

The next morning, the tattoo hurt like hell. I had moved around in the night and ended up sleeping right on top of it. In the shower, I realized it was impossible to clean it; I couldn't reach. There was no way I was going to be able to wash it and put lotion on it three times a day on my own. I would have to ask my handsome bodyguard, a thought that put me in a good mood and even eased some of my pain, psychologically speaking, at least.

I pulled my hair up, and since it was Sunday and I didn't have plans to go anywhere, I put on a leotard to avoid anything touching my tattoo, and slipped some gray sweatpants over it.

As I walked into the kitchen, I was instantly met with the delicious smell of Sebastian's coffee and freshly cooked pancakes. He had his back to me, but when I saw him dressed in gray sweatpants like mine and a simple black shirt, I had the urge to take them off him and search for all the secrets hidden in his tattoos.

"Good morning," I said, taking a seat at the island as I gathered my thoughts. I hadn't forgotten I was still mad at him for having ratted me out to my father. But I had to be honest: I didn't usually stay angry for long, much less with a handsome guy who kept me safe and made me breakfast.

Sebastian turned around and set a plate of pancakes on the counter. "Eat," he said, warm and friendly as ever.

I poured some milk into a mug, then placed it in the microwave for a few seconds. As I waited, I stood right beside him while he flipped another batch of pancakes.

"Do you always make such elaborate breakfasts?" I asked as I dipped my finger in a drip of honey and brought it to my lips.

"It's just pancakes, Marfil—you mix milk, flour, and sugar, that's it."

I took my warm milk from the microwave, then turned to him and said, "Be grateful I even got up to drink this."

"Breakfast is the most important . . ."

"Meal of the day, I know," I said, finishing his sentence. "But I prefer to sleep as long as possible."

"That says a lot about you."

"That I'm charming, for example?" I laughed at my own joke, since he wasn't going to do it, and sat back down at the kitchen island.

He finished making the pancakes, which were apparently all for me, then leaned against the counter, coffee in hand.

"Eat," he barked with a glacial stare.

"Don't you get bored being here all day with me?"

"It's my job."

"And why did you decide to become a bodyguard?"

Ignoring my question, Sebastian walked over to the cupboard, picked up a glass, and filled it with water before returning to his original spot.

"How are the pancakes?"

I chewed slowly as I openly observed him.

"Delicious. Do you not like questions?"

"Do you not get tired of talking all the time? A little silence is nice sometimes."

I pretended to consider his question.

"No, I don't ever get tired of talking. Silence is boring. Why did you decide to become a bodyguard?"

Sebastian stared blankly at me, then took a step forward

and, resting his palms on the counter, bent his head slightly to look me in the eye. "If I told you, I'd have to kill you . . ."

I felt a shiver as I contemplated whether he was being serious. My mind went blank, and I responded with the first thought that popped into my head.

"With kisses?"

Sebastian blinked in disbelief and sat back down.

"Marfil, just eat."

I smiled, pleased with myself. "Doesn't your girlfriend miss you? You're here all day with me, the poor thing must be going crazy," I said casually, waving my fork and congratulating myself for being so subtle in my desperate attempt to get information out of this man.

Sebastian surprised me with a faint smile. "I don't have a girlfriend. Don't worry—no one is missing me."

Inside, I was dancing the conga.

"I'm just a good person like that, concerning myself with people I don't even know."

"Right," he said, taking out his cell phone and glancing at the screen.

An interesting idea then popped into my head. "Technically, Sebastian . . . your job is to take care of me, right?" He didn't answer, so I went on, "But if I could take care of myself, that would make your job easier, right?"

"I don't like where you're going with this."

I set my mug down on the counter and looked at him very seriously. "I didn't like what happened last night with Regan."

"I'll say it again: It's my job."

"I don't mean the fact that you intervened, which I didn't enjoy, but I at least have to thank you for . . . I'm talking about the feeling of not being able to get him off me on my own."

Sebastian narrowed his eyes, waiting for me to continue.

"That move you made on him, or on me the other day.

You're fast, and deadly. I'd love to be *fast* and *deadly*," I added, emphasizing each word.

Sebastian looked at me as if I'd grown a second head. "Marfil, I think I've reached my limits on attempting to understand the things that come out of your mouth."

I glared at him. "If I knew how to defend myself, maybe I would've never been kidnapped. Has that ever occurred to you? Maybe I could've done something to buy time and could've escaped to get help. And maybe yesterday that idiot wouldn't have trapped me against the counter, blocking me so I couldn't do anything besides wait for him to leave me alone or for you to turn up and make him. If I knew how to defend myself, I would feel safer in dangerous situations, don't you think? You never stop reminding me that there are people who want to hurt me, and it's true, but without you all I can do is scream if I get into trouble, like some damsel in distress. I hate that."

Sebastian studied me. "What is it that you want, exactly?"

"I want you to teach me self-defense," I said.

Sebastian didn't respond with a resounding no. Instead, he seemed to consider the idea for a few seconds. "What do I get out of it?"

Wow, I hadn't expected that.

"I can pay you."

"I'm not interested in money. Your father is already paying me plenty."

"What do you want?"

Sebastian set his cup on the counter and, resting his arms beside it, leaned over to look me in the eye. "Three hours," he said after thinking it over.

I stared at him, not understanding.

"Three hours to myself, during which you will stay here, at home, without leaving or getting into trouble."

"You're asking me for free time?"

Sebastian nodded.

"Listen, if it were up to me, you could take all the days off you want . . ."

"Don't get ahead of yourself." He smiled, and I admired the dimples in his cheeks.

"I'm just being a good Samaritan. I don't want to exploit you."

"Three hours and the promise that you'll stay put."

It was an offer I couldn't refuse. Also, three hours alone was a gift for me as well.

"Done," I said, holding out my hand to shake on it.

He stared at me for a second, and I watched, spellbound, as my hand disappeared beneath his long, strong fingers. His handshake was soft, but I made sure to keep mine firm.

"When do we start?" I asked excitedly.

Sebastian hesitated. "Three days, once your tattoo has healed a bit . . . I don't want to hurt you," he said, and it sounded more threatening than sweet.

My God, what was I getting myself into?

I spent the rest of the day studying in my room for midterms coming up . . . for the most part. I also spent a good portion of that time contemplating what to do about my tattoo's aftercare. I had to lotion it, and I didn't know if it would be a good idea to ask Sebastian. Not because he might say no, just the opposite, in fact.

Finally, seeing that there truly was no way I could reach it on my own, I went and gently knocked on his door, which he opened immediately.

"How's it going?" I asked in a friendly tone.

"What do you want?" he asked, patiently observing me as he leaned against the doorframe.

"I tried to put lotion on my tattoo, but I can't reach. Can you help me?"

Sebastian looked at the lotion I had in my hand and sighed. "Come into the bathroom," he ordered, turning his back to me.

We crossed into what was now his bathroom, where he showered, shaved, got undressed . . . Seeing his products caused butterflies in my stomach.

My God, how pathetic. What had this man done to my neurons?

Since I was wearing a backless leotard, there was no need to take off anything except for the loose cardigan I'd slipped on. I stood in front of the mirror with my back to him, waiting with anticipation.

He proceeded to wash his hands, wet a washcloth, and lather it with glycerin soap. "Tell me if it hurts," he whispered, almost as delicately as his touch.

I don't know if I was the only one who felt it, but suddenly the four walls seemed to close in on us; the space became smaller, filled with his presence, his scent, which flooded every corner. I had goose bumps, chilled from the cold water and his fingertips on my bare skin, which caused an instant, involuntary reaction in my body. I blushed as Sebastian's eyes wandered down to the reflection of my breasts in the mirror. To my embarrassment, my nipples were clearly visible under my leotard.

I cursed silently and flinched as he brushed a sore spot.

"Sorry," he said, touching me more gently. He rinsed his hands after washing the tattoo and wet the tip of a towel to remove the soapy residue. "Hand me the lotion," he said in a very calm tone. Too calm, considering I was dying inside.

After handing him the ointment, he squeezed some onto his fingertips and carefully rubbed it into my back. This time the feel of his skin against mine almost caused a short circuit in my brain. I was unavoidably turned on as I felt his body so close to mine.

Time seemed to stop as he ran his hands over my tattoo for what seemed like longer than necessary for one as small as mine. Maybe I was imagining things, which was highly likely.

My eyes met his in our reflection and, to my surprise, his gaze was as intense as mine. To make matters worse, my legs nearly gave out beneath me as he slid his fingers down to the lower part of my spine.

I closed my eyes, suppressing a sigh.

"You shouldn't have done it," he whispered very close to my ear, tightly gripping my side with his free hand. "Your skin is too pretty to mark it up with ink."

"You think so?" I asked, looking at him in the mirror. I could see a conflict being waged behind his eyes. The way his fingers gripped my waist so tightly made me think that, like me, he wanted to take things further . . . much further.

He didn't answer, and the silence stretched out for a few seconds.

Not being able to take his lack of an answer much longer, I raised a hand and pulled down the sleeve of my leotard to expose my shoulder and the upper part of my breast. I knew one of two things could happen: either he would undress me, which I doubted, or he would lift my sleeve back into place.

"Don't do that," he said, responding the way I'd expected.

His fingers grazed my arm as he pulled my leotard up. Once again, his touch gave me goose bumps, and he paused for a second, his eyes fixed on my pale skin, before he ran his fingers quickly back down my arm.

I thought I would melt into a puddle right then and there, until I felt him step back.

"All done. You should go back to studying."

My eyes met his in the mirror. "I should, but I don't want to," I replied, now facing him.

"Am I going to have to drag you out?"

I pretended to consider it. "Would that mean you put your hands on me again? Because if so, go ahead. You have my permission."

Sebastian took another step back. I hadn't realized how close we'd still been until he was right in front of me. "Be careful what you wish for, Marfil, it might be more than you can handle."

His response only inspired my perverted mind, which he must've seen in my eyes because before I could give a clever response, he squeezed my cheeks with one of his hands, impeding me from speaking.

"Please, don't say anything," he said, staring intently at my pursed lips.

"I think I can handle . . ." I started to say, but he leaned down and pressed his lips against my ear.

"It's not going to happen, Elephant. I'll never put this job in jeopardy, no matter how breathtaking you are."

What did he just call me?

"Did you just call me an elephant?" I asked, incredulous.

"Didn't you say they named you after that beautiful animal?" he asked, laughing.

"Are you trying to be funny? I told—"

"I know what you told me, Marfil," he interrupted without missing a beat. "I also remember you saying elephants are your favorite animal. And as a reminder to you, I'll say it again—it tracks." He moved to the door and gestured for me to leave. "But that doesn't make you any less annoying."

"You just said I was breathtaking, now you're calling me annoying . . . Yesterday you said I was unbearable . . ."

"You are."

"And a spoiled brat," I added, moving to the door.

"That's undeniable."

I stopped in front of him. "You can call me whatever you want . . . but you're dying to kiss me."

Sebastian pressed his lips together without taking his eyes off mine. Our attraction to each other seemed to become more obvious in the silence that stretched between us. I stood very still as he slowly leaned over, stopping his face just a few inches from my mouth. I held my breath and closed my eyes.

"You need to leave," he said finally.

I opened my eyes and looked at him in surprise. "What?" I answered. "No."

Sebastian pinched the bridge of his nose and sighed deeply. "Please . . ."

"I want a kiss," I said, crossing my arms.

Sebastian lowered his hand and looked at me in disbelief. "Marfil . . ."

"Don't *Marfil* me. You were just about to kiss me a second ago."

Sebastian seemed to be torn between killing me, kissing me, or pushing me out of the bathroom.

"You can't tell me what to do."

"And you can't start something and leave it half finished," I said, taking a step toward him.

"You can get as close as you want, but you're not tall enough to kiss me," he said without batting an eye.

He was right . . . but his lips weren't the only part of him I could kiss.

Without taking my eyes off him, I gently pressed my lips into the highest part of him I could reach while standing on my tiptoes: his collarbone. I noticed his breathing hitched for a split second.

Suddenly, without as much as a flinch, I had his fingers gripping the back of my neck, pulling my head away, his face leveled with mine.

"You're not used to anyone ever telling you no," he began in a whisper. "But I'm a person with too much self-control for you to—"

I leaned forward without hesitating and pressed my mouth to his, interrupting his lecture.

God . . . my body was overwhelmed with pleasure.

Sebastian stiffened momentarily; I'd caught him by surprise. Key word being *momentarily*. Before I knew it, he began kissing me back, a hoarse groan escaping his throat.

Who had gotten their way?

I had.

Unfortunately, it all came to an end quicker than I wanted to.

"Fuck, Marfil!" he exclaimed, pulling away from me and running a hand over his face. He looked furious. "I can't do this!"

"Why not?" I asked. "Who's stopping you?"

"*I can't*," he said, emphasizing each word.

I removed my high ponytail and let my hair swing loose. Then I proceeded to stay just like that, not a single movement, looking him in the eye.

Time seemed to stand still. We remained silent, locked in a staring contest, until he finally made a decision.

One second, we were staring each other down, and the next his mouth was on mine. This time, his kiss was unhesitating, firm, as if he wanted to make me pay for having caused him to lose all self-control.

He pressed my back into the wall and gripped my waist, as if it were the anchor that kept him rooted to the ground.

Tasting his mouth, inhaling his scent, his tongue more desperate for me than I ever thought possible, I wrapped my hands around his head and twisted my fingers into his hair, trembling as his hands slid up my sides until his palms practically covered my entire back.

"Tell me to stop," he said, his mouth against my moist lips.

"Don't stop, please," I moaned against his mouth.

A curse escaped his lips, and we once again merged into a passionate kiss that left us breathless. He proceeded to trace kisses down my neck, his teeth grazing my throat, then licked me gently, driving me totally wild.

As if this moment couldn't get any better, he picked me up effortlessly and sat me on the counter.

I sighed and grabbed his T-shirt, pulling him to me, wanting to feel every inch of him. I settled for clawing my nails along his back, and when I pressed my tongue into his, his mouth desperately devoured mine.

Were we seriously making out?

I gripped him tightly, wanting that moment to last a lifetime. For the first time in years, I felt alive; for the first time in a long time, I felt something when a man touched me, when a man kissed me.

I rubbed up against his erection and pressed harder into it, experiencing the impossible, wanting more, so much more.

But just as a sigh of pleasure escaped my lips, Sebastian cut the kiss off abruptly, as if suddenly realizing what had just happened, as if unable to believe what we'd done.

"I'm taking my three hours," he said, throwing me one last glance before leaving the bathroom.

I sat frozen in place, my heart beating out of control as the door slammed shut—further cementing the moment coming to an end.

## CHAPTER 13

# SEBASTIAN

I cursed everyone and everything, most of all myself, as I sped to my destination, far away from Marfil. What the hell was I thinking?

I wasn't, and that was the problem.

Filled with rage, I slammed hard on the accelerator, and before I knew it, I was almost outside the city.

I pulled over on the shoulder and took out my cell phone to check on her through the cameras. Marfil was sitting on the couch with Liam beside her. They were talking.

Why the hell did I care?

Who was I kidding? I had fallen into her trap like an idiot. I had given in, completely unable to control myself at the sight of her half-naked body before me, noticing how she reacted to my simple caresses, how her body was more sensitive to my touch than any woman I'd ever been with. She was a fucking nymph, with her bright eyes and dark hair, her body so fucking killer it could give you a heart attack.

I cursed aloud and punched the steering wheel, startling myself as I accidentally honked the horn. How could I have been so stupid? I had to quit. If Cortés found out what had happened, he'd kill me. If he found out about the mistake I'd made, all hell would break loose.

I opened the glove compartment and checked that the 9mm

Glock 19 was still where I'd left it. It was my duty to protect her; that's what I had to do. I could figure everything else out later. But one thing was for certain: I would never again lay a finger on Marfil Cortés.

CHAPTER 14

# MARFIL

I'd forgotten that Liam was coming over that night. Luckily, by the time he rang the doorbell, I had regained my composure and was able to act like nothing had happened between my bodyguard and me.

Don't ask me why, but I didn't tell Liam about the moment I'd shared with Sebastian. Not because I was afraid of Liam's reaction or was expecting him to disapprove, but because it was something I wanted to treasure all for myself. Also, I was almost frightened by the intensity of what I'd felt. The simple brush of Sebastian's leg against the center of my body had given me more intense pleasure than my ex-boyfriend or any other guy I'd ever been with, and I'd done much more with them than with Sebastian.

No guy had ever given me an orgasm, even though I'd been obsessed with trying to find the one who could. Not even Liam had been able to. I had thought I was incapable of having an orgasm, something that happens to a lot of women, feeling like there's something wrong with them when they don't feel the things they hear about in books, songs, and movies. I'd finally accepted the fact, and it was another of the reasons why I didn't want to go all the way with anyone. Why should I let someone else enjoy my body if they couldn't give me the pleasure I craved the most? Did that sound selfish? Maybe so, but I had made up my mind.

And yet, kissing Sebastian had been like merging all of my previous experiences into one. Was it normal for a kiss to feel so intense? Was it common to feel the attraction I felt toward him? Did Sebastian feel the same way about me?

At least I could take satisfaction in knowing one thing for certain: Sebastian would be able to grant me that kind of pleasure, if there was any chance we ever took it far enough.

Liam stayed to watch a movie, and we ordered Chinese food. He told me about his upcoming vacation plans and that he also had an offer for a new financial analyst position on Wall Street. He was nervous, but I was sure they'd hire him, even though he told me that he didn't plan to quit his night job as a club promoter. He didn't do it for the money, more so because he loved feeling like he owned the club, always surrounded by girls, and he wasn't going to give up a position that had brought him so much pleasure. And by pleasure, I mean women in his bed.

As time went on, I started to become more and more worried. Sebastian's three-hour break should've ended long ago, and he still hadn't come home. Eventually Liam had to leave, but he promised we'd see each other next week.

When he left, I felt totally alone, and even a little bit scared as I looked around the empty apartment.

What did Sebastian think of me? Had that kiss meant as much to him as it had to me?

Probably not.

Concluding that waiting by the door was pointless, I decided to get ready for bed. I had to lotion my tattoo again, but I'm sure I did a bad job because I couldn't really reach. I needed his large, strong hands.

I got into bed, reliving the moment we'd shared in the bathroom, and I lay awake, waiting to hear him come home.

Finally, I must've fallen asleep.

---

When I opened my eyes on Monday morning, I felt butterflies in my stomach. I no longer got nervous about guys, but the thought of seeing Sebastian made me so excited, I felt nauseous.

I took a shower, trying again without much success, to wash and lotion the tattoo, then I slipped a lightweight dress over my head, with my favorite boots and a sweater over it. I took a deep breath before going out into the living room. Would he be in the kitchen, like always—with his cup of coffee in one hand and the newspaper beside him on the table?

I couldn't be such a coward.

*Come on, Marfil, act like you do with everyone. Be confident.*

I walked out of my room and headed for the kitchen. There he was, standing facing the doorway as if he'd been waiting for me to appear. He looked so handsome that my mouth dried up.

Suddenly I felt the way I did when my father called me to his office to scold me for something. I remembered how it felt to have Sebastian's body against mine, and I couldn't help but blush like a little schoolgirl.

"Good morning," I said in a weak voice.

*Enough, Marfil. You're a grown woman.*

He didn't answer, just turned his back to me and started doing something.

I got out my favorite mug, heated the milk, then stirred in some honey as I moved to my usual spot, deciding on what to say or whether to wait for him to speak, or to simply do it myself.

"That won't happen again, Marfil," he said, looking out the window, his back to me, cutting through the silence with a knife.

That wasn't the greeting I'd been expecting. All night long

I'd imagined different phrases coming out of his mouth, that mouth that had been literally on mine: *We shouldn't have done it. Your father is going to kill me. I could lose my job.* But never *That won't happen again, Marfil.*

How could he say that? Wasn't he dying to do it again, to touch me everywhere, to devour me?

"I'd like for you to look at me when you speak to me," I said, setting my cup on the counter.

He spun around, and what I saw in his face left me frozen. He looked like a fucking robot, impossibly cold and distant. There was no life, no emotion in those eyes, only ice.

"It was a mistake. I let myself get carried away by the situation."

"What situation?" I was more scared of his response than any of the danger I was in.

"You know perfectly well the effect you have on men. I'm not made of stone, and you're too attractive for your own good. I let you seduce me. I was an idiot, and I'm sorry. But I'm not going to put my job on the line for you."

Wow. That hurt.

"So it's my fault that you did what you did because I seduced you with my body that's 'too attractive for my own good'?"

Sebastian seemed unfazed by my sarcastic tone.

"You know what? For a second I thought maybe you'd be able to see beyond my looks, which apparently drive all the guys sooo crazy, according to you. For a second I hoped I might hear something out of your mouth that made sense, instead of that bullshit you just spouted. But I guess guys are all the same—you only think with your dick."

"What do you want me to say? That I'm in love with you like in one of those books you read? Don't be such a little girl."

I stood up, unable to believe what he'd just said. How the hell did he know what fucking books I read, and what did that have to do with anything? Also, had he just called me a little girl?

"I'd throw this mug at your head right now, milk and honey included. But since I don't want to give you any more reasons to call me a 'little girl,' I'll just tell you that you're an emotionless asshole, and that even if what happened last night was amazing, I have a long list of guys I can spend my free time with, guys who won't run away scared like you did."

I didn't wait for him to respond. I picked up my bag and my keys, then walked to the door. Sebastian, as always, followed me, but I chose to pay him no mind.

On the way to campus, I rode in the back seat because I didn't want to let a rogue tear betray how much his words had affected me. I felt humiliated, that was the word. He had made me feel like a fucking object, but the worst part was verifying that, just like every other guy, Sebastian saw nothing in me beyond my physical appearance.

---

I went through the next two days without saying a single word to him. I didn't even want to see him. I was hurt by what he'd said to me, but I still felt the same intense emotions whenever he got too close, or whenever I simply laid eyes on him, which happened every time I left my fucking room.

Wednesday morning, however, I finally had to speak to him. I'd had a terrible night, I felt sick and miserable, and I was freezing cold. When I didn't come out of my room to have breakfast and go to class, he came to check on me. I ignored his knocks at my door, turning my face away and covering my head with the down comforter.

"Marfil?"

*Yeah, that's my name, asshole.*

"Are you going to class?"

"No," I tried to shout, but it came out as a hoarse groan.

I suppose he heard me because he didn't bother me again until after seven o'clock that evening, when he knocked again. Receiving no response, he barged into my room without waiting for permission.

"I didn't say you could come in. Get out," I protested.

"You've been in here almost twenty-four hours. You haven't even eaten. What's wrong with you?"

"Nothing," I grunted, burrowing under the covers.

I could tell he was moving closer because I heard the sound of his shoes against my wooden floor. He gently pulled back the comforter, and I let out a whimper of pain.

He brushed my arm. "You're burning up."

I didn't want to move. All I wanted was for him to leave me alone. I had a cold, so what? It was no big deal; I wasn't going to die. And anyway, who was he to act all worried about me now?

"Sit up," he practically ordered me.

"Go away, Sebastian. No one asked you to take care of me."

He ignored me again, taking advantage of the fact that I was lying on my stomach and pulling up the back of my shirt.

"Shit, Marfil, it's infected."

"What is?" I grumbled weakly.

"Your tattoo, dammit."

"What are you talking about?" I questioned angrily, pushing him away with the little force I could muster. "I cleaned it three times a day like they told me to."

"Well, you didn't do a very good job. I'm going to call a doctor."

"Don't even think about it. Leave me alone."

He left, and I tried to go back to sleep. But a short while later, I heard the buzzer sound, and soon after, someone came into my room. I cursed Sebastian, but at least he had the decency to turn on the bedside lamp instead of the overhead light.

I felt horrible.

"Good evening, Miss Cortés. I'm Dr. Rockwood."

I gathered all my strength from deep within my soul and pushed myself up to a seated position. The doctor, a man of no more than fifty, stood over me. Behind him—with a worried expression I'd never seen on him before—Sebastian kept his eyes glued to me.

"Your friend told me that you recently got a tattoo, and he thinks it's infected."

"He's not my friend," was my only response.

The doctor ignored my reply as he rummaged in his kit. He gave me a thermometer and told me to stick it under my arm.

"While we wait, why don't you turn around so I can get a look at the tattoo?"

I did as he asked and lifted my shirt. The doctor and Sebastian both winced in unison, making my hair stand on end. Then the thermometer started to beep. When the doctor read it and informed us that I had a fever of over 104, I started to feel worried as well.

"That's a very high fever."

"Do I have an infection?"

"A whale of an infection, Miss Cortés. You need to start taking antibiotics immediately. And with a fever like that, you should be at the hospital until it passes—a day or so, give or take."

"What? No way."

"Marfil, fuck. Do what he says."

"I don't want to go to the hospital. My father will find out about it and about the tattoo. Do you want him to kill me? No, there has to be another solution."

The doctor frowned, accepting the fact he wasn't going to change my mind. "You want to stay here, fine, but I have to warn you, you have an exhausting night ahead of you." Turning to Sebastian, he said, "You, too, young man. You'll need to run her a cool bath."

Sebastian was furious. I could see it in his eyes and in the way he clenched his jaw, but he nodded along to the doctor's orders.

"She's going to need to take this medicine every four hours and apply this cream to the infected area. I'll come back tomorrow to check on her. But if the fever doesn't start to go down, you'll need to take her to the emergency room."

Sebastian agreed as the doctor handed him the prescriptions.

They left the room, and I wrapped the comforter around myself once again. I was freezing, shivering so hard that my teeth chattered.

I must've dozed off, because it was almost an hour later when Sebastian came back with the medication and the antibiotic cream.

"You need to get in the bath, Marfil."

"No fucking way. That doctor is crazy. I'm freezing. I don't want to feel even colder."

"If the fever doesn't go down, you're going to have to go to the emergency room. And I'll gladly drag you down there. So do what the doctor says if you don't want to make me even more mad than I already am."

"Mind your own business," I said, burying my face in the pillow and covering my head with the blankets.

Before I had time to react, he'd lifted me up and was carrying me to the bath. I didn't have the strength to resist. All I could do was murmur insults at him until we reached the bathroom and he sat me down on the toilet. I looked at the bath, and as soon as my arm touched the water, my skin became covered in goose bumps.

"I'll die of hypothermia if I get in there."

"If you won't get it on your own, I'll have to throw you in myself."

I shivered violently.

"I should've cleaned your tattoo for you. I knew you couldn't do it on your own."

"I did clean it. The problem must've been that tattoo artist—who knows what kind of needle he used on me."

Sebastian ignored my comment and placed a hand on my forehead. "You're burning up. Please, just get in the bath."

"I will. But don't leave me." I'm not sure where that came from—maybe I was delirious from the fever—but I asked him to stay . . . and he did.

Getting into that bath in my underwear was the most painful experience of my life. Not only was my tattoo burning like crazy, but I was also shaking like a leaf, sitting in the bath curled into a ball, hugging my knees and cursing everyone and everything, most of all whoever the hell invented tattoos in the first place.

"I hate you," I said over and over, my teeth clacking loudly.

"I know."

After twenty minutes, I couldn't take it anymore. I got on my feet. My hair and body were dripping wet, and I was still shaking violently.

Sebastian stood in front of me, and he couldn't help but look at my soaked body. One glance was enough to see that my wet underwear didn't leave much to the imagination.

"Do you want to take a picture while I freeze to death?"

Sebastian ignored my comment once again and wrapped me in a white towel before helping me out of the tub. He placed me in front of the mirror while he gently dried me off, and I saw how horrible I looked. My face was red from the fever, and my hair hung in a limp cascade that dripped onto the floor.

"I'll leave you to put on your pajamas."

I looked at the clothes he'd set out for me, cursing again between gritted teeth. "Did I mention that I hate you?" I shouted weakly.

When he didn't answer, I stepped into my underwear and slipped on the summer nightgown. I wanted fleece pajamas, with thick socks and a scarf, not something that still left parts of my skin exposed! Annoyed, I dried my hair with the towel and brushed it in under a minute.

On my way to my bedroom, I passed him without saying a word, then got into bed, still trembling, and pulled the comforter up to my ears. "Don't even think about taking away my covers. I swear I'll bite you if you try it."

Sebastian sighed and handed me a thermometer. I put it under my arm, and when it started to beep, I gave it back to him.

"What does it say?" I asked, hopeful. If I'd gone through that torture for nothing, I swear, I was prepared to jump off the balcony, which would almost certainly be less painful.

"A hundred and one," he said, frowning.

I smiled. "It worked."

"It's still a high fever."

"Don't be so annoying. It went down. Now, let me sleep."

"You have to take this first."

He gave me the pill and left my room.

I fell asleep instantly, or at least that's how it seemed. I was exhausted, and felt as if I'd run barefoot through a blizzard, fallen off a cliff, and then walked eight hours straight through the desert.

I opened my eyes who knows how many hours later to a figure moving toward my bed, carrying a tray.

I immediately tensed and felt scared, like I was experiencing déjà vu.

"Don't touch me! Let me go! Help!" I screamed desperately.

"Hey! Hey! Marfil, it's me . . . It's me, Sebastian."

I stopped screaming and looked all around. I was in my room, with no trace of that basement . . .

I stared frightenedly at Sebastian, and he let go of me immediately.

"It's me," he said again in an almost inaudible whisper.

I slowly nodded, then lay back on the bed, my eyes fixed on him.

It had been like two scenes merging into one.

Had I just remembered something from the kidnapping?

"I brought you some tomato soup. You need to drink some water, too. You haven't had any liquids in hours."

He placed his hand on my forehead, and I closed my eyes at his touch. My head was pounding.

I sat up carefully, making sure that my back didn't brush against the headboard, and I drank the soup in small sips.

"How are you feeling?"

I didn't answer. I suddenly felt like I was in some sort of trance, as if I were in danger. I feared for my life, and not because of the fever and the infection. I was afraid of him, of Sebastian, of him being in my room.

"Why are you looking at me like I'm going to hurt you?"

I stared down at the soup. It was hot and delicious, and even managed to warm me up. Or maybe the antibiotic had taken effect and the fever was starting to go down.

"I had a nightmare, that's all."

Sebastian nodded, looking concerned. When I finished the soup, he took the bowl and set in on the bedside table.

"Now I'll put some ointment on your tattoo, then you can go back to sleep."

As soon as his fingertips made contact with my skin, shivers ran up and down my spine. I hadn't forgotten how cold he'd been to me days before, which allowed me to ultimately feel thankful when he finished, turned off the lights, and left.

The night was long and difficult. My fever hadn't taken long to spike up again, and Sebastian had to repeatedly apply freezing-cold compresses to my forehead, making sure my fever didn't rise above 104. I felt weak and miserable. At one point, I even begged him to get in bed with me. He did, although he stayed on top of the sheets. It was easier for him to apply the compresses from that position, but my request came more from my delirious, fevered state than anything else. I might have been hallucinating, but I could've sworn he ran his hands through my hair for what felt like hours until I finally fell asleep.

When I opened my eyes, the light of a new day filtering in through the window, he was no longer in bed with me. I instead found him observing me from the chair in the corner.

I sat up, locking eyes with his.

"How are you feeling?" he asked, also sitting up.

I'm sure I looked as bad as I felt, like a total wreck, but he somehow managed to look more handsome than I'd ever seen him, even with dark circles under his eyes. I wanted to push his messy hair out of his face. I wanted to kiss him all over to thank him for staying up all night with me and taking care of me the way he had. But I couldn't do either.

"Good, much better," was all I said.

Sebastian stood up and looked at me. Before he could open his mouth and disappoint me, I decided what would happen next.

"I'll tell Liam to come take care of me from now on. You can take your free hours, or do whatever you want. I won't be going anywhere for the next few days, clearly."

Sebastian drew his lips together into a fine line but didn't say anything else.

CHAPTER 15

# MARFIL

Liam came over as soon as I called him. He entered my room and whistled like an idiot when he saw me lying in bed, shivering and writhing with body aches.

"I never thought I'd have to say this to you of all people, but you look like shit."

Groaning, I pulled the covers over my head. "I asked you to come make me feel better, not worse, jerk."

I rolled over as I felt him sit down beside me.

"I was just joking. You look adorable when you're sick—your cheeks get all red from the fever."

I hit him with a pillow, although I think it hurt me more than him.

"Can a tattoo seriously make you this sick? I told you, you don't put a bumper sticker on a fucking Ferrari. You tried to go against nature, and now it's paying you back."

"Shut up."

"Can you at least tell me what you got done? Because I could understand if you got a tattoo that says *I love Liam*."

I rolled my eyes, sat up, turned my back to him, and lifted my shirt.

"Very cute . . . Even though you can't really make out the ballerina right now."

"Is it that bad?"

"It's pretty bad."

I put the pillow over my head. Karma strikes again.

"Not to change the subject, but," he began, pulling the pillow away, "your bodyguard is out there in the living room looking super worried. He always has such a stick up his ass, but this time I think you're the one who stuck it there. Did something happen between you two?"

"What are you talking about?" I said, playing dumb. "We don't get along well, that's all."

Liam was about to open his mouth when we heard the buzzer. A few seconds later, someone knocked on my door.

"Come in."

It was the doctor, accompanied by Sebastian. Instead of taking a break like I'd asked him to, he stood leaning against the door, watching me the entire time the doctor examined me.

"You still have a fever, but at least it's under control now. You need to drink plenty of liquids, take the antibiotics, and apply the ointment. The fever is likely to spike in the evening. If that happens," he said, looking now at Sebastian, "repeat what you did last night: Check her temperature every hour and place cold compresses on her forehead to make sure it doesn't go above 104."

I said goodbye to the doctor and lay back down.

The tension in the room was immediately palpable. Liam was staring at Sebastian, who was staring at me. Neither of them blinking.

"You spent all night putting cold compresses on Marfil's forehead?" Liam finally spoke.

Sebastian ignored him, his eyes still boring into mine. "I'll make you some food," he said, then he left the room, closing the door.

Liam looked at me suspiciously. "Tell me you didn't hook up with him, Marfil."

I tensed but shook my head. "We didn't hook up. We had a fight over something dumb, and now he's even colder than usual."

"But he took care of you all night? So now he's a nurse, too?"

"What did you expect him to do? Leave me lying here, burning up? He just made sure I had everything I needed."

"Right . . ."

I didn't want to talk about Sebastian, so instead, I asked Liam to get out my laptop and pick a movie on Netflix.

A little while later, Sebastian came in carrying a bowl of soup with bread and butter. I could tell it irritated Liam.

Sebastian placed the tray on the bedside table and stood over me. "Eat this."

I nodded grudgingly. That must've been enough for Sebastian because he shot Liam an icy look, then left.

"Why do I suddenly feel like I'm not wanted here?"

"Because you're paranoid."

I picked up the tray and sat up to eat. It was a butternut squash soup with carrot and leek, and it was delicious, though knowing Sebastian had made it just for me pissed me off. He had been very caring, it was true, but that didn't erase the words he'd said to me after we'd kissed.

Liam and I watched the rest of the movie while I finished my meal. The last thing I remembered was Liam going to the kitchen and making himself a sandwich. I fell asleep well before the movie ended, curled up under my comforter. I don't even know if it was Liam who put the cold compresses on my forehead or not.

---

I spent two more days in bed, and I gradually began to feel better. Tami came to take care of me the day after Liam. I didn't tell her what had happened with Sebastian. We talked instead about spring break and the possibility of her coming to visit me in Baton Rouge.

"I'd love to. I'll have to see if my parents will mind. Is Liam going?" she asked.

"I doubt it. I invited him, but he has other plans."

If she was disappointed by my response, I didn't notice. We changed the subject, and I asked her how the ballet classes were going.

"The girls are fine; they all miss you. The little one named Lili won't stop asking about you. They weren't at all happy when I told them you'd be gone for a month or so, but the lessons are going well, I guess."

"Are you being careful? I'd feel responsible if anything happened to you . . ."

Tami shrugged. "I go straight to the subway as soon as class ends. It's staying light until later now, so it's not dark when I leave. I do like giving the classes, though. I understand now why you risk going out there by yourself. The girls are amazing."

I smiled, missing my students and wishing I could go back to giving classes again myself.

After Tami left, I felt the need to move my body, do something, so I put on my dance clothes and left my bedroom for the first time in four long days. As I made my way toward the kitchen for some water, my sister called and we talked for the fifteen minutes her school allowed. I missed her, and I was counting the days until I got to see her again.

"What are you planning to do?" Sebastian called, standing in his doorway, looking me up and down as I walked past his room.

I stopped in front of him. "Isn't it obvious?" I answered.

The last thing I wanted was another argument with Sebastian.

"You're not healed yet, Marfil, and you're taking antibiotics. You shouldn't be exerting yourself."

"Physical activity is healthy," I said.

He blocked my path by stretching an arm out in front of me. "Wait a few days—you should be in bed."

"Listen, Sebastian, I understand that you're super concerned with losing your job, but you're going a bit overboard. You're getting paid to keep someone from killing me, not to protect me from myself. I'm going to dance, so leave me alone." I slipped through the space under his arm and moved down the hallway. When I entered my studio, I closed the door behind me and sighed, grateful to be alone in my sacred space. I hit *Play* and stood in front of the barre.

I started with some simple pliés and then stretched on the barre, my torso perpendicular to my leg. All my joints cracked, reminding me how out of practice I was.

The tattoo hurt, and I was afraid that I might've removed the scab. I tried to check it in the mirror, but I could hardly see anything, so I kept stretching until I started dancing. I needed this, needed to do the thing that had inspired me to get the tattoo in the first place.

As I came out of another pirouette, I began to feel dizzy, but I kept going even though I knew I should stop. When I moved into the sixth position, the floor spun at a strange angle, and I fell, my side slamming into the hardwood floor.

Shit.

A second later, Sebastian opened the door.

"I told you not to dance."

He walked over to me, picked me up off the floor before I had the chance to stop him, and carried me out of the room.

"I'm fine, dammit."

After he lay me on the couch, I realized he was angry.

"Go back to bed, please."

"Mind your own business, please."

Sebastian sighed and stood there, staring at me for a moment. "If you like dancing so much, why do you only do it alone in there, where no one can see you?"

His question took me by surprise, most of all because he'd never shown any interest in learning anything about me, other than the meaning behind my name.

"My father and my uncle forced me to stop dancing when I turned fifteen. I stopped training professionally and lost almost all my technique."

"You don't seem to have lost anything . . ."

I narrowed my eyes, confused. He hadn't seen me dance . . .

"The day you taught those girls . . . You didn't seem bad at all."

I leaned forward and started untying my pointe shoes, quickly yet carefully. "That was a dance lesson for twelve-year-old girls . . . It's not that hard."

"Right."

I nodded, eyeing him like a kid does a piece of candy they can't have. That's what he was for me. The way he'd made me feel that day in the bathroom still replayed in my mind every night.

As if echoing my thoughts, he gave me a once-over. I took the opportunity to openly observe him as well, taking in his muscles, recalling the way he'd lifted me off the floor and carried me onto the counter with almost no effort.

"You know what? You'd be a great dance partner," I said without thinking.

Sebastian raised his eyebrows in surprise. "Clearly you're still feverish," he said, placing a palm on my forehead, looking at me like I was delirious.

"I'm not joking," I responded, pushing his hand away and trying to ignore the butterflies in my stomach.

"I guess we'll never know," he said with a blank expression.

Just when I thought the tension in that small room would suffocate us, the doorbell rang, and we both jumped.

Sebastian stepped away from me and walked toward the front door.

I followed.

“Are you expecting anyone?”

I shook my head, annoyed when he put out an arm to stop me from checking to see who it was.

He muttered something to himself, then opened the door, an unfriendly look plastered on his face.

Liam walked past Sebastian without even looking at him and greeted me with a smile. “How are you doing?” he asked, giving me a gentle hug. “If you’re feeling better, I have a proposal for you.”

“I’m doing perfect!”

“Great! Because I have tickets to see Imagine Dragons tonight.”

“What?!” I exclaimed, overjoyed.

“I got them today at work—from a rich dude who knows someone, who knows someone who’s in charge of the tour. It’s a private balcony, great view. What do you say? Are you in?”

“Of course!”

Sebastian shook his head, staring at me with a patient expression on his face. I looked at Liam, and then back at Sebastian.

“How many tickets do you have?” I asked, feeling my euphoria beginning to subside.

“Two,” Liam said, smiling. “One for me and one for you.”

“You can wait for me outside,” I said to Sebastian before he had time to object.

“No,” he replied without a moment of hesitation, then turned and went into the kitchen.

“Sebastian, it’s a private balcony—” I began, but he interrupted me.

“If I’m not with you, I can’t guarantee your safety.”

"Listen, man, I understand you have to do your job, but Marfil's right. It's a private balcony. You can wait outside. Nothing is going to happen to her. I won't leave her side."

Sebastian stopped in front of Liam. "Oh yeah?" he said, his tone suddenly angry. "And what are you going to do to protect her, huh? Do you have any fucking idea how to do my job? Do you think I'm just here following her around because I have nothing better to do?"

Liam gritted his teeth.

"Find another date. Marfil isn't going out tonight; she's still sick."

"No, I'm not!" I cried, furious.

"Look, dude, I know her better than you do. If you try to keep her locked up like this, she's going to—"

"Go crazy," I said, finishing the sentence for him.

"Fortunately, I've been trained to face any type of danger. I think I'll be able to handle a little girl who's mad because she can't go to a concert."

I couldn't believe it!

Liam looked at me, unsure of what to do. I realized I didn't have many options. I couldn't go anywhere without Sebastian, and he was completely unwilling to cooperate; he could easily wait for me outside of Madison Square Garden, just as Liam had said.

My friend finally left, disappointed that I couldn't go with him and trying to think of who else he knew who liked Imagine Dragons.

As soon as the front door shut behind Liam, I glared at Sebastian. "You did that on purpose," I said, stepping toward him, fuming. "I could've totally gone; the problem is that you're so obsessed with the fucking danger I'm supposedly in that you won't let me do the things I'd normally do without you there to ruin all my plans."

"I'm not here to ruin your plans. I'm here to keep you from getting killed."

"No one's going to kill me!" I shouted, totally losing my cool. "They had the chance to kill me and they didn't. If they'd wanted to, I'd already be dead and buried."

"You don't understand a criminal's mind, Marfil. You'd be shocked how twisted it is." He set his glass of water on the counter with a sigh.

I moved closer to him and crossed my arms. "You called me a little girl again," I said, now very serious. "Well, a few days ago, you had your tongue down this *little girl*'s throat. So don't call me that again."

My words took him by surprise. It was as if he'd erased that memory from his mind and couldn't imagine that I hadn't done the same.

"Maybe you're not a little girl, but you're not going anywhere tonight unless I go with you."

"Is that a threat?"

"It's a fact," he said, lifting his glass to his mouth.

I huffed, then stormed into my room, immediately sending a quick text to Liam.

Don't even think about going without me. I'll meet you at 67th and Madison in half an hour.

Afterward, I took off my dance clothes and got in the shower. I was not going to stay locked up. I was an adult, and I needed to feel like one again. I was tired of living in fear, but most of all, I was tired of having Sebastian come everywhere with me. I needed to feel like I was in control of my own life.

I put on jeans, my motorcycle boots, and a dark T-shirt, pulled my hair back into a high ponytail, and grabbed my bag. I knew I couldn't just walk out the front door with Sebastian still lurking around out there, so I opened my window. The building next to mine opened onto the fire escape; I just had to cross over, and the rest would be easy. Like I was back to being fifteen at boarding school, I shoved a pillow under my covers and turned off the lights. If I was lucky, Sebastian would think I was still mad, and he'd leave me alone for the night.

Crossing the ledge was effortless. I'd snuck out of boarding school so many times that I was a pro. The real trick was not being noticed by my neighbors, so I raced down the stairs, silently praying I wouldn't be seen.

Soon, I was walking the city all on my own for the first time in weeks. Despite the adrenaline pumping through my veins, I couldn't help but look all around to make sure no one suspicious was following me.

*You're just being paranoid, Marfil. Prove Sebastian wrong.*

When I finally reached the corner where Liam had agreed to meet me, relief flickered through me as I saw him waiting for me in his gleaming car.

I jumped inside. "Let's go, let's go," I said, looking back.

No one was following me.

"Your bodyguard is going to be fucking pissed," he said with a grin that took up his entire face.

"Not if he doesn't find out," I shot back, feeling a pang of guilt that vanished as soon as I remembered he was the reason I had to go through these measures in the first place.

"What did you do, put a pillow under your blankets?" he joked.

"Exactly," I said, staring straight ahead as Liam navigated through traffic to Madison Square Garden.

Liam laughed out loud, and I smiled. I had no reason to feel guilty. I couldn't let Sebastian get to me. Yes, I'd snuck out. Yes, I had fooled my bodyguard. And yes, I had disobeyed my father's orders, but you know what? I wasn't a little girl, and if I wanted to take risks, that was my decision, not my father's or Sebastian's, but mine.

It took us a little longer than I would've liked, but fortunately we didn't have to wait in line to get in, like most of the concertgoers, since we were VIP. Our seats were amazing; we had plenty of space to dance, and they served us food and chilled champagne nonstop. There were about twenty people total in the private box with a perfect view of the stage.

When the band came out and Dan Reynolds started singing "Whatever It Takes," I took it as a sign that I'd made the right decision by sneaking out. Singing at the top of my lungs, I felt liberated, as if I'd broken free of my chains. Liam jumped up and down beside me, and we felt like the song had been written just for us. I laughed as I sipped my third glass of champagne, my mind clouding over from the alcohol, causing me to forget my problems.

By the time they sang "On Top of the World" and "Radioactive," we were walking on air. My cell phone vibrated constantly in my pocket, but I ignored it. I was drunk and all I cared about was jumping up and down, singing as loud as I could. During the last lines of "Believer," I climbed on Liam's back and hugged him tight as we sang until we were hoarse. Liam and I had great times together, and I would treasure them always.

When the concert finally ended, the musicians left the stage and the lights came on so we could make our way to the exits like a herd of cattle. Liam smiled at me, drenched in sweat, cheeks bright red. "That was incredible, wasn't it?"

"Incredible," I answered, grabbing his arm and following the crowd to the exit.

Out on the street, it was pouring rain. We were immediately soaked, and with all the chaos of people and traffic leaving the concert, I didn't realize that someone was waiting outside.

"Sebastian," I said in a shaky voice when I saw his furious brown eyes boring into mine after I'd practically tripped over him. He took me by the arm and started dragging me to the car.

"Hey!" Liam said, not realizing that it was Sebastian who'd grabbed me.

But before he could do anything about it, Sebastian's fist went flying over my head and crashed into my best friend's face.

I opened my eyes wide in shock. Liam was on the ground, covering his eye with one hand and lifting himself from the sidewalk with the other. I tried to break free from Sebastian, but he picked me up, shoved me in the car, and locked me inside.

"Open the fucking door!" I shouted, horrified to see Liam wobbling as he tried to stand. Sebastian immediately went around to the driver's seat and started the car. "Have you completely lost your mind? Let me out! You just punched my best friend in the face!"

"And I'd do it again ten times over."

My mouth hung open in disbelief. The car was spinning; everything had happened too fast for me to even process.

"How did you know where to find me?" was the first thing I thought to ask.

Sebastian ignored the question as he sped up Fifth Avenue, dodging in and out of traffic like a pro.

"It was my idea. You didn't need to hit him!"

"Whether it was your idea or not, he was the one who took you."

I didn't argue, not because he was right, but because I was drunk and terrified, to be honest. Sebastian seemed possessed, and it was scary, but my biggest fear was that he'd told my father.

In the elevator headed up to my apartment, our eyes met, and I could feel the waves of rage emanating from him. We reached my floor, and I wanted to run to my room like I did whenever I knew my father was going to scold me for something I'd done wrong, but before I could make a run for it, his hand was wrapped tightly around my arm and my back was against the living room wall.

"Don't do that again," he said, his lips so close to mine that my heart started racing.

"Or what?" I replied, challenging him. The alcohol had given me a false sense of courage.

Sebastian grabbed my chin and tilted my head up to meet his gaze. "Or I'll tie you to your bedposts, I swear to God. And I don't give a damn about the consequences."

My breathing quickened as I realized he was being completely serious, but most of all because he was so close I could feel the same intense arousal I had the day we kissed.

I swallowed as he slowly slid his thumb over my cheek.

"Get out of my sight."

He didn't have to tell me twice.

## CHAPTER 16

# MARFIL

The next morning, I woke up with a hellacious hangover. I went into the kitchen, where Sebastian and his delicious breakfasts were nowhere to be seen. I'd woken up early, considering I hadn't fallen sleep until almost three o'clock in the morning, tossing and turning over how guilty I felt. Liam had sent me a picture of his black eye, saying that if he saw my asshole bodyguard again, he was going to break his face.

He wouldn't last thirty seconds against Sebastian, but I didn't want to add fuel to the fire, knowing that Liam's visits to my apartment were going to get a lot more tense.

I was pouring cereal into a bowl with my eyes fixed on the hallway, waiting for Sebastian to appear, when I noticed that the apartment was too silent. I could always hear the murmur of the television in Sebastian's room or the bad music he listened to when he was in there alone.

Setting my bowl aside, I walked down the hall to check if he was still asleep. No one answered when I knocked on his door. I debated as to whether I should open it or wait for him to show some sign of life, but my curiosity won out in the end. The room was dark; the shades were drawn against the sunlight, his bed neatly made.

Had he left, sick of putting up with me?

I went into my studio, which was also completely dark. I was feeling along the wall for the light switch when an arm encircled me from behind, causing my heart to leap into my throat. I tried to scream, but it came out muffled by a giant hand covering my mouth.

My body shook uncontrollably. Someone had broken into my home. Sebastian was probably dead somewhere, and they'd kill me next. Sebastian was right—someone wanted me dead, and I had tempted fate, serving myself up on a platter.

"You're shaking like a leaf and you haven't even put up any resistance, Elephant," he whispered in my ear. "You think what you did yesterday was funny?"

Shit, fuck.

"Sebastian, let me go," I said into his hand, which was still covering my mouth. Despite the fact that I'd relaxed as soon as I realized it was him playing a trick on me and not some murderer who had me trapped in that dark room, I couldn't help but feel a twinge of fear when I heard his deep voice vibrate against my skin.

"I want you to answer me," he said, squeezing me tighter, almost hurting me. "Did you have a good time, while I was going crazy, fearing for your life?"

I flinched. I did have a good time, a great time, but honesty was not always the best policy.

"Mm s'rry . . ." I mumbled into his hand.

"You're going to be even sorrier," he said ominously as he spun me around. He stood in front of me, holding my arms over my head and pinning his body against mine, completely immobilizing me. "You're going to do exactly as I tell you, Marfil, or I swear to God I'm going to make life impossible for you. Do you understand?"

I swallowed.

He grabbed both of my wrists with one hand and used the other to cup my chin, forcing me to look at him. "Answer me."

"I understand," I said. "But now you listen to me: You're not going to touch any more of my friends."

Sebastian smiled in the darkness. “Or what, Elephant?” He laughed.

“Stop calling me that,” I gritted out.

“Would you rather I call you what you are? A fucking spoiled brat?” he went on, holding me tightly as I tried to knee him. “No, no, that’s not the way to do it. You have a long road ahead before you’ll be able to harm so much as a hair on my head.”

“You think you’re so tough, don’t you? All tall with your big muscles . . . You don’t scare me, Sebastian, if that’s what you were trying to do surprising me like that . . . I’ll have you know, I’d let you tie me up whenever you want.”

He showed irritation at my last comment as his fingers wrapped tighter around my wrists.

“Do you want me to tell you what I think?” I said without taking my eyes off him.

“No.”

“What happened in the bathroom between you and me . . . is going to happen again, sooner than you think.”

“You underestimate my self-control, Marfil. I’ve won medals for it.”

“Did you also win a medal for being the biggest asshole in the Navy?”

He smiled, immune to my insults. “I don’t want you to mention that issue again.”

“What, the issue of you kissing me or the issue of you being a monumental asshole?”

“My patience has a limit, Marfil, don’t forget that,” he replied, lessening the pressure on my wrists.

“If you don’t mind, I’d like you to let me go. I have stuff to do.”

Sebastian stared at me with a serious expression, studying my face. He released me and took a step back. My eyes had adjusted to the dark, and I saw how huge his arms looked in the sleeveless shirt he was wearing.

"I'll be in my room, studying," I said without moving.

"Good," he answered, his eyes still on mine.

---

I spent Sunday locked up at home, studying for my upcoming midterms that week. I was really behind in most of my classes, considering all the days I'd missed because I was sick. Still, I felt confident—ironically enough, I *did* have the memory of an elephant and knew I'd pass my midterms with flying colors.

That night, I didn't eat dinner with Sebastian, not because I didn't want to, but because he took his plate into his room, claiming he had to make a call.

That piqued my interest. Who could Sebastian be calling when he wasn't working? Was it really true that he didn't have a girlfriend? Just thinking about it drove me crazy with jealousy. It would be weird if he didn't have girls interested in him, since he was so fucking hot, but I took him for more of a one-night-stand kind of guy. It was hard to imagine him committing to anyone, probably more of the "love 'em and leave 'em" type. He had barely batted an eye when we'd kissed, after all.

God, I wanted so badly for it to happen again.

I bit my lip thinking about it as I walked past his door. What would it be like to have his dick in my hands? I was suddenly very curious. My mind started to imagine how that conversation might go.

*Hey, Sebastian, can I jack you off until I make you come? Or I could do it with my mouth, you decide.*

Yeah, I'm sure he'd think it was as funny as I did, unless he had a heart attack.

I went into my room after eating the dinner he'd cooked, a meal fit for a queen, and I fell asleep almost immediately. What I didn't expect was to find him at my bedside a few hours after I'd closed my eyes.

"Up!" he said, pulling the comforter off me without any warning.

I opened my eyes to see him leaving my room.

What the hell?

I put the pillow over my head, assuming he must've lost his mind after some kind of head injury, karma finally on my side, so I ignored him and tried to go back to sleep. It was still dark out.

He appeared again a moment later.

"Either you get up on your own or I'll wake you up the way they do it in the military."

All I heard was: *Blah, blah, blah.*

Just then, a stream of freezing water landed on my face, causing me to jump so high I fell off the bed.

"What the fuck are you doing?"

Sebastian stared down at me blankly. "Don't you want me to teach you how to defend yourself? Yesterday in your dance studio you proved how helpless you are in the face of danger, so I'll start by teaching you that without discipline, you won't be able to so much as fend off a rabid dog."

I stared at him, unable to believe what I was hearing. "Did you seriously just pour water on my face?"

Sebastian didn't answer my question. "I want to see you in the kitchen in five minutes, dressed and ready for breakfast."

I laughed in his face as I stood up and looked at him like he'd lost his mind. "I don't know whether to punch you or feel sorry for you if you really think I'm going to get up at"—I looked at the clock above my bed—"five thirty in the morning!" I slapped his arm. "Have you totally lost it?"

"You're the one who wanted me to teach you, and I'm going to do it my way."

"Well . . . I don't want you to teach me anymore, thanks."

I got back in bed, but Sebastian wrapped his arm around

me and started to squeeze my neck, leaving me breathless. His other arm wound tightly around my hips, completely disabling me. I couldn't move a muscle; I couldn't even open my mouth.

"Come on . . . What would you do if this were happening for real?"

He lessened his grip slightly so that I could breathe, but without letting me go. I tried to think about how to escape this idiot but felt utterly powerless. I made a move to kick him in the balls, but he pressed me into the mattress and got on top of me so that I was unable to do anything to free myself from him, and I started to get pissed.

"What would you do?" he whispered next to my ear.

As sexy as the situation might have seemed, it was not at all.

"Any guy, *any*, could pin you like this, in this position, in a snap of a finger. I'm much stronger than a normal guy, and that's why I'm giving you a chance to free yourself," he went on, still right in my ear, very serious. "You should know how to get rid of anyone who tries to touch you unwanted, Marfil, and believe me, as beautiful as you are, there will be plenty of guys who will want to try it."

"Let me go, Sebastian," I said into the mattress.

"No," he replied, pressing his hand into my back. "Think, what would you do?"

I thought, trying hard to find a way to get him off me, but I couldn't. It was impossible.

"Scream . . . I would scream!" I answered after a few seconds, pulling air into my lungs.

"Like a little princess?" He was making fun of me.

He'd totally lost it, taking this self-defense lesson way too seriously.

Then I thought of something. He hadn't yet registered it, or maybe he had, but the hand he wasn't using to pin my wrists behind my back was resting on the mattress right beside my face.

Without hesitating for a second, and taking that lesson just as seriously as he was, I lunged my face at his hand and bit down, hard. My unexpected attack, and the pain I suppose it caused, proved effective. I felt his grip loosen a little, then I started thrashing around like a madwoman, rolling under his body.

Somehow, I managed to scramble away and stand up. Just as I was about to lift my leg to kick him in the balls, he moved quickly, dodging my kick. With his good hand, the one I hadn't bitten, he gripped my ankle and pulled, causing me to lose my balance and fall back down, this time against his chest instead of the mattress.

I was furious; I didn't want him to pin me again. I hadn't liked feeling so defenseless, completely at his mercy, so I quickly moved out of the way when he tried to grab me around the waist. The problem was that he was even quicker, and I found myself, once again, lying against the mattress with him straddling my stomach. I went limp and surrendered, panting hard, as if I'd been running for an hour.

He rubbed the hand I'd bitten and frowned slightly as if in pain, although I thought I saw a certain glint of admiration in his brown eyes.

"You have no idea what you're doing, zero technique, but you were savage, you hurt me. We can call it quits for today." He stood up, and after throwing me a quick glance over his shoulder, he left my room.

My chest rose and fell . . . I lay there, analyzing what had happened. His teaching method was far from subtle. But he hadn't so much as flinched, and I was still out of breath from the way the weight of his body had paralyzed me in the blink of an eye.

And then I remembered he'd called me beautiful, but why had he pronounced the word as if it was the worst insult he'd ever voiced aloud?

Unable to get back to sleep, I put on my bathrobe and went out into the living room. I couldn't say exactly what kind of mood I was in, but it hadn't been the best of mornings. Sebastian, on the other hand, was calmly reading the newspaper and drinking coffee. I saw he'd made me my milk with honey and had placed it on the counter in front of him.

Was this some kind of peace offering?

I sat down and waited for him to say something.

He didn't.

"Sebastian, I understand you must get bored being my bodyguard and everything, that you need a little more action in your life, something that makes you feel like Rambo or G.I. Joe or whomever you aspire to be, but I'd appreciate it if you didn't use me for your training sessions, okay? I understand that I was the one who asked you to teach me some self-defense techniques, but waking up at five o'clock in the morning with a glass of cold water in my face did not figure, at all, into my vision." He looked up from the newspaper and rested his eyes on me. "I don't like feeling trapped, so from now on, I'd like the lessons to be a little more . . . gentle, if you don't mind. I know that word doesn't exist in your vocabulary, but—"

He laughed, interrupting my speech, and I set down the cup of milk before it even had a chance to touch my lips.

"Gentle?" he exclaimed, rolling his eyes. "Marfil, this isn't a fucking fairy tale. It's not a game. I'm not trying to show you a good time or help you feel self-actualized. If I'm going to teach you at all, it's so that, if you really need to defend yourself on your own someday, you'll be able to, understand? It was your idea, and it was a good one. As your bodyguard, I should've thought of it myself. You were right; you need to learn to defend yourself, because you should never forget that your life is in danger."

I stared blankly at him, without any clever rebuttal for what he'd just said.

"We can train a little bit every day. I'll teach you some tricks to help you feel safer."

"According to you, I have zero technique . . ." My eyes darted involuntarily to his right hand, where I'd bitten him as hard as I could. I smiled. "Can I see what I did to you?"

Sebastian set down his cup of coffee and frowned. "You look so pleased to see you've hurt me," he said, removing the bloodstained gauze he'd wrapped around his hand to cover the wound.

"Shit!" I exclaimed, ignoring his comment. "I really am a savage. Does it hurt?"

"No."

"What a shame." I brought the mug to my lips and grinned against the edge of it, unable to help myself.

"Before I forget, I'll teach you something else. Come here," he said, gesturing for me to move closer to him.

I did so almost grudgingly. I'd had enough for one day.

He pulled me a little closer, positioning me between his legs. After steadying me, he slid his hand up to my neck and moved my hair over to my right shoulder. "This point right here," he said, carefully touching me in a spot between my neck and my clavicle, "is called the carotid sinus. If you press down hard for thirty seconds, the person will pass out. It won't last long, but it might give you time to escape if someone is trying to hurt you."

He didn't immediately remove his fingers. Instead, he began to trace circles on my skin, causing every single one of my hairs to stand on end.

If he noticed, he acted like he hadn't.

"You just have to press it? Simple as that?" I said, trying to speak normally, trying to act like his proximity and body contact didn't affect me.

"It's not so simple. The person will generally resist, but the first thing is for you to know how to determine the exact location. Give me your hand," he said.

I held it out to him, and he placed it on his shoulder. Then, he guided my thumb to the spot where the carotid sinus was located, and I pushed down gently. His pulse beat right underneath my finger. I could feel the blood racing to his brain . . . or wherever it was going.

Had he noticed my pulse accelerating, too?

I traced two circles on his skin, admiring the cut of his jawline, wishing I could put my mouth, and not my fingers, there. I wanted to bite him, hard, to feel his pulse under my tongue.

Sebastian stood up, interrupting whatever was happening between us in that moment.

"Turn around. I'm going to show you a tae kwon do move that you can use to knock someone out," he said.

I remained rooted to the spot. "What makes you think I'm going to let you use a tae kwon do move on me?"

Sebastian smiled, dimples on full display. "I won't hurt you . . . I promise."

I looked him in the eye and knew he was telling the truth. He spun me around, and I felt him move closer. Just like in the bedroom, he wrapped his arm around my neck and simultaneously looped his other arm around, quickly trapping me in a lethal armlock. I had seen similar choke holds in movies, and whenever someone did it, the person would resist until they fell unconscious on the floor.

"You wrap this arm around their neck and put your weight on the other to apply pressure. Do you understand?"

What I understood was that his chest was making contact

with my body. It's not like it was some romantic embrace, but I was hypnotized by the scent of him.

"These are called pressure points, and when you press them, it causes indescribable pain or momentary loss of consciousness."

I could show him my pressure points . . . and what would happen if he knew how to press them.

He released me, and I turned around to look at him.

"Now you do me."

I couldn't help but think of the double meaning of those words.

"On the couch or in the bedroom?"

Sebastian didn't even blink. I, of course, thought it was hilarious.

"If you're going to make fun of my—"

"Okay, okay, sorry. God, it was just a dumb joke . . . How do I do it?" I said, becoming more serious and looking at him with the eyes of an attacker.

"I just explained it."

That was true, but I had been too distracted by the closeness of our bodies to focus on the words coming out of his mouth.

"If you haven't noticed, you're like a full head taller than me . . ." I said, lifting my chin to look him in the eye. He was solid as a refrigerator.

"The majority of men you encounter are going to be taller than you."

"Are you calling me short?"

"No, Marfil, I'm not saying that. I'm just stating a fact." He seemed to be losing his patience.

"Okay, okay," I said again, stepping behind him. "I'm going to attack you, and you're going to be sorry you showed me your deepest, darkest secrets." I could almost see him roll his eyes.

Shit, he was huge. I wouldn't have been able to hurt him even if I wanted to.

I stepped back to get a bit of a running start, and I jumped on his back. He barely flinched, but I don't think he'd been expecting it. I wrapped my legs around his hips and hung from him like a monkey. Without hesitating or giving him time to object, I did what I thought I had to do: wrapped one arm around his neck as I applied pressure with the other.

"Like this," he said, using his hand to guide mine onto the pressure point and adjusting my hold on him. "Press harder, Marfil; this just feels like a warm hug."

Shit, I wasn't even making it hard for him to breathe.

I did as he said, and he flailed around with me perched on his back.

"This is what anyone would do if they had you on their back," he said, and then smashed my body into the wall. My hold broke as all the air I'd been holding in rushed from my lungs. He hadn't hit me hard, but enough to leave me disoriented.

He grabbed me by the legs so that I wouldn't fall, and I instinctively held on to his neck.

"You shouldn't let this happen. If they start to move around, you should be prepared for an impact."

Of course. As if it were that easy.

He stepped away from the wall and released me. When he turned around, he was utterly composed, as if nothing had happened. I, meanwhile, was panting like an idiot.

"That's enough for today. Go get dressed or you'll be late for class."

I glanced at the kitchen clock and was surprised by how quickly the time had passed. I tried to shake off the sensations aroused in me from having him so close, his muscular back under my body, his hard-as-steel arms around my neck . . .

Oh, fuck, how was it possible for tae kwon do to suddenly seem so sexy?

I went to my room and quickly got dressed. Giving myself one last look in the mirror, I noticed a gleam in my eyes that had never been there before.

*Sebastian . . . What are you doing to me?*

CHAPTER 17

# MARFIL

Spring break finally arrived, and my father sent his private plane to bring me home. I usually only traveled on it if we were going somewhere together, but since I was still in danger—something I tried to forget about but everyone insisted on reminding me—I got to travel like any other rich girl. Gabi, on the other hand, would fly commercial, although they'd told me she'd been assigned a bodyguard as well.

Sebastian drove me to the terminal, where the plane was already waiting for us. I'm not sure why, but I suddenly felt excited for him to see where I'd grown up, my home when I wasn't away at boarding school. Given the size of the house and the level of security, I knew we likely wouldn't spend all day together, though I couldn't help but fantasize about showing Sebastian everything I loved there: the stables, the library, the heated pool, the creek.

But when I stepped out of the car and saw my father's majestic plane, I felt a sense of unease.

Too opulent.

Sebastian stopped to speak with the pilot as I climbed the stairs and sat down in a beige leather seat beside a window that was considerably larger than on a conventional plane. My father and my uncle used the plane for their business trips, but they also took it to their Las Vegas escapades, ones it was best to know nothing about. I didn't even want to imagine the things that had gone on in this airplane.

Sebastian appeared in the door to the cabin, and after throwing me a glance, he walked to the last seat in the plane, the one farthest from me.

I sighed.

We'd continued with my self-defense training, which often involved close physical contact, but no matter how much I'd tried to encourage other kinds of encounters between us, he'd put up a wall taller than the one on *Game of Thrones* and kept things strictly professional. We were getting along better and had become more comfortable with each other, which was to be expected after spending twenty-four hours a day together, not counting the three hours he sometimes took to "clear his head"—his words, not mine. But he was still distant with me, and I didn't like it. I enjoyed teasing him and trying to get under his skin. But Sebastian had infinite patience and an extraordinary talent for ignoring my constant insinuations.

When the pilots and the two flight attendants took their seats and indicated we were about to take off, I unbuckled my seat belt and went to the back of the plane.

I flopped down beside Sebastian, who had his eyes closed, listening to music.

"Go back to your seat, Marfil," he said calmly without opening his eyes.

I fastened my seat belt. "The view is better back here."

Sebastian opened his eyes and looked at me like I was an annoyance. "There are eight seats on this plane; do you really want to sit right next to me? Isn't it enough to have me glued to your side every day?"

His exhausted tone made it sound like he was completely fed up with me. Had I drained all his energy, as my dad often said I did with people?

"I'm scared. I hate takeoff and landing," I admitted, looking out the window.

I actually felt like an idiot because all I wanted was to be near him, yet he seemed to be sick of me.

I moved to stand, intending to return to my original seat, but he took my arm and tugged me back down.

He removed his headphones and turned to me. "What are you scared of, exactly?"

I looked into his light brown eyes, almost the color of honey when the sun hit them directly, as it was in that moment, the sunset bathing the plane in a blinding orangey light. He was looking at me differently now, more like the way I looked at him admiringly, and I knew the cause. When the sun hit mine directly, the green of my eyes was as clear as the water in a cool stream, and if you looked carefully, you could see three turquoise flecks in my left eye.

Sebastian didn't say anything, no comment or compliment, and I preferred it that way. Why? Because it was unusual. When everyone constantly flattered you, compliments became the norm and stopped making you feel special. And so far, that's all he'd given me, at least verbally. No, I wanted him to like me for *me*, not just the way I looked. I craved a different kind of compliment.

"One time, on a trip to Spain, we flew into a storm that almost took down the plane. I was with my father, my stepmother Elisabeth, and my sister Gabriella, who at the time was three years old. They were sitting in the front seats," I said, gesturing toward the grouping of four seats facing each other with a table between them. "They wanted Gabriella to sleep, so they gave her two seats and sat me back here. When the turbulence started, the pilot told us to remain seated, keep our seat belts fastened, and asked us not to move around the cabin.

"I was all alone, and the turbulence was shaking the plane so hard I thought it would break in half. I was terrified, screaming and crying for my father to come sit with me. Gabriella was crying and screaming like crazy, too, and Elisabeth was trying to soothe her while my father shouted at the pilots, ordering them to tell him what the hell was happening. Since no one was paying attention to me, I unbuckled my seat belt. I simply needed to be near my father.

"Right when I stood up, a terrible patch of turbulence jolted the plane so hard that it threw me up in the air, and I ended up hitting my head on the edge of the overhead bin, which had opened with all the shaking." I turned my face to the window before continuing. "Not only did I get a cut on my forehead"—I instinctively touched the scar along my hairline—"but my father hit me for getting out of my seat."

Sebastian had been silently listening to my story, but in that moment, something told me to steal a glance his way. He was tense, his right hand balled into a fist and his jaw clenched tight.

"It was just that once; he never hit me again . . . but it was enough for Elisabeth to file for divorce. They separated two years later, after a brutal custody battle for Gabriella, which my father obviously won."

The plane began to take off. I stared out the window, nervous . . . and then I felt him take my hand. I turned to him, and I smiled at the sight of our hands intertwined, his thumb gently caressing mine. Without a word, I squeezed him tightly, his touch giving me all the strength I needed.

---

I wanted to sleep so the flight would go by more quickly, but an hour and a half later, I was still wide awake. The lights were off and all we could see out the window were the brightly lit cities beneath us. Sebastian had his eyes closed, but I knew he was awake.

"Sebastian . . ." I said quietly.

"Mmm," he answered without opening his eyes.

"You don't happen to have anything that might help me sleep, do you? Some magic pill, like a Valium or something?"

He opened his eyes. "Do I look like someone who self-medicates?"

He did not.

"I'm tired. I want to sleep."

"Then close your eyes and go to sleep."

"I can't . . . I've done everything you're supposed to do to get sleepy . . . I even tried counting sheep, but nothing's working."

"Well, then count elephants. I'm sure that will work."

Had Sebastian Moore just made a joke?

I turned again in my seat. I was uncomfortable.

"Can I lay my head in your lap?"

"No."

Shit.

"Just for a minute, so I can stretch my legs a little," I said.

It was true—I was uncomfortable. I had no ulterior motives.

"We're on a private jet. There are six other very comfortable seats you can lie on without pestering me."

"Didn't you hear my story about the turbulence?" I asked, pointing at the dark sky. "If I go to one of the other seats, all I'll be able to think about is that if we crash, I'll die all alone, with no one by my side. I don't want to die alone. I don't know about you, but I think that would be incredibly sad, and that experience I went through as a kid . . ."

"For the love of God, okay, go ahead, lie down," he said, losing his patience, and lifted the armrest between us. "Just be quiet," he added.

I smiled. "Thanks, Sebastian, you're a good guy."

I rested my head on his thigh and curled into the fetal position in my seat. I was extremely comfortable, even if his leg was hard as a rock, but I didn't care.

I lay there drowsily, unable to fall asleep. After about an hour in that space between sleep and wakefulness, Sebastian began to gently run his long and masculine fingers through my hair, from the roots all the way to the tips. I guess he thought I was asleep because I know he wouldn't have done it otherwise. It was so soothing, I almost purred in my sleepy state as he brushed his hand over my ear.

Had I dreamed it? Had that really happened, or was it just a product of my imagination?

All I know for sure is that I spent the rest of the three-hour flight to Louisiana with my head in his lap.

And I enjoyed every fucking second of it.

---

My father's driver, Peter, was waiting to pick us up at the terminal to take us home. He had always been kind to me and my sister, which was why I ran up to hug him when I saw him.

"I'm very happy to see you, Miss," he said, formal as always. "And it's a pleasure to meet you, Mr. Moore," he added, looking at Sebastian, who held out a hand and helped him load our luggage into the trunk of the Mercedes.

As I sat in the back seat and Sebastian talked to Peter in the front, my mood gradually soured. It was something that happened when I knew I was about to see my father. Our personalities always inevitably clashed, and I had to try hard to make myself "bearable," as he called it. I hated knowing that no matter what I did or said, I would always irritate him.

My home in Louisiana was ostentatious, but it was my only home, and I liked it, especially when my father wasn't there. I smiled as it came into view, excited that I would soon get to ride Philippe, my beautiful horse, whom I adored and missed in equal measures. After the kidnapping, I'd been home for such a short time that I hadn't been able to visit him. I was also excited by the prospect of, after two months of having constant company, finally being able to do something on my own.

Peter parked the car outside the front entrance, and Rob, my father's Saint Bernard, came bounding out to greet us. He was almost as big as a pony. When I was a little girl, he had been terrified of me, but we'd come to a truce when I turned fourteen and stopped trying to ride him. It was also around that time when my father gave me Philippe so that I would leave his poor dog alone.

I petted his ears lovingly, and then went inside to say hello to Lupita, who was waiting in the entryway to welcome me, as always.

"Hi, Lupe!" I said, giving her a hug.

"Oh, my girl, tell me you're doing okay; tell me no one has hurt you again . . ." she said, pinching my cheeks to make sure I was alive and well.

Just then, Sebastian entered, carrying my suitcase and his small duffel bag. We both looked at him, and he held out a hand to introduce himself.

"This guy here is the one who makes sure nothing happens to me, Lupita," I explained, smiling in Sebastian's direction.

"Oh, young man, take good care of her, please. Trouble seems to follow Marfil wherever she goes."

I frowned, but Sebastian laughed and nodded. "I think I know what you mean."

I looked at the two of them, eyes narrowed. "I have no idea what you're talking about. I'm a perfect angel," I said, batting my eyes.

"Angel is the last word I'd use to define you, Marfil," came my father's voice behind me.

I tensed, my natural reaction to him.

Taking a deep breath, I turned to greet him. He gave me a hug, and I inhaled the familiar scent of his cologne.

"How are you?" he asked, stepping back to get a good look at me.

"Good, good," I responded.

My father stepped toward Sebastian. "It's good to see you, Sebastian. How's it going?" He slapped my bodyguard on the back. "I hope my daughter hasn't given you too much trouble."

Sebastian smiled.

I was surprised to see that they already knew each other. Then I remembered the day Sebastian had ratted me out to my father, getting my ballet classes canceled, and my mood shifted.

"Everything's in order, Mr. Cortés, although there are certain matters I'd like to discuss with you."

My father nodded, smiling. "Of course, of course! We'll have a meeting with Logan tomorrow, don't worry. But call me Alejandro, I've told you a thousand times."

A thousand times . . .

Ugh, I didn't like this chumminess at all.

"You two already know each other?"

Sebastian and my father exchanged a glance, and I knew I was being intentionally left out. I expected it from my father, but not from Sebastian.

"You don't think I'd send just anyone to protect you, do you?" my father responded jovially.

I didn't answer, but I did change the subject. "When is Gabi getting here?"

My father frowned at the mention of my little sister.

"In three days."

I nodded and went to pick up my suitcase, but Sebastian got to it before me.

"I'll help you with that," he said politely.

I let him walk me upstairs to my room, eager for the chance to be alone with him. It felt strange having so many people around, accustomed as we were to always being alone together.

"I didn't realize you knew my father . . ." I said as we reached my bedroom door. I opened it and stepped inside, waiting for him to follow.

He didn't.

"He hired me. Of course I know him."

"Logan Price is in charge of security, not my father, but you two seem very friendly . . ."

Sebastian looked at me from the doorway, unfazed. "He likes me, is all."

Yes, clearly . . . But Alejandro Cortés didn't like most people.

"You must've really impressed him, based on the way he treats you."

"The fact that I'm taking care of his daughter doesn't seem like enough of a reason to you?"

I forced a smile. "He isn't usually pleased by anything that has to do with me."

Sebastian squared his shoulders. "Do you need anything else? I'd like to rest."

I remembered the feeling of his fingers in my hair, and I had the urge to shake him. How could he be so sweet and so cold at the same time?

"What rules apply now? Do I have to let you know every time I want to go somewhere?"

Sebastian looked at me as if he didn't understand. "The same rules apply, Marfil. That's why I'm here."

Right.

I didn't pry any further because he was acting strange, and something told me it was better not to know anything about his former dealings with my father. I would've loved to call him out on it, but I decided to let it go, at least for tonight.

He left without another word, and I watched as he disappeared down the hallway.

—

The next morning, I went down to breakfast early. I'd slept fitfully, and had dark circles under my tired eyes, but I would make the most of my day regardless of not having slept. I wanted to walk around my father's property, go horseback riding, and swim in the heated pool in the basement, one of my favorite places.

Lupita greeted me with a warm hug, and as she made me breakfast, she caught me up on the fact that my sister had called every day since my kidnapping to make sure she was up-to-date on any news. She hadn't called me directly because she was afraid I'd lie to keep from scaring her.

"That girl worships you, Marfil," Lupita beamed as she peeled potatoes.

We chatted for a while, then I said goodbye with another hug and the promise not to get into any trouble. Just as I was walking through the living room, I saw Sebastian coming down the hallway that led to my father's office. It surprised me to see him dressed in a suit and tie. The members of my father's security team had always worn that kind of attire, but I was so used to seeing Sebastian in jeans and sneakers. He wasn't alone either, which also took me aback; he was accompanied by a guy a bit younger than him, a bit shorter, but dressed practically the same.

"Marfil, let me introduce you to Louis Wilson," he said in a professional tone as Louis held out a hand. "He'll be with you these next few days until your sister gets here."

I frowned. "You're a bodyguard, too?" I asked as this new Louis guy discretely gave me a once-over. He was handsome but nothing special: blond, green eyes, thin lips, and straight nose.

"Yes, ma'am," he answered, suddenly nervous.

"You can call me Marfil," I said in a friendly tone, then frowned at Sebastian. "Are you leaving?"

"I won't be able to guard you all day, that's all."

"You make it sound like I'm a prisoner," I answered sarcastically.

Louis threw us a curious glance.

"I thought you could use a break from me," Sebastian said plainly.

Or maybe he needed a break from me.

"Oh, okay, I guess you have something more important to do than keeping me alive."

Sebastian refused to take the bait. He pulled me aside and whispered, "Behave. Wilson has potential; he's new at this. Please, don't make him want to quit before he's even started."

"You're so sweet that it makes me want to punch you in the face."

He almost smiled.

"All yours, Wilson," he said, turning back around. "If you need anything, you know where to find me."

Sebastian didn't walk out the front door, heading toward the service quarters instead.

Why the hell did he give his job to Wilson?

I looked at my new bodyguard with an inquisitive smile. "Does everyone call you Wilson?" I asked as I headed outside, and he followed.

"Yes, ma'am," he said.

I shot him a dirty look.

"Marfil, sorry."

"Have you ever ridden a horse, Wil?" I asked. "Do you mind if I call you Wil?"

He shook his head. "You can call me whatever you want. And yes, I know how to ride."

I smiled. Wilson was much nicer than Sebastian.

"Great, because I want to be outside this house as much as possible."

We passed the huge swimming pool, surrounded by lounge chairs and the grill, and headed to the stables. My father raised horses in Montana, but he kept his ten finest Appaloosas at our home in Louisiana, including Philippe. I'd named him after the horse in *Beauty and the Beast*, one of my favorite movies as a little girl.

When we entered the stable, we saw Colin, a man of around sixty who looked after the horses. He knew so much about animals that, even if he wasn't officially a vet, it was as if he was.

"Are you going to ride today, Miss Cortés?" Colin asked.

I nodded, smiling. It was impossible to convince Colin to address me less formally; I'd stopped trying years ago. Without waiting for him to prepare my horse, I made my way to his stall. Philippe was beautiful, white with black feet and a glossy mane. When I went in, he whinnied happily, and I gently rubbed his favorite spot, right between his pretty eyes.

"Hello, gorgeous," I said. I loved this animal.

Colin saddled my sister's horse for Wilson, a very calm black mare named Glitter. Once everything was ready, we got on our horses and headed out into the fields. I looked back at the house, about to take off at a full gallop, when I noticed Sebastian watching us from the second-floor balcony. The warning look he shot me only made me want to take off faster.

*Didn't you say you didn't have time to protect me? Well, then, fuck off, Sebastian.*

Wilson knew how to ride, but just the basics, so I couldn't run Philippe as fast as I would've liked. Galloping at top speed across the adjoining fields and jumping over the stream had been my favorite pastime when I was little, and I was annoyed that I couldn't do it now, but I knew I couldn't make poor

Wilson risk breaking his neck. I wasn't planning to prove Sebastian right. Instead, I gave Wilson a tour of my father's property: We passed the abandoned barn where Gabriella and I played as kids. The ancient oaks looked beautiful in early spring, and the pink azaleas were in full bloom, a beautiful sight to behold.

We got back to the house just as the sun was setting on the horizon. We hadn't eaten anything since breakfast, so we went directly to the kitchen as soon as we dropped off the horses.

I had enjoyed spending time with Wilson. He was sweet and fun, not at all paranoid like Sebastian. Spending time with him had been like hanging out with a friend. My sister would be lucky to have him as a bodyguard.

When we reached the kitchen, both covered in mud and all varieties of leaves, I saw that Sebastian was there with his laptop open and an unfriendly expression on his face. I was instantly reminded of how unpleasant he could be.

"How was your day?" he asked as he closed his laptop and stood up.

Wilson walked over to the fridge and grabbed a bottle of water. I stood observing Sebastian, trying to determine what was going on behind his eyes.

"Fun," I answered dryly.

"I'm glad," he said, then left without another word.

---

I barely saw Sebastian the next day. It was as if he was intentionally avoiding me, which irritated me endlessly. He'd put Wilson on duty as my babysitter so he could take time off and relax. But Sebastian's vacation wasn't going to last long: My sister arrived the next day, and he was going to have to get back to work.

I wondered what the hell he did all day. I imagined him just watching movies, but I saw him going in and out of my father's office on several occasions. And speaking of my father, I only saw him at dinner, where we made small talk and then each went to our respective rooms. Normal.

That afternoon I decided to go for a swim on my own, without bothering to let either Wilson or Sebastian know, since I wasn't even leaving the house. I put on my favorite red bathing suit and disappeared down the long stairs that led to the basement, where the gym and indoor pool were located. It was still a little cold to swim outside, and the heated pool was a luxury I missed while living in New York.

I connected my phone to the speakers, set my towel on one of the chairs, and jumped into the water. I loved swimming, something that always relaxed me, and I was delighted to be alone for once.

Over an hour had passed when I finally stopped, out of breath, and rested on the edge of the pool. I looked up and was surprised to see Sebastian leaning against the wall of the gym. We hadn't spoken since the few words we'd exchanged the other night in the kitchen, after I returned from riding.

I pulled myself onto the edge of the pool and walked over to him, dripping wet.

He kept his eyes on me the entire time.

"How long have you been here?" I asked, picking up my towel and wrapping it around myself.

"Wilson has been looking for you for hours," he said in response.

Was it my imagination, or did he just look at me like he wanted me?

"Two days since we've seen each other and you start out by scolding me?"

"You have to tell us where you're going, Marfil."

I looked at his track pants, his white sleeveless shirt, and I, too, felt a desire for him. I'd missed him, and I hated how cold he'd been with me ever since we'd arrived at my father's house.

"I needed to be alone."

Sebastian pressed his lips together but didn't say anything else.

"Were you going to work out?" I asked as water dripped from my forehead down to my neck, finally disappearing into my bathing suit's neckline.

I knew that'd been the exact trajectory, because Sebastian's gaze traced the water's path down my body.

"I was going to," he answered.

"Has my presence caused you to change your mind?"

"I'm back to work," he answered, looking away, then back at me. "I realized I couldn't leave you in someone else's hands." His eyes paused on my right knee. I had fallen off the horse during a jump that didn't land entirely well. It was just a scratch, no big deal. The cut was already starting to heal.

"It was my fault, not Wilson's," I answered.

"I know," he said, staring at my mouth. "You haven't stopped moving since we got here."

I shrugged. "I like to run wild."

He didn't argue, and I suddenly had the desperate urge to feel his hands on my face, my arms, my hair . . . I needed to feel the way I did when our bodies were in contact.

"You should go back up now," he said, when the tension between us became too intense to bear.

I looked toward the gym. "I think I'm going to stay down here and do some exercise."

"You've been swimming for an hour."

"And you finally answered my first question," I replied as I let the towel fall, standing in front of him in nothing but my bathing suit.

His eyes paused on my legs for a fleeting second.

I leaned over to pick up the sweatpants I'd worn over my swimsuit, and I pulled them on with excessive slowness.

"I think I'll do some kickboxing," I said, walking around him and entering the gym. It was stocked with every type of equipment you could imagine: treadmills, ellipticals, all kinds of weights, stationary bicycles, punching bags . . . I had no idea how to box, but I wanted more time with Sebastian.

He followed me, just like I was certain he would, and watched in silence as I picked out some gloves that I knew would end up being huge on me. I put the first one on and immediately realized I couldn't put on the second one, since my right hand was rendered useless by the glove.

Sebastian stepped in front of me. "Why did you put on those gloves?"

I blinked twice before answering. "Because I'll hurt my hands without them, won't I?"

Sebastian held out his hand. "Give them to me," he said. "If you're ever attacked, you won't be wearing gloves." He pulled them off my hands. "Effective punching and kicking requires a lot of training, and most of all, a lot of strength." Sebastian threw the gloves down and walked to the black exercise mat in the center of the room. "Come here," he said.

I walked over to him, excited to be resuming our self-defense lessons.

"When do you think a woman is most vulnerable during an attack?" he asked.

I thought about it for a few seconds. "When there's a man on top of her."

Sebastian nodded silently. "Lie down."

My heart stopped. I lay down on my back as he stood over me. From that position, he looked even more enormous.

"You're right; a woman is at her most vulnerable when a man has her pinned to the ground. But that doesn't mean she can't get away or turn things around to create a dangerous situation for her attacker." He crouched down and rested his hand on my knees. "Open your legs," he ordered.

I did as he asked, and he placed himself between my thighs.

Okay, yes, I was in a vulnerable position, but that didn't change the fact that I had him between my legs, which was hot as fuck.

He looked me in the eye for a second and lifted my legs. "I'm going to show you what you should do if someone tries to rape you." He said it so seriously that any sexual or romantic thoughts vanished from my mind, and I gave him my full attention. "Your legs are your greatest asset. When someone has you pinned underneath them, they might think the battle is won. It's true they have a lot of points in their favor, like gravity, for one. From this spot, I could easily kill you."

A shiver ran down my spine.

"So, this is the first thing you should do: Cross your ankles around my back, tight, to get a firm grip," he said, demonstrating with my legs. "The next thing you should do is grab me by the back of the neck and pull my head to your throat."

Did he understand that what he was asking me to do caused a whole series of reactions in my body? Reactions I couldn't control?

"Do it, Marfil."

I raised my hand to the back of his neck and was immediately reminded we hadn't been this close since the time we'd kissed. I pulled him to me, as if offering him my neck, waiting for him to kiss it until I moaned with pleasure.

"You have to hold me tightly in place so that you'll be able to do the next move." He lifted his head to look at me. "You have to act quickly, without hesitating," he said, his eyes fixed on mine. "Use your left hand to lift my shirt up to the back of my neck. Hold it there tight. Then use the fingers of your right hand to grip my neck and push your legs into my hips. Lastly, you can cross your other arm and choke me. In six seconds, you'll have cut off my breathing."

I stared at him as if he'd just spoken to me in another language.

"I stopped listening at the part about lifting up your shirt."

Sebastian rolled his eyes and sat up. "We'll do it the other way around so you can see how it works. Come on," he said, taking my hand to help me up as he looked around for something. "Weren't you wearing a shirt?"

I shook my head. I'd slipped pants on over my swimsuit but hadn't brought anything else except for the towel. There was no need to try to hide my tattoo down here; my father had never liked swimming.

"I'll give you mine to show you the move, and then you can try it on me."

*Hold on. You're going to take off your shirt?*

Of course he was going to take off his shirt! He slipped it over his head in a single movement, revealing his chiseled muscles underneath.

Fuck, I became very aware I had only ever caught a glimpse of his body before.

He tossed his shirt to me, but I couldn't stop gawking at him.

"Concentrate, Marfil."

Concentrate? With that half-naked body in front of me?

He had a skull tattoo on his left pec that I didn't like at all. But I stored that image away to analyze it later and did as he asked. I slipped the shirt on over my bathing suit and tried to get my hormones under control. He was turning me on so much. Didn't he realize that?

He lay on the floor and told me to get on top of him like he'd done with me.

Sebastian. Underneath me. Shirtless. Someone pinch me.

Fuck.

I placed myself between his legs, and he immediately wrapped them around me. I was tiny compared to him; his legs double the size of mine.

"The important thing is that you understand what comes next." He put his hand on the back of my neck and pulled me to him. "Once you have me in this position, lift my shirt," he said as he moved his fingers up my back and wrapped the shirt I was wearing around my neck.

My body was pressed against his chest, but I had no time to fantasize. He moved quickly and decisively, the way I was supposed to if I found myself in that situation and wanted to live to tell the tale.

"Lift your head," he told me.

His mouth was just inches away, the smell of him all over my skin, his fingers touching one of the most sensitive parts of my body: my neck.

"With this hand," he said, lifting his right, "grab the shirt, tight." I was immobilized, my head against his. "Then you push your feet into my hips," he said, simulating the movement with his knees, "and cross your left arm . . . like this." As he did this, my head was trapped between his crossed arms. I couldn't move; I couldn't do anything. "The next step is to apply pressure." He did so, and I understood.

Two seconds later, he released me, and I gasped desperately for air.

"Did you get it?"

I nodded, rubbing my neck. "Would that really work on someone like you?"

Sebastian took me by the waist and lifted us both to our feet in one motion. "On someone of my size, yes. On someone like me, no."

Now it was my turn to roll my eyes. "A little arrogant, aren't you?"

"Give me the shirt and lie down," he said, ignoring my joke, seeming to want to get the lesson over with as quickly as possible.

I took off his shirt and threw it at him. Why did he have to be such an asshole?

I lay down, and before I knew it, he was kneeling between my legs.

Annoyed by his indifferent attitude, considering that he was on top of me—*Fuck!*—I tugged on him hard, taking the lessons seriously for the first time. My left hand lifted his shirt—my fingers grazing his bare skin, wishing I could dig my nails in and cover his mouth with mine—as my right hand gripped his neck tightly.

"Now grab—"

"I know," I interrupted, grabbing the collar of his shirt, pushing my feet against his hips and crossing my arms until I had him trapped on top of me.

"Very good . . ." he said, his brown eyes so serious and his mouth once again so close that his breath mingled with mine.

I pressed my arms together and saw the effects up close. I could choke anyone this way . . .

I released him and felt proud of myself to see that he was coughing and struggling for air.

Once he recovered, he placed his palms on either side of my head, and I could see equal pride in his eyes.

"Good work, Elephant."

My breathing picked up, and his gaze moved to my mouth as I unconsciously licked my lips, imagining all the other things that could be done from that position.

"Class is over," he then said, jumping up in one agile motion and killing any type of fantasy that might be going through my mind.

I closed my eyes, trying to get my feelings under control.

When I finally opened them, I was irritated to see that he was still standing over me.

"I should shower and get dressed for dinner," I said, ignoring his extended hand in offering.

Sebastian simply nodded and went to pick up the gloves he'd thrown on the floor earlier.

"Do you promise to stay out of trouble while I work out for a while?"

I threw him a glance over my shoulder, already starting up the stairs.

"I can't promise *you* anything."

---

I took the longest bath in history, and I told Lupita that I didn't feel like going down for dinner. I wasn't in the mood to see anyone, much less Sebastian, who had left me as horny as a teenager, with nothing I could do about it. I needed to get some fresh air to clear my head, and try to forget about my fucking bodyguard.

Shortly after midnight, I leaned out my window and climbed down the willow tree that had served as a ladder for me my entire life. I crossed the backyard and passed the pool to the stables. I couldn't help but look back, making sure no one was following me, that no one had noticed I was leaving the house on my own.

The stables were clean and empty except for the sound of the horses in their stalls and the whisper of the wind. I found Philippe asleep in his, but he woke up as soon as he heard me approach.

"Hello, cutie. Do you want to go for a ride in the moonlight? Do you?" I said, talking to him like a baby as I opened the door to lead him over to the saddles. I laughed as he whinnied in response.

Unfortunately for me, we didn't make it past his stall.

I felt a presence behind me and turned around, frightened, grabbing the first thing I could find on hand, which turned out to be an umbrella leaning against the wall.

Sebastian observed me from the entrance to the stables, leaning against the wooden doorframe.

I sighed with relief.

"An umbrella? Seriously?"

"What do you want, Sebastian?" I said, spinning around to place a saddle on Philippe's back.

"This is what you call not getting into trouble?" he asked, watching as I saddled my horse.

"I don't get you," I said very coldly.

How the hell did he know I was here?

He stepped toward me, into the shadows of the stable that now bathed both of us in darkness.

"I thought I'd made very clear what would happen next time you escaped out of a window."

"Were you spying on me?"

He walked up to Philippe and rubbed his mane without looking at me. "I'm not spying on you; I'm looking out for you."

I tried to climb onto the horse, but Sebastian put an arm out to stop me. "You're not going out riding alone at this hour, Marfil."

I didn't pull away from his grip, but I tensed. "I've done it a thousand times."

"Does your father know?"

I huffed. "Did you tell your father everything you did, Sebastian?" As soon as the sentence left my mouth, I knew I'd put my foot in it. Sebastian didn't have parents. What an idiot.

"It's dangerous for you to be out alone," he replied, ignoring my last comment.

"I'm at home. I'm not in any danger here."

"There's danger everywhere."

He was just a few feet away from me, but I could hardly make out his face through the shadows, which made him look more menacing than normal.

"How did you know I'd left?"

Sebastian seemed to hesitate for a second. "Cameras . . . on your bedroom window. I saw you climb out and almost fall when your foot slipped on a branch . . ."

So they'd put a fucking camera on me. Just what I needed.

"You're unbelievable," I said, trying to get back on my horse.

I almost managed it, but this time he grabbed me by the waist and pulled me down, trapping me between the horse and his chest.

"You're not going anywhere," he said, so close that I felt his breath on my lips.

"Leave me alone," I replied between gritted teeth.

Ever since we got here, he'd been so buddy-buddy with my father and so distant with me. Even today, he acted so indifferent as he showed me how to defend myself, and it all somehow left me feeling betrayed. His days now centered around my dad, and it bothered me, a lot. Sebastian was mine, not my father's . . . That's how I felt. That's what I wanted.

"Tomorrow I'll ride with you wherever you want, but right now you need to get back inside and go to bed."

My breasts brushed against his chest, and all my hairs stood on end. I couldn't help but feel turned on whenever he was near me.

"I'm not tired. My mind is too filled with fantasies to sleep . . . You and me naked in the gym . . ."

Sebastian released me and took a step back, pointing to the house. "Go. Now," he said, his jaw clenched tightly, his tone intimidating.

I knew that referring to what had happened that afternoon

was a low blow. Those moments between the two of us were sacred, veiled in a silence we both upheld. Afterward, we both acted like those glances, those caresses, had never happened, and he avoided any mention of the kiss we'd shared a few weeks ago, denying the attraction that existed between us. And even though he had done everything possible to seem indifferent to me ever since we'd arrived at my father's house, I hadn't forgotten the way he'd run his hands through my hair on the plane until I fell asleep. If he was acting so cold now, it was because of my father, not me.

"Are you afraid my father's going to find out?" I said, now enraged with him for denying what he felt for me, because he had to feel something, I knew it. I could tell.

"Fuck, Marfil," he practically shouted, making me jump. "How many times do I have to tell you? This might be a game to you, but it's my job, dammit!"

I had never seen him so irate. I understood his concern—if my father found out what had happened between us, as innocent as it might have been, he'd have Sebastian drawn and quartered—but it bothered me that I didn't even figure in Sebastian's list of priorities unless he was getting paid. It hurt me more than I wanted to admit.

A flash of lightning momentarily lit up the stables, followed by a loud clap of thunder that made the horses whinny with fright.

"This might be your job, but it's my life. I've done everything you asked me to. Ever since the concert, I haven't caused you any more trouble. But I've gone out riding at night hundreds of times; nothing is going to happen to me."

Sebastian stared blankly at me. "No, you came out here at night, right before a storm, because it's the only way you have of getting my attention. You want to go on a fucking horseback ride at one o'clock in the morning? Go ahead."

I adjusted Philippe's saddle as he turned around without another word.

"What are you doing?" I asked, glaring at him as he brought out my father's horse and started to saddle him.

"I'm going with you. It's that or I drag you back to the house by your hair."

I threw him a poisoned glance, hopped onto my horse, and galloped out of the stable before he could stop me.

The cool wind in my face felt glorious. I had never intended to let Sebastian come with me. I just needed to do exactly what I was doing in that moment: ride, alone, at night, and if I was lucky, through the rain.

Sebastian soon caught up, the asshole, so I had to kick Philippe to make him run even harder. Sebastian had chosen my father's purebred, Marengo—the fastest and most decorated of all the horses my father raised—and he didn't take long to catch up.

I heard him galloping beside me in the darkness, and even though I didn't want to look at him, my eyes darted over, curious to see how he handled my father's horse.

Fuck, it was like he'd been riding his entire life . . .

Just then, the storm that had been brewing finally unleashed its fury. We were instantly soaked. Lightning split the sky overhead, and it soon became impossible to continue at such speed, so I pulled back on Philippe's reins to slow him down.

I had gone riding in the rain many times, but never in a storm like that one. The ground under my feet was flooded. I hated that Sebastian had been right yet again. The problem was that I didn't like being given orders. I had always bristled at authority, whether that be at home or away at boarding school. The nuns had hated me so much that one of the sisters once referred to me as the spawn of Satan. I had always been one to break the rules, that was just part of who I was, even standing up to my father, as far as his strict limits would allow.

I'd lived on my own for two years now, free from any rules, far away from the people who had been trying to tame me ever since I was a little girl—just like the horse I now had beneath me—but no matter what they did, my mother's indomitable spirit always shone through. I did not submit to orders; that's just the way I was.

"Are you happy?" Sebastian shouted, soaked to the bone and extremely mad.

I only glanced at him, water streaming down my face, then I looked up at the sky. I could almost make out the individual raindrops falling fast onto my cheeks. Up there, my mother was smiling down on me, I was sure of it.

I kicked at Philippe's sides.

"Fuck, Marfil, we have to go back."

I ignored his protests and followed a path that I knew well enough not to get lost, even in those conditions. It would be better to wait until the storm had calmed before attempting to go home, so I headed toward the abandoned barn where Gabriella and I had played countless times, pretending we were on important, secret missions full of adventure, with dragons, elves, fairies, and all kinds of mythical, magical creatures.

I saw the barn in the distance and continued galloping until I was finally under its dry roof, sheltered from the storm. Sebastian arrived a minute later. Philippe seemed content to have been taken out in the rain. Marengo, on the other hand, whinnied and shook the water from his hide.

"Have you completely lost your mind?" shouted Sebastian.

I shot him a murderous glance before jumping lightly out of the saddle. There was dry hay in the stable, and the horses moved over to eat, oblivious to the epic battle of wills that was about to play out in front of them.

"I think it's still in place," I said sarcastically.

Sebastian seemed to want to kill me. "Goddammit, you're so oblivious!"

"I guess you've only ever worked with submissive clients before!"

The rain was falling so hard that I had to raise my voice for him to hear me. I was shivering, the storm having blown in an icy wind, which, adding in the fact that I was soaked, was not a pleasant combination.

"This ends here . . ." he said, more to himself than to me. "It ends here. I can't keep doing this."

I looked up in surprise. "What is it that you can't keep doing?"

Sebastian stared me in the eye, and I didn't like what I saw there.

"I'm not going to keep being your bodyguard. I'm not going to keep doing this job under these conditions."

At those words, my heart stopped.

"What conditions are you talking about? A few minutes ago, you said that your job was the most important thing . . ."

"It is. That's why I have to quit."

I clenched my jaw. "That doesn't make any sense."

Sebastian looked at me as if I were an idiotic little girl who had to be indulged. "You're too used to getting your way. You don't respect me. I can't do my job if you're going to do something stupid every chance you get. I try to make you understand the danger you're in, but you continue to think it's all a big joke."

That pissed me off.

"You have no idea what you're talking about, Sebastian. I'm aware of what's happening, although you don't seem to want to tell me much more, like I'm some moron. I'm the one who got kidnapped, remember?"

Sebastian ran a hand over his face, wiping away the excess

water, and looked down at me, cold and distant. "Then why do you make it so hard for me, dammit?"

I held his gaze. He was overreacting. That was just how I was, and he knew it.

"You don't want to quit because I went out alone at night without letting you know. You're just scared now because you're under the same roof as my father, your boss, and you don't want him to find out what's going on between us."

There. I'd said it, I couldn't keep it inside any longer.

Sebastian didn't blink. "There's nothing going on between us," he said coldly.

"You can keep telling yourself that if that makes you feel better." I turned my back to him. I didn't want him to see how much his words had hurt me. I didn't want to give him any more power than he already had.

He spun me around to face him. "I already apologized for what happened. We agreed it wouldn't happen again."

I laughed sarcastically. "We agreed?" I repeated. "I don't remember that part . . ."

Sebastian cursed under his breath without taking his eyes off me. "You can't have everything. I'm just a toy to you, but you have no idea how—"

"A toy?" I said, raising my tone and cutting him off. "You think you know me, but you have no idea. You see what I have, but you don't know who I am, what I want, what I desire . . ."

"I know that if I stay with you much longer . . ." But he didn't finish the sentence, and a part of me knew what he was going to say.

I took a step forward. "If you stay with me much longer . . . what, Sebastian?"

He shook his head, refusing to look at me.

"Why did you run your hands through my hair on the flight? Why did you do it? I didn't ask you to."

He didn't answer, so I stepped closer and shoved him. He barely moved.

"You know how I feel about you. You know it, and you don't care, but then you go and do things that make no sense, like when you took care of me after the tattoo or when you worry that I haven't had dinner and you make me something healthy to eat. You like touching me, Sebastian. You may not even realize how often you do it, but I'm aware of it every single time you brush past me. Do you think I don't notice that you take every opportunity that presents itself to put your hands on me, even if it's fleeting and totally innocent?"

He clenched his jaw so tight in response that the veins in his neck seemed like they were about to explode from the pressure.

"Dammit, Sebastian! I felt more from that one kiss with you than everything else I've ever done with any other guy!"

He fixed his furious eyes on mine. "Stop talking, Marfil."

"Why can't you admit that you feel something for me? Why are you so scared to take what you want?"

"Because you could never give me what I need, not in a million years."

That hurt. A lot. And it made me angry.

I took a step back. "Don't challenge me, Sebastian, because you know I'm up for it." With my eyes fixed on his, I took another step back and, when I knew my body was in full view, removed my shirt.

His gaze shifted from fury to desire when he saw me standing before him in my bra and blue jeans.

"Stop . . ." he said as I undid the first button of my pants. Removing the space between us in two strides, he grabbed my hand as I tried to undo the second button. "Stop," he said again between gritted teeth.

My breaths were coming fast, and his were as well. Our

bodies, soaked by the rain, were so close together now that it gave me goose bumps.

"I don't want to stop. I want you to make me feel like you did that first time. I want to take it all the way . . ." My voice broke off.

I desired him with every fiber of my being. I craved his touch so badly that it hurt, and I would take whatever he was willing to give me. I could content myself with very little . . .

"I can't, Marfil," he said. "It's not good for you to feel that way about me . . ."

My eyes were blazing when I lifted my head to meet his gaze. "You feel the same way," I said in a low whisper. "I know you want me."

I was standing in my bra just a few feet from this tall, muscular, soaking-wet man. I wanted him to kiss me. I wanted him to do the thing we both wanted, needed. So why wouldn't he if my father was nowhere to be found?

"Any guy would want you," he said, his eyes glued to my lips. I knew he was trying to control himself, and I loved seeing how hard it was for him. "But I don't plan to touch you ever again," he concluded before walking away.

"If you don't kiss me, I'll tell," I said, immediately feeling like the biggest bitch on planet Earth. If I hadn't been so sure that he wanted me as badly as I wanted him, I would never have played that card. But I refused to let my father interfere in my life, yet again. Especially knowing that this man before me could drive me wild at the push of a button.

Sebastian stopped and turned slowly toward me. "Don't blackmail me, Marfil, because this could get very ugly."

The look in his eyes scared me, but I gathered my nerves and doubled down. "Didn't you say I was a spoiled brat? Well, maybe you were right. And what I want this instant is your mouth right here," I said, tilting my head to one side and pointing to the part of my neck where my veins visibly pulsed under my pale skin. My voice trembled, but I prayed he wouldn't notice. "And then I want you to move over to the other side. I want you to bite me, gently. I want you to make me moan while your hands explore every inch of my body."

The dark glint in his eyes almost scared me. I couldn't tell if he was turned on or pissed off. He moved closer, and I unwittingly took a step away from him. My back made contact with the wall, and I became nervous at the realization that I had no escape.

"Take it back," he said, placing his hands on the wall behind me and trapping me between his arms, causing me to tremble with fear and arousal.

"Kiss me right now or my father's going to hear all about how you almost gave me my first orgasm."

His eyes blazed, but I saw that he didn't believe what I'd just said. Sebastian seemed to have bought into my reputation at Columbia. I, for one, was dying to make those rumors a reality.

"You're entering dangerous territory, Marfil."

He was so close that I could feel the heat radiating from his body.

"Our relationship has been dangerous from the beginning. Aren't you here to protect me from the bad guys?"

"Protecting you is costing me blood, sweat, and tears."

"Do you want to know how I feel when you're this close to me?" I said, placing my hand on the back of his neck. He let me do it, but he remained still as a statue, the blood I could feel pumping through his veins the only sign that he was a living being. "You can put your hand down there and find out," I said, completely shameless.

He blinked only once before answering. "And do you know how I feel when you try to blackmail me?" he said, moving my hand from his cheek. "I hate you a little more every day."

Before I had time to process his words, his mouth was on mine. Our lips collided and our tongues entwined. Our damp, cold bodies warmed by passion as we kissed desperately, like it was the last time we'd ever kiss anyone.

Finally.

I almost heard our collective mental sighs of relief before he pressed my back against the barn wall. I began to bring my fingers to curl into his hair, but he gripped them tightly above my head, grunting as if in warning.

He lifted me off the ground as he did something magical with his tongue, producing an intense heat between my legs that left me feeling like I might die from desire. The way he kissed . . . Fuck . . . I was right. There was something very real between us, something rare and extraordinary.

I panted as he gripped my chin, drawing back to look at me.

"You drive me so fucking crazy," he said, taking my upper lip between his teeth and tugging gently. "I'd eat you out just to shut you up and stop you from trying to provoke me every second of the day."

My vision was clouded by my intense arousal, by my insatiable desire for this man.

"I'd fuck you against this wall all night long, until you couldn't take any more, if I didn't know you were a virgin," he said.

The comment nearly froze me on the spot. I questioned him with my gaze, but he silenced me with another kiss. He filled my mouth with his tongue and tortured me with the pressure of his body against mine. I wrapped my legs around his hips, and as I leaned into his erection, my sense of pleasure grew larger and louder, demanding to be properly taken care of.

"What? How do I know?" he asked, pulling away from me. "Because it's written all over your face, Elephant. You exude virginity from every pore of your body, no matter how hard you try to conceal it."

I felt myself blush. "I just want you to kiss me," I said, maintaining eye contact.

"Just that?" he asked, peeking down at my lace bra, my nipples standing out under the fabric, aching, like the rest of my body, to feel his touch.

He took my left breast in his mouth, and I let my head fall back, breathless as he slid his tongue over my nipple, kneading my other breast with his hand.

"I'm so mad at you, Marfil. And I tend to lose control when I get mad."

"I want you to lose control . . ." I said, letting out a broken moan as he gently bit my left nipple. "You're always so tense."

He thrust his hips into mine, and I gasped as his erection pressed into my groin. He put his mouth on my neck, sending chills through my body as his tongue, his lips, and his teeth toyed with me torturously. I loved it. I loved everything he did to me. I wanted him inside me. I didn't care about my virginity. I didn't care about the lectures, the warnings, the catechism classes, committing sin. I wanted to commit every sin in the book with Sebastian, and once done, create new ones to commit together all over again.

My feet touched the ground as he trailed kisses from the space between my breasts down to my belly button, just to come back up and suck desperately on my collarbone.

"I could make you come like this," he said, placing a hand between my legs. My jeans brushed up against the hypersensitive skin of my groin, and I quivered with pleasure.

"Sebastian . . ." I felt him unbuttoning my jeans and then his hands slipping beneath my underwear. When his fingers entered me, I closed my eyes and gave in to the immense pleasure overtaking me. "God . . ." I whispered against his earlobe, biting down gently as he penetrated me with his fingers in swift in-and-out movements.

He kept his mouth on mine, his eyes open wide so he wouldn't miss a detail, his fingers keeping a steady rhythm, driving me closer to the long-awaited ecstasy. I grabbed his wrist as an overwhelming sensation flooded into every corner of my being, taking over my senses, leaving me without a single thought.

"Go with it, Marfil," he said gruffly.

If I hadn't been so lost in the pleasure of the moment, I might've noticed that his tone of voice had changed.

I opened my eyes. Who knew what would happen after this? Who knew how Sebastian would behave when the arousal we both felt evaporated into thin air?

But I didn't have time to think . . . My mind went blank as my first orgasm took hold of me at the hands—fingers, really—of this man. I wasn't even aware of the sounds coming from my mouth as Sebastian continued fucking me with his fingers, although at a slower rhythm, ensuring that my pleasure was drawn out, until I'd given every ounce I had to give.

He didn't immediately remove his fingers, applying gentle pressure on my clit instead. Then, as if it were nothing, he brought them to his lips and licked them one by one without taking his eyes off me, and I hungered for him more than ever.

The rain had slowed to a drizzle, and suddenly, I felt my legs go weak. I leaned against him, and he held me firmly against his chest for a few seconds. But then, before I had even fully recovered, he grabbed my wrists and pulled me away from him.

"I did what you wanted," he said coldly, without a hint of desire in his gaze, as if he'd just removed a mask. "Now get dressed, get back on your horse, and go home." Sebastian let go of me and went directly over to my father's horse.

I was still trembling from the orgasm, but Sebastian's hard

gaze had caused any trace of pleasure to vanish from my body, as if he'd just poured a pitcher of ice-cold water over my head.

"Sebastian . . ." I said in a shaky voice.

Oh my God, I was going to cry my eyes out if he didn't come back to me this very instant and wrap his arms around me.

"I told you to get dressed," he said, noticing I hadn't moved an inch.

I felt ashamed and humiliated. His fingers had just been inside me, and now he was looking at me like I was a total stranger, an irritating one at that.

I hurriedly got dressed, more out of embarrassment than anything else. Sebastian faced the opposite direction, giving me privacy, and started petting Marengo.

"Why are you treating me like this?" I asked, wiping my tears with my arm.

He turned back to me. "I'm not treating you like anything," he said with feigned calm. "You blackmailed me, so I gave you what you wanted."

The way he said it sounded so dirty, so horrible, so disgustingly wrong . . .

"You'd never do anything you don't want to do," I answered. All warmth had left my body, leaving me trembling and vulnerable before the man with whom I'd shared something so special and intoxicatingly wonderful.

"You're right about that . . . I let you blackmail me once. Next time, I'll be the one who speaks to your father, and I'll do it to inform him that I quit." His tone told me he was being totally serious.

I needed to get out of there. I couldn't stand to look at his face, his blank, impersonal stare.

I mounted my horse without another word. I didn't stop to see if he was behind me. I simply urged Philippe to run like we were being chased by the devil himself.

I pressed my lips together and blinked back the tears that were clouding my vision.

When I got off the horse and left him in his stall, I ran to the house without looking back. I didn't want to see the satisfaction on Sebastian's face when he saw that I was crying, that I had let him get back at me with such a low, painful blow.

I climbed into my bed and cried myself to sleep.

## CHAPTER 18

# MARFIL

The morning after the "incident" in the barn, I refused to let Sebastian see how much I'd been affected by the way he'd treated me the night before. So I covered my red eyes, pink cheeks, and swollen lips in a magical layer of makeup that left me looking like new. The Dior foundation I'd bought a while back and had hardly ever used worked miracles on my skin.

I went down to the kitchen at noon, radiant, at least on the outside. Inside, all I could think about was how humiliated I was. I had never imagined Sebastian capable of doing something like that to me. Yes, it was true that I had blackmailed him, but it was obvious I wasn't going to actually go through with it. Can you imagine me telling my father that I'd hooked up with my bodyguard? Not a chance. Sebastian knew I wasn't being serious, and although it was wrong to threaten him, I didn't plan on just accepting the way he'd treated me. There was no excuse for it.

We spent the day avoiding each other. The house was large enough that we didn't have to cross paths, but if I left, he'd go wherever I went, so I spent several hours in my bedroom. Everything would be much easier when my sister arrived. She would be a good distraction for me, and if they let us, we might even be able to go into town.

As I was waiting for Gabriella to arrive, I saw Sebastian walking out of my father's office with Logan. They both looked more serious than ever, and I wondered what they'd been discussing that made them avoid my gaze and turn away from me so abruptly.

But I didn't have time to ask, because just then, the front door opened and Gabi appeared with a big smile on her pretty pink lips.

"I'm home!" she shouted, dropping her backpack and running over to me.

I hugged her tightly, genuinely happy to see her, and realized she'd had a major growth spurt in the past few months.

"You're as tall as me!" I said, taking a closer look at her.

My sister was beautiful, a fifteen-year-old young woman who looked closer to being eighteen. She had light brown hair that brushed her shoulders and our father's eyes: light brown framed by thick eyelashes. She had the body of a model—tall and thin, with gentle curves that deepened a little more with each year that passed—her twiggy legs on full display in those shorts she had on. Although that had more to do with her age than anything else. I was so happy to have her there, even though we were only going to be together a few days.

Wilson came up behind her, carrying her luggage, effectively putting an end to our embrace. Then our father emerged from his office to welcome my sister, who had always been closer to our father than I was. Living with her mother half the time had helped reduce the tense moments.

My father hugged Gabriella, looked at me over his shoulder, and then asked us to sit with him in the living room.

"Well, girls, now that you're both here, there are some things we need to make clear," he said as he brought a glass of brandy to his lips.

Gabriella looked at me, and her smile faded. Our father always knew how to spoil our good time.

"Gabriella, your sister was kidnapped and left at the hospital," my father said. Gabriella already knew that, but I guess he wanted to remind us of everything that had happened. "For some reason that I still don't fully understand, someone wants to harm her, and they could easily try the same with you. So I'm going to ask you both to keep your eyes open, and most of all, to listen to your bodyguards. Gabriella, you're safe when you're at school, but you, Marfil, need to continue to do everything Sebastian says. Do you hear me?"

Everything Sebastian says . . .

My gaze drifted to Sebastian, who had just appeared in the doorway. Wilson was standing beside Gabi, looking at us with a serious expression on his face. We both agreed, and Gabriella tried to lighten the mood by talking to us about boarding school. Then my father sent her to bed, and I took the opportunity to ask him if there were any new developments.

"There's not much I can tell you, Marfil," he said impatiently. He'd always hated spending more time with me than strictly necessary. "I don't know who's behind this, although I have a vague idea . . . Listen, the world I move in, when a deal goes sour or someone loses money, things can get very ugly. People will do anything for even just a few thousand dollars, and I move in the millions, do you understand?"

Of course I understood, but why the hell did I have to suffer for his sins?

"I don't think I can take living like this much longer," I said, looking sidelong at Sebastian, who stood at the other end of the room with Wilson and Logan, but I knew they had an ear to our conversation.

"It's the way things are," my father said, standing up and heading back to his office.

*The way things are* . . . What an answer.

I stood up, angry. Sebastian didn't even look at me, which really made my blood boil.

I went to bed without even stopping into my sister's room to talk.

---

The next morning, I woke up in a better mood, happy because I had something to do, a welcome distraction. I'd always been someone who liked to go out and help. I loved being a productive member of my community and finding any way to give back, loved feeling like I was part of something important. So whenever I was home in Louisiana, I volunteered at a nonprofit foundation that had been originally set up to help with the devastation of Hurricane Katrina. I wasn't there when the storm hit, but the hurricane had been one of the most devastating natural disasters in the history of our country, and New Orleans, one of my favorite cities in the world, had never fully recovered, something that still made me sad to think about. Over time, the nonprofit shifted to working with unhoused people, doing the work of finding homes for families going through hard times. The most successful initiative was the soup kitchen, which fed hundreds of families and served as a shelter to children without homes.

My father supported the organization and was one of the top contributors. Many of our wealthy neighbors did as well after I went door to door asking for donations. In four years, I'd managed to help raise a good deal of money for the nonprofit Stronger Together, or ST for short. I loved the organization and the people who worked there. It was a place where I felt valued, and even though I'd had to take a step back to focus on my studies, I always liked to lend a hand wherever possible, especially with preparations for the festival we held every year to raise money.

Before heading out, I dressed comfortably in leggings, a shirt that tied in the back to hide my tattoo, and sneakers. My sister often volunteered as well, but I wasn't going to ask her to come with me today since she'd just gotten home from school and was likely jet-lagged.

To my surprise, I entered the kitchen and found said sister sitting on the counter, talking to Sebastian, Wilson, and Lupita, who was mixing dough.

It was strange to see Sebastian smiling and nodding along as she talked. My sister could be very charming, and I adored her, but I would be lying if I said I didn't feel a pang of jealousy seeing him so relaxed around her. His eyes flitted to me for a second, and then immediately darted away with the look of someone averting their gaze from an eyesore. Wilson, on the other hand, let his eyes linger . . . We'd spent a lot of time together, and I'd noticed the way he looked at me.

"Come in, Mar, we're making cookies," my sister said, gesturing to Lupe.

"*You're* making cookies?" I replied sarcastically, noticing my tone had come out uncharacteristically sour. I wasn't someone who was often in a bad mood. I could get mad, yes, but it passed quickly. Sebastian, on the other hand, frustrated me to the point that I wanted to pull out my hair.

"Well, more like we're entertaining Lupe while she makes cookies," Gabi answered with a smile. "But you like us talking to you, right, Lupita?" she asked.

I ignored them and walked to the fridge, where I took out a bottle of Evian water and stopped at the counter to open my backpack and put it inside. Sebastian sat up a little straighter in his seat, and Wilson watched me out of the corner of his eye.

"I'm going into town. I'll take my car," I announced to no one in particular.

"Can I go with you?!" my sister exclaimed, jumping off the counter.

"I'm going to ST," I answered.

She looked disappointed. "Oh, then I'll just stay here."

"Very nice, Gabriella. I'm glad to see that the thought of helping others gives you so much joy," I answered, dry as a desert.

My sister threw me a guilty look. "Well, if you want, I could—" she started to say.

"Don't worry about it," I cut her off. "Wil, would you mind coming with me?" I said, knowing that he was supposed to be guarding my sister.

Wilson stood up immediately. "Of course."

"No," said Sebastian, taking the last sip of his coffee without even looking at me as he spoke. "I'll go with you," he added, standing in one swift movement.

I crossed my arms and turned toward him. "I don't want you to come with me. I want Wil," I said coldly, refusing to look him in the eye, worried I might falter if I did.

"Wilson is your sister's bodyguard. I'm yours," he corrected me dryly.

"Right, but what does it matter? You're interchangeable, aren't you?" I said, now looking directly into his brown eyes. "It's not that hard to follow me around—anyone could do it."

Boom, I'd just insulted their work. I felt sorry for Wilson, but I didn't care that I was being a bitch.

The vein in Sebastian's neck began to twitch.

"I'll be the one to go with you, Marfil, end of discussion."

I huffed pathetically. "I don't want to go with you!"

My sister stared, as if she didn't recognize me. "Wow, looks like someone woke up on the wrong side of the bed today," she exclaimed, looking to Lupita, wide-eyed.

"I don't mind going with her . . ." Wilson said, adding more fuel to the fire.

Sebastian narrowed his eyes. "You do as I say. I'm your superior," he reminded Wilson in an icy tone.

"My father—" I began, but Sebastian interrupted me.

"Your father has put me in charge of protecting you, so don't waste your time trying to convince anyone. You'll either go with me, or you won't go."

I glared at him and marched to the front door without looking back to see if he was following me, swinging my ponytail around so hard it would've whipped someone in the face if they'd been standing too close.

Once outside, I opened the garage, aware that Sebastian was now behind me. The vehicles parked inside were unimaginable. I had never cared much about brands or the makes of cars, but among the relics of automotive history that my father liked to collect was a Lamborghini, two Ferraris, a Bentley, and a gigantic four-wheeler that he used for hunting.

My adorable lime-green VW Beetle looked ridiculous compared to those cars, but I'd wanted it, and my father had indulged me. He'd planned to give me an Audi, if I remember correctly, but I'd always wanted a Beetle, just like the Barbie mobile I had as a kid.

"You should let me drive," Sebastian said, seeing that I was headed straight for my car.

"No way. It's enough that I have to bring you along," I said, climbing into the driver's seat and finally glancing over at him. "You can follow me in Peter's car."

Sebastian walked around to the driver's side and stopped in front of me. "I don't trust you one bit," he said simply. "I'll ride with you in the same car. You want to drive, go ahead. I've already drafted my will."

"Was that supposed to be funny?"

"What's not funny at all is the level of hostility you're exuding from every pore in your body. If you keep talking to me that way in front of people, you're going to get us both in trouble."

I gave a fake smile. "Sorry, which level of hostility would you prefer, sir?"

Sebastian frowned as he paced over to the passenger's side and got in.

I started the car, blasted the air-conditioning, buckled my seat belt, and drove out of the garage.

My house was a centuries-old mansion along the Mississippi River outside of Baton Rouge. There had been many plantations in the area, cotton farms that were only profitable because of forced slave labor, but my house had belonged to an English nobleman who fled to the North during the Civil War. Knowing that the people who built our home had not participated in slavery gave me peace of mind, but according to the historical record, the English nobleman had been killed before he'd managed to escape.

The road to Baton Rouge was almost always deserted, surrounded by thick vegetation. Truth is, I would've loved to have spent more time here. This was my home, after all. I was a Southerner, although I barely had an accent, since I had been raised in England. But seeing all the nature that surrounded me filled me with a sense of peace that I rarely felt in London or New York. Moving to Manhattan had been more a wish to be far from my father than anything else.

I rolled down the window and felt the wind whip my face. It was a beautiful day, warm, but not hot enough to be uncomfortable. Last night's storm had left puddles all over the ground, but the sky was clearer than ever.

I tried to ignore the person seated next to me, and even though the memory of his lips on my body still made me blush, I couldn't forget his rejection. Angry, I slammed on the accelerator, causing the wind to lash my face so hard, it was almost painful.

"Don't be reckless, Marfil," Sebastian lectured me from the passenger's seat.

"You drive just as fast," I replied, enjoying the speed.

"I never go over seventy-five, Marfil," he said, sitting up in his seat and cursing under his breath as he saw me step harder on the accelerator.

There was never anyone on this road, and the speed was exhilarating.

"Marfil," he repeated through gritted teeth.

I rolled my eyes but tapped the brakes to slow down.

The car didn't respond.

"Slow down. Now," he demanded, not noticing how my body had tensed and that all the blood had drained from my face.

"It's not responding," I said in a thread of a voice.

"This is not funny at all," he answered in an icy tone.

"The car won't stop, Sebastian!" I shouted, now freaking out. Sweat began to drip down my back. I was flying down the road at top speed, and the fucking brakes weren't responding!

Sebastian cursed loudly when he saw that I was being serious.

Trying to take control of the situation, he leaned over me, forcing me to grip the wheel tighter. "Focus on the road," he said with a calculated calm.

"I can't stop! There are no brakes! I can't slow down!" I shouted hysterically, tears streaming down my cheeks.

"Listen to me," he said, squeezing his hand against mine on the wheel. "Stay calm, okay? Everything's going to be fine. There's no traffic, but we have to lose speed before we get to that bend in the road."

"We're going to die!" I shrieked, my foot cramping from the force I continued applying to the brake unsuccessfully.

"We're going to be fine! I won't let anything happen to you, I promise," he assured me. "Now, take a deep breath and do as I say. You have to reduce your speed using the car's engine. Shift into a lower gear."

"I can't!" I answered.

"Shift down gradually into third," he ordered.

I did as he told me, and the speed dropped, but not by much.

"That's not enough . . ." Sebastian said, alarmed.

Just ahead of us on the road was the curve he'd referred to previously. Never, in my entire life, had I driven at such speed, and in that moment, I couldn't help but remember what I'd learned in driver's ed, about how, past a certain speed, a simple turn of the wheel could make the car spin out uncontrollably.

"Sebastian . . . Sebastian, the curve . . ."

"Pay attention: I'm going to pull the emergency brake. When we get to the curve, I want you to turn the wheel to the right, okay?"

"But I'll lose control of the car!" I replied, terrified.

"We're going to skid, and hopefully, we'll lose some speed. Marfil, you have to do it, do you hear me?"

"No, no! Sebastian . . . I'm scared; I can't." I was petrified, my entire body stiff from gripping the wheel so tightly, the car still barreling down the road . . . We were going to crash, I knew it. I was going to die in this car. I was going to die in this fucking car with Sebastian beside me.

"Fuck, Marfil, listen to me, please!"

"I can't see. I can't see anything!" I said, blinking back my tears furiously.

"Take a deep breath," he said, a little more calmly this time. "Everything is going to be all right, I promise."

We reached the curve, and everything happened very quickly. I turned the wheel as Sebastian pulled hard on the emergency brake and the car spun out of control.

The world disappeared.

I felt a hard impact, and I lost consciousness.

## CHAPTER 19

# SEBASTIAN

I knew exactly what was going to happen, and I would've given anything to face that situation alone.

Marfil did as I told her. As soon as we reached the curve, she turned the wheel to the right and I pulled the emergency brake so that, with the help of the rear wheels, the vehicle's speed was reduced.

Needless to say, things didn't go as smoothly as they would have if I'd been the one behind the wheel. When the car started to skid and turn on itself, Marfil lost control. I tried to help, but it was impossible. We crashed into something, which caused the car to flip over with us still inside. The airbags deployed and the windows shattered. The last thing I heard before I hit my head was Marfil's scream of terror.

I lost consciousness for a few seconds, but opening my eyes and finding myself hanging upside down, I knew that the situation was worse than I'd imagined. I turned toward Marfil and saw that she was unconscious, held in place by her seat belt.

Ignoring the sharp pain in my right hand, I unbuckled myself and fell against the door. I cursed under my breath and climbed out the window.

Fuck . . . The car was totaled . . . Flames were coming from under the hood.

Trying to ignore the pain in my arm, I limped around to Marfil's window. She was blinking, half conscious.

"Marfil," I said, trying to figure out how to get her out of there as quickly as possible without hurting her. "Marfil, can you hear me? Elephant, wake up."

Her bright green eyes flew open, startling me. She blinked several times until she finally managed to focus on me.

"Se-Sebastian?" she asked, disoriented.

Gathering all my strength, I managed to slip into the car. "Grab on to my neck, okay? I'm going to unbuckle you and get you out of here."

"It hurts . . ." she whimpered, and I could see a trail of blood trickling from her mouth.

No, fuck.

"Hold on, okay?" I said desperately, reaching for her seat belt as much as the car would allow. I heard the buckle click open, mentally thanking God that it wasn't stuck. Marfil fell onto my back and, ignoring the searing pain in my arm, I pulled her out as best I could on all fours before carrying her far away from the car in case the engine exploded.

"Marfil," I said, setting her down to better examine her.

Her breathing was normal, and I assumed that the blood around her mouth was caused by the cut on her lip, nothing internal. I hoped I was right. The airbag had bruised her cheek, and she had cuts on her arms and legs from the shattered glass. She seemed fine otherwise, but she was still only half conscious, meaning she might've suffered a concussion when she hit her head.

"Hey . . . talk to me, please," I said, pushing her dark hair out of her face.

Marfil blinked again, and, when I helped her to a sitting position, her eyes shifted to the car. "My Barbie mobile . . ." she said, and I held out a hand to help her stand.

*Fuck . . . Only Marfil Cortés would make a comment like that in a moment like this one.*

She met my gaze, and then started crying. I pulled her to my chest in an automatic reflex.

"They tried to kill me . . ." she said, her face pressed into my shoulder, voice breaking.

I tensed as I heard her say it aloud, although I had reached the same conclusion when the brakes first failed. "Don't think about that now," I said as I retrieved my cell phone from my pocket, gripping it tightly. We were in the middle of nowhere . . . If whoever had planned this had followed us here to make sure it had been effective . . . "We need to get over there." I pointed to the edge of the woods. "Can you walk?" I asked.

She nodded, lifting her hand to touch her injured lip and cheek.

"Let's go," I encouraged her, looking all around as I called Wilson. There didn't seem to be anyone for miles.

"What is it, Moore?" was Wilson's response on the third ring.

"Come pick us up, quick. We've had an accident. We're still on the back road, close to where it meets the highway," I rushed out before ending the call.

When we got to the edge of the trees, I took out the gun I had holstered to my waist and forced Marfil to get behind a tree big enough to shelter her.

"What are you doing," she shouted, alarmed at the sight of the weapon in my hand.

"It's just a precaution . . ."

Her eyes searched the woods and the road. "Do you think there's someone here?" There was fear in her voice.

I had no idea. All I knew was that someone close to the family had to have been the one who cut her car's brake line, and that made me furious.

Five minutes later, Wilson appeared with Logan in Cortés's Mercedes. Logan's eyes went wide with shock, and he threw me a look that said everything there was to say.

Wilson pulled out his gun, walking over to us. "Are you all right?" he asked immediately, staring at Marfil as he moved closer to her.

I held out a hand to stop him. "I'll take care of Marfil. You know who to call," I said, looking him in the eye.

Wilson nodded as he walked back toward the car, unable to take his eyes off the destroyed Beetle.

"What the hell happened?!" Logan asked, as livid as I was.

"The brakes," I answered. "It had to have been someone close to the family. If not, I don't understand . . ."

"The car was in the shop last week . . ." he said, then suddenly seemed to remember something. "Son of a . . ." He stopped as his eyes fell on Cortés's daughter. "Get her in the car—we need to get her out of here immediately."

Marfil was quieter than normal. Glancing at her in the back seat, face bruised, pale skin smudged, and lip bleeding, I wanted to kill whoever it was that had tried to harm her. And that fury I felt scared me more than anything else.

When we got back to the Cortés mansion, everyone was waiting for us, sick with worry. The first one to come running out to us was Marfil's little sister.

"Marfil!" she shouted, pulling the car door open.

I moved to help her out, but she stopped me before I could touch her.

"I'm fine, I can manage on my own."

Her mood was as dark as mine, which I could understand. Someone had tried to kill her. This went way beyond a tasteless joke involving animal blood and a threatening message. They had taken harmful action, which meant Marfil Cortés had been marked. It was only a matter of time before another hit was put out on her.

And if she was marked, then I was, too.

CHAPTER 20

# MARFIL

I didn't see my father until after returning from the hospital, where they took X-rays and cleaned the wounds on my face and body caused by the glass. Sebastian, worse off than me, grudgingly accepted a sling for his left arm. I hadn't said a word to him at the hospital, despite the fact that he had stood watching, looking concerned as they examined me, rejecting any medical attention for himself until they'd finished treating me.

Back at home, my father came into the living room, his face ashen and angry as a thousand devils. He shot me a look I didn't know how to decipher, and then gestured for Sebastian to follow him into his office.

Lupita served me tea and cookies, but I wanted to hear what they were saying. Gabi was asleep in my lap after crying the whole time I'd been in the hospital. Logan was inside my father's office as well, and the last thing he'd said with regard to what had been done to my car left me in suspense. Who the hell had taken my car to the shop? There was nothing wrong with it! It was practically new, given I'd barely driven it since I lived so far from home.

After Lupita left the living room, I stood up carefully, trying not to wake my sister. I walked down the long hallway, the taxidermized animals following me with their lifeless eyes, and stopped outside the office door.

"You're going to call Bianic! Do you hear me? You're going

to call that son of a bitch and tell him that he either helps me with this or I swear to God he'll never see another dime."

Who the hell was Bianic?

Someone else spoke, but I couldn't hear what they said because they weren't shouting like my father was . . . I was sure Sebastian would be able to keep his cool.

"You're wrong, dammit!"

I heard something slam against the desk, followed by the sound of a chair scraping across the wooden floor.

"I'm not going to stop until that piece of shit is pushing daisies. Until then, I don't care about anything else!"

I strained my ears. There were some more comments that I only half heard, and then the door opened. I jumped back. Sebastian stepped into the hall and closed the door behind him. When he saw me there, eavesdropping in the dim hallway, he gave me a disapproving look that quickly softened into concern.

"How are you doing?" he asked, delicately cupping my chin to examine my cheek and lip, causing chills to rush through my body.

"Better than you," I said, looking to the wound on his eyebrow that had started bleeding again, staining the bandage they had put on him at the hospital.

He ignored my comment and dragged me away from the door with his free arm, his other still pinned to his chest due to the sling. "You shouldn't be listening in," he scolded me.

I followed him down the hall, noticing he now walked with a slight limp.

"Are you planning to go back so they can take a look at that?" I asked, gesturing to his leg.

"I'm fine," he answered curtly.

"Who is Bianic?" I asked, stopping beside the head of an especially large deer. If he wasn't going to let me worry about his injuries, he could at least give me some answers.

"No one you need to worry about." He sighed, exasperated.

"Of course I'm worried if he's the one you have to ask for help to keep me alive."

Sebastian spun around and took a step toward me. He put a hand behind my ear and ran his fingers through my hair, all the way to the back of my neck. "I'm the one who keeps you alive," he said, a dark gleam in his eyes, as if insinuating otherwise had offended him. Then he seemed to remember where he was, looking down the hallway and putting space between us. "You should be resting," he added, moving back toward the living room, where my sister had fallen asleep on the sofa.

When I saw that Sebastian intended to leave without another word, I grabbed his hand and stopped him, making sure my tone of voice was sufficiently low so that no one would hear me. "I need you to explain what's happening," I said, my eyes unwittingly filling with tears. I tried to blink them back, annoyed, without much success. "My father isn't going to tell me anything, and this is getting out of control. I need to know who wants to hurt me. I get the feeling that you already know, but you don't want to tell me."

Sebastian tightened his lips, but he didn't walk away or drop my hand. He observed me in silence, then wiped away the tears sliding down my cheeks. "This will be over soon, Marfil. In the meantime, you need to stay home."

I took a step back, frustrated, and he released his hold.

"I don't understand how you know more about my life than I do, but you can be sure I'm going to find out what the hell is happening here, because I don't see any police officers around asking about the accident or taking statements about what was, without a doubt, an attempted murder."

Sebastian started to say something, but just then the door at the end of the hallway opened and my father emerged.

"Marfil, I need to talk to you. Come into my office," he said in a sharp tone.

I threw one last defiant glance at Sebastian, then turned my back on him. I retraced the path to my father's office, where he stood holding the door open. Logan left the room, and my father closed the door behind him.

"There's something I wanted to talk to you about," he started saying as he poured himself a glass of brandy. I had not received a single word of concern from him, no explanation, nothing. If I was already angry, his next words left me seething. "I have to meet with some friends tomorrow at the racetrack, and I want you to come with me."

What?

"Dad, are you seriously not planning to say a word about what happened this morning?" I said, raising my voice. Didn't he see my cuts and bruises, my eyes swollen from crying, the terrified look on my face?

"I have said many words about it, of course, just not to you, since you have nothing to do with it and you wouldn't understand."

I had nothing to do with it?!

I opened my mouth, but he lifted a hand to stop me from speaking.

"Don't start, Marfil, please," he said, setting his glass down too hard and spilling most of the brandy onto the papers that covered the desktop. "You wouldn't understand, not in a million years."

"I'm not an idiot—" I began, but he interrupted me again.

"Of course you're not an idiot, but you're a woman!" he exclaimed, looking at me fixedly, then making a sweeping gesture with his hand. "Look at yourself! You haven't stopped crying since you got home. You wouldn't last half an hour in my world. I have to protect you from everything around you, around me.

The world outside is horrible, but I've always given you and your sister nothing but the best! The only thing I ask in return is that you do as you're told for once in your damn life and wait for things to be resolved. You know I have practically my entire staff and other trusted people working to find out who's trying to kill you, and for your safety, it's better if you didn't know anything, understand? Don't make me repeat myself again!"

I clenched my fists. I would tell him to go to hell if it weren't for my fear of him. It was my life; I had every right to know who the hell wanted to kill me and why.

My father sat down and studied me. "As I was saying, I need your help," he began, now in a calmer tone. "You're my oldest daughter, and since you love telling me how mature you are, I want you to come with me tomorrow to a casual meeting with a friend I'm hoping to go into business with."

"What good would I do? That is, if you can tell me, of course."

My father ignored my jab and fixed his eyes on mine. "Your presence there will help lighten the mood."

That was it? That was all he was going to tell me?

"You've always loved horses, and Marengo will be racing tomorrow, so you can just relax and enjoy an outing with your father. You won't have to do anything else, just be there."

I didn't like the idea one bit, so when he asked me to leave, I stood up without hesitation.

"I've taken the trouble of choosing your outfit for tomorrow," he added as a parting comment. "You'll find it on your bed. I'm sure you'll love it. You can thank me later. Now, go rest and recover from today. I need you fresh and pretty for tomorrow."

I hated that he made me feel like a fucking doll, but I knew there was no way to get out of it. I had no choice but to go with him. That's how it had always been; I had never had a choice.

When I got to my room, I saw three large white boxes with blue stripes waiting to be opened. I walked bravely past them to the window, needing a calming distraction from everything that had happened. If I closed my eyes, I could still feel the car starting to roll, the breaking glass, the terror invading me. Luckily, Sebastian had been there and had pulled me out of the car in time, before something worse had happened.

Was I still mad at him?

Why fool myself? What had happened a few hours ago had erased any trace of anger I'd felt toward him.

I sat on my bed and lay back on the pillows. I was exhausted. This was turning out to be the worst spring break ever, and what awaited me the next day made me even more anxious than I already was. My father had never asked me to join him for any social occasion, normally taking one of the many women he slept with. Why did he suddenly want me at one of his meetings?

I took one last look at the boxes of clothes and waited for my fate to arrive tomorrow.

---

I woke up in the middle of the night, tormented by my usual nightmares: the car I was riding in lost control, crashing into all the people I loved, killing them. It took me a few seconds to realize I was safe at home.

I replaced my jeans with the nightgown from under my pillow, then put on my robe and went downstairs to find some food in the kitchen. The entire house was asleep, so I was surprised to find someone up so early, leaning on the kitchen counter, drinking coffee, as per usual.

Sebastian stood up straight as soon as he saw me.

"I came to get something to eat," I explained, hoping he wouldn't notice I'd been crying.

"Were you able to get some rest?" he asked, concerned.

"Some . . . but my head hurts, and I had a horrible nightmare."

Sebastian moved closer under the pretext of setting his cup

in the sink. "Do you want to tell me about it?" He had stopped in front of me, his eyes examining me distractedly, studying each of my injuries.

"Never talk about nightmares before breakfast," I answered, looking at the wound on his eyebrow and his injured arm. We both could've died . . . because of me.

Sebastian smiled. "Why is that?"

"Because they'll come true if you do."

We stared at each other for a few seconds.

"I wasn't aware of that infallible science."

"That's because you're too close-minded," I answered, moving away from him, needing space to think clearly.

I took out some milk from the fridge, then stretched toward the upper cabinet in an attempt to get the honey, which some idiot had stowed way out of reach.

I felt his chest against my back as his arm reached over my head. He grabbed the honey and placed it on the counter, but he didn't move, still pressed up against me.

I closed my eyes for an instant . . .

Despite everything that happened, my body yearned to be close to him . . . to feel his warmth, inhale his scent like a soothing balm. I forgot about everything else with him there beside me, simply letting the seconds pass.

"I didn't say it yesterday, but you were very brave." He ran a hand over the sleeve of my white silk robe, instantly giving me chills. "Even though you were scared, you were able to keep calm and handle the car . . . Things could've gone much worse," he said, his fingers gently caressing my arm.

"I just did what you told me to," I answered in a whisper.

"For once," he replied, and I couldn't help but roll my eyes.

"My father wants me to go with him to the racecourse," I confessed, and I was aware how confused I sounded when I said it.

"I know," he answered, halting his caress.

I turned around, and we stood face-to-face. His hair was messy, having just gotten out of bed, and I was dying to smooth it down with my fingers. "Will you be there?"

He nodded, and I felt somewhat relieved. He must've noticed because, without thinking, he put his hand in my hair and brushed his thumb across my cheek.

"I should've checked the car . . . I'm sorry." He sighed.

Sebastian Moore, apologizing?

"You're not the one to blame for what happened, Sebastian," I said. He removed his thumb from my cheek and gently brushed my lower lip. "That, at least, wasn't your fault."

His eyes met mine, and I knew that my last comment hadn't escaped him.

"It won't happen again," he said very somberly, and I didn't know if he was talking about the car or our encounter two nights before.

He began trailing his fingers softly up and down my arm; still, I didn't respond. Why did he contradict himself? Why, if he would just torture himself over it later?

He lowered his other hand to my waist and slowly began to untie my robe.

I closed my eyes. I should've stopped him. I didn't want to go through that again—experiencing so many intense emotions only to be met with total indifference afterward. This game between us was beginning to feel exhausting.

"I want to kill anyone who tries to hurt you, Marfil," he said, sliding his hand around my waist, allowing himself to indulge if only for an instant, before gripping the white silk of my nightgown in frustration. "I want to do it, and knowing that I can't is killing me," he whispered, burying his mouth in my neck and speaking into my ear. He seemed frightened and desperate, as if part of him was struggling to repress the words that came out of his mouth.

I opened my eyes, my gaze fixed on the kitchen door as he pulled me to his chest, wrapping his good arm around me. I stood there stiffly for an instant, and then relaxed into his comforting embrace.

Had he changed his mind? Had the accident shifted the way he saw things between us?

He withdrew a few seconds later, as if reading my thoughts. "Let me make you breakfast," he said before I could say anything else.

I sat at the counter and watched as he heated milk, added the honey, and handed me the mug before getting started on the pancakes.

"Where did you learn to cook?" I asked, trying to use conversation as a distraction. I still couldn't believe he had hugged me like that. It gave me hope, but I didn't want to make too much of it. Sebastian had shown me that he could get caught up in the heat of the moment and then later act like nothing had ever happened.

"Well . . . I didn't have much of a choice," he said, as if that explained everything.

"I don't understand," I said, stirring my milk.

"I grew up in foster homes . . . They didn't usually take great care of the kids, so cooking was one way I could help out the younger ones. I just so happened to discover that it relaxed me."

Growing up without any type of family must've been hard. I could understand because, although I had a father and a lovely home, I had often felt very alone.

"The most cooking I ever did was when I snuck into the boarding school kitchen and tried to make a fried egg in the middle of the night . . . I started a grease fire and was suspended for three days. My father refused to let me come home because he was busy, so I had to stay locked in my dorm room the whole time."

Sebastian placed a plate of blueberry pancakes in front of me, propped his elbows on the counter, and observed me, perplexed. "I just can't picture you in a boarding school with nuns."

I smiled. "At least one sister left the school because of me, saying that God had placed me in her path as a test, and she wasn't up to the challenge."

Sebastian grinned. "Were you that bad?" he asked, immediately raising a hand before I could respond. "Never mind, don't answer that."

I smirked in return as I popped a bite of pancake in my mouth.

"And you . . . how did you end up in the military?"

Sebastian stole a bite of my pancake and looked pensive as he chewed. "When you turn eighteen, the state stops taking care of you. They put me out on the street. I went through a rough time." I raised my eyebrows questioningly, but he stopped me once again before I could say anything. "That's all in the past now, Marfil. The military was the only thing that interested me, and I didn't have to pay them to take me."

I nodded, glad to be receiving information about him, although something told me he wasn't telling me everything. He observed me as I ate in silence, but I didn't feel uncomfortable or intimidated by his presence. Instead, a blush crept up my cheeks as I remembered the feel of his mouth on mine, his hands against my bare skin, my fingers getting lost in his hair.

"Are you going to tell me about your nightmare now?" he asked when I finished my last pancake.

I looked up from my plate and fixed my eyes on him. "Nothing out of the ordinary," I said calmly. "Everyone dies, and all I can do is sit there and watch as it happens."

Another moment of silence fell over the kitchen, and I stood up, suddenly needing to get out of there.

"I think I'd better go shower," I said.

"Me too." Sebastian nodded, then walked around the counter and followed me into the living room.

Our eyes met for an instant, and I felt an abyss open up between us once again.

---

I'd expected to feel better after a hot shower, but I didn't. Not even when my sister came into my room, excited to open the boxes and help me get dressed. She had always wanted our father to take her with him to the Fair Grounds Race Course & Slots in New Orleans. I had only been there on one occasion, as a rider in an obstacle race organized to raise funds for ST, and still, my dad wouldn't let me stay for the party afterward, which was another reason why I was so surprised by his invitation to join him now.

Gabriella opened the first box and removed a pretty white dress that hit just above the knee and wrapped across my body to tie at one side of my waist, fortunately hiding my tattoo. It was simple, but it was a Valentino, and I knew it had cost a fortune. In the other two boxes were Louboutins with a higher heel than I was used to wearing, and a large navy blue sun hat, with a satin ribbon that matched the dress.

I looked at the clothes unenthusiastically . . . I didn't feel like getting all dressed up, not with how battered my face looked, and definitely not while my head still ached. However, knowing I had no choice but to obey, I sat down at the dressing table and let my sister do my hair. We'd always liked to play beauty parlor, and she was much better at it than me.

"Do you think Daddy is taking you because he can't find anyone to go with?" Gabriella asked as she made two thin French braids that met in the center, leaving the rest of my hair in loose waves to cascade down my back.

"I doubt it," I answered as I looked at my face in the mirror and cursed, wondering how I was going to cover the cuts on my face. If I didn't do it right, people would think someone had beaten me up. The thought made me shudder.

As my sister continued fixing my hair, I began to hide the marks on my skin the best I could and tried to reduce the swelling around my eyes in a way that looked natural but accentuated their color.

"You have to wear this, Mar. You'll be even more of a showstopper," she said, handing me a bright red lipstick.

"You don't think it's too much?"

"Everything about you is too much," she answered, looking at me in the mirror.

I still had to get dressed and put on that damned hat, but my face looked smooth as alabaster under the foundation, and my eyes were extra green thanks to the mascara, which had taken my already long eyelashes to unexpected lengths.

I used the red lipstick that my sister suggested, but only dabbing it onto my lips very lightly so that it looked a little more natural. When I put on the dress and heels, only one thought came to mind: What would Sebastian think when he saw me dressed like this?

I didn't have to wait long to find out, since he was standing beside the car along with my father, who was smoking a cigar as he waited for me to come down. When I stepped out of the front door, they both turned to look at me. My father's gaze held admiration and pride, though not fatherly pride, more like when he bought himself a new Ferrari that made him feel like he was better than everyone else. Sebastian, on the other hand, looked dazzled, as if he hadn't expected to see me that way.

I walked down the steps toward them. "The hat itches like crazy, so I don't plan on wearing it until we get there," I said, waving it like a fan, "and the heels are super uncomfortable,

Dad. They might've cost you a fortune, but they're already rubbing blisters."

And the bubble was instantly burst. My father frowned in disapproval, his normal reaction to me, and Sebastian tried to suppress a smile.

We got in the car, and I realized that Sebastian wouldn't be riding with us as he climbed into the passenger's seat of Logan's car.

"Who is that?" I asked, looking back at the four well-dressed men, including Sebastian—*My God, he looks so good in that jacket and tie!*—who were following in an SUV.

"I hired additional security," my father said, taking out his cell phone as we turned onto the same road where we'd had the accident the day before.

He spent the entire ride talking to someone named Malcolm, and I got so bored that I fell asleep in the back seat until my father shook me awake once we arrived.

Someone opened the door for me, and I immediately felt ridiculous when my eyes landed on the crowd of people entering the racecourse, understanding that the custom of dressing up for the races was a thing of the past. Most of the people there were wearing blue jeans and sneakers. But when we reached my father's private balcony, his social circle was as snobby as he was, and my attire suddenly made sense.

Rows of seats were positioned up front with a great view of the racetrack, and glass doors at the rear opened onto a room furnished with sofas facing a gigantic TV, where servers endlessly passed trays of champagne and canapes.

I began to feel nervous when I noticed Sebastian was nowhere in sight. After scanning the space, I finally spotted him on the other side of the room, looking around with a stern expression. He even had one of those earpieces in his ear. He was all bodyguard that day, and I hated that he had to stand in the shadows, leaving me surrounded by people I didn't know and had no desire to talk to.

As I was lifting a glass of champagne to my lips—I needed to get a buzz if I was going to survive the evening—my father came over to me, flanked by two very tall and attractive men.

"Marfil, let me introduce you to Emilio and Marcus Kozel," he said, pointing to each man in turn. The older man, Emilio, was obviously the father of the younger, more handsome one, Marcus. I held out my hand as my gaze lingered involuntarily on Marcus Kozel. He was very good-looking . . . and he seemed intrigued by me as well. "This is my daughter Marfil, whom I've told you so much about, Emilio."

"And you did not do her justice, my friend," Emilio said, taking a step forward and shaking my hand with an amused smile.

I turned toward Marcus and shuddered involuntarily.

"They told me you were very pretty, but I thought they were exaggerating," he said, kissing my gloved hand instead of following his father's example and simply shaking it.

His hair was very dark, like mine, and he had startlingly blue eyes that left me with a strange feeling when they rested on me.

"People tend to exaggerate," I said, grateful to have my hand back.

Marcus smiled and continued to openly stare at me as if I were a work of art. I had always felt uncomfortable receiving attention from men like him. Although I had to admit that this one was uncommonly handsome.

"Your father told me what happened yesterday with your car," Emilio Kozel said, bringing our attention back to him. "I can't believe anyone would want to harm a single hair on your head. I'm sorry you've had to go through something so traumatic."

"You don't need to be sorry. The idiot who thought they could kill me is the one who's going to be sorry, sir," I said, blushing as I realized I'd shown my anger in front of a total stranger.

Marcus laughed loudly. "She does have a strong personality, Alejandro. I thought you were exaggerating there, too."

My father smiled and sipped from his glass, then said, "It's impossible to exaggerate when it comes to my daughter, Marcus."

"Would you like to take a walk with me, Marfil?" Marcus said, looking first to my father, as if we needed his permission.

"Sure," I answered automatically, hating that he thought I couldn't decide for myself.

"Go on, go on. We old men have to talk business, unfortunately," Emilio Kozel answered, smiling.

Marcus offered me his arm and I took it, verifying that under his perfectly tailored navy blue tweed jacket and khaki pants was an athletic body in perfect physical condition. He was older than me, probably around twenty-nine or thirty, but he was so attractive that it didn't matter. In reality, he seemed to be around the same age as Sebastian, who was staring at Marcus with an unfriendly expression.

*Hmm, this could be interesting.*

Apparently, Marcus didn't seem overly interested in the races because he led me out of the private balcony and outside to the fields surrounding the racetrack. I didn't know if we were allowed to be there, but he assured me it was fine.

"My family all but keeps this place running, so don't worry, we can do whatever we want."

As he said this, I saw that four bodyguards trailed behind us, Sebastian and Logan among them, maintaining a good distance but glancing all around to ensure everything was in order.

Marcus noticed me looking at them and sighed. "They're annoying, I know. Your father told me that you don't like having a bodyguard," he said as we strolled over the freshly cut grass, enjoying the open air.

"I don't like having someone with me everywhere I go, no," I answered, relieved to be able to talk to someone who understood how horrible it was to have their privacy hijacked.

"If you were mine, you'd have five of my best men guarding you at all times." He stopped and looked down at me. "As attractive as you are, you're begging for trouble."

I stopped short and stared at him in disbelief. "You talk about me as if I were an object that can be owned," I answered, rage beginning to flare up inside me.

Marcus seemed surprised by my response. "Please don't misinterpret my words," he said, placing his hands on my shoulders. "I just meant that, considering everything that's happened over the past few months . . . you know, the kidnapping, the car . . ." I tensed, and he went on, "You should have the best security in the world, Marfil."

"I do have good security. Sebastian Moore is in charge of it," I answered proudly.

Marcus's eyes darted to Sebastian for an instant, and he raised his eyebrows. "I know him . . . Good man, they say."

"Who says?"

Marcus seemed to regret having let that comment slip. "Tell me about yourself, Marfil," he said, abruptly changing the subject and ignoring my last question. "Your name, for example . . . Why Marfil?" he asked with an amused smile.

I shrugged, thinking of the last person who'd asked me the exact same question. "My mother chose it . . . Apparently my skin was very pale when I was born," I settled on, not wanting to elaborate further as I had with Sebastian.

Marcus looked me up and down before placing a hand on my heated cheek. "Great nations have gone to war over women like you . . . You could be this century's Helen of Troy," he joked.

I found the comparison amusing; no one had ever complimented me using a reference to Greek mythology before.

"I always felt sorry for her," I said.

"You sympathize with a woman who would leave her husband for another man?"

"I sympathize with a woman who was forced to marry against her will and instead fled with the love of her life, yes."

"You're a romantic, then," he said, lowering his hand, starting to walk again.

"I don't know. I've never been in love," I answered.

Was that still true?

"Well, we'll have to remedy that," he said, stopping under a tree near the stables, where the guards couldn't see us. "Have dinner with me; it'll be a date," he said, staring as if dazzled by me.

The man piqued my curiosity. He was incredibly handsome, charming, and sure of himself. Why not have dinner with him?

Sebastian appeared in my thoughts just then. But he had made it clear that nothing would ever happen between us. I was tired of pining away over him when deep down I knew he was right. I deserved to have passionate romance, didn't I? Could Marcus Kozel be my Prince Charming?

"I'll think about it," I said.

His expression shifted at my response. I imagined he was accustomed to having his offers immediately accepted.

"I get the feeling I'm going to have a lot of fun with you, Marfil Cortés."

Something in his blue eyes told me that his definition of fun would be very different from mine.

## CHAPTER 21

# MARFIL

We finally returned to the balcony and were able to watch the last race. Marengo came in fourth place, but the horse belonging to my father's principal racing rival, Mathew Byrne, came in sixth. Knowing Alejandro Cortés, that was victory enough. My father introduced me to other friends of his, as if it were my debut into society, and I was thankful to Marcus for sticking by my side to help ward off all the guys vying for my attention.

Finally, the time had come to say goodbye. My father and Emilio Kozel walked ahead, and Marcus pulled me aside, out of earshot.

"Marfil, agree to dinner with me," he said for the eighth time, in what had become something of a running joke for the last hour. "I'll hand you a glass of champagne if you have dinner with me. Want me to get rid of all these men drooling over you? Have dinner with me . . ."

I smiled, still uncertain, and just as I was about to decline the offer again, Sebastian appeared.

"We should go," Sebastian said, curt as always. But his expression of extreme distaste as he looked at Marcus suddenly made me more interested. Was he jealous?

"How's it going, Moore?" Marcus stretched out a hand.

Sebastian was a bit taller and more muscular, and he stared at Marcus's outstretched hand for a few endless seconds. "Kozel," he finally said, offering the briefest of handshakes.

"You're in good hands, Mar," Marcus said, calling me by the nickname only my friends and family used for me, but I didn't mind. "I'm sure Sebastian will take care of us the best he can on our date."

Sebastian remained impassive, but I thought I saw a certain tension in his posture that made me think he disliked seeing me with Marcus.

This could be fun, using Marcus to make Sebastian jealous. What could go wrong? Marcus seemed like the kind of guy who had a different woman in his bed every night; he wouldn't take it too hard when I ultimately rejected him. Sebastian, on the other hand . . . I could tell he wanted to punch Marcus in the face and get me as far away from him as possible.

I turned to Marcus with a wide smile. "Fine, I'll have dinner with you."

The waves of hatred emanating from Sebastian were undeniable.

Marcus looked pleased. "I'll pick you up tomorrow at seven?" he asked, completely ignoring my bodyguard, as if he were a houseplant.

Sebastian had said what he had to say, so why was he still standing there, in the middle of our conversation?

"All right," I said.

I could do dinner with Marcus and still have time to hang out with Gabriella all day before she left for her mother's house. With the accident and the visit to the racecourse, I'd hardly spent any time with her.

Marcus took me by surprise when he leaned over, grabbed me by the waist, and pulled me to his chest as he planted a kiss on my cheek.

"See you tomorrow, Miss Cortés. I want you to get all dolled up for me," he said to me, then to my bodyguard, "Moore."

Sebastian didn't respond, and I turned to him as soon as Marcus was out of sight. Sebastian was staring blankly at me without any hint of emotion. "We should go now," he said simply, and started to walk ahead of me.

I followed Logan, who was coming up from behind us, feeling a stab of pain in my chest. That was it? Did he really not care that I was going to have dinner with Marcus?

---

I got home, and my sister greeted me excitedly, wanting me to fill her in about the day at the races.

"Oh, Mar, you're finally going to have a boyfriend!" she exclaimed as soon as I finished telling her about Marcus Kozel.

"No one said he was going to be my boyfriend—we're just having dinner," I clarified as I took off my pearl earrings and set them in a jewelry box on my dressing table.

"Will anyone ever want to date me?"

I looked at her, surprised. "Of course, you're incredible. How could anyone not want to date you?"

"You'll always be the prettier one, you can't deny that," she said, pointing at her pulled-up hair and pink satin pajamas, as if emphasizing her point.

"I may capture people's attention, briefly, Gabi, but they get bored of me quickly. You, on the other hand, are pretty and *fun*—no one's getting bored of you. Anyone would be crazy not to fall madly in love with you."

Suddenly something in her expression made me think she had something to tell me.

"I met a boy," she said a few seconds later, confirming I'd read her correctly. "Dad would never approve. His father owns the candy shop in the town near school. He's older than me, and so cute," she said with dreamy eyes.

I tensed at her comment. "Gabi, you have to be very careful; you can't sneak out of school like you used to. If someone—"

"Yeah, yeah . . ." she cut in, frowning. "That's easy to say when you live alone in New York City and can go wherever you want."

I opened my eyes in surprise. "Gabi, I'm five years older than you, and in case you forgot, I went through boarding school, just like you . . . without any boyfriend in town, I should mention."

"But that was different. Do you have any idea what it's like to be a fifteen-year-old who's still never kissed a boy?"

"My first kiss was at eighteen, so, yes, I know what it's like."

My sister opened her eyes wide in surprise. "Took you long enough . . . Girls lose their virginity at sixteen these days, and I . . ."

My heart started beating faster as I heard her say that. I leaned over and gripped her hands tightly. "Don't even think about it, Gabriella," I said, a little too intense. "Don't even think about sleeping with anyone. You're a baby!"

My sister leaned back, pulling out of my grasp and looking at me angrily. "Don't talk to me like the nuns or like Dad. It's not like you're still a virgin."

I remained silent, trying to erase a certain recent memory from my mind.

When I didn't answer, my sister opened her eyes wider and laughed. "You're joking, right?! You're a virgin?"

"Shhh!" I said. "Yes, I am. And you better stay a virgin, too, or Father will kill you."

"You're so dramatic. As if he would know."

"There are ways of checking, don't you know that?"

My sister lay back on the bed and looked at the ceiling, smiling. "No one's going to check anything. And if Timmy and I decide to do it . . ."

"Gabriella, don't even think about it. You're fifteen years old. You haven't even had your first kiss!"

My sister sat up. "I haven't had my first kiss with a boy, you mean," she corrected, raising her eyebrows. "I asked Laura to teach me. I have to have some idea of what to do when Timmy finally kisses me. It was pretty gross, though, so much spit and tongues touching, all slimy."

*Oh my God!*

"You should only kiss someone who's important to you, someone you feel something for, not your best friend at school."

My sister shrugged. "It's not that big of a deal."

I looked at her worriedly. The only thing that had given me some peace of mind in this whole situation was knowing that my sister was safe miles away and would be responsible enough not to sneak out while the threat still loomed.

That night, Gabriella and I watched our favorite movie in my room. As I lay in bed looking up at the dark ceiling, I couldn't help but wonder what it would feel like to kiss Marcus Kozel, and especially if he could make me feel anything anywhere as intense as the way Sebastian made me feel.

---

The next morning passed without incident. Well, except for the fact that, when I went down for breakfast, I found a gigantic bouquet of red roses. Gabriella and Lupe jumped up and down, insisting that I show them the card, and before opening it, my gaze shifted unwittingly to Sebastian, who was having breakfast at the other end of the table across from Wilson. Our eyes met, and I felt a tingling sensation inside.

Sebastian quickly looked back to his newspaper.

I let out a scoff before opening the envelope and reading the note Marcus had included with the roses.

*From the moment I met you, I haven't been able to stop thinking about you. I'm counting down the hours until I see you tonight, Marfil. Don't forget to get yourself all dolled up for me.*

*Marcus Kozel*

I handed the card to Gabriella so she would stop asking what it said, and I sat down at the breakfast table. Sebastian didn't even blink.

"Wow . . . '*get yourself all dolled up for me*,'" my sister read aloud. "This Marcus guy is a real player, huh?"

"Shut up," I said, yanking the card from her and putting it in my pocket. "You'd better hurry up if you want to spend all day at the creek. I need to be back here by five to start getting ready."

An hour later, we were galloping on our horses with Sebastian and Wilson behind us as we laughed and raced as we often used to do when we were back at home. Lupe had packed us a picnic basket with sandwiches, apples, cheese, and grapes. Sebastian and Wilson didn't want to join us for lunch, having brought their own food, so I didn't have the opportunity to talk to Sebastian until we got back to the stables around four thirty in the afternoon. I took my time brushing Philippe before going in, so when Sebastian entered the horse stall, I knew we were alone.

I tried to behave as if he wasn't there, but it was impossible to ignore him, especially when he walked up to my horse and petted him with infinite tenderness.

I set down the brush and made my way to leave, but he stopped me before I was able to take my first step.

"Be careful tonight," he said, causing me to look back and meet his gaze.

"It's just a date, Sebastian. I've had thousands of them," I responded.

Sebastian tilted my chin up with a single finger, forcing me to look him in the eye. "Marcus Kozel is nothing like any of the guys you've gone out with before. He's dangerous. Be careful," he said again.

I took a step back. "He's the son of my father's friend. If my father thought I was in any danger, he wouldn't let me go. And from what I can tell, he's very happy that I'm going out with Marcus."

Sebastian huffed, then followed it with a smirk.

"Is there anything else you want to tell me without risking looking insanely jealous?"

Sebastian took a step toward me and bored his brown eyes into mine, completely unfazed by my comment. "Yes, there is something else: Don't let him kiss you."

I looked at him incredulously. "Why not?"

"Because one kiss from you will leave him dying for more."

With that, he turned his back on me and left.

*What just happened?*

---

I had to admit that it made me extremely happy to know Sebastian was jealous over my date with Marcus, even if Sebastian had seemed like he was genuinely trying to warn me about him. But I wasn't going to waste my time thinking about that tonight, especially when I felt a mix of nerves and excitement over my date with Marcus. I had chosen a tight, elegant dark green dress that hit at the knee, paired with black heels that made my legs look amazing. I left my hair loose down my back to cover my tattoo and played up my eyes with makeup so that they looked bright green and catlike. I chose to leave my lips nude, except for a touch of pink gloss.

"You look amazing," my sister said admiringly.

I thanked her, kissed the top of her head, and headed

downstairs. I had no idea how the date would go, but I didn't want to stress too much about it. I had gone on tons of dates in the last two years; they didn't intimidate me. The only man who'd ever managed to make me feel truly nervous was Sebastian, but I hoped Marcus would help me put an end to that. With Sebastian, everything was too complicated and too intense. I wanted something easier for a change.

Regardless, this was just dinner. A romantic dinner, sure, but more than likely, I'd either be totally bored or have a good time without anything worth mentioning happening, which was how dates usually went for me.

I stepped into the foyer where both Wilson and Sebastian were waiting, dressed in suits and ties, blank expressions on their faces.

"You aren't both thinking of coming, are you?" I asked, horrified.

"You're taking them both, yes," my father said, appearing in the door to the kitchen. He looked me up and down and gave me an approving nod. "You look lovely, dear. I'm glad to see you're starting a relationship with Marcus. He's a great catch for you. Unbeatable."

"First of all, I'm not starting a relationship with him. I hardly know the guy—we're just going to dinner. And second, why do both of them need to come? Marcus made reservations for two. I can't bring along an entire entourage," I ranted at my father, who smiled in amusement, something uncharacteristic for him.

"Don't worry. Marcus is used to having plenty of security around."

I recalled Marcus's comment about having five men to guard me if I were his, and I suddenly felt less eager to see him again.

It was pointless to argue with my father on that point. I couldn't back out now, so I tried not to let it bother me that

Sebastian and Wilson would be observing every movement I made that night on my date. How the hell was I going to act natural or even attempt to flirt with Sebastian staring at us?

Finally, Marcus arrived. He was dressed a bit more casual than me in dark jeans and a white shirt, but not so much that we clashed. He seemed truly sincere when, upon seeing me, he said I was the most beautiful woman he'd ever seen in his life. I smiled, not letting the compliment affect me.

Even though he would be driving us in his car—a matte black Ferrari, it had to be said—he'd brought his full security detail. Parked in the driveway were two black Mercedes. I eyed them, trying to see who was inside, but he took my hand and pulled me toward his car.

"Don't worry about them. Act like they're not here."

Did he really need that much security everywhere he went? Who the hell was Marcus Kozel?

I looked back at Sebastian, and Marcus followed the direction of my gaze.

"You don't need to come, Moore. I have enough security to protect her. Nothing is going to happen to her while she's with me."

Sebastian looked like he wanted to bite Marcus's head off. "Marfil doesn't go anywhere without me," he said, leaving no room for argument.

"I said," Marcus replied, stepping in front of Sebastian and placing a hand on his chest to stop him from taking a step toward Peter's Mercedes, "that I'll take care of her tonight."

Sebastian was about to push Marcus, but I intervened immediately. "Marcus," I said, taking him by the arm, "I want him to come."

Marcus smiled without looking at me, his eyes fixed on Sebastian, and took a few seconds to respond. "Whatever you say, princess," he said, giving in.

*Princess.* That was a bit much for a first date, but I wasn't going to say anything about it.

He held open the car door for me, and I watched as Sebastian got into the Mercedes. Since when did anyone take three carloads of bodyguards just to go out on a date?

Marcus got in the car, filling it with the scent of his cologne, and I relaxed into the leather seat.

"I'm sorry about all this, but considering the circumstances..."

"It's no big deal," I said as he shifted the car into gear and started out, fast, down the country road that ran past my house—the three security vehicles following closely behind.

"I've made reservations at a restaurant with stunning views of the Mississippi," he said, seeming satisfied with himself. "It has an incredible rooftop, the best steak around, and a spectacular wine list."

I smiled, admiring the countryside as it zoomed outside the window. Marcus drove fast, very fast, but I didn't ask him to slow down. The car demanded to be driven that way.

"So, I realized I never asked you—what's your major in college?" he asked with one arm on the back of my seat and the other on the wheel.

"Economics," I responded.

"Seriously?" He laughed, glancing at me out of the corner of his eye, and then back at the road.

Why was that so funny to him?

"Yes, I'm finishing up my sophomore year," I said, studying his profile. He was very handsome, like he'd been plucked straight out of a Christian Dior ad.

"What do you do?" I asked, curious, as I took in the gold Rolex on his left wrist and the ring with a lion's head on his right hand.

He looked at me for a moment with an amused expression on his face. "I buy and sell companies," he explained. "I purchase bankrupt businesses for one dollar and take on all their debt."

"One dollar?" I asked incredulously.

"Yes," he said simply. "Then I restructure them, make a deal with the banks to settle the debt, and sell to the highest bidder."

"It sounds risky," I said, looking out at the sun setting over the trees and the empty, winding road lit up only by the car's headlights.

"All business is risky," he replied, shrugging. "Do you like ballet?" he then asked.

I sat up straighter in my seat and shot him a questioning look. Was my tattoo visible? Had my father seen it?

He pointed to the ballet slipper pendant hanging around my neck.

"Oh," I sighed in relief. "Yeah, I love it."

"You dance?" he asked.

"Yes, although not professionally," I said, unavoidably thinking of my mother.

"It's in your blood, isn't it?"

I looked at him in surprise.

"Paulina Kozlova was a friend of my parents. If I'm not mistaken, it was my father who introduced her to yours."

"Your parents knew my mother?" I asked in disbelief.

"Yes. I knew her, too, although I couldn't have been more than eight or nine years old . . . She once danced for my family, a private show at our home in Moscow . . . I remember that half of Russia was in love with her. She was very beautiful." I nodded, becoming misty-eyed. "I never believed that anyone could be more beautiful than her . . . until I saw you." He looked at me, and the intensity of his gaze was so hypnotizing, I hadn't even realized we'd arrived at the restaurant. Marcus stretched out a hand and wiped away one of the tears sliding down my cheeks. "Will you dance for me . . . sometime?"

My heart raced. "Of course," I answered quietly.

Marcus grinned and walked around to open the car door for me. When I got out, I saw that Sebastian was already standing beside the entrance to the restaurant. Something in his face changed when he saw me, and it took me a moment to realize it concerned him to see me step out of the car with moist eyes, so I smiled to put him at ease.

Between Marcus's three bodyguards and my two, a total of five well-dressed men followed us into the elevator that would take us directly to the rooftop terrace to have dinner. Marcus was able to behave as if they weren't there throughout the ride up, but that was harder for me to do. Especially when I felt his hand on the lower part of my waist and the possessive way he pulled me toward him in front of everyone, in front of Sebastian.

Once outside the elevator, I relaxed as I took in the restaurant; it was gorgeous, with sweeping views of the river. The seating was intimate, with tables situated along a huge window but screened off from each other to provide a sense of privacy that few restaurants could offer. I was relieved to see that the bodyguards would not have a clear view of us on our date, but it was still awkward to have Sebastian there, and I regretted not having accepted Marcus's offer to leave my bodyguards behind.

We sat down and an elegantly dressed waiter offered us menus. Marcus ordered wine, which arrived a few minutes later, and slid closer to me.

"Did you like the flowers?" he asked as he served me some wine.

"They're beautiful, thank you," I said, bringing the glass to my lips, enjoying his attention.

"Your father told me that you live in New York," he commented, after taking it upon himself to order for me.

I nodded, admiring his handsomeness. Up close, he looked a bit older than Sebastian. I don't know why I was so obsessed with their ages, but I needed to know what league I was moving in.

"Do you live alone?" he asked as he slid his arm across my back.

"Yes, but it's a very safe area," I said, taking another sip. I was nervous, but I didn't want him to think that he intimidated me.

"Your father told me that Sebastian Moore shared the apartment with you . . ." he said, without taking his eyes off me.

"Well, yes. He moved into the staff room a few months ago," I explained.

"Then why did you say that you live alone?"

I didn't like the way he was looking at me. It made me feel tense and uneasy.

"Why did you ask if you already knew?"

"Touché," he said, lifting his glass to his lips.

The waiter brought the first course, and from there the conversation became more casual, more relaxed. Marcus was a true gentleman at all times, and he seemed to be genuinely interested in the things I said. Even so, I realized I was holding back with him. I hadn't let my true personality shine through, and I knew part of it was because this man was a friend of my father's. Whereas with Sebastian, I was one hundred percent Marfil from the first second I met him. I didn't like the realization that, with Marcus, I was trying to conduct myself the way I knew he expected a woman to behave, but I tried not to get too worked up about it.

By dessert, Marcus was practically glued to my side, his hand caressing the sensitive skin of my neck. "I brought you a gift," he said after we finished sharing a slice of chocolate cake. He opened his jacket and slipped his hand inside to produce a black velvet box.

I opened my eyes in surprise. "You didn't need to get me anything," I said, feeling suddenly nervous.

"I enjoyed choosing it. Take a look," he said. "I noticed you weren't wearing any type of jewelry, just that necklace. A woman like you deserves diamonds and sapphires, Marfil."

I opened the box and sat looking at the necklace, unsure of what to say. My heart was pounding in my chest, and not in a good way. I didn't like jewels. They reminded me of my mother, of the reason for her death.

"It's . . ." I tried to find words. "It's too much. I can't accept it," I said, running my fingers over what I was certain was an authentic diamond.

"Nothing is too much for you," he said, taking it out of the box. "Will you allow me?"

I was going to say no. I was going to explain that I didn't wear jewels, but before I knew it, my ballet slipper necklace had disappeared from my neck, replaced by something that had likely cost thousands of dollars.

When I tilted my head toward him, his eyes shone with some indecipherable emotion.

"I want you to be mine, Marfil Cortés," he said, rubbing my knee a little too forcefully.

"You're going too fast," I replied, stopping his hand as it began to slide up my thigh.

Marcus halted his caress and fixed his eyes on my lips. "When I want something, I simply take it," he said, very sure of himself.

"That's quite an ambitious motto." I unclasped the necklace. "But you won't win me over with flowers and jewelry, Marcus."

I'd feared that he'd be offended, but he simply let out a small laugh. "That only makes me want you more," he admitted.

The waiter came to remove our dessert plates, and I took the opportunity to ask for the check.

This time, Marcus laughed loudly. "You're ready to go so soon?"

"My sister is leaving tomorrow, and I promised her I wouldn't be out too late."

"It's fine," he said, handing his black credit card to the waiter.

Minutes later, as we waited for the elevator, my eyes met Sebastian's, and I felt a stab of pain in my chest. Marcus took me by the hand and didn't let go until we reached his car.

We rode back in silence. It wasn't uncomfortable, but it made me question whether it had been a good date or not.

When we reached my house and he turned off the engine, I knew he would try to kiss me.

"What would you say if I told you I wanted to see you again?" he asked, turning toward me.

I smiled automatically. "I would say you're looking at me right now."

Marcus leaned closer, his hand on the back of my neck and his scent filling my nostrils. A part of me wanted to jump out of the car and rush inside, but another part of me wanted to see if he could make me feel the way my bodyguard did.

He closed the distance and kissed me. Seconds later, his tongue was tangled around mine, probing further than I was comfortable with. I tried to pull away, but he gripped me tightly until he finally released me.

We were both out of breath, and I could tell with a simple glance how excited he was.

"Marfil . . . my new drug of choice."

Our eyes met, and he kissed me again, this time more delicately.

"Go back inside before I kidnap you again myself."

I shot him a questioning glance.

"Bad joke, sorry."

"Thanks for everything," I said, then got out of the car without looking back.

Wilson had disappeared inside, but Sebastian stood waiting

at the front door, holding it open for me. I felt strange, unable to look him directly in the eye, as if I'd betrayed him.

"Good night," Sebastian said, turning around to go to his room.

"Wait," I said eagerly.

He looked back at me blankly, not revealing anything.

"You don't have anything to say, Sebastian?" I asked, hating that everything I'd been hoping to feel with Marcus came to me now in that instant, torturously, just by simply having Sebastian near me, his body mere inches from mine.

"You make a great couple," he said, walking around me to continue on his way.

He hadn't even made eye contact with me. He was angry, I could tell. I would've been, too, but it didn't matter one way or the other. He might be bothered that I went out with someone else, but he still stubbornly refused to touch me because he was my bodyguard, and that made me angrier than anything else. Why didn't he speak up and say I belonged to him? Why couldn't he at least admit that he felt something for me?

I woke up a thousand times in the night, my usual nightmares interspersed with scenes of Marcus suffocating me with a diamond necklace as Sebastian stood watching from a distance, without intervening, without even blinking. I called to him, stretching out an arm to show that I needed him, but he just looked on, impassive, as a crushing sense of loneliness pressed down on me.

## CHAPTER 22

# MARFIL

Friday morning, my sister left to spend the rest of her spring break with her mother and stepfather. It made me sad to say goodbye, knowing I wouldn't see her again until the month we always spent here in the summer.

Marcus Kozel and I went out again that night, not alone but with a group of his closest friends, who he wanted to introduce me to. They were nice and I felt comfortable around them. After an hour of friendly chatting and an intense kiss outside my house, he said goodnight, promising that he'd visit again before the end of my stay to say goodbye.

Things with Sebastian had cooled considerably. I avoided him and he avoided me, a major feat, given that we were forced together all the time. And even though Marcus showed an avid interest in me, Sebastian was the one who occupied my dreams. As much of a catch as Marcus might be, and as happy as my father was with me for the first time in my life, I couldn't keep going out with him while another person consumed my thoughts. It wasn't fair to him.

I would tell Marcus how I felt and suggest we just be friends. That was my plan when he came to see me early Saturday morning.

"One thing's for sure, you can really ride," he said as we galloped together through my father's fields.

"How about a race?" I said, throwing him a glance over my shoulder.

"Last one to the barn owes the other one a kiss!" he shouted, catching me off guard as he galloped past at top speed.

I followed automatically, but he had a head start and beat me there.

Sebastian and Wilson were coming up behind us, but they stayed outside to give us privacy. I didn't need to look at Sebastian to know he had on the same poker face he'd been wearing for days.

"You lost," Marcus said, walking over to help me down from my horse. When my feet touched the ground, Marcus bent over to kiss me, but I reared back with all the subtlety I was capable of. "Aren't you going to give me my prize for winning?" he said, trailing kisses along my neck without my permission.

"Marcus . . ." I started to say gently, looking at the spot where, days prior, Sebastian had behaved quite unprofessionally with me.

"Oh, come on, princess," he said, placing his hands on my hips and pulling me to his body, wanting more. "Give me something to remember you by . . ."

He was a good kisser, but I didn't feel anything. Also, kissing me right there, with Sebastian outside, made me uncomfortable.

His hands roamed my body and cupped my breasts.

I stiffened.

"You're going too fast, Marcus. I don't . . ." I began, but he placed his mouth over mine, shutting me up with a kiss. His tongue felt like it was about to poke my tonsils out, and I was immediately disgusted. I pushed him away, but the more resistance I applied, the harder he forced himself against me.

"You drive me crazy," he said, squeezing my ass so hard it hurt.

"Let me go!" I shouted, angry and scared, upon noticing that my attempts to distance myself from him were completely unsuccessful. I couldn't get him off me, and none of what Sebastian had taught me to defend myself could be put into practice in that moment. "Fuck, Marcus!"

"I deserve something in exchange for following you around all these fucking days, don't you think?" he said, thrusting his erection into my groin and blocking my attempts to kick him.

"Let me go, you fucking—"

He covered my mouth with one of his hands as the other squeezed my left breast, hard.

Never in my life had I been treated that way. Not even Regan had dared to go that far. My heart pounded and fear coursed through my veins. I knew in that instant that it didn't matter what I said. If he could, he'd take me right then and there, against my will.

"Sebastian!" I screamed at the top of my lungs when Marcus moved his hand from my mouth to rip my blouse open.

"Be quiet, fuck!" Marcus growled in a terrifying tone.

I sobbed soundlessly, barely able to breathe. Then I heard a loud click. Marcus stopped. I opened my eyes, trying to see through my tears, when Sebastian came into view. He had his gun aimed at the back of Marcus's neck, who, to my surprise, smiled, as if amused.

"Get away from her," Sebastian ordered in a measured tone.

Marcus laughed and slowly stepped away from me. I rushed to stand behind Sebastian, arranging my clothes back into place.

"Who the hell do you think you are, telling me what to do?" Marcus said as he turned to face Sebastian without a hint of fear in his blue eyes. The gun was now pointed directly at his throat. "You gonna shoot? Huh, Moore?"

Sebastian kept the gun steadily pointed at Marcus, the twitching muscles in his back the only sign of any tension in his body. "Get out of here," Sebastian said.

Marcus laughed again and turned to me, huddled behind Sebastian. "Tell your father I'll be calling in his debt sooner than planned." His eyes blazed into mine, so dark and menacing that I felt true terror. How had he gone from Prince Charming to total psychopath? To make matters worse, I'd been right. Men only wanted me for my body. The rest didn't matter. It had never mattered.

Once Marcus left, riding back to the house, escorted by Wilson, I discouraged Sebastian from doing or saying anything else. I couldn't handle it right then. Sebastian had warned me about Marcus, and I'd ignored him, like always.

"Marfil . . ." he said, approaching me from behind after making sure they had left. "He'll never lay a hand on you again."

I turned around to face him and saw that he was still fuming, his fists tightly clenched at his sides.

"I forgot all my tae kwon do," I said. "You're going to have to teach me better."

Sebastian didn't smile. He simply looked at me and closed the short distance that separated us. When he reached me, he lifted a hand to wipe the tears from my cheeks. "I'll teach you anything you want," he said, stroking my face with his rough thumb. His eyes shifted to the spot where Marcus had ripped my shirt open, exposing my pink bra. Without a word, he took off his jacket and held it open so that I could put it on. He stepped in front of me and slowly zipped it up, without taking his eyes off me. "If he touches you again, I'll kill him." He said it as if it were an undeniable fact.

I shivered, fully realizing for the first time that my life had changed. I hadn't wanted to admit it, but Sebastian had been trying to warn me all along. Ever since the kidnapping, from one day to the next, my life had ceased to be the normal drama-free life of any ordinary college girl, to one fraught with threats and dangers.

"I want to leave this place," I said, wrapping my arms around myself. "I want to go back to New York and forget about all of this."

Sebastian stood silently observing me. I took a step toward him and, without asking for his permission, I rested my cheek against his chest, still hugging myself. When he wrapped his arms around me, squeezing me tightly, I knew that no matter what happened, Sebastian Moore would protect me; he would never let anything bad happen to me. He was the only man I could trust. He was the only man I'd ever desired . . . would ever desire. And that certainty, I would later learn, meant absolutely everything.

---

Sebastian said that he would speak to my father about Marcus. I had no idea what Marcus had been referring to when he said that he'd be calling in the debt sooner than expected. I also didn't understand how he could've dared force himself on me, knowing that his father and mine were friends. But the thing that surprised me the least was the fact that my father didn't say a word about it to me. I was very upset, and I wanted to leave as soon as possible, so I asked Lupe to change my flight to leave earlier than I'd planned.

Spring break had ended horribly, and I simply needed to be home, back to my routines, to try to forget about everything that had happened and feel like I had control of the things around me.

The only true benefit of that short vacation was that I was now sure of three things. First, that my life was still truly at risk; second, that my father hid an unimaginable list of secrets; and third, that I was beginning to fall hopelessly in love with my bodyguard.

## CHAPTER 23

# MARFIL

Sebastian traveled beside me in first class on the flight back to New York. Without my asking, he held my hand and didn't let go. I was nervous, apart from everything that had happened since my kidnapping, I also had no idea where things stood between us. Living with him had already been intense before. Now, after everything we'd gone through that last week, and knowing for sure that I was starting to have strong feelings for him, I had no idea how to behave in his presence.

A full-fledged war was raging inside my head. My life, as I'd known it, had changed. My list of priorities now included the man seated beside me with his eyes closed, gently rubbing his thumb across my palm. I wanted to bury my head in his chest, to sleep curled up against him, to let him run his hands through my hair until I drifted off, just as he'd done on the flight to Baton Rouge, but something inside me had changed, too. Nothing was the same as it had been before the trip, not only because I'd experienced an attempted murder firsthand, but because of everything Sebastian had done and said during our time there. All that had hardened me, had made me realize that, if I didn't protect my heart, I might experience the biggest heartbreak of my life.

But whenever I closed my eyes, I still felt his body close to mine, his mouth on mine, his hands on me, and my heart pounded at the memory of that exquisite pleasure.

We barely talked on the flight back to New York, and when

we reached the airport parking lot without a word, I knew that Sebastian was going to behave as if nothing had happened, that his attitude would remain the same as always. Instead of making me angry, it made me sad. I wasn't going to keep putting up with his isolation, lack of communication, and distance; I couldn't do it anymore.

In the car, I rested my head on my hands and looked out the window at the imposing buildings that rose up in the distance. It didn't matter how long I'd lived there; I always felt like a tiny ant in that city.

It took me longer than it should have to realize we weren't heading to my apartment. Instead, we were crossing the Brooklyn Bridge in the opposite direction. I peeled my eyes from the road and turned to Sebastian as he parked outside a red-brick restaurant near the East River. Despite often rubbing elbows with snobby, prejudiced people who disliked Brooklyn, Tami and I loved it. Our favorite neighborhood was Bushwick. We often walked its lively streets, popping into galleries to see works by unknown but highly talented artists.

"What are we doing here?"

Sebastian cut the engine and turned to me. "We're here to eat the best hamburger in New York."

That was the last thing I expected to come out of his mouth. Before I could say anything, he got out of the car and started walking to the entrance.

I caught up to him just as he stopped to open the door for me. "Why are you bringing me here?" I asked before going inside.

"Why do you think?"

I blinked, confused. "Because you want to fatten me up so you can eat me?" I answered, noticing that my mood had lifted and a smile tugged at my lips.

Sebastian looked at me for a few brief seconds. "I brought you here because I needed to see you smile."

My lips froze, and I felt a thousand butterflies begin to dance inside me. He didn't wait for me to answer; he just gestured with his head for me to enter the restaurant, and I did.

The place was casual, almost a fast-food joint, but it was not without its charm.

We sat at a table in the corner, and I said I'd have whatever Sebastian was having. When they brought the food, however, I quickly regretted my decision.

"Did being nice for the first time in your life impair your ability to count?" I said, unable to fathom the quantity of food the waiter had placed before us. "There's only two of us."

"I eat for four," he replied, meticulously positioning the plates in front of us.

It was funny to me how obsessive he could be sometimes, as I'd observed in our time living together. It wasn't that he was a clean freak, but with certain things like food, he insisted that everything always be perfect.

I picked up a fry and realized something was missing. I stood up, intending to go to the counter, but Sebastian grabbed me by the wrist and narrowed his eyes at me.

"Where are you going?"

"To get something. I'll be right back," I said calmly.

Sebastian hesitated for a few seconds, scanned the restaurant, and then let me go. That fleeting touch reignited my desire for him, but I did everything possible to keep it under control.

When I got back to the table, he was already on his second burger. He looked displeased as I placed a bowl of vanilla ice cream between us.

"You haven't even tried the hamburger and you're already going straight for dessert?"

I sat back down, and without taking my eyes off him, picked up a fry and dipped it in the ice cream.

Sebastian simply frowned.

"Mmm . . . delish," I said, grinning from ear to ear, picking up another fry and repeating the process.

"Just when I thought you couldn't be any stranger . . ."

"Try it," I said, picking up a fry, smearing it with ice cream, and holding it up to his lips.

"No, thanks," he replied, ignoring my outstretched arm.

"Come on," I said, watching as the ice cream began to drip down my finger.

Sebastian looked at me, then at my hand, and I couldn't help but notice his eyes had an unfamiliar gleam to them. Without looking away, he leaned in and brushed his lips against my fingers before he took the bite, the tip of his tongue tickling my skin as he licked away the drip of ice cream.

I froze. His dark eyes blazed as he released me and sat back in his seat. My breathing was ragged and my heart beat wildly in my chest. Unlike Sebastian, who picked up his plastic cup and took a sip as if nothing had happened.

"Did you like it?" I asked, pretending that what he'd just done hadn't affected me in the slightest, but cursing silently as my trembling voice betrayed me.

Sebastian's eyes sparkled. "Very much."

Was he flirting with me?

"Eat up," he said, back to doling out orders.

I shook my head and smiled as I bit into the hamburger. "Wow, it's delicious!" I exclaimed, licking my lips.

Sebastian nodded.

As we continued eating, I thought about how I could broach the subject of what was going on between us without starting another fight. I was blabbing away senselessly, trying to get up the nerve to ask him, when the restaurant doorbell jingled, and his eyes shifted away from me, all the fun he'd been trying to fake fading instantly.

I followed his gaze slowly, and saw a young woman entering

the establishment, looking at the menu. Then she noticed us, paused, and immediately made a beeline for our table, as if we had summoned her over. She was livid, and Sebastian seemed to feel similarly enraged by the sight of her. Before I had the chance to ask who she was, Sebastian stood up and intercepted her in the middle of the restaurant.

"What the fuck do you think you're doing here?" she spat.

"Please, Samara . . ." I heard Sebastian say in a low voice so that I wouldn't hear.

I turned back around so as not to seem nosy, but I continued watching them through the mirror on the opposite wall.

Who the hell was this woman?

Sebastian said something to her that I again couldn't hear, as she shook her head and looked toward me with revulsion. I was so confused by her reaction that I didn't realize Sebastian was struggling to keep her from coming over to where I was seated.

She reared back, her blond hair swishing around her thin frame.

"Fuck, Samara," Sebastian said as she stopped before me and looked me directly in the eye.

"Stay away from him." She threw Sebastian a look of abhorrence, then directed her attention back to me. "He's dangerous. Trust me, you should stay away from him," she repeated. "When you least expect it, he'll ruin your life and leave you before you even know what hit you."

"That's enough!" Sebastian broke in, holding her firmly by the wrist, clearly losing his cool.

I jumped out of my seat.

Samara's eyes filled with tears, but she released herself from his grip.

"You've been warned," she said, looking at me and then back

at Sebastian. "And you . . . go to hell," she said to him. Then she left without another word.

Sebastian stood eyeing the door, as if afraid she might reappear. Then, all of a sudden, he seemed to remember that I was still there, and he returned to the table.

I stared at him, trying to figure out what the hell had just happened and why this woman had bothered him so much. Was she his girlfriend? His ex?

I shuddered at the thought.

"Who was that, Sebastian?" I asked, seeing that he wasn't planning to say anything.

He didn't immediately answer, seeming to only register my question after a moment, as if his mind was racing a thousand miles a minute.

"No one," he said dryly. "Are you done?"

I looked at my tray, still completely full, and his, half the food untouched.

"Let's go," he added without waiting for me to respond.

I didn't say a word, my intuition telling me that it was better to keep quiet for now, although I wasn't going to allow him to pretend like nothing had happened.

Sebastian got in the car and sped onto the highway. I stretched out a hand to lower the volume, and he lashed out at me, livid. "Fucking leave it!"

"Don't talk to me like that," I answered, shutting the radio off. Silence flooded the car, and I turned to face him. "Who the hell was that woman?"

Sebastian didn't answer, he just stepped harder on the accelerator.

I looked out the window, alarmed by how fast he was going. "Sebastian, slow down."

He didn't even acknowledge me. The man at the wheel was

not the Sebastian I knew; he had a completely deranged look in his eyes, as if that woman had awoken that dark, frightening man inside him.

"Sebastian, slow down, fuck!" I shouted as the speed approached suicidal.

It was as if he couldn't hear me, as if he weren't able to hear anything beyond whatever was playing inside his head. I punched his arm, shook him, but his eyes didn't stray from the road for an instant, even though it was clear he wasn't seeing anything in front of him.

I started to panic. The scene was too similar to the accident a few days prior, reviving the same sensations, but the person now putting me at risk was the last person I would've believed could harm me.

I screamed hysterically as a large truck passed just inches from us, forcing Sebastian to swerve, barely avoiding collision. I buried my face in my hands, no longer able to watch what was happening.

Samara's words replayed in my mind: *He's dangerous . . . stay away from him.*

I noticed that the car was slowing to a stop. I lowered my hands from my face, and without even stopping to look at him, threw open the door and jumped out of the car.

"Marfil!"

I stared him down, shooting daggers from my eyes. He walked over and tried to touch me, but I pushed him away.

"What the fuck is wrong with you? Have you lost your mind?"

Sebastian looked sad and full of regret, guilt painted all over his handsome face. "I'm sorry," he said, trying to pull me toward him, but I reared back.

Sebastian had exited the highway, where the cars zoomed past in the distance, the Manhattan skyline visible on the horizon. Where the hell were we? Had we gone that far from the city?

"Don't get any closer to me, Sebastian," I said when he tried once again to close the distance between us.

He stopped and looked at me, sorrowful, his perfect face lined with concern. "I don't know what came over me . . . I'm sorry, truly," he said, rubbing a hand over his face.

"Who is Samara?" I asked in a voice cold as snow.

Sebastian lowered his hand and looked at me, clenching his jaw. "No one you need to concern yourself with."

I stared at him in disbelief. "She just told me that you're going to ruin my life. Who the hell is she to you?" Seeing him with her had upset me, had affected me more than I could understand, and I needed the truth.

"Marfil . . . please," he practically begged. What did he expect? For me not to ask about her? "You should've never met her. You should've never seen that."

"I just want to know who she is—if she's some nutjob who doesn't even know you, if she's your little sister or your fucking lover, Sebastian. I just want to know who she is."

He stood in stubborn silence for a moment, until he finally chose to answer me. "I'll tell you. Then we'll get back in the car and go home. After that, we won't talk about it again. Ever."

What?

"Promise me." He seemed totally serious.

"Okay," I agreed, although inside, I knew it was a promise I couldn't keep.

Sebastian took a deep breath and then looked me in the eye. "She's my ex-wife."

## CHAPTER 24

# MARFIL

Sebastian had been married?

You can imagine my reaction. I took a few seconds to process, then I walked past him and got back in the car. I felt angry and betrayed, even though Sebastian and I were nothing. In my heart, however, Sebastian was all mine, it was that simple. I couldn't conceive the fact he'd ever belonged to someone else, that he had once vowed to spend the rest of his life with a woman whom he thought was the love of his life. Although, given her attitude toward him, maybe she'd been the one to end things; maybe it was Sebastian who was still hopelessly in love with that pretty blonde.

This drama was honestly the last thing I needed right now. I tried to rewind back to that moment of closeness we'd had at the hamburger place, his lips brushing my skin, his eyes promising something more. But it was all eclipsed by a fact I'd been trying to deny since the moment I met him: Sebastian, whether I liked it or not, had a personal life outside of his job protecting me.

He seemed relieved that I was making good on my promise not to ask any questions. For the first time since we'd met, I did what he wanted me to do: I kept quiet. I only broke the silence as we entered the city, and I realized that, after everything that had happened—at my father's house, with him, with Marcus, with his ex-wife—I didn't want to be around him. I needed space.

"Take me to Liam's, please," I said without looking at him.

He turned to stare at me for a few seconds before fixing his gaze back on the road. "I don't think that's a good idea."

"I have a key to his apartment, just like he had a key to mine before you took it away from him. He's my best friend, and I need to see him. I need . . . I'm sorry, but right now I need some space from you." Danger be damned.

"Marfil, you can't be aw—"

"I won't leave his apartment," I interrupted.

Sebastian pressed his fingers to his temples and threw me a defiant, calculated glance. His eyes rested for a few seconds longer than necessary on me, and then, sighing, he looked back at the cars ahead of him. "Give me the address."

I told him, then immediately sent Liam a message letting him know I was on my way to his apartment and that I needed to spend the night. I had no idea whether he was alone, or if he was already asleep for the night, but I knew he would welcome me with open arms, and that was all I needed.

When we got to Liam's building in the Financial District, a few blocks from Wall Street, Sebastian got out of the car and came to meet me as I stepped onto the curb. I looked at him and once again heard the woman's words of warning echoing through my head. *He's dangerous.* Was he? It was clear that he could be, but not with me, even after tonight . . . Sebastian was the one who protected me from the bad guys . . . wasn't he?

I was about to cross the street, but he held my arm. For a second, I thought he might open up to me, explain what had happened with his ex and that she was nothing to him now, confess that, against all his attempts to deny it, he felt the same way about me that I did about him.

But nothing like that came out of his mouth when he opened it to speak. "Don't do anything stupid."

I blinked. "Something stupid like falling for you?" I said without thinking.

"Marfil—"

"Don't worry," I cut him off, ready to walk away, wishing I could erase his expression of panic from my mind. "You've made it abundantly clear you're only interested in one thing from me."

I expected him to stop me, to tug again at my arm and tell me I was wrong. But he didn't do either of those things, and I felt myself go pale.

I ran across the street to my best friend's building and rushed through the front door. When I got into the elevator, I was starting to hyperventilate, and I used the few seconds it took to reach Liam's floor to steady my breathing.

Liam's apartment was dark upon entering, completely empty. I wandered down the long hall to his bedroom, then took off my clothes, grabbed one of his T-shirts, and got into his bed. It took me a while to get to sleep, but exhaustion eventually won out.

My nightmares weren't the usual ones. They didn't have anything to do with my mother or her death, but everything to do with a Sebastian who abandoned me, a Sebastian who turned his back on me. No matter how many times I called out to him, he just kept walking away. He walked and walked toward a tall, beautiful blond woman, took her hand, and led her into the darkness.

---

I awoke to the dazzling light of a new day. It took me a second to remember where I was. In Louisiana? My apartment? Where? Then Liam stepped into the room, shirtless in pajama bottoms, with a steaming cup of coffee in his hand.

"I have to admit, I love seeing you between my sheets," he

said, walking over to the bed, handsome as always, then sitting down next to me.

Why couldn't I just fall in love with him? He was perfect for me, and I adored him.

"Why are you looking at me like that?" he asked, leaning against the headboard and staring at me with curiosity.

"Like what?"

"Like you're thinking impossible thoughts."

I couldn't help but smile. He knew me so well.

"Why are you in my bed?"

I pulled the covers up to my chin. "I wanted a bit of normalcy."

"In your life?" Liam laughed. "Babe, that word has never come close to defining you."

I sighed.

"Can I ask you why your bodyguard is parked across the street, sleeping in his car in the freezing cold?"

I sat up quickly. "What are you talking about?"

"I saw him early this morning when I came home from the party."

I stood up and went to the window, where I could see the entrance to the building. It was true—Sebastian's car was still parked there, with him inside, I supposed. I was instantly flooded with guilt and quickly searched for my clothes to get dressed.

"Where are you going?"

"Home. I had no idea . . . It doesn't matter. You're right, my life is shit."

Liam laughed loudly. "I said that?"

I ignored him, angrily hopping into my pants to pull them up, then buttoning them.

"Hey," he said, standing up and stepping toward me, "I can go down there and tell that asshole to get lost. You could skip class, we could order in some pizza and watch a movie. You decide."

I shook my head. "Another time. Right now, I'd better go home and face the consequences of . . ." I fell silent, realizing that I'd said too much.

"Consequences of what?"

I avoided his blue eyes, fixing my gaze on the window.

Liam sighed deeply. My silence must've given me away.

"Marfil . . . are you seriously in love with that idiot?"

Was it that obvious?

I picked up my bag. "Don't make a big deal over it, okay?" I answered, annoyed.

Liam shook his head. "I always knew this moment would come."

I spun around to look at him. "What?"

"I knew you would end up falling in love with the first guy who rejected you, a guy your father would never approve of, and that you'd fall hard. I knew it as soon as I saw the way you look at him."

"And how do I look at him, if you don't mind telling me?"

Liam leaned against the dresser and crossed his arms. "You look at him like you expect him to rescue you from the life you were born into."

I stood in silence, processing what he'd just said to me.

"I don't need anyone to save me. When are you guys going to get that through your heads?"

I left without waiting for his response.

When I stepped out of the building, Sebastian opened the car door and got out.

"What the hell are you doing here?" I said.

He didn't bat an eye. "It concerns me that you haven't realized by now that I'm not going to leave you unprotected."

He looked annoyingly handsome, even in his disheveled state

and the fact that he'd surely slept like shit. I wanted, I *needed*, to touch him, feeling that longing more intensely than ever.

"You said you would wait for me at my apartment."

"I said no such thing."

His self-control was unnerving as fuck.

I huffed angrily and got in the car.

Sebastian got in after me and gave me a look that made me think he had something more to say, but then he seemed to think better of it, starting the car.

When we got back to the Upper East Side and entered my building, there was a giant bouquet of flowers on the front desk beside Norman, who looked at Sebastian somberly.

"Miss Marfil, these flowers arrived for you," he said, then looked to Sebastian. "Mr. Moore, I haven't touched them or brought them up, just as you instructed me to do with anything that comes for Miss Cortés."

"Very good, Norman. Thank you," he said as I moved over to the flowers and, with shaky hands, picked up the card inside.

*I'm sorry. Please forgive me. Have dinner with me.*

*Marcus*

Before I could tear the card into a thousand pieces, Sebastian pulled it out of my hand and read it without my permission. He didn't say anything, just stuck the note in his pocket.

"Get rid of them, Norman," he said, then followed me into the elevator.

He stood behind me, so I couldn't see his expression, but I supposed it was as dark as mine. That asshole Marcus had just ruined my day, and it was only ten o'clock in the morning.

My intention had been to lock myself in my room as soon as we entered the apartment, but Sebastian stopped me with his deep, baritone voice. "Marfil, wait a second."

I turned slowly toward him.

"It was unfair to make you promise not to ask any questions about Samara," he said, taking me totally by surprise, "but there are just things in my past that I prefer to leave there. Do you understand?"

The way in which he said her name, with such familiarity, such intimacy, left me unsettled.

"Do you love her?"

"Yes."

My heart stopped beating.

"But I'm not *in love* with her."

That phrase, that clarification on his part, could mean so many things.

"What happened between the two of you?"

Sebastian stepped closer. "I can't tell you," he said, looking at me sadly, as if he wished to tell me so many things but couldn't.

I pressed my lips together. We were back to keeping secrets.

"But I want to make one thing clear," he said, lifting a hand to my cheek. "I will never hurt you or place you in danger. You know that, right?"

I nodded. He seemed to want to say more, but something kept him from going on. I could see it in his face, and I was dying to know why. His fingers slid down to the back of my neck, giving me chills, and for a second, the only sound was the sighing of our breath and the beating of our hearts.

"I fucked up, Marfil . . . Everything I promised myself I wouldn't do . . ." His mouth hovered dangerously close to mine as he said this. "I swore I would stay out of it. I swore . . ."

"What are you talking about?"

He rested his forehead against mine and closed his eyes as if what he was saying pained his soul. "How am I going to continue with this if . . . ?"

"Sebastian . . ."

He opened his eyes when he heard me say his name.

"What are you talking about?" I asked again, alarmed to see him so upset.

"Nothing. Don't listen to me." He stepped away, collecting himself.

I studied him for a few seconds, trying to decide whether I should push the issue, given how upset he was. "I'm scared," I confessed, and his attention returned to me. "It's all just too much sometimes. I feel like I'm going to explode, but just knowing you're here makes all the fear go away."

My words seemed to have had a strange effect on him.

"You shouldn't feel that way," he said in such a low voice that I could've misheard him.

"Something tells me everything that's happened in this past month is only a foreshadowing of something even more horrible about to happen."

His eyes gleamed, and I could tell he was conflicted as he once again cradled my face in his hands. "Listen to me, Marfil," he said, looking me straight in the eyes. "You shouldn't trust anyone, not even me."

Of all the things he could've said, that was the last thing I expected to hear come out of his mouth.

"You can't tell me that you'd never hurt me and then say that you can't be trusted."

Sebastian clenched his jaw, and I saw the veins in his neck stand out.

"They're two different things," he said very somberly, barely moving his lips.

"Are you dangerous?" I asked, remembering Samara's words.

He closed his eyes for a second before answering. "Not to you . . . I would never hurt you."

His words were a comfort to me. I smiled, as I noticed that

his hands were still on my face and his mouth was only inches from mine. "Did you really spend the night in the car?"

He seemed to relax, realizing that I didn't want to keep listening to him talk about secrets, trust, and bitter ex-wives.

"Ask my back." He lowered his hands and stretched to his full height.

"Does it hurt?" I asked.

"What do you think?"

"I think I could give you the best massage of your life and leave you feeling like new."

"Oh yeah?" he answered, playing along with me for the first time since we'd met.

"I can show you, whenever you want, wherever you want."

"I think I may have tempted fate too much already."

My eyes moved involuntarily to the sling he still wore on his left arm from where he'd been injured in the car accident.

"Are you going to be able to do your job with only one arm?" I asked, more out of curiosity than anything else.

Sebastian looked at the sling and frowned. "Haven't I been doing it? Don't worry, this is coming off soon—I'll be like new again in a few days . . . But I can call in someone to help me out if you think that . . ." he began, very serious.

"No! I don't want anyone else in here."

Sebastian gave me a half smile in response to my panic at the notion of another version of him lurking around my apartment. "Are you hungry?"

I nodded, the anxiety I'd been feeling since the night before slowly beginning to fade.

"Well, then help me out."

I followed him into the kitchen, where we washed our hands before continuing on with anything else.

"You can start by sifting the flour," he said as he opened the fridge.

"Sorry, what?" I asked, blinking several times.

Sebastian rolled his eyes and took a carton of eggs from the fridge. "You have to sift the flour before you mix the other ingredients into the pancake batter. Come here, I'll pour it in while you just tap the sieve so it falls through."

I ambled over to him, feeling totally clueless. "It was more fun when you did all the cooking by yourself," I said, looking at his injured arm and frowning. "Are you sure you really hurt yourself that bad? I swear I've seen you move those fingers a few times."

"I'm not paralyzed; it's just a sprain. Start sifting, will you?"

I followed his instructions, and together we made some fairly decent pancakes.

"Wait, I want to make one shaped like the United States!" I said after a few batches.

"Marfil, you tried four times to make one that looked like Mickey Mouse. Do you really think you'll be able to make one shaped like an entire country?" He'd clearly lost his patience with me.

"Give me that," I said, yanking the pan out of his hand at the same time as he was pouring the last batch in. I couldn't help but laugh at the two of us covered in flour, egg, and batter. Whenever he cooked on his own, he didn't get so much as a hair out of place.

"What's so funny?"

My laughter almost turned into a howl, smudging my face with batter as I covered my mouth.

Sebastian stared at me, and finally, an amused grin spread across his face.

"From now on, this is my territory. I don't want you anywhere near this stove, do you hear me?"

"No way! I've just discovered my deep love for cooking."

Sebastian shook his head, picked up the frying pan, which

was still on the hot burner, and flipped the last pancake in the air. Then he strategically balanced two plates on his right arm and placed one in front of me on the table. When I looked down at my plate, I felt a warmth flood through my body. He'd made the last pancake in the shape of an elephant, tusks and all, and it had come out perfectly.

I looked at him out of the corner of my eye, but he just ate his pancakes as if he hadn't just made the sweetest gesture.

I smiled silently and started to eat my breakfast.

CHAPTER 25

# SEBASTIAN

The storm was drawing near, literally. I read the forecast and saw that a blizzard was moving in as I waited for Marfil to finish getting ready to go to class. It had been a week since we'd returned from that disaster of a spring break. So much had happened at Alejandro Cortés's house. Even though it didn't surprise me, having run into an asshole like Marcus Kozel, I never could've imagined being intimate with Marfil in that abandoned barn.

I tried every day to act like it had never occurred, employing all my willpower to keep from falling for her, to keep my hands and my body as far away from her as possible. I'd even kept my cool as that moron Kozel continued accosting her daily with flowers, trying not to let my old self rear his ugly head once again. I had already let Marfil see much more of me than I'd ever wanted to show her. The encounter with Samara was the worst thing that could've happened, and I'd totally lost it, furious with myself for being so stupid.

Marfil came into the kitchen and smiled, radiant as ever in a miniskirt, leggings, and a wide sweatshirt that left her shoulder exposed when she moved. I couldn't help but feel that, despite our situation, Marfil Cortés belonged to me and no one else. One look at her, and a strong urge to kiss her came over me. The fact that I couldn't touch her left me in a foul mood, and I often took it out on her.

"It's thirty-seven degrees outside," I said, looking sullenly at her outfit.

"Now you're a weatherman?" she replied, sharp as always, but with a smile on her face. She didn't wear much makeup, although her lips always had a layer of gloss that made it look like she'd just licked them.

"I'm the man who's not leaving here until you put on a coat," I answered, taking my cell phone out of my pocket and looking at the screen in order to keep from staring at her.

"Sometimes you're even worse than my father," she said, turning around and walking back to her pigsty of a bedroom.

*If you only knew . . .* I thought to myself.

She stepped out a minute later, wearing a pink wool hat, matching scarf, and a leather jacket.

"Happy?"

I didn't answer. I simply walked to the door and held it open for her. As she passed, she paused for a second beside me.

"Thanks for your concern over my well-being," she said, standing on her tiptoes and giving me a kiss on the cheek.

I felt my body tense at that innocent contact. That was another thing—Marfil now took certain liberties, leaving me constantly anxious. I was incapable of rejecting those seemingly harmless gestures, even though we both knew that she was playing games with me. But a brief touch, a caress, a kiss on the cheek was nothing, right?

I grunted in response, and as always, she continued on as if nothing had happened.

In the car, I turned on the heat and the radio to listen to the news. Apparently, I wasn't the only one worried about the imminent snowstorm. Temperatures had dropped dramatically in just a few hours, something unusual considering it was almost April.

"This weather is crazy," Marfil said with a worried expression. She took out her cell phone and began typing rapidly. I would've liked to ask her who she was texting, but I kept quiet and continued driving.

We reached campus, and it came time to separate since she still didn't want anyone to think there was anything between us. I observed her from a distance, sitting at the back of her classes, admiring her wit, her constant smile, the way she was so feminine yet so tough at the same time.

She'd been arguing with her professor for the past ten minutes about how to proceed during an economic crisis, and how the mistakes made during the last recession could've been easily avoided.

"The problem is greed, and the fact that the country's largest banking institutions took on too much risk without a big enough financial cushion to support them."

The professor, a former banker himself, looked fed up with her. Luckily, it was time for class to end, and he dismissed us before I had to intervene to defend her. Marfil gathered her books, put them in her Prada bag, and waved goodbye at the classmate seated next to her. As I leaned against the wall outside the classroom, waiting for her, a small group of female students stood glancing at me and whispering. Over half of them had already introduced themselves to me, their intentions obvious, but my monosyllabic responses were enough to keep them from trying again.

Marfil exited the classroom, and just as she'd been doing every day for the past week, she stopped to talk to me as if we were friends.

"How'd you like the lecture today?"

"Very educational," I said, looking ahead, checking every doorway and dark corner, eyeing anyone who looked suspicious.

"Professor Benet is a tight-ass, like you, but deep down he knows I'm right."

I nodded, and we continued walking toward the exit, when a group of girls intercepted us.

"We've talked to everyone in all our classes, and you'd be surprised how many people want to participate," one of them said.

"Excellent!" Marfil replied, tucking a strand of hair behind her ear. "The more people, the better. Did you tell them where we're going to meet?"

"We're going to meet on the stairs of the Met and start from there."

"Great." She nodded. "Don't forget to dress warmly. If my personal weatherman is correct," she said, glancing at me, "it's going to get colder."

I frowned as I listened to the conversation.

"What is it you're planning to do, exactly?" I asked, ignoring the other girls.

"We're going to pass out food and blankets. With the snowstorm coming, a lot of unhoused people are going to have a really awful time. Not everyone will have shelter . . ." she began as my frown deepened. "We're trying to get as many people as possible to bring donations."

This was unexpected. Even if Marfil Cortés had good intentions, however, I wasn't going to let her walk around in those weather conditions. But I didn't say anything, because I knew it would cause a conflict, and I didn't want to make a scene on campus. As soon as we got in the car, I told her what I thought about it: "You're not going."

"Of course I'm going."

"I said no."

"Sebastian!" she argued, slapping her legs, frustrated. "I'm the one who organized it, I have to go. I have experience with this kind of thing through ST. It's what I do, direct action and fundraising, like I was trying to do the morning my car was tampered with. I wasn't able to help out there, but I can here."

"You just gave the reason why you're not: You were trying to help out when you were almost killed. We're not going to repeat the experience," I answered, remaining calm.

"Don't you get tired of always having the same fight?" she said, looking at the road and then going on without waiting for my response. "I tell you I'm going to do something, you give some single-syllable negative response, I insist, you say no again, I end up sneaking out the window, and—"

"You're not going," I cut her off.

I felt her eyes on me.

"Can we at least try to come to a compromise?" she asked, exasperated.

I turned brusquely onto our street. "No."

"We can go just for the first round. It'll still be daylight. Tons of people are coming out; it's basically going to be like a school field trip. You'll be with me the whole time, and we can both help restore a bit of humanity to society." She sighed. "I truly meant what I said the other night—I feel safe with you around, no fear. So, please?"

I parked the car, cut the engine, and faced her. "One hour," I said, angry with myself for being incapable of saying no to her, and angry with her because she always insisted on getting her way. "One hour, Marfil, do you hear me? I don't want you out of the house tonight in that storm. All hell's going to break loose."

She smiled sweetly. "That's exactly why it's so important to lend a hand, despite the risk."

---

Two hours later, we were at Tami's art studio surrounded by tons of people coming and going, dropping off blankets, food, gloves, umbrellas, and other warm clothing to be handed out that afternoon. Marfil hadn't stopped moving since we arrived. The space was large and mostly empty, except for the artwork that lined the walls and the cans of paint stacked up in the corners. Tami had spent the last half hour trying to organize everyone into groups while Marfil mapped the areas they were going to cover.

I moved the boxes people had left, never losing sight of the main entrance or anyone present. A little while later, that asshole Liam arrived. He came in emptyhanded, and after pulling Marfil aside to tell her something, she jumped into his arms, overjoyed. He picked her up, spun her around, and then set her back down.

My entire body tensed, and an irrational rage forced me to look away, trying to control the jealousy I felt every time I saw her with him. My eyes then fell on Tami, who was staring at Liam and Marfil from the other end of the room. Based on her expression, I could tell she was also displeased by that public display of affection.

When she noticed that I was observing her, she immediately returned to folding blankets.

I'd had to look into Tami's past—just like I'd checked up on everyone who was part of Marfil's life—and I had to admit that reading the report about her had made me feel sorry for that angelic girl, seemingly so fragile.

She was now struggling with a box on a high shelf, and I decided to go over to give her a hand.

"Thanks, Sebastian," she said, her cheeks red from the exertion. She was very small, no more than five feet tall, and I hated knowing everything she'd been through.

Was Marfil aware of her best friend's past?

"It's nothing. What else can I do to help you?" I asked.

"Yes, Tami, what else can we help you with?" came Liam's voice from behind me.

Tami shot daggers at him. "I don't want your help. I didn't even give you permission to come here."

"When you say *here*, are you referring to this shithole you call a studio?"

Tami remained silent, and Liam and I watched, surprised, as her eyes filled with tears.

"Hey, asshole! Leave her alone," I said, stepping in front of her.

Liam looked me up and down. "Look who it is. The little toy soldier."

I didn't let that moron ruffle my feathers. Too many years of training to lose it all over some idiot.

"Liam, can't you see you're not wanted here?" Tami said, stepping out from behind me.

Liam glared at her, the hurt visible in his eyes. Tami's words had affected him more than he'd ever admit. Still, he managed to compose himself before speaking. "Marfil told me we were meeting here to help pass out donations . . ."

"What's going on over here?" Marfil said, walking up to the commotion. Her smile froze as she noticed how tense the three of us were, her gaze shifting from Tami to me and then Liam.

"Your little friend wants me to leave."

"Tami!" Marfil exclaimed angrily. "Liam just brought in ten boxes of provisions, and he got a big group of his coworkers together to help pass them out . . ."

Tami looked like she wanted the ground to swallow her whole. But I'd heard the way Liam had antagonized her. Tami hadn't known about the boxes, and she had every right in the world not to allow certain behaviors.

"If you want, I can tell them to take the donations away and go home," Liam said, staring at Tami.

He liked her. I could tell by the way he looked at her. But she'd never fall for someone like him.

"No!" Tami practically shouted, fidgeting nervously.

Liam gave an evil grin.

"Enough, Liam," Marfil said, finally intervening. "We're thankful for your help—go tell your friends they can come up."

Liam nodded, his eyes still on Tami. "You're not going to thank me?"

I wanted to punch him in the face.

"Those in need will thank you, don't worry," Tami said.

Liam smiled as if what she'd just said was somehow funny. "People like you, Tami? Don't worry, I've got what you need."

"Get the fuck out of here," I said, as I stepped in front of him, unable to stand by any longer.

He moved to push me, and I acted so quickly that, when his face hit the floor, Marfil and Tami were the only ones who noticed. No one else was even aware of what was happening in that corner of the room.

"Leave her alone, did you hear me?" I said very quietly in his ear. "You'll never get with her, not in a million years."

Liam squirmed uncomfortably, and I released him.

"This bodyguard gig is working out great for you, isn't it?" He got quickly to his feet, apparently unaware that I could kill him using just one hand. "Watch out, Mar. It looks like there's something going on between your best friend and your little soldier."

Marfil looked at us, and I cursed between my teeth when I saw a shadow of jealousy cross her face.

How the hell had I gotten myself mixed up in this childish drama?

Liam walked away, and Marfil shot us a look that I didn't know how to interpret, before turning around to continue organizing boxes.

“Thanks for defending me,” said a small voice behind me.

“You don’t have to thank me for anything,” I said, facing her and observing the way her blue eyes followed Liam across the room. “Tami, he likes you. You know that, right?”

Tami blinked and looked back at me. Then her cheeks went bright red, and she shook her head. “He doesn’t like me . . . He hates me. He can’t stand me . . . And I can’t stand him,” she stammered.

I nodded and went back to lifting boxes. My part in that drama was over.

When it finally came time to make our rounds—I had chosen our route myself to make sure it was as safe and as short as possible—I was amused to see that Marfil was still so angry and jealous over something so stupid. I couldn’t believe she really thought I liked her best friend.

We went out in a group of ten people, and when we got to our designated area, we divided into pairs to walk around and pass out coats and hot food to anyone who needed it.

The cold wind was so intense that it seemed to blow straight through the coat I had on. Marfil walked beside me, her red jacket and pink hat like a target, catching the attention of anyone passing by. I let her take the lead, watching as she talked to the people on the street, brightening their days with her smile, offering not only blankets and food, but her kindness, her warmth. Who wouldn’t be awestruck by her?

“Ma’am . . .” she said to an older woman who seemed to have already hunkered down for the storm, huddled onto a section of cardboard. When she opened her eyes and looked at us, I saw something in her expression . . . Hope?

My heart sank.

“We have blankets and some delicious hot soup a good

friend of mine made," she said to the woman, leaning over and offering her a hot thermos.

"Oh, child," the woman said, accepting the blanket as if we were offering her a lifeline.

"Take some more warm stuff," Marfil said, picking up another blanket, a hat, a scarf, and some thermal socks. "Here, it's going to get even colder. This will help you get through the night."

The woman accepted the items and slowly began to put on all the clothing Marfil had offered her.

"Are you warmer now?" Marfil's voice shook, and I had the urge to comfort her.

"Yes, thank you so much, child. Thank you so much," the woman said, taking Marfil's gloved hands and smiling gratefully.

Marfil nodded and stood up. We said goodbye to the woman and continued on our way, but I noticed that Marfil was uncharacteristically quiet. It started to snow, and I pulled her into a doorway for a few seconds.

She was crying.

"Hey . . ." I said, leaning over to wipe her tears with the tips of my gloved fingers.

"It's so unfair . . ." she said in a faltering voice.

"What's unfair?"

She shook her head and closed her eyes to clear her vision. "I have so much, and she . . ."

"We don't choose the life we're born into, Marfil," I said, understanding how she felt. "What you're doing today is what makes the difference . . ."

She laughed bitterly. "It doesn't matter what I do, how many blankets I pass out. What about all the people who won't have anything tonight? What about everything else I could do?"

"You can't save the world."

"I'm selfish . . . and spoiled, you're right about that. And I'm a bad person . . . I'm . . ."

"Stop," I said, taking her chin in my hand. "Why would you say that?"

She looked up and fixed her eyes on mine.

I felt a chill run down my back. I knew it wasn't the time, but she was just so mesmerizing, so beautiful . . .

"Before . . . I hated Tami for a few seconds. I hated her because I thought that . . ."

I nodded silently.

"I know there's nothing between you, but just imagining it . . ."

"You're human, Marfil, and you're still young. But the fact that we sometimes have dark feelings doesn't make us bad people."

"What we're doing here tonight . . . we do it to feel better about ourselves, at least partly. Isn't that horrible?"

I shook my head. "Nothing is purely selfless, Elephant," I said, rubbing her cheeks, which were bright red from the cold. "But small actions can make a difference. There are a bunch of people out here who will have you in their prayers tonight, and that's never a bad thing."

Marfil sighed. "I'd bring her home with me if I could, you know?"

I frowned. "Who?"

"The little old lady."

Oh God, I could just picture it . . .

"I know, I know. But please, promise me you're not going to let any strangers into your apartment, no matter how sorry you feel for them."

She rolled her eyes, but she promised she wouldn't.

## CHAPTER 26

# MARFIL

We walked the streets, handing out donations for a couple of hours. Sebastian had wanted to keep it shorter, but I begged him to let me stay longer. When he saw that my teeth were chattering and my lips were blue from the cold, he forced me to get in a taxi that was thankfully still in service. By the time it dropped us off at the place we'd parked, I was truly freezing.

That's when I saw him.

A medium-sized puppy was curled up on the curb beside our car, his fur covered in snow and frost.

My heart shattered.

"Sebastian," I said, pulling at his coat to get his attention.

He followed the direction of my gaze and stopped. "Marfil. No."

I ignored him and approached the dog with caution. He was shaking so hard that he hardly noticed when I walked up and crouched beside him. "Hey, buddy," I said. He looked at me with big, sad eyes.

"Marfil," Sebastian said, bending down, "dogs can handle the cold. Don't you see all that fur? It's like he's wearing a warm coat. He is, in fact."

"We can't leave him here," I said, petting his head. His tail began to wag slowly, and he stuck out his tongue to lick my hand. "Poor thing!"

Sebastian cursed aloud, and when I stood up, the dog did as well. The creature was filthy, frozen, and malnourished.

"Please, Sebastian," I said, turning to him. "Don't be cruel. I can't leave him here. You said I couldn't bring people back to the apartment, and I didn't even object! But this little dog needs me."

"Dammit, Marfil," he said, but then he held open the car door.

I got in the back seat, and the dog clumsily climbed in beside me. Sebastian turned on the heat, and the dog started licking me.

"Don't let him do that. He might have some disease," Sebastian warned, but I ignored him.

The dog was adorable, gray with black legs. One of his floppy ears was also dark. I felt sorry for him, with his matted coat and skinny body.

"I'm going to feed you until you can't eat another bite," I said, feeling a warmth in my heart that I hadn't noticed had been missing. Seeing all those people on the streets and knowing that there was so little I could do had affected me deeply. Sebastian was right: I couldn't save the world, and I couldn't bring every stranger home with me, but I could save this little dog from freezing to death on the street.

My father had always forbidden us from bringing home stray animals and became furious if we disobeyed. We'd once found a little piglet with an injured foot; he'd escaped from the neighboring farm. My sister and I brought him in and wanted to keep him as a pet. Our father had him slaughtered and butchered, and then forced us to sit at the table while he ate it for dinner, to teach us a lesson. I still remember my nausea, which lasted the rest of the night.

When we got back to the apartment, Norman looked at the dog with curiosity. "Miss Cortés . . . you got a pet?" he asked.

"Yes," I said, holding my head high. This stray was no purebred, but I was no snob.

We went up to my apartment, where it was warm inside, since the radiator turned on automatically when the temperature dropped below fifty-five degrees. I truly understood, more than ever, how fortunate I was. My father could be an asshole, but he had always given my sister and me everything.

Sebastian hung his coat up without taking his eyes off the dog, who had waltzed into the apartment like he owned the place. I smiled. He walked around sniffing everything—his snout stuck to the floor—and then circled the rug three times and lay down beside the small electric fireplace in the living room.

"Do you see how smart he is?" I said, pressing the button to ignite the flames.

Sebastian groaned something in response and looked at us.

"We have to give him a name."

"You're going to name him?"

"What do you think of Rico?"

"Why would you call him Rico?"

"I don't know . . . It's the first thing that came to mind."

Sebastian walked over and studied the dog with a serious expression. Rico sniffed him. "He's kind of ugly."

"He's not ugly! He's unique."

Rico barked, as if agreeing with me, and Sebastian smiled for the first time all day. "You should take him to the vet; he's malnourished. And you're going to have to house-train him and walk him . . ."

I rolled my eyes. "I know how to take care of a dog, thanks." I stood up, and Rico followed me into the kitchen. "What should I feed him?"

Sebastian raised his eyebrows, as if saying I was already proving him right. "Don't give him too much—his stomach must be the size of a marble. We'll give him a little bit of chicken, to see how he does with it, but tomorrow you need to take him to the vet."

I nodded, looking lovingly at Rico. "Want me to give you a bath while Uncle Sebastian makes you something to eat?" I asked in a singsong voice.

"You gave Uncle Sebastian the rest of the day off. Don't push it." He turned around and headed down the hallway.

"Come on, Sebastian," I begged, looking at Rico, who barked to back me up. "You're really going to leave me alone in the kitchen?"

He seemed to think better of it, then turned around and threw me a poisoned glance. "I'll make him a chicken breast, and after that I'm done."

I smiled as I walked to my room, Rico on my heels.

"One for me, too, okay?"

I didn't hear what he said because I quickly closed the door behind me, took off my coat, and carried Rico into the bathroom. I didn't really want the dog in my tub, but I knew Sebastian would refuse to let me wash my new four-legged friend in his shower. I turned on the hot water, adjusting the temperature to keep from burning him. He barked when I put him in the water and grabbed the showerhead to wet him. As soon as he was fully soaked, Rico shook his fur, splashing me with water and grime.

I went through almost an entire bottle of shampoo before the water finally ran clear. The dog's fur was now bright white, and I smiled contentedly at the result. I picked up the hair dryer and started to dry him as he ran back and forth, opened his mouth to feel the air, and barked like crazy.

"What the hell are you doing to that dog?" Sebastian asked, entering the bathroom and picking him up before he could dash out the door.

"Help me out!"

Between the two of us, we dried him off, and I brushed his fur with my hairbrush. The transformation was incredible.

"Rico, you're gorgeous!" I said, looking at his white, wavy fur. He was such a mutt that it was impossible to tell what breed he was, but to me, he was beautiful.

We went into the kitchen with Rico following along beside us. Sebastian placed some chunks of chicken in a cereal bowl and brought it closer to Rico, who sniffed it, hesitant at first, then began to eat slowly. It made me sad to think about the things this dog must've experienced and the fear and the cold he must've felt.

I noticed there was a plate on the counter for me—grilled chicken breast, tomato salad, and cooked carrots—and I turned to Sebastian with a smile. "What would I do without you?"

He didn't respond, he just leaned on the kitchen counter and watched as I ate.

When I finished, he took my plate and put it in the dishwasher. Rico had returned to his spot on the rug and was dozing beside the fire. It made me happy to see him getting used to my apartment so quickly.

"You should go to bed," Sebastian said, posing it more as an order than a suggestion.

I walked over to pet Rico. "What if he's scared to be in a new place?" I said hesitantly. "Although he seems pretty comfortable."

"Anyplace is better than the street, Marfil, believe me."

I stopped petting Rico and looked up at Sebastian for a few seconds, wishing I had the ability to read minds.

"Can I shower in your bathroom?" I asked.

Sebastian frowned.

"My tub is all full of Rico grime," I explained.

"Shower wherever you want. I'm going to bed."

How sweet. I missed the other Sebastian.

I went to get my pajamas and knocked on his door. He told

me to come in, and I eventually found him standing in his closet, the door open, pulling a white cotton T-shirt over his head.

"Do you need me to show you how to turn on the water?" he asked. "It's the same as yours."

I rolled my eyes as I went into the bathroom and closed the door. I took off my clothes, aware of the fact that he was just steps away, and turned on the hot water. Unsurprisingly, all of his products were perfectly lined up. I sniffed his shower gel and felt a tingle of pleasure; it was like smelling him. Wanting to have him as close to me as possible, I rubbed that familiar scent, *his* scent, all over my body.

Finally, I turned off the water and stepped into a cloud of steam—I loved a super-hot shower. I dried off, pulled on a simple white camisole with thin straps, and stepped into my pink cotton pajama pants. I squeezed the excess water out of my hair, then left the bathroom.

Sebastian was sitting up with his laptop open on his knees, which he closed as soon as he saw me.

"Why do you always do that—are you watching porn or something?"

"Go to bed, please."

"I thought you were going to sleep."

He set his laptop on the table, sighing. "I don't go to sleep until you do."

I walked slowly over to him and sat beside him. "How do you know when I fall asleep?"

"It's enough to know you're in your room."

I smiled, remembering the time I snuck out the window. Then I thought about how he must've freaked out that night, and the smile faded from my face.

"I like your bodywash," I said, sitting very still. He looked me in the eye for the first time since I'd come out of the bathroom. "I smell like you."

He took a deep breath and ran a hand over his face.

"Does it bother you when I say things like that?"

"What bothers me is the way I feel when you say it."

My heart sped up. His eyes were still closed, and I took advantage of the fact that he wasn't looking to move closer to him.

"Why do you make me feel like it's wrong to want to touch you or to feel something for you?"

He opened his eyes and looked at me. "Because it is." He was being serious.

"Why?"

Sebastian sighed again. "Marfil, I can't do my job if we keep this up."

"How does the fact that I want to kiss you affect your work?"

Sebastian looked to my lips and then back to my eyes. "It would be a distraction."

"No, I can kiss you only when we're at home. Outside the house, you'll be able to concentrate as much as you want."

Sebastian smiled, and my heart fluttered as if I had a hummingbird flapping its wings inside my chest.

"It doesn't work that way, Elephant," he said, moving my hand away when I tried to hold his. "We can't, it's that simple."

I pursed my lips, annoyed, but also sad.

"You should be going out with some college guy," he added an instant later.

"You're not being serious," I replied, unable to believe what he was saying.

He stood up, walked to the door, and opened it for me. "I'm being very serious."

I instantly felt lonely without him beside me.

"Are you saying you wouldn't be bothered to see me with other guys?"

"I'm not saying anything, Marfil. I'm not here to participate in your life; I'm here to protect you. That's it."

I stood up and walked over to him. "That's not it and you know it, but I'm not going to keep insisting."

"I'm glad you finally get it."

"I'm a slow learner, I guess," I replied in the same cold tone.

"Go to bed."

"Of course, Mr. Moore."

I walked down the hallway toward the living room, angry and hurt.

Rico lifted his head as soon as he heard my footsteps and looked at me from his spot beside the fireplace.

"Do you want to sleep with me?"

The dog jumped up, wagging his tail happily, as if he'd understood me.

I heard Sebastian's door shut behind me, and I sat down on the couch with Rico. I hugged him tightly and began to cry. Why did everything suddenly seem to revolve around the way I felt for Sebastian? Why couldn't I just forget about it, the way he did? I guessed that was what it meant for me to be in love: suffering like an idiot since no one would ever take me seriously enough to love me back.

CHAPTER 27

# MARFIL

We took Rico to the vet, who gave him several shots—including rabies—dewormed him, and put him on a special diet for the next month. Then we went home so that I could change, drop the dog off, and meet Tami on Fifth Avenue to go shopping. We needed to catch up. I hadn't liked the interaction I'd witnessed the night before between Liam and her, and I wanted to ask her if she was okay.

Despite having grown up together—she'd been at boarding school in England since age nine—and having spent years sharing the same dorm room, the same dreams, being for each other the family we didn't have, I had always felt that Tami had something locked away inside her that she never let anyone see.

I once tried to ask her about it after confessing tearfully what I'd gone through as a little girl—how much I'd wished to have my mother with me, the fact that I still had nightmares about her being killed right in front of me, my strained relationship with my father—but she assured me she had nothing to tell: She was simply a lonely child from a rich London family who had shipped her off to boarding school like so many other parents.

I knew she was lying, and at first it hurt my feelings that she refused to open up to me, but I wouldn't force her to confess her secrets. I could tell that there was a wall between us that never allowed her to fully trust me, but I still loved her. Just looking at Tami made you want to hug her, make her laugh, or soak up that special aura that always surrounded her.

That's why I couldn't understand what the hell was going on between her and Liam. He was a good guy, truly, my best friend, and he was always on his best behavior with me. I had often asked myself what I would've done if I hadn't met him in my first year of college. We were a unit; he knew everything about my life, and I knew everything about his. He could sometimes be presumptuous and a bit of a jerk, but I knew it was all a façade. It was simply the secret weapon he used to get girls, and fuck, did it surprisingly work.

But I also knew that my experience was exactly that: mine and not hers. Another reason why I wished she would open up to me. I wondered if she thought it useless to do so, that I would take Liam's side over hers, and it made me sad to think I'd failed her as a friend.

When I first introduced Liam and Tami, I had the fantasy that they might hit it off and maybe even fall in love. At the time I was going out with that asshole Regan, so I saw everything through rose-colored lenses. I believed in true love and all that crap, but I soon discovered that love is shit and it only makes you suffer. I was living proof of that.

My eyes wandered involuntarily to the back of the coffee shop, where Sebastian was seated, watching the doors and windows of Pret a Manger, a British café chain that Tami and I loved because of the banana cake. I had barely exchanged two sentences with my bodyguard since our brief conversation the night before, and he certainly wasn't going to be the one to break the ice. He had rejected me, it was that simple, and I wasn't taking it very well.

"It's fine, honestly," Tami told me for the fourth time, taking a sip of her coffee. "The fact that he's your best friend and you get on so well doesn't mean it has to be that way with me. He and I are very different, and his personality drives me crazy."

"I never thought it possible that someone could drive you crazy, to be honest."

"Well, there's a first time for everything, or a first person, more like," she said, looking out the window at the view of Central Park.

We'd spent the better part of the afternoon buying clothes, shoes, and accessories. It had been ages since I'd updated my wardrobe, and I'd forgotten how fun those outings could be. We knew a personal shopper, Tina, who adored us and always filled us in on the latest fashion trends.

Sebastian seemed like he was about to go insane after the hours we'd spent browsing couture, and I secretly enjoyed torturing him in that subtle way.

Tami and I were surrounded by shopping bags, and I had finally led the conversation in the direction I wanted it to go. "If Liam said or did anything offensive, you know you can tell me, right? I'll give him a good chewing-out for you. It won't be hard at all now that Sebastian is teaching me self-defense and a bunch of other martial arts nonsense."

Tami smiled, showing off the dimples in her porcelain cheeks. "I'm sure I injured his fragile fucking ego when I threw him out of my studio."

Hearing her curse, I sat back and laughed. "Who are you, and what have you done with Tami Hamilton?"

She shrugged and glanced over at Sebastian. "Is there something going on with you two?"

I sighed. "I wish . . . but no." I hadn't told her what had happened between us, and although Liam had guessed, I hadn't wanted to go into detail.

"Sebastian defended me yesterday," she said, looking back

down at her coffee cup. "I liked the feeling of someone taking care of me. You're lucky to have him."

I made a mental note of that comment, adding it to the collection of information I'd been gathering the entire time I'd known her.

"I know," I answered, pinching off a piece of banana cake. "And to be honest, I was jealous," I admitted as I chewed.

Tami seemed to regret having said anything about him. "Listen, it's not that I like him or anything!"

I smiled. "I know, don't worry. The problem is me. I'm obsessed with him."

"That's not the problem; you're just not used to anyone saying no to you."

"Is my hair green?" I answered.

Tami frowned and looked at me as if I had suddenly lost my mind. "No."

"See? I can hear the word no without any problem. I didn't make a scene," I said coldly.

Tami sighed. "Now you're angry. I shouldn't have said anything."

"No, no, fuck. I'm sorry, it's just that sometimes I think Sebastian's right, and I really am a spoiled brat who can't take no for an answer."

"You're not a spoiled brat. You were just born with a level of privilege that made it easy for you to get everything you want."

"That's not true," I answered quietly, almost in a whisper.

"I loved helping out yesterday. We should do things like that more often," she said, subtly changing the subject. "People turned out in incredible force. I didn't expect it."

I smiled. "I've been thinking about trying to open a branch of ST here in New York. Wouldn't that be amazing?"

We continued talking about the project and about girls' ballet classes for another half hour; we had both always been interested in helping others, feeling guilty for having so much, I guess. We were always the first to raise our hands when they asked for volunteers for the charity drives at school, and we also came up with the Smile Box idea, where all the students wrapped a shoebox filled with presents for a specific age group. Those boxes were later passed out at Christmas to children in need. The program was so successful that we received an award at school. Since then, the Smile Box has been a Christmas tradition.

When we finished our coffees, Tami ordered a ride, and Sebastian and I were once again alone, walking back to where he'd parked the car.

"It's such a hassle to go everywhere by car. We should take more taxis or order Ubers," I complained. Sebastian was still looking at his phone, where I supposed he had an app that told him where he'd parked. It was seven thirty, and I needed to let Rico out to do his business. Also, I wanted to show him all the toys I'd bought at a super-posh pet store.

When we finally got home, almost without a word to each other—although I'd delivered a few lines because I was incapable of remaining silent—I got a call from my father. To my surprise, he was in New York and wanted to meet me the next day for brunch.

"You're already here, now?" I asked, starting to panic.

"I arrived an hour ago. I was going to pick you up for dinner, but I'm exhausted. I'll see you tomorrow, okay?"

I nodded and said goodbye, frowning.

"What's wrong?" Sebastian asked, breaking his silence after being mute all day.

"Nothing," I answered, and I went into my room.

---

I woke up early the next morning to be ready to meet my father at ten o'clock for brunch at the Plaza Hotel. He always stayed there because one of his best friends was the son of the owner, so he always got the best suite.

I took a quick shower, knowing that Sebastian had been awake since at least seven thirty. He went out running at that time and then later again if I wanted to run in the evenings. By the time I entered the kitchen, he'd already done a thousand things.

I was wearing one of the dresses I'd bought the day before, cream colored and very pretty, although with how unpredictable the weather was being, I had to wear leggings underneath along with a coat, scarf, and boots.

Sebastian frowned upon seeing me dressed up.

"Where are we going?" he asked as Rico bounced around, begging for food.

I leaned down and scratched the dog behind the ears. "To brunch. My father wants to see me."

"Your father is here?" he asked, surprised.

"You didn't know?" I asked innocently. Weren't they supposed to be best friends?

He disappeared down the hall without a word, and I assumed he was going to change out of his track suit—a shame, since seeing Sebastian in head-to-toe Adidas always caused my brain to short-circuit.

He reemerged fifteen minutes later, showered and dressed in a suit and tie, which I hated because it created distance between us. In that uniform, he was a bodyguard, nothing more.

"All you're missing is the earpiece," I said, trying to annoy him.

"I don't need it. I'm not connected to anyone."

"I was joking," I answered dryly, turning my back on him and walking out the door, when Rico barked to get my attention. "Oh, shit, I have to take him out," I said, realizing that I didn't have time to walk him.

"I took him out this morning," Sebastian informed me.

"You didn't have to do that," I answered as I followed him onto the elevator.

"I do a lot of things I don't have to do, Marfil. What's one more thing on the list?"

Was that a jab at me?

"Yeah, you do things you shouldn't. Like touching me, for example."

Sebastian pushed the button to stop the elevator. "Enough," he said through gritted teeth, furious. His neck was inches from my mouth, and I could see his Adam's apple moving up and down to the rhythm of his rage.

I fixed my eyes on his. "Why does it bother you so much? Just because you're capable of forgetting what happened between us doesn't mean that I can."

"Well, you should."

"An elephant never forgets," I said, lifting a hand to caress his neck, more to provoke him than anything.

But before I could touch him, he pinned my hand against the wall of the elevator. "Keep it up, and I'm not going to be so friendly, Marfil. You and I both know you don't want the old me to come out."

I felt his breath against my cheek, making the hairs on my arms stand on end.

"The old you, the dangerous heartbreaker who drives a hundred miles an hour on the Brooklyn-Queens Expressway? Would the old you be less afraid to touch me or kiss me or say dirty things in my ear? Because I wouldn't mind seeing that Sebastian again."

"Believe me," he said, his lips so close to mine they were almost touching, "you wouldn't be able to handle that Sebastian even if I gave you lessons."

He abruptly released my hand and stepped away, then

pressed the elevator button again for it to begin moving. I stood behind him, trying to keep my heart from beating out of control. He went straight to the car without looking in my direction, and we rode in moody silence for the twenty minutes it took to get to the Plaza Hotel.

They knew me at the Plaza, since I often met my father there when he came to the city. Brunch was served at The Palm Court—inside, not outside, due to the weather—with spectacular views of Central Park and the surrounding buildings. Gorgeous, ostentatious, extra, possibly, but that was my life, especially around my father. I was used to it.

My father spotted me as soon as I stepped out of the elevator and entered the restaurant. He walked over to me with a wide smile.

Why the hell was he so happy?

"You look lovely, as always," he said, kissing me on either cheek.

I smiled in response as he nodded dryly in Sebastian's direction. I shot Sebastian a glance as well, but he was in poker-face mode: He transmitted absolutely nothing.

My father put his arm around my shoulders and guided me to a table. Only a couple feet in, and I stopped dead in my tracks when I saw who was already there, waiting for us.

*Boom, boom, boom.* My heart pounded in my ears, as if trying to remind me I was strong and healthy and I could run away if I needed to.

"You remember Marcus."

My legs continued propelling me forward of their own accord, even as Marcus Kozel pushed back his chair and stood up with a smirk as he leaned in to greet me.

What the hell was he doing here? Why had my father invited him? Didn't he know what his friend's son had tried to do to me?

I looked at Sebastian, whose eyes showed what he felt: rage. His fists were tightly clenched at his sides and his lips were pressed into a hard, thin line. But he just stood to one side, observing the scene.

"You're even more beautiful than the last time I saw you," Marcus whispered in my ear, and I swear I almost vomited right then and there, on the immaculate carpet.

My shock and discomfort were obvious, but my father simply pulled out my chair and remained standing until I sat. The plates were empty, but their glasses were full; they had been drinking whiskey.

"It's nice to see you. How is school going?" my father asked me cordially.

I was so overwhelmed that I answered with a simple "Fine" as the waiter came to take our orders. "I'm not hungry," I said coldly, recovering slightly from the unpleasant sensation of seeing that asshole again. This was the same guy who had tried to force himself on me, the same guy who hadn't stopped harassing me with flowers and cards every day since I'd returned to New York.

"Bring her blueberry pancakes," Marcus instructed the waiter. "You have to eat," he added, turning to fix his glacial gaze on me.

Just then, my father took his cell phone out of his pocket. "I need to make a quick call. Start without me. I'll be right back," he said, leaving the table.

I watched as he stopped beside Sebastian and they exchanged a few words. Then, throwing me an uneasy glance that I didn't know how to interpret, Sebastian followed him out of the restaurant.

"Have you enjoyed the flowers I've been sending you?" Marcus asked, taking my hand.

I yanked it away. "Don't touch me."

Marcus smiled, unfazed by my hostility. Of course not. He knew what he'd done, although it didn't seem to matter much to him. "Come on, Marfil," he said, raising his glass to his lips. "It's time you forgive me, don't you think?"

"You forced yourself on me," I said firmly.

"I did no such thing," he replied calmly. "I kissed you. It's not the end of the world."

"You ripped my shirt open. You wouldn't let me go. You tried to rape me."

"Don't be childish," he said in a serious tone, seemingly affected by my words. "Do you really think I'd do something like that? I just wanted to get a look . . . It's not such a big deal. It's like test-driving a car before buying it."

My eyes bulged with rage, and I moved to stand, but Marcus was quicker and dug his fingernails into my wrist.

"Sit down," he said, trying to hide his fury.

I did as he said because I knew that my father was about to return, and I needed to understand what the hell made this son of a bitch think he had the right to treat me as if I were a fucking piece of meat.

He released me and took another sip of his drink.

"I'm going to be very clear," he said, setting the glass back on the table. "I want you to be mine."

I would've laughed out loud if I hadn't seen how serious he was. Did this man have mental problems?

"That's great that you have things you want, asshole, but welcome to the twenty-first century. Women are no longer goods to be purchased, understand?"

He didn't seem offended by my insult. Just the opposite, in fact. I got the feeling he was amused by me standing up to him, as if no woman had ever dared to do so before.

"Anything can be bought for the right price, Marfil."

"Do you think I want or need your stupid money?"

"Maybe you don't, but your father does."

I stared at him, trying to understand what he was saying. Just then, the waiter brought the food, and I had to swallow back bile. I looked around for Sebastian, my father, anyone. I needed to get out of there, to erase that conversation from my mind, but another part of me wanted to know more.

"Do you know who my father is, how much he's worth? He would never use me to get anything. You're being ridiculous."

"Do *you* even know who *I* am?"

"A sexist asshole who thinks he's king of the world?" I would've been proud of my response if it hadn't been for the consequences.

He grabbed my hand and tugged it under the table.

"If you insult me again," he said, twisting my hand so hard I gasped in pain, "you'll have eight fingers instead of ten for the rest of your life."

"Let go of me," I said as tears sprang to my eyes. I don't know why the hell I didn't scream, why I didn't shout for help, why I didn't take off running.

Sebastian would kill him . . . Sebastian, where the hell was he?

"There's no one here to save you. I'll be the one in charge of you from now on, do you understand?" He dug his fingernails into my wrist with so much force that I had to bite my lip to keep from screaming.

"You can't—"

"A person with a lot of money usually also has a lot of debts. And that can create dangerous enemies," he continued, smiling as if telling an amusing anecdote over brunch with friends. "It's like a house of cards: one card falls, it all collapses. You don't want that to happen, do you?"

"I want you to stop hurting me," I said through gritted teeth.

"Oh, I'm sorry. All you had to do was ask."

I let out the breath I had been holding in, cradling my hand against my body.

"Your life, your father's life, your adorable little sister's life, all depend on me now," he calmly explained. "I'm lending a hand out of the kindness of my heart. Your father and mine are old friends—they've been doing business together for I don't even know how many years, and you know the best part? I've only asked for one thing in return," he went on, turning to me. "You."

"My father would never . . ."

"Oh, please! Let's not talk about the things your father would do, princess. We'd be here for centuries."

"What does that mean?"

Before he could answer, my father returned, smiling as if he'd come to close the best deal of his life. "You didn't need to wait for me to start eating."

"Dad . . ." I said in a trembling voice, turning to face him.

The look he gave me made it clear that he knew perfectly well what was going on at our table.

"I suppose Marcus must've filled you in on our new business deal."

"Oh, yes," Marcus said, cutting into his eggs Benedict and slowly savoring a bite. "Although we still need to tie up certain loose ends; you know how these things go."

"That's true, we don't want to be hasty . . ."

I felt the room begin to spin.

"Marcus has offered to cover all your expenses here in New York, Marfil," my father went on. "Things with the family business are complicated right now, which is why we should be thankful to have a lifelong friend willing to offer his help."

"I don't want you to pay for anything. I'm perfectly capable of supporting myself."

Marcus looked to my father without a word.

"Don't be ridiculous," my father said, chuckling. "Do you know how much a New York apartment costs? How much I spend on your tuition alone?"

My world was crashing down. I was disgusted with myself, with everything I had, with what was happening right under my nose.

"I don't want any of that, I—"

"Enough, Marfil," Marcus cut in. "You insult me. I came here to lend a hand to your family, and it seems as if you'd rather throw yourself off the tenth floor of this building than accept it."

Exactly.

"You don't have a say in this," my father interjected. "We only told you so that you'd know how generous the Kozels are being, helping us in these complicated times. Also, let's not forget that you're still in serious danger."

"Then fucking fix it! Don't drag me down with you."

"Lower your voice," my father hissed.

"I can assure you that you'll be safer than ever," Marcus chimed in.

I shook my head at Marcus's words. I needed to get out of there, to wake up from my nightmare, return to reality.

"What the hell do you want from me? Say it plainly one fucking time."

Marcus leaned over the table and looked into my eyes. "Another chance. For you to forgive me, to start over from scratch."

"No," I said, but my voice was trapped in my throat, and it came out as a hoarse whisper.

"Marfil, Marcus has shared with me the feelings he has for you. That's one of the reasons he wants to help us. He's just asking that you get to know each other."

I took a deep breath, understanding that I wasn't going to get anywhere with either of them. All I could do was try to make sure this nightmare of a brunch was over as quickly as possible.

"Can I think about it?"

My father opened his mouth to answer, but Marcus spoke first. "Of course you can," he said with a friendly grin that made me want to claw at his face. "We'll talk it over. Things will get better, you'll see. Your father's just going through a rough patch. He'll get through it." He continued, this time directing it toward my father, "Don't worry about a thing, Alejandro."

They then changed the subject, talking about the stock market and an upcoming trip to Latin America. At one point, once I'd completely checked out of their conversation, my eyes scanned for Sebastian and found him standing beside the door, looking as tortured as I was.

When they'd finished eating, I finally spoke up after an hour of muteness. "I'm not feeling well. May I go?" I hadn't taken a single bite of the food in front of me.

My father didn't give Marcus the chance to respond. "Yes, you can go," he said, standing up and leaning down to give me a kiss on the cheek.

Marcus also stood and helped me with my coat. I felt dirty as his fingers brushed the bare skin of my neck. I stormed out of the restaurant, passing Sebastian without so much as a glance in his direction.

"Marfil . . ."

"No," I said, taking a step back as he tried to touch me. "Don't talk to me. Don't touch me. Leave me alone."

## CHAPTER 28

# MARFIL

We reached my apartment in total silence as I wiped away the stupid tears that would not stop streaming down my face, and felt the rage pounding in my ears, increasing with every second that passed. I wanted to scream, cry, and break things. I felt humiliated, as if I were an object that could be handed over to close a deal, someone who didn't have an opinion or feelings.

Inside my apartment, I tried to dart past Sebastian, but before I could get three steps through the door, he gently grabbed my wrist.

"Marfil . . ."

"Let me go!" I shouted, totally losing it. "You left me all alone! With him! How could you?!" I continued shouting, pushing at him over and over. "You said that if he ever touched me again, you would kill him!" I shoved his chest so hard that it hurt my wrist, still sore from when Marcus had twisted it. I rubbed the spot where he had dug into me with his nails, breaking the skin.

Sebastian looked down at my hand. "Did he do that to you?" he asked, brimming with latent rage, dropping his mask of self-control.

"Yes!" I shouted, moving away as he tried to touch me. "I called him an asshole and he practically broke my hand. What do you think of that?"

"Let me see."

"No!" I shouted again.

I had just been reminded of everything I hated about men, and I had betrayed each and every one of my values by not screaming at the top of my lungs when that son of a bitch hurt me. Why hadn't I slapped him in the face as soon as those horrible things came out of his mouth? Why hadn't I done anything? Out of fear! I was cowardly; I was weak. I wished I were strong enough to deal with him myself, but I wasn't. That's why I had a fucking bodyguard!

"Why did you leave?" I shouted hoarsely, pushing him again.

This time he wrapped his arms around me and held me against his chest, his arms squeezing me tight as his breath came fast in my ear. I knew I could've kept hitting him for hours and he wouldn't have complained, but I stopped because my hand hurt.

"I couldn't do anything else," he then said against my head. "I work for him now, understand?"

I froze.

"Do you think I wouldn't kill him with my bare hands if I didn't know that standing up to him would mean losing my job and not being able to protect you?"

I took a deep breath, trying to slow my racing heart.

"Do you think I wasn't repressing the urge to storm into that restaurant and kill him every second I had to stand outside?" His mouth was in the space between my neck and my ear. "Tell me exactly what happened," he demanded, brushing his lips across the most sensitive part of my neck as he noticed that my rage was giving way.

I took another deep breath, trying to find the words. "He bought *me*, that's what happened."

He tensed. "What the hell do you mean by that?"

I felt my body give out, collapsing into his arms. Sebastian held me close as the last of the adrenaline drained from my body, leaving me exhausted.

"My father made a deal with him in order to settle some debts . . ."

"Did he explain the deal?"

I shook my head. "Marcus just said he was going to help my family because our fathers had been friends for so many years and he just wanted one thing in return: for me to give him another chance."

Sebastian remained silent.

"This is all so surreal. Now he's paying my rent, my college tuition, my expenses. It's as if . . ."

"You belong to him," Sebastian practically growled.

I wiggled my way out of his embrace and glared at him, angered by his words. "I don't belong to anyone."

Sebastian brushed the hair off my forehead in a gesture that felt like a soothing balm. "Of course not," he said, looking me in the eye. "Will you let me get a look at those scratches, please?"

I nodded.

He took me into the kitchen and sat me at the island as he looked for the first aid kit. I winced when he lifted my hand and inspected it very carefully, seeming to know what he was doing.

"It's probably just a minor sprain," he said, rummaging in the silverware drawer until he found a small wooden spoon, the kind that comes with ice cream. "I can take you to the hospital or I can make a splint for you myself. I've done it more than once."

I nodded, feeling helpless, mistreated, and lower than I'd ever felt in my entire life. Rico remained seated beside Sebastian during the entire process, never taking his eyes off me. It was as if he knew something horrible had happened and he needed to be close to protect me or make sure that I was all right.

When Sebastian finished, he brought me a glass of water and a painkiller.

"Drink this," he ordered, standing behind me, "it'll help with the pain."

I nodded and silently swallowed the pill.

Sebastian then examined my cuts and scrapes from the car accident, almost fully healed. He seemed to be fighting a battle inside himself.

When our eyes met, it was as if he understood me completely, as if he could see how destroyed I was.

"I'm sorry," he said, very serious. "I need you to forgive me."

I looked down at my hands without a word.

"I never imagined he'd touch you in a public place, and your father came out to—"

"It doesn't matter," I cut him off, staring down at my knees.

"Yes, it does matter," he insisted, gently lifting my chin so he could look me in the eye. "It won't happen again, Marfil. I promise you."

I nodded, drawn in by his intense stare, as if he desperately wanted to share all the secrets his eyes held. I caught a glimmer of something unexpected in his gaze, and in a second, his lips were on mine.

His kiss started out gentle, comforting, if only for a moment . . .

Before I knew it, my hands were moving of their own accord, tugging him closer, demanding more. Everything had changed. This wasn't like every other kiss. We were devouring each other, completely lost in the moment. And for the first time, Sebastian had kissed me without having to be persuaded.

Seconds later, his tongue slid inside my mouth, causing us both to involuntarily gasp with pleasure. He tugged at my lower lip with his teeth, his hands rubbing my knees, then moving toward my thighs. And when I slipped my hand inside his shirt, he let out a moan that set my entire body on fire.

"I want to kill him," he said against my lips.

I felt tears sliding down my cheeks, and he wiped them away with his kisses.

"Please don't cry," he begged me, gripping the back of my neck as if I were his anchor.

Our mouths met once again, our bodies perfectly in sync, as if we were made to kiss each other for the rest of our lives.

He understood what I was asking of him. I didn't even need to open my mouth. His fingers dug into my thigh, and I began to pant. I needed him to keep going, to continue down that path. He nuzzled into my neck and left a trail of wet kisses on my shoulder, then started over again. I began to quiver as his hands slipped under my dress, caressing me.

"This is the way you deserve to be touched, Marfil. As the priceless work of art that you fucking are," he said, slowly applying pressure against the most sensitive part of my body.

I needed him. I needed him like I needed air to breathe. I let out a moan choked with emotion as my pleasure mounted, and my hips began to grind against his fingers.

"Why are you so quiet?" he asked, kissing along my jawline, his fingers picking up speed against my clit.

"You can do the talking . . . for once . . ." I said, panting.

"I should be giving you this pleasure every fucking day," he said, pulling back and looking me in the eye.

I was soaking wet, about to come, and I closed my eyes in anticipation.

"Look at me," he demanded, gripping me firmly by the chin with his free hand, slowly sliding a finger inside me.

"More," I begged.

Sebastian smirked, then did as I asked, inserting another finger. His movements were slow and deliberate at first, teasing. He was taking his time, while I was seeing stars, so close to orgasm. But then he stopped and brought his fingers to his lips.

"You have no idea how delicious you taste."

"Please, I need you inside me."

He used one hand to level his body over mine as he whispered, "As you wish."

Before I had time to even blink, his fingers were back inside me, only this time, he used his thumb to rub my clit as his fingers penetrated me.

"Don't stop," I groaned. "Just like that."

"Open your eyes."

I did as he said, and all it took was one look from him to make me come. He squeezed my arm as I let out a scream that I'd been holding in for far too long. The waves of pleasure lasted a few infinite seconds until I collapsed against his shoulder, exhausted and panting, relishing in my orgasm.

He nuzzled my neck, and I knew why he'd taken things further. He wanted to make it up to me, to make up for everything: for rejecting me, for not giving me what I'd been begging him to give me all this time. But most of all, I knew he was being devoured by guilt over not having gotten me out of that restaurant before Marcus had hurt me.

"This is the point when you usually reject me," I whispered once we'd both caught our breath.

"I don't reject you."

I leaned back to look him in the eye.

"It's complicated, Marfil," he then said, his attitude shifting, although still rubbing my back.

Yes, it was.

If it was true that Sebastian now worked for Marcus, being fired would be the least of his problems when that asshole found out there was something between us. It scared me to think what could happen to him. Marcus was dangerous, I now understood, and my father . . .

"What kind of business is my father involved in with Marcus, Sebastian?"

His fingers stopped moving and his eyes went dark. "I'm not going to answer that." He removed his hand from my back, and I instantly felt cold, missing his touch.

I hopped down from the counter, my legs still shaky, and faced him. "I need to know. This has gone beyond anything I could've ever imagined. Do you think I'm an idiot? That I didn't see the way Marcus behaved this morning?"

"That's exactly it, Marfil. They're dangerous people, and it's better you don't get involved."

"Do you include my father in that category?"

Sebastian shot me a questioning glance. "He's your father; you tell me."

Of course my father wasn't dangerous. He was demanding, authoritarian, complicated, but not dangerous! Not at least to the degree Sebastian was insinuating.

"He's my father, yes, and I love him, even if he's gotten himself into trouble. But I don't think I need to be afraid of him."

Sebastian rested his hands on the kitchen counter and looked at me for a few seconds without saying a word.

"I guess it makes sense for you to trust him. He's your father."

I didn't like his tone.

"Don't be condescending with me," I said, stepping back and leaning against the opposite counter.

He came over to me and cradled my face in his hands. "I'm not," he said in a calming tone. "I'm being totally serious."

I avoided his gaze and stared at the wall behind him. "There's a difference between being dangerous and being involved in dangerous dealings," I said.

His brown eyes glistened. "I agree with you there."

We looked at each other for a few seconds, and then he took my bandaged hand and kissed it.

"Everything's going to be all right," he said, transmitting a calm that I now know he didn't feel.

"I don't want to see him ever again, Sebastian," I said in a trembling voice. "I don't want him to touch me or even look at me ever again. The way he spoke to me . . ."

Sebastian took a deep breath to steady his emotions and hugged me like he knew I needed him to. "Don't worry," he said, smoothing my hair, "everything's going to be all right."

---

We spent the rest of the day at home. I tried to get ahead on schoolwork while taking breaks to play with Rico. Sebastian seemed more somber than usual, which I could understand, but I was happy about our moment of closeness, feeling like we'd turned a corner with our relationship. I still felt an unfamiliar mixture of disgust and fear every time I thought about Marcus, but at least Sebastian was there to give me a hug and make me feel better every single time.

That night, I knocked on his door. He told me to come in, and I found him punching his punching bag, without gloves, shirtless, seemingly so full of rage that I wondered if seeking him out had been a good idea . . . But when he saw me, he picked up a towel and wiped it across his face without taking his eyes off me, coming to a halt where I stood. Without warning, he bent down and kissed me, while his hands gripped my waist and pressed my back against the wall. He was furious, and I didn't understand what could have happened, apart from the events that morning, to make him feel that way.

I could feel how aroused he was as he lifted the back of my dress and slipped it over my head, leaving me naked except for the little black bra and panties I was wearing. My breathing picked up as his hands were on my skin.

"What happened?" I asked, almost breathless, as he kissed my neck and jaw. "Sebastian," I whispered as he brushed his free hand over my soaking-wet underwear.

"Don't talk, Marfil," he said quietly, shutting me up with a deep kiss.

I ran my hands up his back and chest, until I reached his neck, then pulled him to me and enjoyed the warmth of his lips, the caress of his tongue . . . so intimate that I melted in his arms.

He lifted me and carried me over to the couch, positioning me on top of him, and continued kissing me, although at a calmer pace. He seemed to gain control of himself as his caresses became gentler.

I wasn't sure I liked the change in intensity.

"Can I talk now?" I whispered in his ear, kissing his lobe.

He grunted as I stuck my tongue in his ear, taking in the salty taste of his skin.

"I'll let you do whatever you want today, Elephant." He sighed, burying his hand in my long dark hair and pulling it back gently to meet my gaze. "You know I'd do this all day if I could, right?" he said, sitting up until the tips of my hard nipples brushed against his incredible pecs.

"You have my permission," I said, marveling at his handsomeness, his strength and masculinity. God, I was so attracted to him, it drove me crazy . . .

He leaned back and stared up at the ceiling, as I admired his square jawline and his Adam's apple. I wanted to kiss him again and never stop.

"How is your hand feeling?" he asked after letting out a deep sigh.

I looked down and started fiddling with the splint.

"Stop, don't mess with it," he scolded me. "And put this on." He handed me his T-shirt.

"First you get me naked and now you want to put clothes on me?" I said as he slid the shirt over my head, ignoring my weak attempts to push him away.

"I lost my head. I'm sorry," he said, helping me into the sleeves.

I observed him, feeling something very different from the desire I felt only minutes ago. My God, I loved him. I loved him, and I couldn't do anything to protect myself from that feeling.

"Can I ask you something?"

Sebastian let out a breath, then nodded.

"How old were you when you married Samara?"

My question took him by surprise; it took me by surprise, too, to be honest. But I needed to understand his past and what had compelled Sebastian to get married. I needed to know whether he'd truly gotten over her, what the hell had happened . . .

"I was twenty and she was eighteen," he answered.

Wow . . . he'd been my age.

"Why didn't it work out?"

Sebastian ran a hand over his face, frustrated. "Apart from the fact that we were so young?" he asked but did not wait for a response. "I don't know, Marfil, I did things . . . I made decisions that affected us both, and everything just went to hell . . ."

I thought for a few seconds about his response.

"Why does she think you're dangerous?"

Sebastian fixed his eyes on me. "I already told you I was raised in foster care, and Samara was, too, so we've both been through things . . ." He paused for a second, then went on, "You could say there was a time when we moved in environments that weren't suitable for kids . . . That leaves its marks . . . It can affect your character and judgment," he continued, distractedly caressing my leg. "The way you see me now, I had to do a lot of work on myself to gain this level of self-control . . ."

"It's hard to imagine you any different," I said as he fell silent. "The Sebastian I know is obsessed with self-control . . ."

"The military helped me tame that part of myself, although I'd be lying if I said I never lose control and go back to . . ."

I recalled the scene he'd made in the car and understood what he was talking about. "Being scary?"

Our eyes met.

"Do I scare you?" he asked worriedly.

I shook my head, even though deep down I knew I was lying; he had scared me that time in the car.

"Although . . . knowing you could kill someone with only one hand is kind of terrifying," I said jokingly.

He smiled.

"You could teach me," I added immediately.

The smile faded from his face. "I still question whether teaching you self-defense was a good idea."

"What if someone tries something like this again?" I said, lifting my hand with a frown.

Sebastian clenched his jaw. "Go for their eyes," he said simply, before adding, "Jab your thumbs into their eye sockets until you perforate their brain."

I shuddered.

"Too much for you?"

"Man . . ." I began, and he smiled again.

"You should go to bed, it's late."

I rolled my eyes. "Don't be a party pooper," I replied. "Should we watch a movie?"

Sebastian looked as if he was wondering how we'd gotten here. Something as simple as sitting on the couch to watch TV meant an enormous shift in our relationship.

"And then you'll go straight to bed?"

I thought about it. "Only if you let me pick the movie."

I climbed off his lap reluctantly and reached for his laptop, which was lying on the table.

His hand flew out and picked it up before I got the chance.

"Give me a second." He closed the tabs so quickly that I wasn't able to see anything, except for one name: Lucas Miranda. "What do you want to watch?"

I took his laptop, smiling, and searched for the movie.

"You're going to love it . . ."

We settled onto the couch. I set the laptop on the coffee table, making sure we could both see, then wrapped my arms around him and rested my head on his chest. He didn't seem perturbed by the way I curled up next to him, invading his personal space.

The music began, and I instantly got goose bumps.

"Seriously, Marfil?" he asked, and I couldn't help but smile. "*The Bodyguard*?"

"You can't tell me it's not funny . . ." I said, holding back laughter. "It's one of my favorite movies."

The movie started, and Sebastian began to run his fingers through my hair, from the roots all the way down to the tips. I closed my eyes, feeling every caress in the center of my soul.

What would happen with us? Could we maintain this thing we had, whatever it was? I didn't like that it was Marcus's angry face and not my father's that appeared in my mind when I imagined starting a relationship with Sebastian.

Fucking Marcus. I hated him for what he'd done to me, for the way he'd spoken to me, for the way he'd forced himself on me and hurt me, but most of all, I hated him because my fear of him was threatening to invade all the most important aspects of my life.

## CHAPTER 29

# SEBASTIAN

Marfil fell asleep twenty minutes into the movie, but I sat there, enjoying the feel of her body next to mine as thousands of unconnected thoughts battled it out in my brain. I stared at her for the entire two hours and ten minutes that the ridiculous movie went on, captivated by how pretty she was. In reality, the word *pretty* came up short, but I'd learned over the last several weeks that it wasn't her appearance alone that made me lose my head; it was the whole package. Her sweetness, her interest in helping others, even her angry outbursts, but most of all, her way of seeing the world, like it could be kind in return, even after everything it had taken from her.

She'd been hurt; she'd been treated like a simple object; she had been forced to endure her own father turning her over to a man whom he knew to be capable of anything, who had forced himself on his daughter. And yet Marfil Cortés was still able to smile. Still able to believe in kindness, in hope, in love, even if she gave it to someone unworthy of it.

I knew I was entering dangerous territory, that the consequences of being with Marfil could cost us both dearly. It scared me think about it, but I felt a strong urge to protect her, well beyond my job description as her bodyguard. Those of us in this line of work knew we could end up giving our lives to save the people we protected. That aspect of the job had always given me pause. But with Marfil, I didn't even question it. There was no other possibility: If I had to take a bullet to save her, I would do it without hesitation. And I'd die happy.

That was worrying.

When the movie ended, I carried her to her bedroom. She was light as a feather, and I couldn't help but think it would do her good to add a few pounds to her thin dancer's frame, but I had learned she didn't place much importance on food.

Suddenly awake, she leaned her head back as we passed through her doorway. "Are you practicing what you learned from Kevin Costner?" She yawned, holding tightly to my neck.

"Shh," I said, hoping she would go back to sleep. Alone, in her dark bedroom, things could get out of hand.

I deposited her on her bed, but she didn't let go of me.

She tugged at my neck until my face was mere inches from hers. "Sleep with me," she asked, her lips so close to mine that I could smell her exquisite, natural fragrance, feel her breath against my mouth, and most of all, an intense desire to bite down hard on her lower lip.

"Marfil—" I began, but she interrupted me.

"I just want to sleep, truly."

*Maybe so, but the problem is me, not you,* I thought to myself.

"No." I took her hands and peeled them off me. I needed to get away from her, to clear my head, get my thoughts in order . . .

I left her room, unaware of what I was missing out on. If I could go back in time to that instant, not a single person would've been able to get me out of that room.

---

I woke up early, like always, and went for a run, taking advantage of the fact that Marfil was still asleep, checking on her through the app that let me view the cameras inside the apartment. Central Park was full of early risers like me, people who wanted to take advantage of the first hours of the day before the park got too full. I had taken Rico with me. The dog seemed to be recovering nicely and was full of energy, which was to be expected given the vet had said he was a little over a year old.

I stopped to play with him, throwing the ball as I thought about everything that had happened with Marcus Kozel. Momentarily blinded by rage, the ball flew much farther than I'd intended it to. Rico took off like a bullet, and I had to run to keep from losing sight of him. The last thing I needed was to lose Marfil's dog.

I was returning to the apartment when I saw an Audi—pretty much identical to the one Cortés had given me—parked outside the entrance to the building. Just then, my cell phone started ringing. It was Marcus. I took a deep breath, trying to steady myself before answering the call.

"Moore?" he asked calmly over the background noise of what sounded like a bar. "I don't have much time. I'm just calling to inform you that from now on, you'll have another two men working with you to guard Marfil."

Shit.

"I don't think that's necessary—"

"It doesn't matter what you think," he cut me off. "I'm in charge here, remember? And that girl is worth too much to let anyone do anything to her."

I clenched my jaw at the sight of two men in nice suits climbing out of the Audi.

"And Sebastian," he said, now in a different tone, "I assume Cortés has brought you up to speed on the changes. If you fuck it up . . . I'll kill you."

I gripped my cell phone so tightly, I was surprised it didn't snap in half.

## CHAPTER 30

# MARFIL

I woke up with a smile on my face. I had so many reasons to be unhappy, but Sebastian Moore eclipsed them all. I had always heard that being in love made you see the world through rose-colored lenses. Well, I didn't exactly have a filter over my eyes, but I was happy. The night before, even though we hadn't taken things any further, had been super special. Sitting together to watch a movie, like a couple, had made me start to feel hopeful, so much so that the night's events carried into my dreams, which had been filled with scenes of us together. Unfortunately for me, I'd woken up just when things were getting interesting, and my body was left wanting more.

Sebastian was prone to change his mind according to the direction of the wind, but I wasn't going to fall for his misdirection this time. I showered quickly, with only one idea in mind: I wanted to sleep with him.

The situation my father had placed me in with Marcus made me realize that I couldn't go on living under the premise that what Alejandro Cortés believed was correct. I was twenty years old. I was an independent woman. I could listen to my mind and body and stop waiting . . . for what? It was ridiculous.

I silenced the voice that told me my father would kill me, and I walked out of my room naked, covered only in a white towel.

Sebastian was on the phone, and it took me a few seconds to realize he was fighting with someone. When he saw me, three separate emotions seemed to cross his face. The first, surprise; the second, fear; the third, anger.

"What the hell are you doing?" he said in place of his usual *good morning*.

What a slap in the face.

"I'll call you back," he said into the phone, and then walked toward me, his eyes black with rage. "Go into your room right now and put some clothes on," he hissed.

Well, I definitely hadn't achieved the desired effect.

"What's wrong with you, Sebastian?"

"Get dressed, Marfil, or you'll be late for class," he said, his eyes communicating urgency.

I felt ridiculous and humiliated as I turned around and went into my bedroom.

What the fuck was wrong with him?

I put on my leggings and my favorite black sweatshirt and left my room, steaming mad. It was true that Sebastian had never been one to easily fall victim to my charms, but did he have to be so rude?

I shot him a curt glance when I walked out and found him seated, waiting for me.

"Are you going for a run instead of class?" he asked, now in a normal, cordial, yet still cold tone.

"That's my plan, yes," I answered, crossing my arms and facing him. "And what's yours? Are you going to keep on treating me like this? Aren't you exhausted from all these mood swings?"

"Not now, Marfil," he said, staring fixedly at me.

I frowned, my anger reaching new heights. Sebastian stood up and walked past me, forcing me to follow him. He stopped and leaned against the wall, looking as serious as I'd ever seen him.

"Why do you have to be like this, Sebastian?" I said, hurt. "I never know what to expect from you. One day you kiss me, and the next day you ignore me! I'm so sick of it! I'm sick of sounding like a broken record."

He didn't say anything.

"Yesterday you took off my dress, and today you're upset that I came out wrapped in a towel?" I continued, raising my voice. "Am I a fucking plaything to you?"

"Of course you're not," he said very quietly, barely moving his lips.

"Well, it seems like it," I answered, hating his attitude. "Last night I asked you to sleep with me, and you just took off with a single-syllable response."

"I had something to do."

"What?"

He didn't answer, he simply observed me. It was all so ridiculous! I needed to get out of there.

"Where's Rico?" I asked.

"I took him out earlier. He's sleeping."

I glared at him and left the apartment, furious.

We waited for the elevator without even looking at each other. Then, when the doors opened and we stepped in, he took me by the arm and gently pressed me into the mirror.

"I couldn't say anything inside the apartment," he said, briefly stroking my cheek, leaving me confused. "You're not a plaything. Haven't I made it clear that you matter to me? But things have changed."

"What?" I asked, not understanding what he meant. "What are you talking about?"

The elevator stopped and the doors began to open. Sebastian jumped back, as if my skin suddenly burned him. I followed him out, more confused than ever.

Seated before Norman in the lobby were two very large men in nice suits. They both stood as soon as they saw me, and I instinctively stopped short.

Sebastian didn't step away from me, but when he opened his mouth, my stomach nervously flipped inside.

"Marfil, this is Jakov and Egor," he said, gesturing toward them. The two men stared blankly at me. "From now on, they'll be working with me on your personal security detail."

I scoffed and glared at Sebastian with a rage that I knew shouldn't be directed at him. "No fucking way," I said, backing away from him.

Sebastian stepped in front of me, blocking my view of the two gorillas. "Marfil," he said in a low voice, "there's nothing we can do; he ordered it."

"He's no one, fuck," I said, pushing Sebastian away and dashing out the door.

I raced toward Central Park, almost getting run over as I crossed the street. When I finally glanced back, I saw Sebastian and the other two men glaring at me as I moved farther away and they were forced to stop for traffic.

My head was spinning. Everything was changing. Everything was happening too fast and I didn't understand anything.

*If you were mine, you'd have five men guarding you.*

I ran faster still. The adrenaline was coursing through my system, and I felt as if my world were collapsing all around me without being able to do anything about it. I stopped at one of the many bridges and climbed onto the rocks underneath, tucked out of sight. I didn't want to see anyone, especially not Sebastian.

Did he support this? Had he approved or even requested more men? How long had he known about it?

It didn't take long for Sebastian to find me, and when he did, he didn't look angry, just relieved.

"Come out from there, please," he said, out of breath from running.

"I want to be alone, Sebastian," I said, looking down at him.

"I asked them to wait at the apartment. You and I need to talk."

"Oh, now you want to talk?" I asked, not intending to move an inch. "Fine, let's start with how you found me here," I said, suspecting that I wasn't going to like the answer one bit.

Sebastian sighed. "You have a tracker on your cell phone," he said calmly. "I can follow it from an app, but I'm the only one with access to it."

Fuck. That explained a lot.

"That's how you knew where I was the day of the concert."

He didn't say anything, which was enough of a response.

I climbed down from the rocks and stood in front of him. "Were you ever planning to tell me?"

"If I had, and you wanted to get away from me, it would've made things pretty easy for you, don't you think?"

I looked away... It was true, I had snuck out... If I had known, I could've simply left my phone at home and he would've never known where I was. Also, considering more recent events, my little escapade that night could've ended very badly.

"Why more bodyguards?"

"Marcus wants to keep you in line, and me, too."

My eyes returned to him. "You? Why?"

Sebastian seemed to debate whether to tell me or not. "We've known each other for a long time... To sum it up, we don't get along too well."

"How do you know him? Did you work for him as a bodyguard?"

"The less you know, the better, Marfil."

"God!" I groaned, frustrated. "How long are you going to go on hiding things from me? And what was with your attitude this morning? You could've warned me, but instead you just acted like some asshole who can't say more than three words at a time, and..." My brain was trying to connect the things he'd just told me, and something finally clicked.

I couldn't talk inside the apartment.

Sebastian was looking at me with his usual poker face.

"Was there someone else in the apartment this morning?" I asked in horror.

Sebastian stepped toward me and held me by the arm.

"There was no one else physically in the apartment, besides the two of us, but that doesn't mean he couldn't see us."

I opened my eyes wide.

"He installed cameras?!"

His silence said it all.

I pulled out of his grip and tried to control the panic attack I was starting to have. Marcus couldn't have had his men install cameras without my realizing it; I would've heard it!

I spun around and faced Sebastian. "You put them in, didn't you?" I shouted. Suddenly, everything made sense. "That's why you always knew what I was doing or came in at just the right moment every time I needed you! That's how you knew I fell while I was dancing! That's why you were always able to get ahead of my every movement!"

Sebastian still didn't say anything, and it made me even angrier.

"You've been spying on me?!" My God, I felt so humiliated! The other night, when I'd cried myself to sleep over the way he'd treated me. How many times had I stopped in the hall outside his room, trying to decide whether to knock? Had he been watching me standing there like an idiot? "I hate you, Sebastian!" I shouted.

He held me back before I could run away again, although what did it matter, since he could just track me through my cell phone? Knowing him, he'd probably be able to track every single person who mattered to me.

"Let go of me, dammit," I shouted, pulling away. "You lied to me!"

"I was just doing my job."

"Your job is shit! You can't invade my privacy without telling me!"

"It was necessary, Marfil. I didn't put any cameras in your bedroom and bathroom, but the rest of the house had to be under surveillance."

"You should've told me!"

Sebastian clenched his jaw tightly. "You're right," he finally said, looking me in the eye. "I was going to, but when I met you and I saw how opposed you were to the idea of having a bodyguard, I knew you'd try to outsmart my surveillance. I'm really sorry, but my priority has always been keeping you alive." He brought his hand up to my cheek. I tried to turn my face away, but he held me firmly. "It was only to keep you alive, Marfil," he repeated, staring at me intensely.

My heart was pounding out of my chest. I was so angry, so scared . . .

"Did you watch me in my studio?" I asked, daring him to lie to my face. We both knew the truth, and I wanted him to admit it.

Sebastian stammered, nervous for the first time since we'd met. Finally, he opened his mouth to speak. "Getting to see you dance was an unexpected bonus."

I shoved him as hard as I could. "You had no right." That was something private, something special to me. I couldn't believe he had been watching me do it all this time. If I had known . . .

"It's true, I had no right," he said, a fierce look in his eyes, "and I also had no right to touch you or kiss you or to feel any of the things I feel for you, but that's the way things worked out."

I had so badly wanted to hear those words from him, but it wasn't enough. I couldn't let them make me forget the reality of the situation. I didn't trust him. Sebastian Moore had too many secrets, and they seemed to be related to my family and to Marcus Kozel. I didn't want any part of it.

"This is over," I said, feeling the weight of each word as my heart broke into a thousand pieces.

Sebastian's eyes went dark, but his face remained impassive. "You're finally being sensible."

I laughed, feeling miserable.

"And now what?" I asked, controlling the urge to cry.

"Marcus has access to the cameras," he explained. "That's why I treated you that way this morning."

"I want you to take them out, all of them!" I shouted furiously. I wasn't going to let that psychopath watch me whenever he felt like it.

"I can't."

I shook my head as my mind spun, trying to process everything. "This is a nightmare."

"It will only be for a little while," he said in an attempt to console me.

I glared at him. He wasn't the one being watched!

"I want you to take the camera out of my dance studio."

Sebastian opened his mouth, but I interrupted him. "Make up some excuse, Sebastian!" I shouted. "He's not going to watch me dance. I refuse."

Sebastian thought about it for a few seconds before he spoke again. "I can try to rig the system for a little while, but I'll still need to have access," he said, leaving no room for objections. "I'm sorry, but the room opens onto a fire escape."

I pursed my lips and repressed a desire to tell him to go to hell. "Well, I hope you enjoy the show," I said instead.

I turned around and started running home. Sebastian followed, and as the wind blew my tears away, my mind began devising a plan to make each and every one of my bodyguards wish they'd chosen another profession.

## CHAPTER 31

# SEBASTIAN

Marfil tried her best to make our lives a living hell. Knowing now that there were several cameras watching her at home, she refused to spend time there, choosing instead to sleep over at Tami's, and then packed up to go stay with that asshole Liam. This meant that I had to remain posted outside their apartments, night after night, in the company of those two muscleheads.

The little time we were in the apartment, I watched her through the cameras more than anything because she refused to say a word to me. Her rebelliousness only seemed to increase with every day that passed: She stuck her middle finger up at the cameras on a daily basis after discovering the location of each and every one of them, and when she danced in her studio, she alternated between pirouettes, obscene gestures, and erotic dance moves that drove me crazy.

She seemed to know that I watched her from the moment she went in to the moment she came out, and she enjoyed slowly torturing me. It was the only time we were ever alone, even if there was a camera between us, and she had a single objective: to piss me off.

That day, for example, we'd just come back from Liam's house. Marfil was seated in the back seat, and Egor and Jakov followed in their car. Not only was I exhausted from having spent the night in the car, but knowing that she'd slept over at Liam's drove me crazy. Marfil knew it, and when she got out of the car, she made sure I saw the bright red hickey on her porcelain neck. I slammed the door so hard it almost fell off. I needed to control my jealousy before it gave us both away. Marcus Kozel could observe us whenever he wanted, and for all I knew, he was glued to the cameras twenty-four hours a day.

Marfil entered the apartment, totally indifferent to my mood, and shortly thereafter, sauntered past my door, wearing another one of those black leotards that left so little to the imagination. She looked me directly in the eye before entering her dance studio, closing the door behind her.

I scrolled to camera number ten and observed her. She no longer danced facing the mirror, instead looking fixedly at the camera. She began to move, and I knew it would be no classical ballet routine today. I watched as she opened and closed her legs, tracing impossible figures on the floor. Her body was a work of art, something that could've caused a riot if she'd ever been allowed to dance on stage.

My breathing started coming fast as I caught another glimpse of that hickey on her neck. She'd pulled her hair back to leave her bare skin exposed, telling me to go fuck myself for being such an idiot. She did a few more impossible pirouettes and then stopped, leaned against the barre in front of the camera, and, panting, stared into it.

I turned off all the cameras and entered her studio.

## CHAPTER 32

# MARFIL

I hadn't really expected him to come into my studio, convinced he would resist the temptation. I had tried to make it hard for him, but Sebastian Moore had an enviable resistance.

All week, I had done my best to provoke him by any means necessary. I was pissed at everyone, especially him, for having lied to me, and for sitting back and letting Marcus watch me whenever he wanted. A part of me hoped that Sebastian would just forget about his job and take me away . . . but nothing could be further from reality.

Staying over at Tami's and at Liam's had been mean of me. I knew that he'd have to wait up all night in his car, that he wouldn't sleep well for days, but my anger was greater than everything else. I refused to let Marcus watch me through his spy cameras! And although I knew I was being childish by provoking Sebastian, like with the hickey that went too far, it was just so easy. There was nothing I wanted more than to penetrate his armor of self-control. We had broken off whatever it was we'd had between us, and I hated how quickly he'd given up, how little he'd been willing to fight for me.

He came into the studio, slamming the door behind him, and stopped in the middle of the room. "Is this what you want?" he asked, pupils dilated and breath agitated. "You like seeing me like this?"

I barely blinked. "I love seeing you like this."

He pressed his lips together and took two long strides

toward me. He stopped briefly, looked deeply into my eyes, trying to transmit everything his mouth couldn't say. Then, cupping my face, began to plant soft kisses along my lips. I panted as I felt his erection against my stomach, and smirked up at him. He didn't say anything, simply sucked on my bottom lip, hard, and moved down to my neck.

"Sebastian . . ." I began.

"Don't say anything," he ordered me, pinning my wrists behind my back as his mouth kissed the spot where Liam had given me the hickey after I'd begged him to help me make Sebastian jealous.

Liam had refused at first, annoyed. Something had been up with him lately, but after pestering him for half an hour, he finally gave in just to shut me up.

That morning with Liam, I had laughed throughout the entire process, but the feel of Sebastian's lips sucking at my skin instantly made me wet. I rubbed myself against his pants, desperate for any kind of friction to help me ease the pain I felt at not having him inside me, but Sebastian immobilized me.

"Tell your little friend that if he touches you again, I'll kill him." He released me when he saw that I was wriggling uncomfortably and took two steps back. "Don't toy with me, Marfil," he said as our chests rose and fell in unison.

"You started this game," I answered, controlling the urge to throw myself back into his arms. I was still furious with him, and now disappointed, for more reasons than one. "Did you get a good night's sleep?"

Sebastian shut me up with a glance. I was being a bitch, and we both knew it, but my pride was injured, and it made me want to provoke him. Because of him, a man who'd hurt me and tried to rape me now had the access codes to the cameras Sebastian had installed all over my apartment without my knowledge!

"As soon as I walk out that door, this little game of yours is over," he said, stepping toward me again. "I'm your only ally here; don't push me away." He kissed me hard, then walked away.

Deep down I knew he was right.

I wiped away a single tear of rage from my cheek before he saw it on his computer screen, and picked up dancing where I'd left off, staring into the camera.

---

I decided I couldn't keep crashing with my friends any longer, and the days in the apartment became unbearable. I now had three men built like refrigerators following me everywhere, including around campus. Egor and Jakov ignored my complaints about their wardrobe choices and continued to wear those black suits and ties, including those earpieces they used to communicate with each other and Sebastian.

Sebastian was . . . unrecognizable. If he'd been hermetic before, he was now cold as winter in the North Pole and much stricter with what he allowed me to do. He literally had his eyes on me at all times, and his habit of worriedly scanning every space we entered only increased, causing me to be suspicious of everything around me.

"Are you sad you can't come in?" I said, closing the door to the women's bathroom in his face.

I had gone to lunch with Tami and was trying to convince her to come out with me that night. My life had become a living hell, and I needed to go out drinking and dancing.

I touched up my red lipstick and ignored Sebastian entirely as I walked back to our table. We were at Catch, a restaurant Tami and I both loved.

"So, what do you say?" I asked her for the fourth time. "The plan is to go to PHD. We can have a glass of champagne or the drink of your choice, some fried mozzarella, which I know you love, and then do some dancing."

"I don't know." Tami sighed, putting a bite of maki in her mouth. "Is Liam going to be there?"

I rolled my eyes in response. "He's the one putting us on the list. But don't worry, he's going to be working all the tables in the VIP section, so he'll hardly be with us, I promise."

"Why the hell does he still work as a club promoter?"

"Because he likes the nightlife, ladies, and alcohol," I explained, shrugging as I took a sip of my drink. "And he gets paid to go out partying," I added.

Tami's expression made me laugh. I worried sometimes that Liam would get burnt out, working in the clubs at night in addition to his day job, but he seemed to enjoy it.

"I think I'll pass tonight," she answered, looking disgusted.

"Come on, Tami! Liam is great. You just need to loosen up around him. He can tell you're judging him, and that makes him want to mess with you. Don't play his game! Can't you see that's what he wants?"

"Why? Explain to me why he would enjoy harassing me?"

I thought about it for a few seconds.

"Maybe he likes you . . ." I had never considered the possibility before.

Did Liam like Tami? Wow. And what about her? No, that was impossible.

"Don't be ridiculous," she answered dryly.

I didn't push the issue, but I made a mental note to ask Liam about it later. If he liked Tami and he hadn't told me, I was going to kill him!

We finished lunch and said goodbye, Tami grudgingly agreeing to meet at PHD, a club located on the rooftop of Dream Downtown.

Inside the car on the way home, I informed Sebastian of my plans.

"Is it really necessary for you to go out tonight?" he asked, frowning, his attention fixed on the road.

"Yes, it's necessary for my mental health."

He shook his head but didn't say another word.

When we got home, I went straight to my room, the only space that still belonged to me, where I could do whatever I wanted and not have to answer to anyone. That night, Marcus Kozel was going to find out what kind of woman he was dealing with.

I put on the sexiest dress I had—super short, black, hugging all my curves—and bloodred heels that lifted me a few inches off the ground. I would've loved to see Marcus's face when his lackeys sent him their report for the night.

I pulled my hair up into a high ponytail and took my time doing my makeup. I used a dark eyeshadow that brought out the color of my eyes and spent extra time making sure my lips were perfectly lined. When I walked out of my room, Sebastian observed me without a word. I was glad not to have to answer any comment from him because, even though a part of me had dressed like that for him, we were still barely speaking to each other.

"Are the gorillas downstairs?" I asked as I checked my bag and touched up my lipstick in front of him.

"Egor and Jakov are waiting, yes," he patiently corrected me, his gaze pausing on my legs.

We left the apartment and stepped onto the elevator, where we stood against opposite walls and glared at each other.

"Don't fuck up my night, Sebastian."

"Don't do anything stupid and we won't have any reason to."

He looked very handsome in his dark jeans and gray sweater.

Simple was sexy, something I hadn't realized until I met him. The fact that he cared so little about fashion or his appearance made him even more attractive. I looked at his arms, his hands, remembering the places they'd been, and felt a sudden heat travel through my body, stopping at my cheeks.

"I wish I could read your mind . . ." he said, staring at me.

"You wouldn't like what I'm thinking, believe me," I answered.

He moved closer and placed his hands against the wall on either side of my head. "No? And why's that?" His face was so close to mine that I could feel his breath on my lips.

Just then, the elevator doors opened, and he stepped away from me with his characteristic calm. I recovered my composure and pushed past him without another glance. No way would I fall for him again.

The night wasn't cold at all, the late spring storm having given way to more typical April temperatures, and the city was beautiful. I didn't fail to notice the fact that Sebastian held the door open for me or the gentle brush of his fingers on my waist as I passed.

I didn't want to talk to him, and I was more nervous than normal, so I pretended to call Tami, talking to myself for the entire drive to the hotel as he kept his eyes fixed on the road.

It didn't take us long to get there, thankfully, and I jumped out of the car as soon as he pulled over. Tami was already waiting for me along with Stella and Lisa, who all turned to stare at the entourage trailing behind me. I smiled, pretending this was all perfectly normal, and greeted them.

"Are you guys ready to get drunk tonight?" I asked excitedly.

Stella and Lisa laughed as we waited for Liam to come out to get us. Tami seemed a little nervous, but she was more beautiful than ever, with her platinum-blond hair styled into loose curls that fell almost down to her ass. Her dark jeans and sexy white top accentuated her body in all the right places, and she was wearing heels, something unusual for her.

"Hey, you look incredible," I said, looking her up and down.

"I don't know, I . . ." she said nervously.

I rolled my eyes and grinned from ear to ear as I saw Liam emerge.

He smiled back and, noticing Tami, stopped and frowned. "What is she doing here?" he asked very rudely.

"Liam!" I scolded him, and his face cracked into a grin to show that he was joking.

He laughed at the expression on Tami's face, suddenly pale. "Come on, don't look at me like that," he said, looking her up and down admiringly.

Tami glared at him and stepped next to Stella, looking away.

Liam chuckled, then any semblance of happiness faded from his face as he spotted Sebastian. "You're still here?" he asked, then took notice of the two gorillas. I had already told Liam everything . . . well, almost everything, and he knew that I now had three bodyguards with me everywhere I went.

Sebastian didn't respond, busily staring down the street, no doubt making sure everything was in order. "Come on, get inside," he said to the other girls and me.

Stella and Lisa happily did as he said, and I followed, only coming to a halt when I noticed Liam had stopped in front of Tami, blocking her way.

I rolled my eyes. Seriously?

"Say one thing that you like about me and I'll let you in," he asked arrogantly.

Tami huffed and crossed her arms. "You're insufferable."

Liam turned around to leave, but she yanked at his sweater to stop him. He glanced at her hand on his arm. Sparks were flying; how had I not realized it before?

Tami looked at him timidly, unsure what to say. "I like your shoelaces."

Liam laughed loudly, leaned toward her, and whispered, "That won't cut it."

I looked on in amusement.

"Okay, okay!" she said again, and Liam gave her his full attention. "I like your back," she admitted, turning red.

I almost laughed out loud.

Liam smiled. "My back?"

"Yes," she said, now as red as a tomato. "I like not having to look at your face," she added, and I could tell she was annoyed by the way her fists were clenched tightly.

"Can we get everyone inside?" Sebastian interrupted the scene.

Liam looked toward him and lifted the rope to let Tami through. He whispered something to her that I didn't catch, and Tami stormed past me, seething.

"You could give it a rest for one night, couldn't you?" I said, irritated.

I turned to follow my friends into the elevator, then looked back again as I heard Sebastian arguing behind me. "We're with her," he said calmly.

"A thousand dollars each," the bouncer told him.

"A thousand dollars to get in?"

I walked over to them. Liam seemed unaware of what was happening as he let some other girls in, greeting them each with a kiss on the cheek. "Yes, a thousand dollars to get in," he repeated rudely.

"They're with me, John." The bouncer knew me, so I didn't think it would be a problem.

"Your girlfriends are with you; these guys have to pay," John insisted with an unfriendly expression.

"Liam?" I called out to him, trying to intervene as I saw that

Sebastian was taking out a credit card angrily. I wasn't such a bitch that'd I make him pay a thousand dollars to protect me.

Liam walked over, grabbed me by the waist, and kissed me on the cheek, very close to my lips. "What is it, babe?" he asked, looking only at me and ignoring the situation playing out right before his eyes.

"Let him in, Liam," I said in a low voice so that only he could hear me.

"Are you sure?" he asked, looking unhappy.

I nodded silently, and Liam turned around, taking his hands off me. "John, he's with me," he said, and Sebastian put away his wallet with an irritated sigh. "The other two can wait outside. I don't want to fill up the club with soldiers."

Sebastian seemed fine with that arrangement, and I practically jumped for joy. Without Marcus's lackeys watching . . . No, I wasn't going to throw myself at Sebastian, as much as I might've wanted to. I was still angry with him.

I saw that Sebastian was giving them instructions, indicating points along the street that I supposed they were meant to watch. The seriousness of his tone made me nervous. I didn't want to be scared, but it was sometimes impossible, considering recent events, on top of what I'd learned about my father.

"Let's go up," Liam said, tugging at me.

"Hold on," I said, waiting for Sebastian.

I could tell by the look in his eyes that something wasn't right. I had no idea what it was, but I felt a shiver run down my spine.

Without even realizing it, as soon as he reached us, I moved to stand right beside him. I felt safe with him next to me. Liam frowned as we walked to the elevator that would take us to the rooftop bar.

"What's wrong?" I asked Sebastian.

"This place has too many entrances."

I could tell he was in a bad mood, and I imagined he didn't enjoy seeing Liam so close to me either. I didn't say anything, and when the elevator doors opened, I went directly to join the other girls, who were serving themselves from the bottles of tequila and vodka that had already been placed at our table along with a bucket of ice, orange juice, and raspberries.

I preferred tequila, at least when I intended to get nice and drunk.

Tami was seated on one of the sofas with a glass that looked like it contained only orange juice.

"Tell me there's at least a splash of tequila in there," I said, leaning over to sniff her drink.

"Don't be a pest," she said, moving her glass away before lifting it to her lips. I followed the direction of her gaze and saw that her eyes were fixed on Liam, who was flirting with a large-breasted woman at the bar.

"Come on, let's dance," I said, dragging her to the center of the dance floor.

Aside from Tami taking ballet with me at school as an extra-curricular activity, she also did fencing and field hockey. She was a total athlete, so she knew how to move her body. The two of us had always been the ones to create the choreography for our class Christmas pageant, putting lots of hard work and energy into it.

It had been ages since we went dancing together because Tami didn't like to go out. We were polar opposites—she was a platinum blonde, and I was a brunette; she was short, I was tall, and so on and so forth. I still wondered how I'd been able to convince her, but I was happy to have her there with me.

It didn't take long before all eyes were on us. Tami and I were great dancers and knew how to have fun together; it was inevitable for guys to try to butt in.

I tugged on her waist to save her from a guy who was drooling over her as she stared down another one who was coming up behind me. We laughed, and I dragged her over to the bar. I needed another drink, immediately.

"Two tequila shots, please," I said to the bartender. Tami shook her head. "Don't be boring!" I insisted, and I thanked him for bringing salt and lime.

"You know how I get when I drink alcohol," she said, looking repulsed by the shot I'd shoved in her face.

"I love drunk Tami; she lets herself get lost in the moment." I raised my glass in the air. "To getting out of your head and letting loose for once," I said as we clinked glasses and downed the shots. We laughed and quickly stuck the limes into our mouths.

Tami's eyes then wandered to some point behind me, and her face fell. "You'll never guess who just walked through the door."

I turned to see who she was referring to, and there was Regan, flanked by his buddies.

"Shit," I said, turning back around when our eyes met across the room.

"He's coming over," Tami said with a frown.

And sure enough, two minutes later, I felt a hand on my waist. "Hey, baby," he said, spinning me around.

"Don't call me that," I said, removing his hands from my body and turning around to order another drink. "Do you want one, too, Tami?"

Tami nodded without taking her eyes off my ex.

"Hey, come on, Marfil. When are you going to forgive me?"

I arched my eyebrows in response.

"You know I would've never made any bet that had to do with you, baby. You can't believe all the rumors."

"What about the video they showed me with you admitting everything, asshole?" I said, accepting the drink from the bartender. "Let's go, Tami."

"What an idiot," Tami said, her cheeks already pink from the alcohol as we walked away.

My eyes unwittingly searched for Sebastian. Had he noticed the guy who'd just come up to me was the same dude who'd forced himself on me at that party?

I finally spotted him beside one of the windows, a blond woman standing next to him, very close.

Flirting on the job?

I finished my drink and went back for another. When I returned to the table, I saw that Liam had sat down beside Tami and was talking to her. She was staring straight ahead, scowling, her third drink now half empty. Liam seemed to be proving her right about him, talking to her in a tone somewhere between angry and annoyed. Tami saw that I was watching them, said something to Liam, and jumped up. "I think I need more of this," she said, pointing to her now-empty glass.

I walked her to the bar, where we ordered another shot. If we continued on like this, we were going to get trashed. I could see it coming.

"Hey . . . what's up with you and Liam?" I asked very seriously, or at least as seriously as the alcohol would allow.

Liam observed us from the sofa with an unfriendly expression.

"Nothing," she said, turning her back to him.

"Tami, I've seen the way you look at him. It took me a while to realize it, but I'm not a total idiot," I said, trying to ignore the scene taking place across the club: Sebastian was still talking to the blond girl, and she seemed to be moving closer and closer to him.

"Look, I don't want to talk about that right now, okay? But I promise I will when I'm ready."

That's just how Tami was, very reserved. Liam needed to

know that getting through to Tami was going to take a lot more than a bit of flirting and a few compliments.

"Fine, let's dance," I said, jerking her arm.

The music was good, a mix of rock and Latin hits. I don't know how much time went by, but before I knew it, Liam had joined us on the dance floor. The problem was that, instead of dancing with my friend, he pressed his body against mine.

"Liam . . ." I said, trying to pull away, but then his mouth moved down to my neck, to the spot where I still had a mark from the hickey I'd received a few days ago.

Tami stopped, gave me a heartbroken look, and then walked away.

Both Liam and I stretched out our hands to stop her, and Tami had no choice but to stumble back to us.

"Don't get me wrapped up in your mess!" I shouted at them, stepping away.

I left them arguing and, trying to gather the courage I didn't feel, went directly to the corner where my bodyguard was about to hook up with some random girl. When I reached them, I stuck my fingers through the blond girl's belt loops and pulled her away from him. She tripped, spilling her drink onto her dress.

"What the fuck are you doing?" she said, shaking herself off.

I stepped beside Sebastian. "Get out of here," I said, looking her in the eyes.

She was a bit taller than me, but I didn't care. I knew martial arts now thanks to Sebastian, or at least that's what I told myself as she lunged toward me and I grabbed her by the hair.

Sebastian immediately picked me up me by the waist and carried me to the other side of the club. "Have you lost your mind?" he shouted over the loud music, setting me down.

"You're working!" I shouted back, furious that he seemed to be on her side.

"Why do you care how I do my job?"

I crossed my arms. "Because my life depends on it, genius."

"You're drunk, Marfil. I assure you that I haven't lost sight of you for a second."

"Oh, okay, so you can look at tits and watch me at the same time? Very talented."

Sebastian exhaled through his nose. "Marfil . . ."

He tried to turn his back on me, but I grabbed his wrist.

"Do you like her?" I asked in a pathetic tone. I needed to stop drinking immediately.

Sebastian looked me in the eye for a few seconds and leaned down to speak into my ear. "The only girl that interests me here is you."

He walked away before I had the chance to kiss him.

I looked around, searching for Tami, but I couldn't find her, or Liam for that matter. I smiled at the thought of them starting something. Although, knowing Liam . . . I feared he might hurt her. I'd have to have a very serious chat with him about it.

I went over to where Stella and Lisa were dancing in the center of the dance floor with two very hot guys. I joined in and let my drunk mind take control.

Somehow, I found myself alone on the dance floor a short while later. Well, I wasn't exactly alone. There were tons of people dancing all around me, but my friends had gone to make out with their respective hook-ups.

I scanned the club for Sebastian and wished more than anything that he wasn't my bodyguard. I wanted to be able to walk over to him, whisper that I loved him, and wrap my arms around him as we moved to the music.

Why didn't he come over and dance with me? What harm could it do? He'd just been standing there all night letting that blond girl try to flirt with him, too polite to tell her to go away . . . or maybe he liked her and was lying to me. None of what he'd said to me before mattered, if he cared about me at all, he'd have done something, thrown everything away for me. He should've been my boyfriend, not my bodyguard, and he should've put that asshole Marcus in his place. But he chose his job.

I felt someone embrace me from behind. I closed my eyes, and for an instant my fantasy became reality.

"Just looking at you gets me hard, baby," said a voice that sounded nothing like Sebastian's. Regan had found me again.

"How romantic," I said, annoyed.

"You're so hot," he said, stroking my cheek.

I shuddered, disgusted by him.

"I'm sorry for what I did," he said, moving closer. "I didn't know what I had until I lost it."

Regan had been the first guy I'd ever thought I was in love with, and he broke my heart. His apology meant something, as much as I wanted to deny it. A first love always cuts deep, although in reality, it hadn't been love at all. I now knew that with total certainty.

What I felt for Sebastian was ten times stronger than what I'd ever felt for Regan, and it wasn't even the half of what I might be able to feel in the future. Love had invaded every part of my body. I knew that if Sebastian remained at my side twenty-four hours a day, if he let down his guard, if he touched me, kissed me, and allowed himself to be with me . . . he could easily become the man I gave my heart to.

Before I realized what was happening, Regan had dragged me over to a less crowded corner of the club.

"Do you remember our first kiss?" he asked, taking my face in his hands and placing his lips very close to mine.

Why was I letting him touch me?

"I remember the last one," I said, a sick feeling in my stomach. We'd been dating for months and had gotten more intimate than ever, kissing, touching, undressing each other. I thought I was going to finally lose my virginity with him, was seriously considering it, despite all my hang-ups. He'd kissed me in the car at the door to my building and told me he loved me. The next day, I found out who he truly was.

His mouth now pressed into mine, feeling slimy and disgusting. His tongue jabbed at me violently; his hands groped me clumsily, without any tenderness or feeling.

Sebastian was the only man who knew how to touch me, the only man who could give me what I wanted.

I pushed Regan away, hard, but he only pressed tighter against me. I wasn't scared this time; I was prepared. I would put the things Sebastian had taught me into practice . . .

But before I had time to put my new skills to the test, Regan was no longer in front of me. Sebastian had shoved him away, knocking him hard to the floor. He said something to Regan and then turned back to me with eyes blazing.

"Hey," I shouted angrily. "I could've handled it on my own! If you always intervene, how do you expect me to learn?!"

"We're leaving," he said, grabbing my hand tightly and hauling me to the elevator.

I tried to break free, but he gripped me tighter, hurting me.

"Let me go!" I shouted, digging my heels into the floor.

But he didn't let go, and before I knew it, a security guard had come up to us from behind, intending to get Sebastian off me.

With a movement so quick my eyes couldn't even register it, the security guard was next on the floor, touching his bleeding mouth in surprise.

I stood there in shock, my eyes wide as saucers, shouting all kinds of obscenities. Sebastian wrapped an arm tightly around my waist and picked me up to carry me into the elevator, where he set me down before I had time to even process what had happened.

"Are you crazy?!"

"I saw someone . . . We have to get out of here."

I looked at him, wondering if he really believed I was that stupid.

"You're jealous; that's the problem."

Sebastian looked at me in disbelief for a second, and then panic flashed across his face as the elevator doors opened to two men, both pointing guns at us.

Sebastian pushed me back, covering me with his body, and someone fired before I had time to understand what was happening. I screamed at the top of my lungs as I fell to the floor and curled up against the wall.

Sebastian acted quickly. With one dry blow to the wrist, he knocked the gun from one of the attacker's hands, then proceeded to knock him out with a punch to the head, as the other man picked up the gun and pointed it at me.

"Sebastian!" I shouted as loud as I could, terrified.

The next thing I heard was a howl of pain and a hollow blow, then I felt arms lifting me from the floor. Sebastian took me by the hand, and we rushed out into the street like a bat out of hell.

"Marfil!" came a voice from behind me.

I turned around and saw Tami running toward us. Liam was behind her, his eyes full of fear. I had no idea what they were doing out there. I hadn't seen them since they'd disappeared together earlier.

Sebastian stopped for an instant to look around, and that's when I saw them: Egor and Jakov lay on the ground, dead.

"Oh my God!" I shouted in horror, covering my mouth with my hands.

Then everything seemed to happen in slow motion. Tires screeched on the asphalt as a car skidded around the corner and stopped in front of the spot where we stood. Sebastian pushed me back inside, causing me to fall to the floor as he aimed his gun at a man, who was pointing his own gun at us.

We heard the sound of gunfire as people began running and screaming in all directions. One of the screams sounded like a voice I knew well.

"TAMI!" I shouted with all my might as I rushed toward her and fell beside her. "Oh my God! Oh my God!"

My friend lay on the ground, blood pooling around her. She'd been shot in the side.

Liam dropped down beside her as well and frightenedly applied pressure to the wound as he shouted for someone to call an ambulance.

"Tami!" I shrieked, tears clouding my eyes. I felt a hand lift me from the ground. "NO!" I shouted, pulling free with all my might.

I'd kill them. I would kill whoever did that to her.

Sebastian swept me into his arms and was carrying me to the car before I had time to react. He deposited me in the passenger's seat and jumped behind the wheel, starting the engine and pressing the accelerator all the way down. "Fuck!" he shouted at the steering wheel. His eyes darted between the rearview mirror and the side mirrors as he turned the wrong way down a one-way street and then barreled through a pedestrian area.

"I want to go back, take me back!" I shouted. "They shot Tami!"

"I know, I know," he said, keeping his eyes fixed on the road. "There's an ambulance on the way. You couldn't stay there, Marfil; they were going to kill you."

"Take me back!" I shouted hysterically, pulling at the handle to open the door but finding it locked.

"They'll kill you!" he shouted, shutting me up.

I looked frightenedly in the rearview mirror, but the car was shaking so hard that I couldn't really see, forcing my hands to grip the armrests.

What was going on? Did we have a flat tire?

"Hey, relax . . ." Sebastian said, now speaking more calmly.

Seeing the concern in his eyes, I understood that the car wasn't shaking; I was. My entire body was trembling violently, and my teeth had begun to chatter. Someone had tried to kill me, and they shot Tami instead. She could be dead . . .

Sebastian sped up a ramp to a parking garage with sweeping views of the city skyline. He stopped the car, took a cell phone out of the glove box, and quickly dialed a number. Someone answered almost instantly.

"They just hit us . . . Three men, they couldn't have been over thirty years old . . . Yes, outside the Dream Downtown . . . She's fine," he said, briefly glancing at me. "Talk to Suarez to get the security camera footage, the one from the left elevator . . . Okay."

I tried to follow that conversation, but my brain kept replaying the scene I'd just witnessed, the images of my friend bleeding out on the ground. I took out my cell phone and called Liam, but it went straight to voicemail.

"Take this," Sebastian said, removing his sweater and forcing me to put my arms in it. Even in my current emotional state, I couldn't help but notice it smelled like him. "You're in shock; try to calm down. Tami is going to be all right; I'm sure of it," he said, cranking the heat to its maximum setting as he checked the time on his watch.

"How do you know?" I asked.

"I've seen a lot of bullet wounds. Hers wasn't one of the bad ones." I looked at him, terrified. He pushed his seat all the way back and pulled me onto his lap, wrapping his arms around me. "You're safe," he said as I buried my face in his neck and my tears stained his clothes. "Don't worry, everything's going to be all right. I promise." He rubbed my back until we heard the sound of a car coming up the ramp behind us. "Stay here," he ordered, placing me back in my seat before he got out of the car and closed the door behind him.

I watched through the side mirror as a man as tall as Sebastian greeted him with the same serious and intimidating demeanor as Sebastian's.

What was happening?

Five minutes later, the man left, and Sebastian got back in the car beside me.

"Who was that?"

Sebastian started the car and drove away. "No one."

"No one?!" I shrieked in disbelief.

Sebastian seemed much more concerned with the messages coming into his cell phone than with explaining things to me.

"Stop the car!" I said, looking down at my hands, which wouldn't stop shaking.

He ignored me.

I pulled at the door handle, and this time it opened. I jumped out as he slowed to a stop. I had just seen two men dead at my feet. I had just seen my best friend bleeding out on the ground because of me. I now knew how my mother must've felt right before she died, the way anyone feels when they have a gun pointed at their head. Having gotten out alive only made me more scared because it meant that this was truly just the beginning . . .

Why hadn't I listened from the start? Why did I have to be so stubborn, caring more about having a normal life than my safety . . . my friends' safety?

Sebastian jumped out of the car and raced over to me.

"What the fuck is happening?" I shrieked, turning on him.

Sebastian lifted his hands, trying to calm me, as if I were a frightened animal he had to approach with caution. "Marfil, I know you're scared, but we have to get out of the city."

I looked at him, open-mouthed. “What?! No!”

“There are a lot of things you should know, and I promise I will explain everything, but we have to go, now.”

“Where?”

“I’ll take you to my apartment in New Jersey. I’ll explain everything there.”

I wiped my tears with my forearm, looking at him mistrustingly. “I want to talk to my father,” I said in a broken voice.

“You will, I promise, but we have to go.”

I looked around. New York suddenly seemed menacing and dangerous. This city, which had taken me in two years ago, welcomed me with open arms, helped me discover who I was, had now betrayed me. I didn’t want to go. I didn’t want to lock myself away somewhere and wait for . . . what? For them to stop trying to kill me?

I got back in the car and managed to connect with Liam on the way to New Jersey. Tami was in the operating room; the bullet had perforated a blood vessel, but they were doing everything possible to save her life.

I cried for the entire forty minutes it took to reach Sebastian’s apartment as he checked the mirrors nonstop, more nervous than I’d ever seen him, continuously throwing me worried glances.

Sebastian’s building was located on the corner of a quiet street. There was a park across from it and a coffee shop on the corner.

I followed him up the stairs to apartment 4B. Sebastian unlocked the door, and I walked into a small loft that, upon first glance, consisted of a large bed on one wall, a small kitchen, a couch, and a large TV. Several boxes were also scattered around, as if he’d recently moved in.

“You live here?” I asked, moving through a space that belonged to him for the first time.

"I did," he said simply as he went into the kitchen to get a glass of water and rummaged for something in a drawer. "Drink this," he said, handing me a pill.

"What is it?" I asked, mistrustingly.

"A sedative," he replied as his eyes looked to my bloodied knees. I hadn't even realized that I'd hurt myself when I fell to the ground beside Tami. "I'll clean you up. Wait here," he said, standing and moving into what I supposed was the bathroom, only to return a few seconds later with a first aid kit and started cleaning my scrapes.

"You didn't tell me you were from New Jersey," I said, trying, unsuccessfully, to keep myself from trembling.

Sebastian didn't answer. He simply went to a closet and took out a thick gray blanket, which he then draped over my shoulders.

"You know exactly what's going on here," I said after he'd finished cleaning my wounds. He sat down beside me and looked more serious than I'd ever seen him. "You know who's trying to kill me, and you also know what my father's gotten himself into."

"You should rest, Marfil," he said, tucking a strand of hair behind my ear.

"Why do I feel like what you know is going to destroy me?"

Sebastian looked at me unblinkingly. "Because it will."

## CHAPTER 33

# SEBASTIAN

It took forever for Marfil to fall asleep. I couldn't get her to close her eyes until after Liam called to say that her friend was in stable condition. The operation had been successful, and they expected Tami to fully recover within a couple of weeks.

I should've listened to my instincts. I should've gotten her out of there as soon as I saw that car parked on the corner and that man staring at us. I should've dragged Marfil home kicking and screaming if I had to when I realized it would be impossible to guard all the entrances to the hotel. But I didn't do any of that, because I didn't want to have to fight her. I wanted her to have the most normal life possible. I wanted her to be able to go out and have fun if she wanted to, but for weeks, things had been anything but normal.

Now Marcus was the one in charge. I had been able to manage Alejandro, but Marcus was totally different, and to make matters worse, Marfil was Marcus's new obsession. I knew things would end badly the night she first went out with him. Alejandro Cortés knew exactly what he was doing by introducing his oldest daughter to one of the most powerful men in the country. I'd bet good money Alejandro had been keeping that ace up his sleeve from the day he first laid eyes on his little girl. In the world her father moved in, beautiful women were common currency. And Marfil was his goose that laid the golden egg.

I gripped my glass so tightly that it cracked in my hands,

cutting me. I cursed between gritted teeth and ran my hand under the water. Blood gushed out, making the cut seem worse than it was. I wrapped my hand in a kitchen towel, and I looked at her.

As soon as she learned the truth, she would hate me. Watching her sleep was a privilege I would never get again, so I treasured this moment for as long as I could.

What was I going to tell her? The whole truth or just part of it?

I closed my eyes, thinking about what would happen to me if I failed in my job.

I couldn't fail.

I had to move forward as planned.

## CHAPTER 34

# MARFIL

It was still dark out when I opened my eyes. I didn't immediately remember where I was, but then I found Sebastian dozing on the couch beside the bed, and the terrible scenes of the night before returned to me.

The first thing I did was check my cell phone. Liam had written to say that Tami's parents would arrive the next day and that he would stay with her until then. He wanted to know what the hell had happened. He told me the police wanted to interrogate all witnesses, and that Sebastian and I needed to present ourselves to make a statement. I responded, saying I'd talk to Sebastian about it.

Sebastian, attentive to my every movement, opened his eyes as soon as I sat up.

"I didn't mean to wake you," I said, seeing that he was making his way over to me.

"I was awake," he said, stretching out a hand to gently take hold of a loose strand of my hair and run his fingers through it. "I'm sorry about all of this, Elephant." He sat down on the bed beside me.

I closed my eyes as I felt his lips brush my cheek. He kissed me tenderly and then sat back to look at me.

"Were you able to get some rest?"

I thought about the nightmares I'd had during the hours I'd been asleep, and I knew that I hadn't rested much at all. I felt even more exhausted than before, but I didn't think it necessary to concern him, so I nodded. I knew he was dreading the talk that was coming, but he had agreed to help me understand what the hell was going on.

Sebastian sighed, and for an instant, it seemed like he was reading my mind. Our eyes met, and something inside me stirred.

"When I look into your eyes, I feel like I'm looking into the eyes of an angel," he said, slowly rubbing his thumb over my bottom lip. "If only you weren't so beautiful, in every sense of the word."

His comment seemed out of place, given the circumstances. I was about to respond, but his lips brushed gently against mine.

I sighed, and he took that as an opportunity to deepen the kiss, touching me in a way that made my heart race. I hadn't been expecting that, but I also wasn't complaining. He leaned me back onto the bed, his body on top of mine. It was the first time we'd been alone in bed together, completely alone, with no cameras to register our movements through the apartment.

He had given me one of his shirts to sleep in, with nothing on underneath. The temptation must have been too much because he wasted no time running his hand up my leg until it rested on my knee. My breathing accelerated at his contact, his closeness, imagining all the possibilities.

"What I feel for you terrifies me, Marfil," he confessed, his mouth hovering over mine before kissing me again.

I felt my heart flutter when he admitted he felt something for me, and gave in. I slid my hand up the back of his neck and buried my fingers in his hair, pulling him closer to me, arching my body to be in contact with his.

"I'm scared that I don't know anything about you, at least not fully, and yet I feel the way I do . . ." I said in a trembling voice.

"You know much more than you should, believe me."

He pressed my body into the mattress, giving me exactly what I wanted. Feeling his weight against me—his body so large and mine so small by comparison—made me want him in every sense of the word.

I slipped one of my hands inside his shirt and felt his torso, hard and chiseled like a marble statue. All his muscles were perfectly defined, and I wanted to run my lips, my tongue along every nook and cranny. I tugged on his shirt, and he helped me take it off him.

Were we really doing this? Right now?

I couldn't shake this strange feeling that he wanted one last chance to have me before he told me the truth that would push me away forever. The thought terrified me, and I hugged him tight, not wanting to ever let go.

I was enthralled by his strength, his perfection, knowing that he had to try so hard to control himself with me, that he would kill for me. It turned me on to think about how strong he was, everything he knew how to do . . .

"Teach me, Sebastian," I said, pulling back from his mouth and meeting his gaze. "Teach me how to pleasure you."

The look he gave me said it all. He picked me up and flipped me around so that I was now straddling him. "Kiss me," he demanded.

I leaned down and kissed his lips. Then I left a trail of wet kisses along his neck, over his sculpted pecs, and on each one of his well-defined abs until I reached his obliques.

He looked so serious seeing me on top of him, inching closer to that part of him I was dying to taste . . . My fear vanished. I forgot about all my problems, what might happen to me, the terrible truth he promised to reveal. All I wanted was to pleasure this man whom I loved. For the first time, I wasn't being selfish. For the first time, I was thinking about him instead of myself and what I felt when he kissed and touched me.

I unbuttoned his jeans, and he helped me take them off him. His erection strained against the fabric of his boxers, demanding my attention. He looked at me, encouraging me to go on, as if giving me permission.

Seeing that I was unsure of what to do next, he took my hand in his and placed it on his dick. He was hard, and I gripped him tightly on pure instinct.

"Slowly, beautiful," he said, exhaling through his nose and squeezing his eyes shut. "Like this," he said, showing me how to touch him.

I was shocked by the feel of him in my hands. I had only touched Regan and Liam, and that had been two years ago . . . Touching Sebastian, seeing his reaction, how his breath hitched.

I didn't hesitate.

I took him in my mouth, and I heard him curse under his breath, shaking beneath me. That turned me on. I caressed the tip of his dick, slowly running circles with my tongue. Sebastian slid his hand to the back of my head, gripped my hair, then began guiding my movements and setting the pace, though I was in no hurry. I wanted to enjoy that experience as long as possible.

Sebastian, however, seemed to think differently.

He flipped me around again and climbed on top of me. I didn't know whether to be upset or in awe of his command. Not that I had too much time to dwell on it. With one swift motion, he lifted my shirt and started kissing me everywhere, stopping on my breasts and sucking on my nipples as his hand slipped inside my underwear and applied pressure to the most sensitive part of my body.

"You are exquisite," he said, trailing his tongue from my neck all the way into my belly button. All the while, his huge pupils looked like they wanted to devour me.

I squirmed excitedly under his weight as he lowered himself little by little, until his mouth was between my legs.

"God . . ." I said, closing my eyes as he ran his tongue over my clit. I was going to explode. I was going to explode into a thousand pieces.

I writhed with intense pleasure, unable to remain still, until he lifted my legs and placed them on his shoulders. I was too excited, and he was all too willing to give me what I wanted.

"Don't move," he said, pulling away from me for an instant.

"Sebastian . . ." I said in a weak whisper as he tasted me again.

This time, however, it was as if he'd been hungry for more. He buried his tongue in my pussy, then sucked on my clit as he inserted a finger inside me. Slowly at first, then picked up speed. His tongue devoured me as his fingers fucked me.

"Fuck . . . Sebastian . . . I'm so close."

The way his mouth touched me, the way his tongue knew exactly what to do to drive me crazy . . . the pleasure was too much to handle. The orgasm came on quickly, as I shouted his name loudly.

Sebastian pulled back and looked at me, very serious.

It took me a few seconds to recover, but my body wanted more, needed more.

"What are you waiting for?" I asked, longing for him to take me, to make me his once and for all. I wanted him inside me.

Unfortunately for me, he ran a hand over his face in a gesture I knew all too well.

"You're a virgin, fuck," he said, very serious.

"And?" I argued, sitting up and tugging him by the neck.

He kissed me fiercely, and I felt his hard dick against my groin.

I quivered.

"It's better we wait," he said, and I could tell by his expression that it tortured him.

"Are you crazy?" I said, arching myself against him.

"Stop," he said, pressing my body to the mattress with a hand against my stomach.

"Fuck me, Sebastian," I ordered him, taking his hard cock between my hands.

"Don't talk like that," he said, biting my lower lip, more as a distraction than anything else.

What the hell was wrong with him?

"You don't want me to talk like that because I'm a little princess who always gets what she wants?"

Sebastian took my wrists in one hand and pulled my arms over my head, pinning me to the mattress.

"Yes, you are a little princess, my little fucking princess, to be precise. And even though I'm dying to fuck you, I can't do it right now. Not without you knowing everything that I am, everything that I do . . ."

The term "little fucking princess" wasn't the most romantic thing I'd ever heard, and it wasn't how I saw myself. I was no princess, and I hated to be called that, but hearing him say I was *his* drove me wild.

"I know who you are, Sebastian," I said, looking into his brown eyes. "You're the man I love. That's who you are."

Sebastian closed his eyes, and instead of reciprocating the *I love you,* he simply pulled away from me and flopped down beside me on the bed.

"You don't know what you're saying . . ." he said, his eyes fixed on the ceiling.

My declaration of love seemed to have hit him like a bucket of ice-cold water. He stood up and put his jeans back on.

"I know what I'm saying because I'm the one who feels it," I said, pulling at the sheet to cover myself, suddenly feeling very exposed.

"You have no fucking idea, Marfil," he said, shooting me a

venomous glance. "You're in love with someone who doesn't exist."

"You're a hologram and you didn't tell me?" I asked sarcastically.

He looked at me condescendingly and walked away from the bed to place both hands on the kitchen table. "I've done things that would horrify you," he said after a long silence, looking at me very seriously.

"You were in the military; it's normal you'd think that. The things you must've had to face . . ." I started, but he let out a laugh.

"My time in the military is the least of it."

He was starting to scare me. I knew that Sebastian had a difficult childhood and a dark past. Everything indicated he had struggled to get to where he was now, but that didn't mean he was a bad person.

"Stop demonizing yourself."

Sebastian was about to say something when his phone began to ring.

I took the interruption to slip his T-shirt and my underwear back on. Why had such an intimate moment between us turned into a stupid debate about whether Sebastian was a good or bad person? It was ridiculous.

I could hear him arguing with someone, and as soon as he hung up the phone, he punched the kitchen window, which cracked, causing my heart to jump into my throat.

I stood up from the bed and moved away from him until my back was against the wall.

Sebastian turned toward me, his hand bloodied, the mask of hatred on his face slowly giving way to regret. He walked slowly over to me. "I'm sorry," he said, holding out his hand.

I allowed him to caress my cheek, maintaining eye contact. "Tell me the fucking truth once and for all, Sebastian."

He hesitated but finally nodded. "You're not going to like what I have to say, but considering the way things are going, you'll find out soon enough anyway. You're too smart not to."

I didn't say anything, waiting for him to continue.

"Your father is a drug lord, Marfil." He said it without hesitation, like someone ripping off a Band-Aid. Better to get it over with quickly so it hurts less, or so they say. But my world stopped, and the words that had just fallen from his lips echoed in my brain. I was unable to process them.

"That's a lie," I said, crossing the room to the opposite wall.

"No, it's not," he said, looking at me sadly.

I hated that look with all my being.

"How do you know?"

He pressed his lips together and let out all the air he was holding in. "Because I am, too."

CHAPTER 35

# MARFIL

"I started out on the streets. We had nothing, and selling weed was the easiest way to get money. I lived in a neighborhood where drugs were common currency, and I did what I had to do to help take care of myself and the other kids who lived with me."

I listened to him without moving a muscle. He didn't come over to me, and I didn't want him to either.

"I started out at fourteen. Samara knew, and she hated me for it, but the money I brought home from selling drugs helped to feed her." The look in his eyes as he spoke told me that it pained him to remember those times. "Once you get into that world, it's very hard to get out. The gangs control everything: who you talk to, who you hang out with, who you sell to . . . and if you squeal or try to leave, they'll kill you." He stepped closer to me and stretched out his tattooed arm. "I was an addict at age sixteen," he admitted. "Heroin."

I closed my eyes as I felt them fill with tears.

"Your father came across me," he then said, and I looked back at him. "He was the one who helped me get clean. He saw potential in me, a potential that no one else had ever seen; everyone had always treated me like scum. He paid off the drug boss I worked for, and he advised me to enlist in the military. He sent me a little extra money every month, and when I finished my service at the top of my class, he paid to train me in everything I know. I was good, Marfil, the best."

I wanted to plug my ears. I didn't want to know more. I didn't want to find out things that would make me hate him.

"For the first time in my life, there was something I was good at. I had found my place . . . Your father offered to let me work for him. It was nothing like my previous experience, selling drugs on the streets. Your father controls one of the largest drug routes in the country. Your uncle is the head of one of the most important cartels in Colombia."

"Stop," I said, wishing he would shut up.

He didn't stop speaking, but he remained at a distance. "A few months ago, a branch of the Russian mafia in Miami tried to take one of your father's routes from him. We planned an operation to intervene. I was the one in charge of carrying it out, strategy being my strong suit, but everything went horribly wrong. We didn't know who we were up against, and the son of one of the most powerful Russian drug bosses in the world ended up being killed in the shootout. That was a few weeks before you were kidnapped. We can't even be sure that it was one of our bullets or one of theirs, but from that moment, all they've wanted is to get revenge on your father."

*An eye for an eye.* Now I understood.

"That's why they want to kill me."

He nodded silently and took two steps toward me.

I raised a hand to stop him. "Don't come any closer."

Sebastian seemed prepared for my rejection, but even so, I could tell my words pained him.

"So they're the ones who kidnapped me?" I asked, although it didn't make sense. "They could've easily killed me."

I caught a glint of something in his eyes, but he quickly hid it.

"We still don't understand the kidnapping. We've even considered the notion that it was someone else. But it's obvious that you are in real danger, and that's why your father has allied with Marcus Kozel. He's the only one who can take on the Russian mafia."

I shook my head, unable to believe what he was saying. I had thought my father might've defrauded people, owed them money, which was why he needed Marcus's help. But the Russian mafia? Narco trafficking?

"What the hell are you telling me, Sebastian?"

"The truth."

"The truth is shit!" I said tearfully. He stepped closer. "Don't even think about touching me, fuck!" I shouted, turning to the door.

I needed to get out of there. I needed to get away. I would go to London. I could ask Tami to let me stay at her house. Her parents would take me in, yes . . .

He stopped me before I could unlock the door. "You wanted the truth, Marfil? This is the truth," he said, squeezing me to his chest.

I tried to pull away. I wanted to leave. I couldn't trust anyone. I couldn't trust anything Sebastian or my father or anyone in my family told me . . . My God, my sister!

"Gabriella!" I shouted, terrified.

"Your sister is safe. She doesn't know any of this. It's not about her."

"Let me go, dammit!" I shouted.

He released me, but he stood in front of the door to keep me from trying to leave.

"How can you tell me all this and stand there so calm? How have you been able to lie to my face for months?"

"I was doing my job," he said, and that made me so furious that I shot out a hand and slapped him across the face.

He held his breath and clenched his jaw tightly. I stared at him, unable to believe what I'd just done.

"Do you want to do it again?" he asked.

I took a step back and a sob escaped my throat. "I can't believe you lied to me like that . . . that you let . . ."

"What I feel for you is no lie."

"But you aren't even capable of telling me what you feel for me!"

"Because I never should've touched you, Marfil!"

"But you did!"

Sebastian was losing his cool, and I felt like I was suffocating.

"I never planned to fall in love with you, Marfil. Ever."

In spite of everything he'd just told me, his confession caused my heart to race. It was incredible how the heart and the mind could go in two totally opposite directions. My mind despised him, still trying to assimilate everything he'd just confessed to me, but at the sound of the word *love* from his mouth, my heart melted, and there was nothing I could do to stop it.

"I hate you," I said, wishing the words were true.

Sebastian kept his composure. "I didn't expect anything less."

I turned my back on him and wrapped my arms around myself.

Why was all this happening to me? Why did my father have to be a drug lord? Why couldn't I have been born into a normal, everyday family? Why couldn't I have an affectionate father who looked out for me, who took care of me and protected me? Why couldn't I have a mother who fed me chocolate ice cream and gave me advice about my fears and ambitions? My mother . . .

"My mother wasn't killed in a robbery, was she?"

Sebastian moved closer and stopped in front of me. I could feel the warmth of his body, but it did nothing to thaw the icy shell around me.

"You're going to have to ask your father that, Marfil . . . but I doubt it."

My mother had been killed for being married to someone like my father, and I was now following in her footsteps.

"Is that why you and your wife separated? Because you're a fucking drug dealer?" I spat.

"That, and a long list of other reasons."

I laughed. "Of all the things that could've come out of your mouth . . ."

"This is the only thing that would keep you away from me, I know."

I lifted my head to look him in the eye. "I can understand that my father does it, you know? I never thought he was involved in something as big as this, something as terrible, but deep down I knew there was something that didn't add up . . ." I whispered to the man in front of me, the man who had taken care of me, who had guarded me in my sleep . . . "But I never thought that you were like him."

Sebastian remained silent.

"It's clear that you're not who I thought you were. You forced me to live a lie, and I'll never forgive you for it."

"I always knew you were smart," he said, looking at me very seriously, "but don't judge me so quickly. Not everyone is born with a silver spoon in their mouth."

"A silver spoon? You mean a stolen spoon."

"Neither one of us can change what we're born into, Marfil, or who our parents are. I was left in a dumpster at just one day old; you were born surrounded by drug dealers and murderers, but you had twenty years to grow up oblivious to that world and learn to look down on it. I couldn't afford the luxury: I had to do everything I could to survive."

"It's always possible to choose a different path."

"Says someone who's spent five minutes in my world."

"Sorry for not being a fucking criminal!" I shouted, angry that he'd now turned against me. I stepped away from him, but he stopped me, pulling me closer, and I glared at him.

"One day you'll understand everything, I promise."

"And what is that supposed to mean?"

"Not all of us are cut from the same cloth."

"No one is forcing you to be a fucking drug dealer!" I shouted, wrestling away from him.

"You think it's easy to get out? Do you have any idea the things I've seen? They'd kill me for just thinking about it!"

"My father would never—"

"Your father is a murderer, Marfil, just like the rest of us."

"Are you hearing yourself?"

He nodded without letting go of me. He held the back of my neck and placed his mouth close to mine. "There's not a day that I don't regret everything I've done, and I assure you there's not a day that I don't try to make up for it."

I stood completely still, searching his eyes for the truth. "How?"

Sebastian closed his eyes for an instant, as if afraid I might see into his soul. "I'm still here, aren't I?"

"Are you saying that you're trying to redeem yourself by getting into my pants?"

"Enough!" he said, shooting me a furious glance. "Don't talk about what we have, fuck. You know perfectly well that you're not just another chick to me. For the love of God, I could've fucked you the first week we met, and look where we are, months later!"

"Are you insinuating that I'm easy? Is that what you're saying to me right now?"

"I'm insinuating that what I feel for you is the only thing keeping me here, risking my life for you, do you understand?"

"Well, then, go! I don't want you to protect me; someone else can do it. I don't need you! Not anymore!"

Sebastian took a few seconds to process my words, and then he released me. "Well, your wish is about to become reality. I'm not going to be guarding you anymore."

What? No.

"What do you mean by that?"

Sebastian took his cell phone out of his pocket. "I have orders to take you to Marcus's house. He'll be the one making the decisions about your safety from now on. Apparently, my work last night was unacceptable. He's replacing me."

I started shaking my head as soon as I heard him say Marcus's name. "You can't leave me with him . . ."

Sebastian pressed his lips together, and the rage we both felt seemed to give way to alarm and fear as he took my face in his hands and rested his forehead against mine. "It'll just be a little while . . . Let me figure out a way to solve this."

My eyes filled with tears, and I looked at him, terrified. "He'll kill me, Sebastian."

"No, he won't. He wants you for himself."

"He'll hurt me!"

"Do what I'm asking, Marfil. I promise I'll get you out of there."

"NO!" I shouted, pulling away from him and rushing over to my purse. I picked up the phone to dial 911. "I'm going to call the police."

Sebastian looked frightened for the first time, moving closer to me and reaching for the phone. "Don't do it, Marfil! They'll discover your location—they'll come for you. Hang up!" He shouted so loudly that I jumped, and the phone fell from my hands. Sebastian picked it up before I could react and put it in the back pocket of his jeans. "No one can know anything about this. They'll already be looking for us because of what happened at the club! Don't you realize?"

"Don't include me in this! I'm not a drug lord! I'll tell the police everything I know and leave it in their hands!"

"You'd be dead before you could count to three."

"Don't say that!" I sank to the floor and hugged my knees to my chest.

*God, wake me up from this nightmare.*

Sebastian walked over to where I sat and crouched down next to me. "I'd give my life for you, Elephant," he said in a conciliatory tone. "I wouldn't take you to Marcus if I thought he might seriously hurt you. As much as I hate to say it, it's the safest place for you right now."

"Since when is the home of a murderous narco rapist a safe place for anyone?"

Sebastian waited a few seconds before responding. "Ever since the Russian mafia set out to kill you."

I looked at him, terrified.

"I know it all sounds horrible. I'm not saying Marcus is a great guy, but he has a lot of resources, and he won't stop until he gets rid of everyone who wants to harm you."

"Why would he go through all that trouble?"

Sebastian looked at me as if the answer were obvious. "Because he thinks he's in love with you," he said coldly.

Just the thought made me want to gag.

"There has to be another way. Don't take me to him, Sebastian. Don't leave me, please," I begged, leaning into him and letting him wrap me in his arms. Suddenly, everyone was an enemy, and Sebastian, the only person I could trust, wanted to turn me over to my abuser.

He embraced me for what could have been hours, but I finally let go of him and went into the bathroom. I sat on the floor in there for an hour and a half, thinking over all my options. There weren't many. I thought about Elisabeth, Gabriella's mom. Did she know any of this? Is that why she ended up divorcing my father? But then I remembered Harold, her new husband, who was a cop . . . Elisabeth wouldn't hide something like that from him . . . But how could she not have known? My father was an expert liar, that was clear, and it was also true that he had companies all over the world, fronts for laundering all the dirty money he made from drug trafficking, I now knew.

I decided not to go to Elisabeth. Not only would it put her in danger, but the last thing I wanted was for Gabriella to find out. My sister loved my dad so much. She needed to stay in London, far removed from all this.

I felt as if someone had suddenly stolen my life away from me. I called Liam to find out how Tami was doing and because I needed to hear his voice. I wanted to beg him to come get me, to take me somewhere far away, but I knew I wouldn't even make it half a block.

And then there was Sebastian . . . Finding out he belonged to that horrible world had possibly pained me more than learning that my father was one of the most dangerous narcos in the country.

Not only had Sebastian lied to me, but he made me question whether any of what we'd shared had been real. He'd always warned me that he was no good for me, but I'd thought he was referring to the fact that he was my bodyguard, that he worked for my father, or our age difference . . . I never imagined it was because he was a murderer . . . That's how he had referred to himself: *Your father is a murderer, Marfil, just like all the rest of us.*

Finally, there was a knock on the bathroom door. I looked at it, trying to determine how I felt about the man waiting on the other side.

"Open up, Marfil," he said, tapping gently with his knuckles. "Don't make me break it down . . ."

I stood up and unlocked the door. There he was, wearing a black sweater I'd never seen on him before. Narco or not, he was still incredibly handsome and sexy. I stared at him, and he stared back at me. I closed my eyes as he gently caressed my cheek with his thumb.

"I'm so sorry," he whispered in my ear. "I'm sorry, Elephant," he said again, kissing the sensitive skin of my ear.

I felt momentarily comforted, until I remembered what he was planning to do, and I shoved him away. "Don't kiss me again, Sebastian."

I moved away from him and walked over to the bed, where I curled into a ball. I had no idea what awaited me or what his new orders were. But I knew that he had made up his mind to leave me with Marcus because I had never seen him so devastated or concerned.

"Drink this," he said a little while later, giving me a glass of water and a pill, just as he had before.

"I don't want to relax. I'm fine."

"You need to rest."

"What I need is to wake up from this nightmare."

Sebastian simply looked at me with the pill in his hand. Finally, I picked it up and put it in my mouth. I needed to sleep without seeing the faces of my dead bodyguards lying on the ground or my best friend bleeding out on the concrete or Marcus's dungeons waiting to swallow me up.

I fell asleep immediately, and when I felt him lift me in his arms, I knew he hadn't given me the same pill as before. He wasn't carrying me to bed, but to the car.

The last thing I saw before my eyes closed involuntarily was a single tear sliding down Sebastian's cheek.

Maybe I'd dreamt it.

## EPILOGUE

# SEBASTIAN

Marfil slept the whole way to Newark Airport. This time I wouldn't be with her on the flight to hold her hand during takeoff and landing. But it wasn't only that I had to leave her—I had to let her go.

I spent over half an hour seated beside her in the car, waiting patiently for her to wake up. In front of us was Marcus Kozel's private jet, where everyone was waiting for me to give the okay for her to get on the plane that would take her a thousand miles away.

Marfil began to stir beside me, and I prepared myself for whatever might happen. She slowly opened her eyes, and they shone with love as she saw me beside her. That gleam had driven me crazy for months and would torture me every second until I could see her again. But then she seemed to remember the past hours, the recent events, and a dark shadow crossed her face, erasing any sign of happiness, hope, or relief at seeing me.

"Where are we?" she asked, looking all around and stopping on the plane parked a short distance away. It was a Dassault Falcon 7X, one of the best private planes in the world. It cost almost fifty million dollars, a price tag that demonstrated just how much money was generated by the business I was a part of.

"Newark Airport," I said, afraid to meet her gaze. I didn't want to know what was going through her mind, how scared she must be. The fact that I couldn't do anything to change it made me want to kill someone, to kill everyone and escape somewhere far away with her.

"Did you drug me?"

I locked the car doors before she could take off running. I needed to have a few minutes with her. I needed to make sure she understood what was going to happen.

"I just gave you a stronger sedative; I needed you to be rested . . ."

"And you needed to be able to bring me here by force."

She turned to open the door, and finding it locked, she glared at me with her beautiful eyes. She was angry, but more than anything, I could tell that she was terrified over everything that had happened, how everything had gone to hell.

"Open the fucking door, Sebastian."

"I will. I just need you to understand why I've brought you here."

"I'm not going to get on that plane."

I sighed and turned to fully face her. "It won't be for long . . ."

"I'm not getting on that plane," she repeated with enviable resolve.

"It's waiting to take you to Miami. It's the only place you'll be safe, at least until we know how we're going to proceed . . ."

"I'm not getting on that plane!" she screamed as she pulled at the door handle. She started crying, and I felt repulsed with myself.

"Marfil, listen to me!" I shouted, realizing she was starting to have a panic attack. I gripped both her hands in mine, forcing her to meet my gaze. "It's only for a little while. I'll get you out of there."

"Why should I believe you? You've been lying to me since the day I met you."

"You have to believe me because I'm in love with you. I

love you. Do you hear me?" I said, holding on to the back of her neck and pulling her toward me until my forehead rested against hers. Her breathing hitched, and my heart sped up in response. "If there were anyplace safer for you right now, I would take this car and drive away with you. But there isn't, and I'm not going to let them kill you, do you understand?"

Marfil blinked several times, trying to clear her eyes. Seeing the fat tears on her cheeks pained me deep in my soul.

"You're lying again . . ." she whispered, shaking her head.

"Why would I lie to you when I could be killed for feeling the way I do about you?"

She looked up to meet my gaze, and I felt something deep in my stomach.

"Why didn't you tell me before?"

"Because I hoped it would go away. Because I was trying my best not to fall in love with you, Marfil. But the more I resisted, the harder I fell."

She closed her eyes, and I wished I could run away with her, hide her, and tell her the whole truth. But I didn't do any of that. I simply waited.

She took a deep breath and looked up at me. "I'm not going to say it back to you, Sebastian. You won't hear those words come out of my mouth . . . Never again."

That sentence was like a dagger to the heart, but I expected nothing less. I knew Marfil Cortés well enough to understand that she would never forgive me for what I was about to do.

"You're as beautiful and cold as ivory . . . but I will always be ebony."

"It doesn't matter what we are. You will always be the man who left me in the hands of a criminal."

Without my realizing it, she'd reached behind me to push the button that unlocked the doors and opened hers. She jumped out and took off running. I managed to catch her several yards away. As fast as she might be, I would always have longer legs.

"Let me go!" she screamed, thrashing in my arms.

"Don't make this even harder, Marfil!"

She tried to bite my arm, and I held her tighter so that she couldn't reach me. "I'm not going!" she sobbed.

"You have no choice . . ." I said quietly in her ear. She gradually seemed to accept the inevitability of the situation and stopped moving. When I saw that she had stopped resisting, I released her and turned her around to face me. "I'll figure out a way to fix everything. Just give me some time."

Marfil was breathing hard, and it pained me to see her eyes filled with tears. I couldn't help but pull her toward me and embrace her. She resisted at first, but then she slipped her arms under my jacket and hugged me back.

A second later, she had pushed me away and was aiming my gun directly at my head. I cursed aloud and carefully raised my hands in the air. Marfil was crying, and her hand was trembling as she tried to get used to the weight of the gun.

"Ma—"

"You're going to take me home . . ."

"I can't . . ."

"Find a way!"

We stared at each other for what felt like hours.

"You're not going to shoot me," I said quietly, calmly. I wasn't afraid for me, but for her. Seeing Marfil wielding a gun was my worst nightmare turned reality. "Give me the gun, beautiful."

She blinked back tears so she could see better. Then she gripped the gun in both hands. "I'm not going to Marcus Kozel's."

I took a step forward.

"Don't move!" she shouted, but I ignored her and continued advancing. "Sebastian, if you keep . . ."

I stepped toward her until the gun pressed into my chest. I looked her directly in the eye. "You're not going to shoot."

It took Marfil only a few seconds to completely collapse. I took the gun from her and pulled her to me. This time she actually hugged me, and I had to muster up all my self-control to keep from breaking down then and there, just like her.

"Have faith in me, Marfil," I said into her hair. "I'll get you out of there, I promise." I looked her in the eye, trying to communicate a thousand things and hoping that she'd be able to read everything I wanted to transmit with my gaze.

Seeing that she didn't respond, I kissed her desperately. Who knew when I would see her again.

"One day you'll understand everything, Elephant. I promise."

"Stop making promises you can't keep." She stepped away, looked at me with so much pain, and then turned toward the plane that stood waiting for her. She took several deep breaths before she spoke again. "Goodbye, Sebastian."

I watched her walk away, her long dark hair whipped up by the wind. She didn't look back. She didn't falter when she reached the plane. She was leaving, and there was nothing I could do about it.

I took out my phone and sent a quick, bitter message. It was done. There was no turning back. I had just let the woman I was in love with step into the jaws of my worst enemy.

When you sell your soul to the devil, falling in love with an angel can only lead you straight to hell.

# ACKNOWLEDGMENTS

Here I am again, writing the acknowledgments for a new novel, and this is one I have a special affection for. It's not easy to leave behind characters who've been with you for years and connect to new ones, but Marfil and Sebastian have stolen my heart, just like Nick and Noah did before them. I owe a huge debt of gratitude to all the people who encouraged me to write something new, who sent me messages every day saying: *When are we going to see another book by Mercedes Ron?*

First of all, I want to thank the team at Penguin Random House for their continued trust in me, for working to make my novels incredible, and for providing the scaffolding that allows me touch the sky. Thank you, Rosa, for having opened the doors to such a huge, special home. Thank you, Ada, for being my star editor, for listening to me and encouraging me whenever I need it. I hope to always have you at my side along the way.

I could thank so many people at Penguin: thanks to Manuel, for listening to all my opinions about cover art and tweaking the image, the color, the size . . . I hope you don't hate me! Thanks to Conxita and Alba, for helping expand my work to new horizons, which I'm sure in time we're going to reach successfully. Every time I get a message from you guys, my heart races! Thanks to you all, because if it weren't for you guys, *Drawn Together* wouldn't be in bookstores today.

I want to thank my father, for helping me with issues I didn't understand, for sitting with me in the living room, pencil and paper in hand, helping me create a world, a task that's still difficult for me even now.

To my mother, my best friend, for always being there, no matter how far away or how many problems or unexpected events may arise. You're my role model.

To my sisters, the set of three, for cheering on my every achievement, for talking about me proudly to everyone they meet, and for loving me as I am: crazy, enthusiastic, and sometimes a little annoying.

To my cousin Bar, for being my right hand, my example of perseverance, my Wonder Woman. You're incredible, and don't let anyone ever tell you differently.

To Ana, for joining me on that trip that helped make this book more special. Our months in New York are still tattooed on my skin, literally, and they wouldn't have been the same without you. I don't know how you do it, but our trips make my books turn out exactly the way I hoped they would. Thanks, Wachi, for also helping me with the cover. Your Photoshop skills are impressive, especially considering that I don't even know how to insert a title. To my friends, all of them: Alicia, Irene, Alba, Ana, Patri, Blanca, Gala, Laura, Eva, Andrea, Miriam, because you inspire me every day. You are my example of strong women, fighters, and dreamers. Don't ever let anyone take your dreams. You are all special and you deserve the best. Thank you for being who you are.

Thanks to all of my "Culpables," my family, for your enthusiasm, your memes, your comments . . . Everything you do is incredible to me. Thank you for having gotten me to where I am today. You're the best thing that could've happened to me, and I love each and every one of you.

And lastly, although I've surely left out a ton of names, I want to thank you, my readers. Thank you for trusting in me, for having paused in the bookshop, maybe intrigued by the cover art or the summary of the plot. I hope I was able to entertain you, to make you fall in love, to laugh and also to suffer a little, because, let's be honest, it wouldn't be one of my novels without a bit of suffering.

Mercedes Ron is a *New York Times* and #1 internationally best-selling author of the My Fault trilogy, with more than five million copies sold worldwide, published in twenty-two countries, and with eleven Amazon Prime Originals. Born in Argentina, she lives in Seville with her husband and beloved dog.

Marfil and Sebastian's story continues in this thrilling sequel from Mercedes Ron

# *Drawn Apart*

Coming 2027

AVAILABLE IN PAPERBACK, EBOOK AND AUDIO